Praise fo
The Alphabet

"Adler-Olsen meticulously constructs the Alphabet House . . . and the stomach-turning evils of Nazi culture to create a pitch-perfect thriller atmosphere." —*Booklist*

"This is a suspense/thriller to beat them all. Not only does it offer action, but readers will start waiting for the rabbit to jump out of the hat and change everything." —*Suspense Magazine*

Praise for
Jussi Adler-Olsen and the Department Q novels

"Adler-Olsen merges story lines . . . with ingenious aplomb, effortlessly mixing hilarities with horrors. . . . This crime fiction tour de force could only have been devised by an author who can even turn stomach flu into a belly laugh."
—*Publishers Weekly* (starred review) on *The Purity of Vengeance*

"A sordid tale . . . inspired by actual events during a dark period of Danish history. Ah, but there's more, so much more in this frenzied thriller."
—*The New York Times Book Review* on *The Purity of Vengeance*

"When your series relies on cold cases, it's not always easy to craft plots that have both historical interest and an air of urgency, but it's something Adler-Olsen is very good at." —*Booklist* on *The Purity of Vengeance*

"This series has enough twists to captivate contemporary mystery readers and enough substance and background to entertain readers with historical and literary tastes." —*Library Journal* (starred review)

"Plan on putting everything else in your life on hold if you pick up this book." —*The Oregonian* on *The Keeper of Lost Causes*

THE
ALPHABET
HOUSE

A NOVEL

JUSSI ADLER-OLSEN

Translated by Steve Schein

DUTTON

DUTTON
An imprint of Penguin Random House LLC
375 Hudson Street
New York, New York 10014

Previously published as a Dutton hardcover, 2015
First paperback printing, March 2016

THE LIBRARY OF CONGRESS HAS CATALOGUED THE HARDCOVER EDITION OF THIS BOOK AS FOLLOWS:

Adler-Olsen, Jussi.
[Alfabethuset. English]
The alphabet house : a novel / Jussi Adler-Olsen; translated by Steve Schein.
pages cm
ISBN 978-0-525-95489-7 (hardcover) 978-1-101-98397-3 (paperback)
1. World War, 1939–1945—Fiction.   I. Schein, Steve, translator.   II. Title.
PT8176.1.D54A4413   2015
839.813'74—dc23   2014018577

 Printed in the United States of America

10 9 8 7 6 5 4

Set in Maxime Std
Designed by Alissa Rose Theodor

AUTHOR'S NOTE

This book is not a war novel.

The Alphabet House is an elementary story about breaches that can arise in all types of personal relationships, from daily life in a marriage or at the workplace to extreme settings like the Korean War, the Boer War, the Iran-Iraq War, or in this case the Second World War.

There are several reasons why I chose this war to provide the novel's framework. Primarily because I am the son of a psychiatrist and grew up in the surroundings of "insane asylums," as they were called in Denmark in the late fifties and early sixties; and although my father was extremely progressive and a new thinker in his field, I couldn't avoid witnessing firsthand how the mentally ill were treated in those days. Many of them had been in the system since the thirties and I was interested in the methods of treatment and the doctors and hospitals during that period, and especially during the war. I got to know a few patients who—through the eyes of a naïve, alert child—I suspected of simulating their mental illness.

One of these chronically mentally ill patients basically coped with life in the hospitals by uttering only two sentences. "Yes, you've got a point there!" was the one he used the most. He wasn't sticking his neck out here. Then he could enhance and round off practically any situation with a sincerely relieved "Oh, thank God!" He was one of the patients I suspected of having retreated from society into the calm and peaceful world of medical treatment facilities by using some obscure form of simulation.

But is it possible to preserve oneself and one's mind in a situation like this if one isn't really ill? It's hard to believe, especially considering some of the hefty methods of treatment used at the time. Wouldn't our verbally limited patient become ill sooner or later?

My father met the patient again after a period of many years. It was in the seventies, by which point the world had become freer in many ways. This had also had its effect on our man. He'd added a third sentence to his repertoire: "Up yours!" He'd kept up with the times.

And again I found myself wondering: Is he ill or is he well?

My desire to combine these two objects of my fascination—the possibly mentally ill individual and World War II—was enhanced by a conversation I had with one of my mother's friends named Karna Bruun. She had worked as a nurse in Bad Kreuznach under Professor Ferdinand Sauerbruch and was able to confirm and expand upon some theories I'd developed.

In the summer of 1987, under the starry Italian skies of Terracina, I outlined my fledgling story for my wife. Then, as now, I had the greatest admiration for authors for whom research and literary expertise were inseparable. She believed my story would be worth this kind of effort.

It took me almost eight years to realize.

In the course of this period I've been grateful to Det Treschowske Fideikommis for their assistance in the form of a travel grant to Freiburg im Breisgau, where a large portion of the story unfolds; to the military library in Freiburg; and to Oberarchivrat Dr. Ecker from Stadtarchiv Freiburg.

Since then, my wife, Hanne Adler-Olsen, has been my tireless muse and critic, constantly nurturing my faithfulness to my original ambitions.

In the perusal of my manuscript by my capable and wise friends— Henning Kure, Jesper Helbo, Tomas Stender, Eddie Kiran, Carl Rosschou, and not least of all my sister, Elsebeth Wæhrens, and my mother, Karen-Margrethe Olsen—the story underwent a multilayered process that made it both shorter and more profound. All elements were assessed and pondered over until the story came to fruition as I'd hoped.

Jussi Adler-Olsen

PART I

CHAPTER 1

It wasn't the best weather in the world.

Cold and windy, with poor visibility.

An exceptionally bleak January day, even for England.

The American crews had already been sitting on the landing strips for some time when the tall Englishman approached. He was still not quite awake.

Behind the group a shape rose halfway to its feet and waved to him. The Englishman waved back, yawning loudly. Functioning in daytime was difficult after such a long period with nothing but night raids.

It was going to be a long day.

At the far end of the airfield the planes were taxiing slowly toward the southern end of the landing strips. Soon the air would be full of them.

The feeling was both exhilarating and oppressive.

The orders regarding the mission came from Major General Lewis H. Brereton's office in Sunninghill Park. He was requesting British assistance from Sir Arthur Harris, marshal in the Royal Air Force. The Americans were still impressed by the British Mosquitoes' discovery, during their November nighttime bombing of Berlin, of the Germans' most closely guarded secret, the V-1 missile sites at Zemplín.

The choice of British personnel had been left to Group Captain Hadley-Jones, who entrusted the practical work to his next-in-command, Wing Commander John Wood.

The latter's task was to select twelve British flight crews. Eight of them were to function as instructors and four as supporting crews with special photo-reconnaissance duties under the 8th and 9th American Air Forces.

Two-seater P-51D Mustang fighters had been equipped for this task with radar and sensitive optical instruments.

Only two weeks had passed since James Teasdale and Bryan Young had been chosen as the first crew to try out this equipment under so-called "normal conditions."

In short, they could expect to go into action again.

The raid was planned for the eleventh of January, 1944. The targets were the airplane factories at Oschersleben, Braunschweig, Magdeburg, and Halberstadt.

Both men had protested about having their Christmas leave curtailed. They were still suffering from combat fatigue.

"Two weeks to figure out this bloody machine!" Bryan shook his head. "I don't know a thing about all those gadgets. Why doesn't Uncle Sam do his own dirty work?"

John Wood was standing with his back to them both, bowed over the document files. "Because Uncle Sam wants *you!*"

"That's no argument, is it?"

"You'll live up to the Americans' expectations and come out alive."

"Is that a guarantee?"

"Yes!"

"Say something, James!" Bryan turned toward his friend.

James fingered his silk scarf and shrugged. Bryan sat down heavily.

It was hopeless. They had to go.

The entire operation was calculated to take a good six hours. A total of about 650 four-engine bombers from the 8th American Air Force were to bomb airplane factories, escorted by the P-51 long-distance fighters.

Bryan and James were to break away from the other P-51s during the attack.

During the past couple of months, there had been persistent rumors of an increased influx of building craftsmen, engineers, and highly specialized technicians—as well as hordes of Polish and Soviet slave laborers—into the region of Lauenstein, south of Dresden.

Intelligence had learned that some kind of construction was going on in the area, but not what kind. They had a hunch it might be factories for producing synthetic fuel. If this were the case, it would be a dangerous development that could lend impetus to new German V-bomb projects.

Bryan and James's job, therefore, was to thoroughly photograph and map out the area, including the railway network around Dresden, so Intelligence could update its information. After completing their mission they were to rejoin the formation on its way back to England.

Many of the Americans who were to take part in the raid were already seasoned air warriors. Despite the cold and the impending takeoff, they were lying half stretched out on the uneven, frostbitten earth some people called a landing strip. Most of them were chatting away as though they were on their way to a dance or relaxing at home on the family sofa. Here and there a few sat hugging their knees, staring dully into space. These were the new and inexperienced airmen who had not yet learned how to forget their dreams and control their anxiety.

The Englishman strode between the sitting figures toward his partner, who lay stretched out on the ground with his arms behind his head.

Bryan gave a start when he felt the gentle kick in his side.

Snowflakes drifted above them, settling on nose and brow as the sky became more and more overcast. This expedition would differ very little from one of their night raids.

Bryan's seat vibrated gently under him.

The radar screen showed the surrounding air space to be thick with signals from the planes in the formation. Each echo that signaled a plane's position was clearly distinguishable.

Several times during training they'd joked about painting the windows over and flying on instruments alone. The equipment was that precise. It was a joke they could just as well have taken seriously on this flight. According to James, the visibility was "as clear as a symphony by Béla Bartók." The windshield wipers and nose of the plane penetrating the snow clouds—that was all they could see.

They'd been arguing. Not about the crazy idea of changing duties and equipment at such short notice, but about John Wood's motives. According to Wood they had been chosen because they were the best, which James was willing to accept.

But Bryan blamed his friend. There was scarcely any doubt in his mind that John Wood had picked them because James never protested while on active duty. And on this operation there had certainly been no time for questioning orders.

Bryan's reproaches irritated James. There were worries enough already. It was a long trip and they were handling new equipment. The weather was terrible and there was no one to support them once they left the rest of the formation. If Intelligence was correct in assuming that important factories were under construction, the target area would be very heavily guarded. Finally, it was going to be an extremely difficult task getting the photos back to England.

But James was right. Someone had to do it. Besides, it couldn't be much different from the bombing raids on Berlin.

They'd made it this far.

Bryan sat silently in his seat behind James, doing his job irreproachably, as always. The vibrations gradually shook loose his combed-back hair. Bryan's hairstyle was his most distinguishing feature. Freshly combed, he looked almost as tall as James.

Between Bryan's map and measuring instruments hung the photo of a WAC by the name of Madge Donat. In her eyes, Bryan was an Adonis.

He'd stuck with her for a long time.

As if responding to the authoritative cue of a conductor's baton, the Germans began greeting the arriving planes with an antiaircraft overture. James had foreseen the barrage a few seconds previously and given Bryan the signal, so they managed to change course. From that moment until some unpredictable time in the future their fate was out of their hands.

Unprotected and on their own.

"We'll be scraping the ass off this machine if you want us to fly any lower," Bryan grunted twenty minutes later.

"If we stay up at two hundred feet, your pictures won't come out," came the reply.

James was right. It was snowing over the target area, but the wind was constantly forcing the flakes to whirl upward, creating holes through which it was possible to photograph. Assuming they were close enough.

No one had been interested in their presence since they'd turned away from the barrage over Magdeburg. Apparently they hadn't been observed. Bryan would do his utmost to see they weren't.

Many planes had crashed behind them. Far too many. In the midst of all the noise, James shouted back to Bryan that he'd seen German fighters firing rocketlike things. A short flash followed by a totally devastating explosion.

"The Luftwaffe isn't worth a shit," an American pilot had bellowed out the previous evening, a broad Kentucky grin on his face. Perhaps experience had taught him something different now.

"And then 138 degrees to the south!" Bryan was following the sea of snow beneath him. "You should be able to get a glimpse of the main road out of Heidenau. Can you see the crossroads now? Good. Then follow the turning toward the ridge."

Their speed was down to scarcely two hundred kilometers per hour, which in that weather made the entire fuselage complain audibly.

"You've got to zigzag over the road here, James, but watch out! Some of the southern slopes could be steep. Can you see anything? You should have a good chance between here and Geising."

"All I can see is that the road seems quite wide. Why would that be, in such a deserted place?"

"That's what I was wondering. Can't you swing southward now? Look at those trees! Can you see how dense they are?"

"Camouflage netting, you mean?"

"Possibly." If there were any factories here, they must have been dug into the hillside. Bryan doubted that. Once such a building was discovered, the earthworks wouldn't provide sufficient protection against intense precision bombing. "This is a wild-goose chase, James! There's nothing in the vicinity to suggest recent building."

If possible, they were to follow the railway line northward toward Heidenau, turn west toward Freital and follow the railway line to Chemnitz, then turn north and later northeast along the railway line to Waldheim. The entire network was to be photographed in detail. By Russian request. Soviet troops were exerting heavy pressure near Leningrad and were threatening to roll up the entire German front. According to the Russians, the railway junction at Dresden was the Germans' umbilical cord. Once severed, the German divisions on the Eastern Front would soon be lacking supplies. It was merely a question of how many cuts were necessary in order to be effective.

Bryan looked down at the railway line beneath him. There would be nothing to see in his photos but snow-covered rails.

The first explosion came without warning and with incredible force, only a half meter behind Bryan's seat. Before he could turn around, James was already forcing the plane into a fast vertical climb. Bryan fastened the snap hook in his seat and felt the cockpit's tepid air being sucked out from under him.

The jagged hole in the fuselage was about the size of a fist; the exit hole in the roof, like a dinner plate. A single round from a small-caliber antiaircraft gun had hit them.

So there was something they'd overlooked after all.

The engine screeched so loudly during the steep ascent that they couldn't tell if they were still being shot at.

"Is it serious back there?" James screamed. He appeared satisfied with the answer. "Then here we go!" Almost instantly James had looped the loop, tipped the plane on one side, and put it into a vertical dive. After a few seconds the Mustang's machine guns began ticking away. Several antiaircraft muzzle flames pointed directly up at them, showing them the way.

In the midst of that deadly blaze there had to be something the Germans were extremely reluctant to have outsiders know about.

James swung the plane from side to side in order to confuse the enemy while the German gunners on the ground tried to get them in their sights. They never saw the guns, but there was no mistaking the sound. The Flakzwilling 40 made a bloodcurdling noise all of its own.

When they were close to the ground, James leveled the plane with a jerk. They would only have this one chance. The entire area was two to three kilometers wide. The camera needed a steady hand.

The landscape whipped along beneath them. Gray patches and white swirls alternated with treetops and buildings. Tall fences encircled the area they were flying over. Several watchtowers fired machine-gun salvos at them. Slave laborers were kept in camps like these. Tracer-bullet fire from a forest thicket in front of them made James instinctively dive still lower, straight toward the trees. Several rounds from his machine gun made it past the tree trunks, silencing all resistance from that quarter.

Then, grazing the tops of the fir trees, James flew the plane right over a gigantic grayish mass of camouflage netting, walls, railway cars, and scattered heaps of materials. Bryan had plenty to photograph. A few seconds later they again banked upward, and away.

"Okay?"

Bryan nodded, patted James's shoulder, and prayed that the guns below them were their only opponents.

They weren't.

"Something funny's going on here, Bryan! You can just see it if you sit up straight. It's the engine cowling! Can you see it?"

It wasn't difficult. A triangular bit of cowling was sticking straight up into the air. Whether it was caused by the dive, a hit, or blast waves was immaterial. It wasn't good under any circumstances.

"We're going to have to really slow down, Bryan. You know that, don't you? There's not much hope of getting back to the bomber formation now."

"Do what you think is best!"

"We'll follow the railway line. If they send fighters after us, they're probably thinking we'll make off due west. You keep an eye on the air around us, okay?"

The trip back was going to be endless.

The countryside beneath them gradually became flatter. On a clear day they would have been able to see the horizon to all sides. Had it not been for the snowstorm, they would have been audible kilometers away.

"How the hell do you imagine we'll get home, James?" asked Bryan quietly. Looking at the map was useless. Their chances were slim.

"Just keep your eye on that little screen," came the reply. "You can't do much else. I think the cowling will stay put so long as we stick to this marching pace."

"Then we'll take the shortest way back."

"North of Chemnitz. Yes, please, Bryan!"

"We're crazy!"

"Not us! The situation!"

. . .

The railway line below them was no minor branch line. Sooner or later an ammunition train or troop transport would turn up. Small, easily aimed twin cannons or Flak 38 twenty-millimeter antiaircraft guns would be able to finish them off quickly. And then there were the Messerschmitts. For them, the Mustang was easy prey. *Close combat. Shot down.* That's how brief the report would be.

Bryan thought of suggesting they land the plane before the enemy did it for them. His philosophy was simple and practical. Captivity was preferable to death.

He took hold of James's upper arm and shook it slightly. "They've spotted us," he said quietly.

Without further comment James let the plane lose altitude.

"Naundorf ahead. Here you go north of . . ." Bryan saw the enemy only as a shadow above them. "There he is, James, straight above us!" James tore the plane away from low altitude with a violent wrench of the controls.

The whole plane was vibrating with protest as he accelerated. During the sudden ascent the hole behind Bryan practically sucked the cabin empty of air. James's machine guns started rattling even before Bryan had seen their target. A merciless salvo into its belly paralyzed the Messerschmitt instantly. The explosion that followed proved fatal. The pilot never knew what hit him.

There were several bangs that Bryan couldn't quite place, and suddenly they were lying level in the air. Bryan glanced at James's neck as if he expected to see it react in some special way. The draft blasting through the shattered front windscreen meant the triangular bit of cowling had been torn off during their brutal ascent.

James shook his head without making a sound.

Then he slumped forward with his face turned to one side.

The roar of the engine increased. All the airplane's joints rattled in time with the fuselage's descent through the air strata. Loosening his harness, Bryan threw himself over James, got hold of the control stick, and forced it toward the lifeless body.

A delta of small blood streams trickled down James's cheek, emanating from two long superficial gashes above and in front of his ear. The piece of metal had hit him in the temple, taking most of his earlobe with it.

Without warning, another piece of cowling came loose with a bang and tumbled over the left wing. Creaking sounds told Bryan there was more to come. Then he made a decision for them both and pulled James free.

The cockpit canopy almost exploded off, sucking Bryan out of his seat. In spite of the howling, icy wind, he grabbed James under the armpits and pulled him out onto the wing in the lacerating air. At the same moment the plane disappeared from under them. Jerked out into space, Bryan lost his grip on James, who plunged downward like dead weight, but he still felt the life-redeeming tug of James's rip cord. For a second James lay poised in midair with arms hanging limp as a rag doll's. Then his chute opened with a sudden jerk. His flapping arms made him look like a fledgling just out of the nest, tumbling through the air for the first time.

Bryan's fingers were like ice as he tugged at his own parachute rip cord. He heard the crack of the chute opening above him as shots began rattling toward him from the ground, sending faint, treacherous flashes of light up through the snowy haze.

The plane banked and plunged slowly earthward behind them. Anyone searching for them would have to do a thorough job. Until then, Bryan had to make sure that James, the small fluttering gray ball, did not disappear from sight.

The ground rose to meet Bryan with unexpected brutality. Hard plow furrows were like concrete gutters in the severe frost. As he lay moaning, the wind filled his chute again and dragged him over the earthen ridges, ripping his flying suit to pieces. The powdery snow froze any bloody scrapes to ice before he could register the pain.

Bryan had seen James hit the ground. It seemed violent, as if his body had been crushed from the waist down.

Contrary to all regulations Bryan let his chute blow away from him as he hobbled over the furrows. Isolated fence posts marked an old corral. The horses were gone, slaughtered long ago. James's parachute had wedged itself between the bark and wood of one of the posts. Bryan glanced around.

There wasn't a sound. Amid cascades of whirling newly fallen snow he took hold of the dancing parachute with both hands and with even tugs guided himself along the seams and straps toward James.

It took three shoves before James slid onto his side. The zipper of his flight jacket gave way reluctantly. Bryan's icy fingertips dug down under the rough clothing. The warmth he found there was almost painful to the touch.

Bryan held his breath until he felt a faint pulse.

The wind finally subsided and the snow stopped drifting. All was quiet for the moment.

James began panting feebly as Bryan dragged him toward a thicket. Sky could be seen through the treetops. Alongside the trunks lay debris from generations of storms, offering shelter and cover. "With so much unutilized fuel around, there's not much chance of any people living here," Bryan said to himself.

"What'd you say?" came a voice from the limp body as it was being dragged through the carpet of snow.

Bryan dropped to his knees and carefully pulled James's head toward his lap.

"James! What happened?"

"Did something happen?" His eyes were still not focusing. He stared up at Bryan, his gaze wandering the air above him. Then he turned his head and surveyed the black-and-white landscape. "Where are we?"

"We crashed, James. Are you hurt bad?"

"I don't know."

"Can you feel your legs?"

"They're cold as hell!"

"But can you feel them, James?"

"You bloody well bet I can. They're cold as hell, I told you! What's this godforsaken place you've dropped me into?"

CHAPTER 2

The morning sky was deceptive. There was a starlit strip just above the horizon, but the heavens looked altogether threatening.

They could see around for several kilometers, but unfortunately that meant they also could be seen.

The remains of James's parachute lay in the middle of a field so vast that its crops would be able to feed a whole village. Clear, dark drag marks led straight from the field to the thicket where they were hiding.

All this was starting to worry Bryan, now that he knew that James wasn't in as bad shape as he could have been. The frost had stopped his ear from bleeding long ago and the cold had considerably reduced the swellings on his face and neck. They had been extraordinarily lucky.

Now it looked as if their luck had run out.

The frost that had cracked the corners of their mouths was gradually working its way farther into their bodies. If they were to survive, they would have to find shelter.

James listened for planes. From the air, the debris they left on the field would clearly bear witness to what had happened. If any planes spotted them, the faded-green bloodhounds would soon appear.

"As soon as we've gathered up the chutes I think we ought to make for the hollow over there." James pointed northward at some dark-gray patches, then looked back again. "If we go south, how far do you think it is to the nearest village?"

"If we're where I think we are, we'd be making straight for Naundorf. It's probably a couple of kilometers away. But I'm not sure."

"Then the railway line is south of us?"

"Yes, if I'm not mistaken. But I'm not certain." Bryan glanced around again. There were no landmarks. "I think we should do whatever you suggest," he said.

. . .

A good bit farther along the first windbreak the snow lay in drifts, helping to conceal the two of them. They followed the row of trees for a few minutes until the first hole in a snowdrift appeared. James was gasping heavily for breath, and while Bryan stuffed the parachute through the hole and down into the ditch, James pressed his folded arms tight against his chest in a vain attempt to defeat the cold. As Bryan was about to ask him how he was doing, they both stopped instinctively to listen. The plane appeared a short distance behind them, dipping its wings slightly as it swept over the thicket they had just left. By then they were lying flat on the ground. Then it swung southward over the field and behind the trees. For a while the droning of the plane grew deeper, as though it were leaving again. James raised his head from the snow just enough to breathe.

A whistling sound had them instantly craning their necks. There were some small, dark patches of sky above the trees. Out of one of these the plane turned up again, this time flying straight at them.

James threw himself on top of Bryan, forcing him down into the snowdrift.

"I'm freezing my ass off," said Bryan indistinctly from under him, his face buried in the snow. He tried to smile. James looked down the length of Bryan's back, pursing his lips at the sight of the lacerated flying suit and the cakes of snow slowly melting with the warmth of his body, then streaming down over his hips and thighs.

"You just keep freezing for a while," he replied, tilting his head upward. "If that guy's spotted us, it'll be plenty hot soon enough!"

Just then the plane roared over them and disappeared.

"Who was that clown? Could you see?" asked Bryan, trying to get the snow off his back.

"Possibly a Junkers. It seemed kind of flimsy. Do you think it spotted us?"

"If it had, we wouldn't be alive now. But it must have noticed our tracks."

Bryan grabbed hold of James's hand and pulled himself upright. They both knew it could all be over soon. If they reached the village, they might have a chance. Hopefully the villagers would understand they weren't a threat, which wouldn't be the case if they were spotted by the plane or one of the patrols that had inevitably already been dispatched to ferret them out.

They simply wouldn't have a chance.

They ran for some time without stopping. Their movements were clumsy. Every boot step in the frozen earth sent a jolt up their spine. James didn't look too good and he was deathly pale.

Far behind them came a gentle hum. They glanced at each other. From in front of them came another sound. A different sound, more like a heavily loaded train.

"Did you say the railway line was to the south of us?" panted James, pressing his ice-cold hands to his chest again.

"Jesus, James, I said I wasn't sure!"

"You're some navigator!"

"So maybe I should have studied the map rather than heave you out of that idiotic Yankee soup can?"

James didn't answer. Putting his hand on Bryan's shoulder, he pointed toward the bottom of the grayish slope that stretched in both directions, and from which came the unmistakable pumping sound of a steam locomotive. "Maybe now you have a better idea where we are?"

A single nod from Bryan made him relax. Now that they knew where they were, the question was whether that would help them. They squatted down behind some bushes prickling with dry, dead branches. The straight stretch of track lay like thin stripes in the white landscape. The distance to the railway was six or seven hundred meters and fairly open.

So they had been south of the railway line all the time.

"Are you okay?" Bryan tugged gingerly at James's fur collar, so he turned his head and faced him. James's pallor made the contours of his skull stand out even more clearly. He shrugged and turned his attention back to the railway line. It was growing gradually lighter and the shadows in the hollow of the slope took on animated shapes. A magnificent yet terrifying sight. Small gusts of wind carried the sound of the enormously long train up to them. Car after car glided past like a deadly lifeline between front and fatherland. Snorting armored locomotives, endless freight cars protected by big guns, machine-gun nests hidden behind sandbags, and grayish-brown troop cars from which no light escaped through the rolled-down curtains. As soon as the train had passed, new sounds heralded another one on the way.

There were only a few minutes between each transport. In this short space of time, during which the airmen's knees were beginning to go to sleep beneath their doubled-up bodies, thousands of human fates must have passed by. Exhausted, battle-scarred veterans westward; frightened and silent reserves eastward. Just a few bombs on this stretch daily, and the Russians' job on the hellish Eastern Front would be a bit easier.

Bryan felt a tug at his sleeve. James put his finger to his lips and sat perfectly still, listening. Now Bryan could hear it too. The sounds came from behind them on both sides.

"Dogs?"

Bryan nodded. "But maybe only in the one group."

James turned down his collar and straightened up a bit. "The other group is motorized. That was the humming sound we heard before. They must have got off their motorcycles where we crossed the ditches."

"Can you see them?"

"No, but it won't be long."

"What should we do?"

"What the hell *can* we do?" James squatted down again and rocked back and forth. "We've left tracks even a blind man could follow."

"We give ourselves up, then?"

"Have we any idea what they do with shot-down pilots?"

"You haven't answered my question. Do we give ourselves up?"

"We've got to go a bit out into the open so they can see us, else they might think we're up to no good."

Bryan felt the treacherous slap of the wind as soon as he started down the slope after James. It made his cheeks tingle.

A few rapid strides and they were out in the open. They stood waiting, facing their pursuers with their hands in the air.

Nothing happened to start with. The sound of voices stopped and all movement in front of them ceased. James whispered softly that the soldiers might have passed behind them. He half dropped his arms.

This was when they started shooting.

The dull, graying winter darkness was to their advantage. Falling heavily to the ground they lay side by side, flat on their stomachs, staring at each other questioningly.

Bryan immediately began worming his way toward the railway line, glancing constantly over his shoulder at James, who was struggling on knees and elbows over the knolls and frozen branches with a wild look in his eyes. The wound beside his ear had opened up again and with every move small red spots mixed with the whipped-up frosty snow.

Short rounds from a machine gun ticked crisply, blasting the air above them to pieces. The soldiers were shouting as they fired.

"They're going to let the dogs loose," James panted, gripping Bryan's ankle in front of him. "Are you ready to run?"

"Where to, James?" A wave of heat moved down Bryan's diaphragm and his guts contracted spontaneously in panicky defense.

"Over the railway line. There's no train just now." Bryan raised his head and checked out the long, treacherous open slope. And then what?

James got up and grabbed hold of Bryan just as a long burst of machine-gun fire ceased. The slope was steep. It was extremely dangerous to charge down it in their stiff boots, not to mention their stiff, frozen feet that were incapable of feeling any unevenness in the ground. The bullets started whistling over their heads again.

Bryan reached some flatter ground a hundred meters farther on and glanced quickly behind him. James was running after him as if all his joints were frozen, fingers splayed and his head cocked backward. Behind him a torrent of soldiers poured softly over the hillside and slithered down the first steep incline on their backs as they approached.

This delayed the soldiers a bit and the shots ceased for some valuable seconds. When they started firing again they were off target. Maybe the bastards were already tired! Perhaps they would leave the rest of the work to the dogs.

Lithe and muscular, the barking killing machines broke rank without hesitation as they'd been taught.

When Bryan reached the bottom of the slope he could see a fair distance in both directions in the pale morning light.

In front of him two trains were approaching, one from each direction, thus preventing them from disappearing into the windbreaks on the other side of the tracks. A strong explosion made Bryan jump. James had managed to draw his Enfield revolver on the run. A sprawling black patch in the snow behind him confirmed that James had wounded an attacking dog.

The three remaining dogs made instinctively for the two men's tracks and headed straight for James's back.

In its thirst for blood, a German shepherd had torn itself away from its master so the chain entangled between its legs slowed it down somewhat, compared to the two Dobermans.

The snow whirled around Bryan and James again. The scattered gunfire was sure to get them before long.

James fired again. Bryan fingered the flap of his revolver holster and took hold of the butt. Then he stepped to one side and took aim as James dashed past him.

For a fatal second the dog James had just wounded was distracted by Bryan's maneuver, snapping in the air just as the shot rang out. The animal rolled over several times before lying still. Without hesitation the other dogs made instinctively for Bryan's arms and chest. He was knocked over, managing to shoot one of them as it fell on him, but not wounding it seriously.

He struck a hard blow to the neck of the German shepherd on his left with his revolver butt. It fell beside him, lifeless. Jumping to his feet, he faced the first animal, which was already springing toward him.

The instant the dog seized hold of his arm, it began shaking its victim. It had no intention of letting go in this lifetime. A hard kick from Bryan lifted the cur off the ground, making it possible for him to turn his hand and fire his revolver. As the animal's body hit the ground, he slid and dropped the revolver. Then the submachine guns began rattling again. There was no longer any danger of them hitting their own dogs, since all three were now lying stretched out in the snow.

James was about forty meters ahead, stooping as he ran, his leather jacket hanging loosely on his shoulders. His whole body quaked every time his foot hit the ground.

Then, a few hundred meters farther down the hollow to the east, another patrol came into view. Their aim was unsure but their very presence left Bryan and James no other alternative than to keep running straight down toward the railway line and the two trains that would soon block their path.

Bryan was out of breath, casting his head from side to side in an attempt to catch up with James. A crazy idea had struck him. If they were hit, which seemed inevitable now, it would nevertheless be better to die close to each other.

The first train to cross their path arrived from the east along the line nearest them.

The locomotive crew watched passively as the patrols gained on them from behind and from the sides. One after another, the absurd sight of brown wooden cars with red crosses painted on them rumbled past in the barren white countryside. Not a single face was to be seen in the cars' few windows.

Next, two joined armored locomotives pulling their gray-green string of cars came snorting along the far eastbound track and soon disappeared out of view behind the foremost locomotive of the hospital train. The soldiers on the roofs of the armored train's rear cars had already caught sight of Bryan and James and were making a move, but couldn't fire at such an oblique angle for fear of hitting the hospital train.

Bryan took long strides forward, stepping in the boot prints James had made a moment before. James's labored breathing in front of him made a whistling sound. Bryan slowed down and looked back.

James reached the train just as two cars were passing. He picked up his pace and reached for the nearest handrail. In a flash he was caught in a grip so far down the metal railing that it was impossible to swing his foot up onto the bottommost step. The sweat in his palm had instantly frozen to ice. He was just about to lose his balance and fall under the axles when Bryan caught up and tried to grab hold of him.

The hard shove forced James forward, toward the nearest stepladder. Running awkwardly sideways, he swung his free arm around like a windmill so as not to lose his balance. After a few whirls he lost his Enfield as it was flung up over the train in a wide arc. Then he stumbled and was dragged along the railroad ties for a moment, fastened to the car by his frozen hand. Every time a railroad tie struck him, he swung dangerously close to the wheels. Then, with a superhuman effort, he kicked out one leg and regained his balance. Bryan took a few more running steps and sprang onto the front of the car, grasping the handrail so briefly that only a tiny piece of skin froze to it and was torn off.

"I've got hold now!" shouted James, hauling himself upward so violently that he was almost flung sideways into the metal steps.

Diagonally behind them the advance guard of the first patrol came into sight, their faces blue with frost and far too tired to keep their balance in the gently drifting snow. One of the soldiers tried to grab the stepladder to the roof of the last car, but he tumbled forward in the attempt, tripping along on his toes. Finally he stumbled, somersaulting heavily over the railroad ties.

Then he lay still.

Meanwhile, the armored train had passed them in the other direction and the hospital train was still accelerating.

Only then did their pursuers give up the chase.

CHAPTER 3

Faint, dancing silhouettes of naked trees appeared on the hilltops south of the rumbling train.

James had gradually recovered his breath and was stroking his friend's back. "Sit up, Bryan. You'll catch pneumonia!"

Both men's teeth were chattering.

"We can't stay out here," said Bryan, who lay flat on the icy car platform.

The track curved gently toward a row of hills, allowing them a brief view of where they were heading.

"If we stay out here, we'll freeze to death or be picked off when we pass a station. We have to jump off as soon as we can."

Bryan stared blankly in front of him as he listened to the accelerating thumping of the rail joints between him. "Bloody business—all of it!" he added quietly.

"Are you hurt?" James didn't look at Bryan. "Can you get up?"

"I don't think I'm any more the worse for wear than you are," James replied.

"At least it's a good thing we wound up on a hospital train. We've got beds just inside that door."

Neither of them laughed. James reached for the handle and wriggled it a bit with his fingertips. The door was locked.

Bryan shrugged. The idea was crazy. "We'll just get shot the instant we open the door. Who knows what's behind there?"

James knew what he meant. No one trusted a red cross when it was painted on something German. They'd been misusing that sign of mercy for a long time, which was why Allied fighter pilots no longer spared transport trains like this. James and Bryan knew this all too well.

And what if it really was a hospital train? The Germans' hatred of Allied pilots was understandable, just as James and Bryan had good reason to hate the pilots in the Luftwaffe. They all had much too much on their conscience to find room for mercy. All of them who were taking part in this demented war.

A single glance from James drew a nod from Bryan. His eyes showed nothing but sadness.

Their luck was no longer interminable.

The train rushed past a level crossing with a jolt. James stuck his head out cautiously and looked ahead. It was morning, but still dark. The countryside lay sleeping. There was no clue as to what the next curve, or the curve after that, might bring.

Sounds of movement were beginning to come from inside the car. Morning had arrived. Now the medical orderlies could start their work. Behind Bryan and James the sliding bolt rattled in the latch connecting the platforms of the two cars.

A quick tap on his woolen collar made James look up. Bryan drew himself in completely behind the door and signaled to James to do likewise.

A second afterward the handle turned. A very young man stuck his head out, drew in a breath of fresh air, and sighed contentedly. Thank God the wind was coming from the north, so the orderly had to step all the way to the edge of the platform with his back to them before unzipping his fly.

Bryan laid his hand on James's arm as it started trembling nervously, but James withdrew it and transferred his weight onto the leg best situated for a sudden leap. The orderly bent his knees a little and farted. Then with satisfaction and relief he shook the last drops of urine out into the wind.

From Bryan's position it looked as if James didn't move until the orderly turned around. The blow fell mercilessly across the German's dumbfounded face and he toppled backward. A dull thud and the body's abrupt angles signified the orderly's death against a naked elm trunk standing in solitary majesty on the embankment they'd just passed. The body continued its fall and disappeared behind some frosted scrub.

It would not be discovered for the time being.

Bryan was appalled. Never before had they stood face-to-face with the death they had so often inflicted upon others. James leaned against the vibrating end wall. "There was nothing else I could do, Bryan. It was him or us!"

Bryan pressed his forehead to James's cheek and sighed. "It won't be easy to give ourselves up now, James!"

The chance of doing so had otherwise been perfect. The young medical orderly had been alone and unarmed. But it was too late for regrets. What was done was done. The tracks rushed past beneath them and the bumps from the rails ticked faster and faster.

If they jumped off now they would be pulverized in the fall.

James turned his head and put his ear to the door. All was quiet inside. Experience had taught him to dry his palms on his trousers before he gingerly took hold of the handle of the rattling door. He put his finger to his lips and stuck his head halfway through the crack in the door.

Then he signaled for Bryan to follow.

The light was dim inside the car. A partition marked the transition to a larger compartment from which muffled sounds and a tiny chink of light reached them. Just below the ceiling hung some shelves stuffed with jars, bottles, tubes, and cardboard boxes of every conceivable size. In the corner was a footstool. This was the domain of the night orderly.

The kid whose life they had just taken.

James cautiously unzipped his jacket and signaled to Bryan to do likewise with his flying suit.

Soon they were wearing only shirts with torn sleeves and long underpants. James had flung the rest of their clothes off the car platform, out into the wind.

They were just hoping that anyone seeing them in such a getup wouldn't immediately shoot them.

The sight behind the partition made them stop dead in their tracks. Scores of soldiers lay packed closely together in narrow steel beds or on gray-striped kapok mattresses jammed against one another on the floor. A narrow strip of bare wooden planks led down to the other end. It was the only way they could go. Several expressionless, sleepy faces turned toward them without any apparent reaction. Many of the shapes lying there were still in uniform. None were privates.

There was an oppressive stink of urine and feces blended with the faint, sickly smells of camphor and chloroform. Many of the badly wounded men lay there making gurgling noises, jaws hanging. But none were complaining.

Walking slowly past with measured steps, James nodded at those in which he could see a bit of life. Thin, unwashed sheets were all that shielded them against the cold.

One man reached out weakly toward Bryan, who smiled weakly in return. James almost fell over a protruding foot. He put his hand to his mouth to stifle his cry of surprise and looked down at the soldier. The gaze that met him was cold and lifeless. The officer had presumably lain dead on the floor all night and was still lying there, clutching a gauze compress.

The gauze bandage was clean, but along the mattress were clotted crusts of the blood that suddenly and profusely must have left the poor devil.

James whisked the roll of gauze out of the dead man's hand and put it up to his lacerated earlobe, from which blood was streaming again. Just then they heard a rumbling and clanking sound from the end of the car from which they'd just come.

"Let's go!" whispered James.

"Can't we just stay where we are?" asked Bryan, as they stood in the passageway. Most of the floor here was covered with used surgical dressings that left a sickly stench.

"Haven't you got eyes in your head, Bryan?"

"What do you mean?"

"The officers in this car are wearing SS insignias. All of them! What do you think will happen if it's SS soldiers who discover us first, instead of the medical orderlies?" He flashed Bryan a dark smile. Then his lips tightened and his gaze hardened. "I promise I'll get us out of this, if you just leave the decisions to me!"

Bryan was silent.

"Is that okay?" James's expression became urgent.

"It's okay." Bryan attempted a smile. A bucketful of chrome-plated instruments jingled at his feet. An indeterminate dark liquid splashed up its sides.

Everything seemed to indicate that this train's main purpose was to take Germany's sons home in—rather than to—German soil.

If this was an ordinary hospital train, the Eastern Front must be hell on Earth.

· · ·

The next carriage was not dark. Several lightbulbs shone down over the two rows of beds that were packed together along the walls.

James stopped behind one of the beds to tip up the patient's chart. Then he nodded to the patient, who was in another world, and went on to the next bed. At the sight of the next chart he stopped abruptly. Bryan walked cautiously up to him and glanced at the chart.

"What's it say?" he whispered.

"It says 'Schwarz, Siegfried Anton. Born 10/10/1907, *Hauptsturm-führer.*'"

James let the chart fall and looked Bryan straight in the eyes. "They're *all* SS officers! This car, too, Bryan."

One of the patients nearest them had already been dead for some hours. A resourceful orderly had secured his maimed arm to an overhead beam so it was undisturbed by the sporadic jolting. James looked at the man's armpit and grabbed Bryan.

A scream from the car they'd just left aroused the man whose chart they had just studied. He looked at James and Bryan with saliva bubbling in the corners of his mouth.

Farther along the train, where the cars were coupled together with coarse, dark-brown, concertina-pleated canvas, they sensed the next car was different. The sound of the rails was more subdued. The door handle was made of brass and the door slid open without creaking.

Here there was no partition. A few lightbulbs shed their yellowish glow over ten beds placed in parallel rows so close together that the nursing staff could scarcely wedge themselves between them. Glass bottles containing life-sustaining liquids hung over the beds and clinked faintly against the metal stands. It was the only sound that came from this car. But voices could clearly be heard from the next carriage.

James squeezed in between the first beds and bent over the nearest patient. He stood for a moment regarding the sick man's chest, which rose and sank almost imperceptibly. Whereupon he turned around without a word and put his ear to the next patient in the region of his heart.

"What the devil are you doing, James?" protested Bryan as quietly as he could.

"Find one who's dead—but hurry!" said James without looking at him as he swept past to listen to the next one.

"You don't intend for us to lie in those beds, do you?" Bryan didn't believe this crazy notion for a moment.

The look James sent him as he briefly straightened up gave him no reason to think otherwise. "Got a better idea?" was all his eyes seemed to say.

"They'll kill us, James! If not for the orderly, then for doing this."

"Shut up, Bryan. They'll kill us anyway, on any pretext they can get away with. You can be sure of that!" James suddenly stood up from the next bed and shoved the body forward into a sitting position. Then he stripped the hospital shirt off over the man's head and let him fall back again, arms dangling heavily and limply over the sides of the bed.

"Help me with this," he ordered as he pulled a hypodermic needle out of the dead man's arm and whipped the blanket off him. A rotten stench made Bryan gasp.

Next James pushed the body farther forward, forcing Bryan to grab hold of it. The dead man's skin was bruised and cool, but not cold. Waves of nausea made Bryan hold his breath and look away as James wrenched at the clasps of the nearest window, his knuckles hard and white.

The icy air from the half-open window made Bryan feel faint and almost fall. James pulled the body partly out of Bryan's grasp, raised its left arm slightly, then glanced underneath and at the soldier's face. He was not much older than they were.

"Help me now, Bryan!" The corpse's arms stuck limply up in the air as James got hold of it under the armpits. Bryan grasped the feet and pushed. Then James leaned as far back as he could to get the body off the bed. Whereupon he took a deep breath and pushed the soldier upward with all his might, resting the head momentarily on the narrow metal edge of the windowframe. Not until Bryan released his grip and the body flapped passively through the air and plunged through the thin ice of a drainage canal did the truth dawn on him.

From here on, there was no return to innocence.

James quickly moved to the other side of the bed and took the next patient's pulse. Then he repeated the procedure, tipping the man forward.

Without a word Bryan took hold of the body and tossed the blanket to the floor. This man was not bandaged and was slightly smaller and stockier than the previous one.

"But he's not dead," Bryan objected, hugging the warm body as James pushed the man's arm back and up, staring at his armpit.

"Blood type A-positive. Remember that, Bryan!" Two faint markings in the armpit revealed the work of a tattooist.

"What do you mean, James?"

"That you resemble him more than I do, and that from now on you're blood type A-positive. All SS officers have their blood group tattooed in their left armpit and most of them have the *SS* sign in the right one."

Bryan stopped short. "You're mad! They'll discover us instantly!"

James didn't react. He turned up the two bed charts and studied them in turn. "Your name's Arno von der Leyen. You're an *Oberführer*. I'm Gerhart Peuckert. Remember that!"

Bryan stared at James incredulously.

"*Oberführer*! Yes, you heard right." James looked serious. "And I'm a *Standartenführer*. We've risen in the ranks, Bryan!"

A few moments after they'd undressed and let their clothes disappear the same way as the two soldiers, the sudden rushing sound of wind from a nearby house told them they had passed a level crossing.

"Take it off," said James, pointing at the identity tag that had been hanging on Bryan's chest for over four years.

Bryan hesitated. James tore the tag off with a quick jerk. Bryan had a sinking feeling as James flung the two tags out into the emptiness and closed the window.

"What about Jill's scarf?" said Bryan, pointing at the silk cloth with its embroidered heart that was still hanging around James's neck. James didn't reply. Instead he pulled the hospital shirt he had taken off the dead man over his head.

Still expressionless, James flung one leg over the excrement-littered bed and lay down on top of it. Taking a deep breath, he collected himself, stared briefly at the ceiling and without turning his head, whispered, "Okay. So far, so good. Now we lie here, get it? No one knows who we are and we're not going to tell them. Whatever happens, remember to keep your bloody mouth shut! One single slip and it'll be the end for both of us."

"You needn't tell me that, dammit!" Bryan looked with displeasure at the stained sheet. It felt damp as he lay down. "I'd rather you told me what you think the orderlies will say when they see us. We can't fool them, James."

"If you just keep your mouth shut and pretend to be unconscious they won't suspect anything, don't worry. There are probably more than a thousand wounded men on this train."

"The ones in here seem to be special. . . ."

A clanking metallic sound from the car in front made them stop short and shut their eyes. The sound of steps grew louder, passed them by, and continued into the next carriage. Bryan opened his eyes a fraction and caught a glimpse of a uniform as the figure disappeared.

"What about those needles?" Bryan said quietly. James glanced over his shoulder. The rubber tubing hung limply beside the bed. "You won't get me to stick one of those in my arm."

The expression on James's face sent shivers down his spine.

James was out of bed without a sound and grabbed hold of Bryan's arm. Bryan stared wildly at him. "No, you don't!" he hissed, horrified. "We have no idea what was wrong with those soldiers. It might be dangerous!" A second later, Bryan's gasp told James that such deliberations were now superfluous. Bryan stared incredulously at the needle that was buried deep into the bend of his elbow, the rubber tube still swinging. James had thrown himself back into the neighboring deathbed.

"You needn't be afraid, Bryan. Whatever the soldiers suffered from won't kill us."

"How do you know? They didn't have any wounds. They could have had terrible diseases."

"Would you rather be shot than take that chance?" James looked down at his own arm and tightened his grip on the needle. He turned his head to one side and pressed the needle into a random vein, making him almost pass out.

Just then the rear door of the car opened.

Bryan felt his heart beating treacherously loud as the sound of footsteps merged with voices. He couldn't understand the words. For him, they were merely sounds.

Scenes from happier times at Cambridge suddenly flashed through his mind.

In those days James had been too busy studying German, his main subject, to partake in typical college foolishness. Now he lay there reaping the benefits of understanding what was being said. Bryan was plagued by qualms of guilt. If he could, he'd gladly give all those hours of laziness and all his springtime flirts and other frivolous pursuits in exchange for being able to understand a fraction of what was being said in that railway car.

In his frustration Bryan dared to open his eyes a tiny crack. A few beds away several people were bowed over, studying an upturned chart.

Then a nurse drew the sheet over the man's head as the others moved on. Cold, clammy sweat broke out along Bryan's hairline and trickled slowly down his forehead.

A buxom older woman led the way and cast appraising glances over the sides of the beds as she shook the metal ends. Apparently she was in charge. At the sight of James's ear she stopped and wedged herself in between Bryan and James's beds.

She muttered a couple of words and bent farther down as if she were about to swallow James up.

Straightening, she turned and glanced at Bryan just as he was closing his eyes. "Please God, let her go past me," he thought, promising himself not to be so careless again.

The click of her heels disappeared behind him. He scowled from beneath almost-closed eyelids. James still lay quietly on his side with his face turned toward Bryan, eyes closed, without the slightest trace of a blink.

Perhaps James was right in thinking the staff couldn't tell one patient from another. At any rate, the senior nursing officer had walked past them without comment.

But what if it came to a closer inspection? When they had to be washed, for example. Or when they simply had to pee. Or shit, for that matter. Bryan dared not think that thought through to the end, already feeling a treacherous pressure mounting in his abdomen.

No sooner had the senior nurse checked the last bed in the car than she clapped her hands loudly and gave an order. In no time there was complete silence.

After a few minutes Bryan half opened his eyes again. James lay staring at him meaningfully.

"They're gone," whispered Bryan, glancing down the row of beds. "What happened?"

"They're leaving us till later. There are others who are worse off."

"Can you understand what they say?"

"Yes." James put his hand to his ear and looked down at himself. The cuts on his body and hand were not conspicuous. "What do your wounds look like?"

"I don't know."

"Then find out!"

"I can't take my shirt off now!"

"Try! Remove the blood, if there is any. Otherwise they'll suspect something's wrong."

Bryan glanced at the needle. He looked down the passageway, took a deep breath, and pulled the shirt sideways over his head so that it hung loosely on the arm with the needle.

"How does it look?"

"Not too good." Both arms and shoulders needed a good wash. The cuts were not deep but a gash in Bryan's shoulder continued onto his back.

"Wash it off with your hand. Use spit and lick your hand afterwards, but hurry up!"

James raised himself up a trifle. He nodded slightly when Bryan's shirt once again hid his shoulder wound. His lips tried to form a smile but his eyes were intent on something else. "We'll have to tattoo ourselves, Bryan," he said, "as soon as possible."

"How do we do that?"

"You prick some dye under the skin. We'll have to use the needle."

The thought made him nauseous. "And the dye?"

"I think we can use the dirt under our nails."

An examination of their hands revealed that the amount of dirt was at any rate sufficient. "Don't you think we'll risk getting tetanus?"

"From what?"

"The muck under our nails!"

"Forget it, Bryan. That's not our biggest problem."

"Can you imagine how painful that would be?"

"No, I'm wondering what to tattoo."

The clarity of this statement took Bryan by surprise. At no time had he thought of asking himself that question. What should they tattoo? "What's your blood type, James?" he asked.

"O-negative. And you?"

"B-positive," Bryan replied quietly.

"Sorry to say," said James wearily, "but listen. If we don't tattoo 'A+' they're bound to find something's bloody wrong sooner or later. It's written in their medical records, isn't it?"

"And what if they give us the wrong blood? That's dangerous as hell!"

"Yes, I suppose it is." James spoke very quietly. "You do as you like, Bryan, but I'm tattooing 'A+.'"

The pressure in his abdomen confused Bryan, diverting his attention. He couldn't hold out much longer. "I need to pee," he said.

"Then pee! There's no need to restrain yourself here."

"In the bed?"

"Yes, dammit! In the bed, Bryan. Where else?"

Sudden movements from the car behind them made them shut their eyes and freeze their position. Bryan was lying uncomfortably with one arm beneath him and the other slantwise over the blanket. He wouldn't be able to urinate now, even if he wanted to.

Nature's own regulating mechanism saw to that.

By listening to their voices, Bryan guessed there were as many as four nurses. Most probably two nurses saw to one bed at a time. Bryan dared not turn his head.

At the far end of the compartment one of the nursing teams lowered a dead man's bed guard. They were presumably going to remove him.

The team nearest Bryan was chatting intimately and working efficiently.

He caught a glimpse of them pulling the shirt off the patient in front of them, exposing his legs and genitals. They stood bent over him, rotating their arms in rubbing movements, never pausing or hesitating, with the sole object of getting the job over with.

The nurses at the back of the car had already wound the sheet around the dead man in the third bed and were about to turn him onto his back.

As they pulled the soldier into the middle of the sheet a sound came from him that made all four nurses stop what they were doing. A long wound, stretching from one shoulder up over the back of his head, had begun bleeding. Without paying attention to it, one of the women drew her nurse's badge out of her collar and jabbed the pin into the man's side. If this drew any protest from the patient, Bryan couldn't hear it. Whether they considered him to be dead or not, they kept on wrapping him in the sheet.

He had no idea how he and James were going to be able to keep still enough to not arouse suspicion. Bryan looked at the nurses' dispassionate faces as they worked. And what if they stuck a pin into *him*? Would he be able to lie motionless? Bryan doubted it.

He shuddered at the thought.

It gave Bryan a start when the nurses skipped James and made straight for him. They ripped the blanket off him in one movement. A single firm grasp made him roll over on his back.

The women were young. He felt embarrassed as they parted his legs and began to wipe around his anus and under his scrotum with firm movements.

The water was icy cold and the shock almost made his thigh muscles quiver visibly. Bryan concentrated as hard as he could. If only he could avoid arousing suspicion. "Keep your armpits covered," he told himself as they turned him around again.

One of the women pried his buttocks apart and felt the sheet between his legs. They exchanged a few words. Perhaps they were surprised the sheet was still dry. Then one of the nurses bent over him and a second later Bryan sensed the whir of a slap heading for his cheek. In that fraction of a second he registered the fact that he was about to be struck and told himself to relax. The blow fell hard on his cheekbone and across his eyebrow without his moving a muscle.

And now the pin, he supposed.

He let his mind go, far from the nightmarish reality in the pitching train, and felt the pin being thrust into his side.

He grew cold. But not a muscle moved.

This would be more difficult next time, if there were a next time.

Then the train car began to sway, making the beds creak. From the far end of the room came the sound of a thud. The two nurses who had just reached James's bed shouted out and rushed back to where they'd come from. The corpse they'd just wrapped up had fallen to the floor. Gingerly Bryan slid his arm down to the tender spot on his thigh where they had jabbed him with the pin. On the bed beside him lay James, quiet as a mouse with his shirt halfway up over his head, looking at him with eyes wide open in a chalk-white face.

In spite of himself, Bryan managed to mouth that there was nothing to fear, that he should relax and close his eyes. But James was far away in a state of anxiety and dread.

Insidious, traitorous beads of sweat trickled down James's face. Several repeated jolts of the car made the nurses topple forward and drop their heavy, dead burden. Their loud complaints made the other two nurses rush to their aid. James gave a start as they ran past and he began panting in short gasps under his blanket.

Two more violent jolts made the whole carriage quake and Bryan was thrown to the edge of his bed. James drew his legs up under him, convulsively clutching his sheet.

As the train continued to jolt along, Bryan stretched his arm toward James in order to calm him, but James didn't appear to notice. Instead, a scream began to form itself deep inside his throat. Before it had a chance to pass his lips, Bryan sat up and took hold of the steel basin the nurses had left by the bed in front of James's half-naked body.

The water splashed up against the wall as Bryan slammed the basin down on his friend's temple. The nurses turned around when they heard the sound, but could see only Bryan, whose body was hanging limply halfway over the edge of the bed. The washbasin lay on the floor, upside down.

As far as Bryan could tell, James gave the nurses no cause for suspicion as they washed him. Chattering softly, they finished what they were doing, engrossed in conversation and without the slightest interest in the armpit's missing tattoo.

As soon as they left, Bryan took a good look at James. The mutilated earlobe and the bruises across his face made his otherwise fine features look crooked and added years to his age.

Bryan sighed.

According to the picture imprinted in his mind as they jumped on the train, they had to be in the fifth or sixth railway car. Behind them were carriages as far as the eye could see. If circumstances demanded their jumping off the train in daylight, they could be passed by as many as forty cars. They were hardly likely to make such an escape without being discovered. And where would they hide, hundreds of kilometers behind enemy lines?

The worst thing, however, was that they no longer could give themselves up. One could say they already had three human lives on their conscience. What difference did it make that one of their victims had already been dead and the other dying? Not wearing the correct uniform, they would be treated as spies and tortured to make them divulge everything they knew. Before being shot.

Despite the misery Bryan had witnessed during the war, he felt injustice had dealt them an unreasonably hard blow. He was not ready to die. There was still a lot to live for. Fleeting images of his family evoked sadness and despair, but also warmth.

At that moment Bryan's body relaxed for a moment, allowing his bladder to empty itself freely and soothingly.

The train had gradually resumed its normal, steady rhythm. The pale wintry sunlight edged into the carriage, muted by the matted windows. Voices presaged new examinations.

Several personnel moved silently out of the path of a man in a white coat who towered above them and made purposefully toward the first patient. Here he turned up the chart with a roughness that shook the end of the bed. Making a short notation, he snatched the paper out of its frame and handed it to a nurse.

None of the patients were examined. The tall medical officer merely leaned over the foot end of each bed, exchanged a few words with the nursing staff, gave some instructions, and hurried on. He looked with respect at the chart at the fourth bed where Bryan lay, whispered a few words to the senior nurse, and shook his head.

Afterward the doctor pointed with a jabbing movement at the head end of James's bed, whereupon a young girl sprang forward and raised it up. Bryan did all he could to breathe quietly and imagine himself far away. If they listened to his heart now, they would find his chest in explosive turmoil.

They talked for some time at the foot of Bryan's bed. He could recognize the senior nurse's sharp voice and sensed that she'd been dissatisfied with his reactions and general condition. The bed shook silently as someone went to stand close behind him. Then strong hands took hold of his sleeve and pulled him over on his back. A gentle fingertip tap over his eyebrows was followed by another. Bryan was sure he had blinked. He almost stopped breathing.

Voices blended and then quite unexpectedly a thumb descended on his eyelid and pried it open. A flickering glimpse of the concentrated beam of a flashlight directed at his eyeball blinded him completely. Then they slapped him on the cheek and shone it again.

Cold air swept over his feet, and hands took hold of his toes as the doctor drew back his eyelid again. Repeated small pricks in his toes apparently told them nothing. Bryan lay stock-still and was terrified.

He was totally unprepared when they pressed a cloth soaked in ammonia to his face. The shock bored into his brain and respiratory system with great effect. Opening his eyes wide, Bryan turned his head away from the cloth and into his pillow, gasping for breath.

Through the film of tears a pair of eyes appeared close to his head. The doctor said a few words to him and slapped him gently on the cheek. Then they straightened him up and raised the head end of the bed another couple of notches so that he was confronted with the enemy in a half-sitting position.

Bryan chose to fix his gaze on the wall behind them and received the next blow with wild, wide-open eyes. "Hold your breath. . . . Don't blink," he told himself. He and James had often whiled away the time in the summer cottage in Dover with contests of will such as this.

The next blow was harder. Bryan made no resistance and let his head rock backward as easily as if it were coming loose. The group of medics dispersed after some discussion, leaving a single person beside his chart, where scratching noises were replaced by a smack as the frame fell back into place.

Bryan kept his eyes open. During the rest of the ward inspection he noticed they were keeping him under constant observation. Then his eyes slowly closed.

He scarcely felt the injection they gave him as he dozed off.

CHAPTER 4

C'mon!" The voice sounded far away, merging as if with the sounds of summer and layers of mist. "Wake up, Bryan!"

He felt as though he was swaying and the voice became deeper and louder. Then he felt his arm being shaken. It took some time before Bryan realized where he was.

The train car was quiet now in the semidarkness. James's cautious smile was followed by a final shake of Bryan's arm. Bryan smiled back.

"We'll have to whisper." Bryan nodded; he'd understood. "You were unconscious when I woke up," James continued. "What happened?"

"I knocked you out," said Bryan, trying hard to concentrate. "And then they examined us. They looked at my pupils. And I opened my eyes. They know there's something about me that doesn't fit."

"I know. They've been looking at you several times."

"How long have I been unconscious?"

"Try to listen, Bryan!" James withdrew his arm. "The car in front of us is full of soldiers. They're going home on leave but I think they've also been instructed to keep an eye on the patients."

"Home?"

"Yes, we're going farther into Germany. We've been on the move all day. During the last hour or so we've been moving quite slowly. I don't know where we're headed, but we're stopped at Kulmbach now."

"Kulmbach?" With great difficulty Bryan tried to follow what James was saying. Kulmbach? Had the train stopped?

"North of Bayreuth," James whispered. "Bamberg, Kulmbach, Bayreuth. You remember that, don't you?"

"God knows what they injected me with. My mouth's completely dry."

"Pull yourself together, Bryan!" A few shakes made Bryan open his eyes again. "What happened when they washed us?"

"What do you mean, 'happened'?"

"The tattoos, man! What happened?"

"They didn't look."

James threw his head back on the pillow and stared at the ceiling. "We've got to do it now, while there's still some light."

"I'm freezing, James."

"You're right. It's goddamn cold in here! They've aired it out. The floor was covered with snow just now." With his eyes still on the ceiling, James pointed at the floor. "See, it's still there. You can understand why the soldiers next door have their coats on."

"Have you seen them?"

"They come in here at intervals. A couple of hours ago they were looking for the orderly we threw off the train. They also know there was an incident with some British pilots who'd been seen jumping onto the train. The dog patrol must have reported it."

"How?" Bryan felt reality rising up inside him faster than he could keep up with it.

"I don't know how. But they know. And they've been looking for us. But they haven't found us, and they won't, either."

"What about the orderly?"

"I don't know." With no further talk James sat up and seized the needle in his left arm. Closing his eyes, he pulled it out as the drops of nourishment from the tube mixed with blood and dripped down onto the sheet. Bryan raised himself on his elbows and tried to watch what James was doing. With a small knot in the rubber tube to stop the flow of liquid, James rolled his shirtsleeve up over his shoulder. Then he scraped a couple of fingernails clean with the point of the needle and with tiny movements pricked the dirt in beneath the thin skin of his armpit.

James began looking ill again. The color drained from his cheeks and his lips turned blue. The needle went on pricking. More and more red drops appeared among the light covering of hair on his armpit. It took a lot of pricking to write an A+.

"I damned well hope it doesn't get infected," whispered Bryan, pulling his own needle out. "But if it does, I'd rather be on the safe side. I'm going to tattoo my own blood type, James."

"You're mad," James protested, though it didn't appear he was going to try to coerce his friend. He had enough worries of his own.

Bryan felt he had thought things through well enough. Of course there was a risk attached to writing B+ instead of A+. But the blood-group signs resembled each other so much that anyone would think the person writing the case notes must have made a mistake. If they ever compared the two, they would be puzzled at most, and then be sure to correct the notes. He was certain of that.

In this way they could cram blood and other stuff into him without the risk of making him seriously ill. After all, that was the most important thing. The possibility that they might not look at his armpit at all, but go by what stood in the case notes, was a thought Bryan chose to ignore. So he began scraping under his nails.

The tattooing went very slowly.

Twice they were interrupted by a clattering sound coming from the car in front. The second time, Bryan instinctively pulled his needle under his blanket. A shadow flickering in the corner of his eye made him shut his eyes.

Some sounds over by James's bed revealed the presence of yet another person who had come to inspect them. At the first lurch of the train, Bryan let his head roll limply to the side facing James's bed. There he caught a glimpse of the black-clad officer.

Bryan felt his loathing transformed into cold shivers that distracted him from the pain in his armpit. He clutched the needle so that it disappeared inside his hand, hoping James had managed to be equally cautious.

The SS security officer clenched his hands behind his back and stood looking straight down at the face of the "unconscious" man. There were some metallic sounds and shouts from outside. Not even a sudden jerk of the train could make the officer move.

Several jolts from behind were followed by loud bumps and slight pitching movements. The train was changing tracks. When the railway workers were finally finished, the black-coated officer turned on his heel and disappeared.

Later that night another of the black-clad men entered the car and made straight for the bed on the other side of James. He stood there for a moment, shining his flashlight in the man's face. Then he stiffened, half smothered a cry, and rushed toward the rear carriage.

A few moments later he returned with several others. A white-coated man James and Bryan hadn't seen before tore open the patient's shirt at the neck, exposing his chest.

After listening for a few seconds, he removed his stethoscope and instantly exploded in a paroxysm of rage that created considerable confusion. The nurses gesticulated and retreated backward. Then the security officer appeared, slamming the door behind him. He instantly issued some commands and struck the nearest nurse in the face without hesitation. After more stormy exchanges, the soldier who had started the whole affair rushed out of the car, returning immediately with reinforcements. In the meantime the patient was carried out, followed by guards and nurses.

The growl of a truck motor and the lengthy screech of brakes echoed along the railway platform to merge with the feverish commands outside. Inside the train the patients were once again left to themselves.

"What happened?" Bryan asked.

James put his finger to his lips. "He's dying. He's a *Gruppenführer* and the security officer was furious," answered James, almost inaudibly.

"*Gruppenführer?*"

"Lieutenant general!" James smiled. "Yes, it's strange. To think I've been lying next to a bloody Waffen-SS general. I can damned well understand the staff are upset. Mistakes have consequences in a place like this!"

"Where are they taking him now?"

"The security people are driving him to Bayreuth. There's a hospital there."

Bryan licked his fingers again, rubbed gingerly at the clotted blood in his armpit, and sucked his fingers clean. It was important not to leave any trace of their work.

"Do you know what worries me most, James?"

"No." A foul odor escaped from James's bed as he turned around and pulled the blanket up over him.

"What if the sick men are on their way home to their families?"

"I think they are."

The confirmation made Bryan close his eyes. "And what makes you think that?" he asked, doing his best to control himself.

"When they carried the general out I heard the word '*Heimatschutz*.' I don't know what it signifies, but in direct translation it means 'home protection' or something like that. That's where we're bound, as far as I can see—home protection!"

"Then they'll discover us, James!" Bryan hissed.

"I suppose so."

"We have to get away. This is completely crazy. We know neither what we're supposed to be suffering from nor where we're heading!"

James's face was almost devoid of expression. "Stop getting me worked up, Bryan, okay?"

"Then just tell me one thing. Do you agree that we have to get away from here? Tonight, for example, if the train moves off again?"

In the long silence that followed, the sound of the truck could be heard, fading slowly as it headed away from the station. The voices outside had moved farther down the tracks. The patient on the other side of Bryan moaned briefly, then sighed deeply.

"We'll freeze to death," James finally replied, "but you're right."

Before morning any thought of escape had evaporated. Three women in civilian clothes entered the front end of their car and quietly opened the door to the front platform and the icy-cold air outside. Just in front of Bryan's bed they were received by the doctors who resignedly reciprocated their "Heil Hitler" and instantly began to argue. The women hardly spoke, letting the senior medical officers cool down. Then the entire team made a round of all the beds, accompanied by the doctors' scattered comments. They stood whispering for a moment beside Bryan's bed and then disappeared into the next car.

"Gestapo. Those women are from the Gestapo," James said as soon as the carriage door slammed. "They've come to guard us. 'Round the clock! And they've been threatened with reprisals if anything more goes wrong. We've landed in fine company, Bryan. We're important to them, but I just don't know why."

From then on, one of these women sat permanently on a chair at the far end of the car. Even when a convoy arrived just before the train departed with several stretchers bearing lifeless, desolate bodies to fill up the empty beds, the female guard made no sign of moving. It was not her duty to help, not even if it meant merely giving the stretcher-bearers a bit more room to get past her.

The women said nothing when they relieved one another, which, as far as Bryan could judge, took place every other hour. A new one simply came in and sat down, and only then did the old guard leave once she had been replaced.

Not being able to talk to James overwhelmed Bryan with a sense of insecurity. They had agreed to try to escape, but what now? Every time Bryan stole a glance at James, he saw only the immobile outline of his body under the white material.

The train was running at full speed again and the rushing sounds of passing trees in the train's slipstream were proof of its being too late to jump off, even without a guard to prevent them.

So they were going to be found out. Only a very simple calculation involving a couple of unknown factors was needed in order to reckon when and where that would be.

Since climbing onto the train they might have covered 200 kilometers at the most. If Bryan shut his eyes he could visualize a clear outline of Germany and all its geographical features without much difficulty. The 200 kilometers was the known quantity, and the destination the unknown. It could be a day or two before they got there or it might only be a question of hours. It all depended on the destination, the speed, the number of stops, and the traffic on the line, not to mention the possibility of air raids.

The lights were swaying gently above him in a faint milky haze when Bryan awoke. James's arm was still hanging over the edge of the bed. He had shook Bryan's bed in order to wake him. "You're restless," he mouthed, looking worried. Bryan didn't know what he'd been doing and was suddenly jerked back into reality. It was seldom he snored and as far as he knew he'd never spoken in his sleep. Or had he?

The nurses had already started the morning ablutions. They didn't look at all cheerful compared with the previous day. Dark circles under their eyes and a characteristic transparency of the skin clearly showed what they'd been through. Without sleep, with the responsibility for hundreds of patients and hard-pressed by the charge of negligence in caring for the dying general, their eyes revealed stress and their hands moved mechanically.

This was Bryan and James's third day in enemy territory. "Thursday, the thirteenth of January, 1944," Bryan imprinted on his memory, wondering how long he would be able to keep track of the days, and how long his enemies would allow him to.

Suddenly the activity in their carriage was transformed into confusion as the security officer made his swaggering entrance to review his troops. It was unnecessary for him to tyrannize them. Bryan lay with his head turned to one side and noticed how James was slowly and imperceptibly clenching his fist. Was it fear or anger?

Bryan couldn't even interpret his own state of mind.

The two nursing teams reached Bryan and James simultaneously. This time they tugged so hard at the sheets that their bodies spun around. A slamming noise indicated that James had crashed into the edge of the bed during the maneuver.

Bryan tried to keep his left armpit covered by his arm as they dried him. This time the icy water was a relief. The crusts of urine and nocturnal defecation had stopped stinging but instead had made the skin swell and itch. Only the nurses' fingernails on the sensitive skin of his scrotum caused him discomfort.

The sheet was new, unbleached, and as yet unwashed. A tickling pleasure over its smoothness merged with irritation caused by the stiff folds passing down along his side. He had to remain in this position until they all had gone. In the meantime he could watch the nurses working away on James.

The blow he had given James must have caused the wound under his ear to reopen. Long stripes of disinfectant mixed with traces of blood pointed up his cheek toward the dark patch. A small fragment of skin had been torn from the base of the earlobe and lay on the piece of gauze beside him. The security officer was watching and stepped closer as they dabbed on the iodine. His surveillance made the nursing assistant nervous and she came to squirt a drop of the golden-brown liquid onto James's forehead.

As the nurse and her assistant hurried on, the security officer stepped still closer and stood watching the drop as it slowly trickled down toward the corner of James's eye. Millimeter by millimeter the stinging liquid brought them closer to the catastrophe of being discovered. James must have realized he was being watched, otherwise he would have wiped the drop away, turned on his side or shut his eyes extra tight. Passing the bridge of the nose, the drop was free to run.

Just as it would have run into his eye, the black riding breeches moved in front of Bryan's face. With a light flick of his thumb he smeared the drop to one side and up into James's eyebrow. Then he crossed his hands behind his back and gently rubbed the iodine-tinted thumb clean.

Despite two days without food Bryan didn't feel hungry, and apart from the discomfort of his dry mouth he didn't feel thirsty, either. So the nourishment he was receiving through the tube must have been sufficient for the time being.

Sixty hours had now passed since their last normal meal. A good fifty-five hours had passed since their crash and they'd been lying in bed not quite fifty hours. But what would happen when another hundred and fifty hours had passed? When would they have a rubber tube forced down their throat, and how would they manage it without reacting at all? The answer was blatantly simple. They wouldn't!

Bryan had to make sure he was never subjected to that treatment. Which meant it was necessary for him to awaken from his sham apathy. The same went for James. Abandon his comalike state and do as the others.

This would give them many advantages. They'd be able to follow what was going on around them and hold up their morale by signaling to each other. They could pretend to be slowly recovering. Once they got that far, they would be able to feed themselves, sit on a bedpan, and maybe even get out of bed.

Perhaps they would even be able to escape.

Again Bryan was left with the same question: What were they supposed to be suffering from, and why were they lying there at all?

The large majority of patients had no sign of injuries. Of course, a few serious wounds could be hidden from view under the blankets, but during the morning ablutions the naked bodies had so far given no hint as to what was wrong with them. One thing was sure. They were all apparently deeply unconscious, and this must have a cause. A couple of them had bandaged heads. These cases were obvious. There was every possible reason for them to lie still. But how about the rest?

What had been the matter with the two naked, dead men they had thrown off the train? And what were he and James supposed to be suffering in their stead?

What would it signify if they suddenly began opening their eyes and reacting to their surroundings? Would it matter? What consequences might it have? New analyses? X-ray examinations? And what would they say if all they found were two fit, unwounded craniums?

All the questions as to who they were, what they suffered from, and what would happen if their families came to visit them, led to one, logical conclusion.

Bryan had to open his eyes.

They would have to play the game as well as they could.

CHAPTER 5

The more Bryan thought about it, the more certain he became that he had done the only right thing. He had opened his eyes cautiously, making his "new" condition known. During the course of the day the orderlies and soldiers passed through the car constantly without paying any attention to him.

Beside him James lay completely motionless. Presumably he was asleep, maybe making up for the long night's vigil. Every time one of the Gestapo women watching over them stretched or dozed off for a moment, Bryan flung his arm over toward the neighboring bed, trying to attract James's attention. Once James turned his head and sighed deeply. Otherwise nothing happened, which worried Bryan more than the slamming of the door when the SS soldiers made their rounds.

The security officer showed up regularly.

The first time Bryan felt the cold eyes scrutinizing him, his heart stood still. The second time, he made sure to keep his gaze fixed solely on the neutral shadows on the ceiling. But even though the black-clad figure stared straight into Bryan's open, dead eyes several times, not once were his suspicions aroused.

Bryan had plenty of time to look around. Now and then a faint ray of sunlight broke through the flickering shadows on the window above him and settled in diffuse waves on the death-marked faces in the neighboring beds.

Time dragged on.

The train had been running quite slowly since sunrise. Sometimes it almost stopped. Each time sounds of nearby cars and human activity were heard indicated they had passed through yet another town.

As far as Bryan could reckon, they had to be traveling southwest and had already left Würzburg far behind. They could be making for Stuttgart, Karlsruhe, or one of the other towns not yet paralyzed by bombardment. It was only a question of time before these monuments to past grandeur would also be razed. Their mates in the Royal Air Force would come during the night and the Americans during the day until there was no reason left to come.

Bryan lay waiting for James to wake up. By now it was almost dark. The next guard to come on duty looked tired. This was already her third watch. She was a beautiful woman. Not nimble and young, but with the same compelling radiance as the smiling older women with flowing bosoms that Bryan and James used to undress with their eyes on the sands of Dover. Bryan forced himself not to look. This woman—his guard—was not smiling. She was already deeply marked by all she had gone through. But she was indeed lovely.

The woman stretched and let her arms drop heavily to her sides as she stared into the twilight at the shadows of the snow that again was falling in large flakes. A life of privation and inevitability was reflected in her gaze. Then she got up slowly and went over to the window. For a moment she was lost in thought with her forehead resting against the misted pane, enabling Bryan to act.

James lurched as Bryan hit him. Several tentative shakes had not been sufficient.

James's transition from sleep to rude awakening took place with no sudden movement or sign of surprise. It was this self-control that Bryan had always so greatly admired.

The still-drugged eyes calmly followed Bryan's gestures, trying to read the exaggerated movements of his mouth. Then his gaze clouded over and his eyelids grew heavy, stubbornly safeguarding the comforting sleep from which he'd just emerged. Bryan's eyes flashed a warning as to what might happen if he didn't pull himself together.

James began to nod his comprehension. "Keep your eyes open," said Bryan's sign language. "Pretend to be crazy," said his lips. "Then we'll have a chance," his eyes pleaded, hoping James would understand.

"You're the one who's crazy," mimed James calmly in return. He obviously disapproved of Bryan's suggestion.

"And if it comes to an interrogation, what can they do if we don't answer?" Bryan tried to continue his silent reasoning, but James had already decided.

"You first!" James gesticulated, as though the case were settled. Bryan nodded.

In a way, he was already in full swing.

That night the light in their car was switched off, though not before the doctor had made his rounds. The Gestapo woman returned his respectful greeting with a curt nod and followed his every movement. It all happened within the space of a few minutes.

Having taken the pulse of one of the new arrivals, the doctor glanced along the row of beds, inspecting each patient in turn as he strode past. At the sight of Bryan, who lay with wide-open eyes and his blanket half on the floor, he made an about-face in the middle of a stride and summoned the guard. After a heated exchange she rushed out the back of the car, leaving behind the echo of the door as she slammed it shut.

The doctor and nurse who had been fetched from the rear carriage bent over the bed, their heads almost touching Bryan's face.

It was extremely difficult for Bryan to figure out what they were doing, compelled as he was to stare stiffly into thin air. Only once did they enter his field of vision, offering a clue other than the physical maneuvers to which he was being subjected.

One thing happened after another. First they shone a light in his eyes, then they shouted at him. Next they struck him on the cheekbone and talked to him in subdued tones. The nurse laid her hand on his cheek and exchanged a few words with the doctor.

Bryan was waiting for her to reach for her sharp tool, the nurse's badge on her collar, but couldn't afford to turn and face her. He held his breath, waiting tensely for her to jab him. When she did so he reacted by rolling his eyes so the carriage ceiling revolved like a carousel and made him dizzy.

The next time she jabbed him he repeated the act, showing the whites of his eyes as they jerked from side to side in their tear-filled sockets.

They discussed him briefly, shone the light in his eyes again, and finally left him alone.

. . .

In the middle of the night James began humming tonelessly with his mouth wide open. The guard glanced up instantly, looking around in confusion as if she were expecting an enemy invasion to come from all directions at once.

Bryan opened his eyes and managed to turn slightly onto one side before the light was switched on. The sudden contrast blinded him for a moment. He, too, had been in his own world.

The illusion was extraordinarily successful and effective. Not only was James's expression vacant, foggy, and quietly manic, but it also had a trace of pain and apathy about it. The total impression was grotesque and repulsive. His hands lay relaxed on top of the blanket, but they were curled at the wrist and filthy with excrement. Lumps of shit stuck to his nails and brown smudges ran all the way up under his arms, clinging to the light covering of armpit hair. Blanket, pillow, sheet, bed guard, and shirt—everything was smeared with a stinking, sticky mess.

James had finally given way to nature's call.

The guard stepped back in revulsion, her arms held tightly to her chest.

The doctor, nurses, assistant nurses, and security officer had all returned to their quarters. The last thing Bryan heard before he dozed off again into a light, vigilant sleep was James's plaintive, atonal, and eternal humming, growing fainter and fainter. The injection they'd given him had started to work.

CHAPTER 6

The sensation of flies dancing on his eyelids and the gentle rocking of a pitching sea in a summer wind with cold spray settling like dust on his cheek had been competing for a long time with irrelevant sounds and an increasingly severe pain in his back. Then, in the trough of a wave, the water rose and hit him in the corner of the eye. Bryan blinked and felt the next splash more distinctly. The strange, massive pain in his back was spreading down his thigh.

Big, feathery snowflakes whirled over his face as he opened his eyes and drowsily tried to tune in to reality.

A narrow strip of snow-laden sky emerged above him, separating the station roof from the stationary train. Around him, stretchers were being removed. SS soldiers were getting off the front end of the train, one by one, their packs and rifles slung over their shoulders.

A couple of them hopped over the edge of the platform and walked farther along the tracks, chatting and joking casually with helmets and gas masks dangling from their backs.

Soldiers on their way home.

With a grating, screeching sound the rear car was detached from the rest of the train to reveal a view of hills and the town's buildings that were emerging from the mist. Another couple of snowflakes landed on Bryan's cheek, momentarily blending dream with reality. He raised his back a bit to lessen the effect of the coldness radiating from the ground and slowly looked around for James in the jumble of stretchers on the platform.

A row of vertical posts supported the station's half roof, creating a passage of less than two meters toward the wooden building. Stretchers were standing up against the wall in scattered blankets of snow. Some of the patients had already been taken away. Bryan fell back resignedly, imagining that he and James had already been split up. The dry rumble of an engine started up as yet another truck backed up to the chute at the far end of the platform.

Several men appeared and inspected the recumbent patients. Slapping their arms sharply against their bodies to shake off the loose snow in the folds of their coats, they grabbed hold of the nearest stretchers. After a while Bryan's was the only one left on the platform, apart from a stretcher that was half-hidden by a mail truck. At the end of his blanket the sharp imprint of naked feet stuck up, crowned by a dark, reddish patch. Bryan looked down his body and cautiously wiggled his toes. The piece of colored paper was pinned to the edge of his blanket, shining like a splash of blood against the white background.

Through clusters of wind-driven snowflakes another building was discernible in the distance. The majority of the railway cars had been moved there. Small black dots were calling out happily as the cars approached. Bryan recognized the mood. He, too, knew what it was like to be received by family and friends after a long period of active duty. He prayed wistfully that it would happen again.

Then a door opened in the wooden building behind him. Two elderly men in civilian clothes helped each other light cigarettes in the doorway, then ambled toward the locomotive without closing the door behind them.

A moment later, soldiers slowly began to stream out of the foremost train car. Not cheerful, expectant lads on their way home to Mom's cooking or a sweetheart's embrace, but weary, stooping men whose forward movement was propelled solely by the constant push from behind. A man on the platform received the first of them, took hold of his arm, and led him along the train past Bryan. The rest followed passively, escorted by armed soldiers in overcoats.

The men getting off the train were SS officers from all the different corps. Elite German soldiers, authentic Nazi heroes. Bryan could scarcely tell one from the other. Suddenly his distaste surfaced. Distaste for all those collar insignias, skull and crossbones, riding breeches, stiff-peaked caps, medals, and decorations. Here was the enemy he had learned to hate and fight against so savagely.

The stream of expressionless soldiers and bobbing stretchers continued toward the pallid, whitish light of the opening at the far end of the platform. Another truck was backing up to the skids.

Its arrival was drowned out by the crunching sound of boots in the frosty snow. The last man in the column shouted at the escort in front and pointed at Bryan and the other stretcher.

Some soldiers took hold of them and followed the sagging flock of men.

At the end of the train they put the stretchers down for a moment. It took time to fill the truck up. A railway worker started to walk across the rails, knocking the switch points with a long pole as he passed. A soldier shouted at him threateningly, gun raised. Dropping the pole in the snow, the man slithered back the way he came, finally disappearing behind a big sign that towered between the sets of tracks. FREIBURG IM BREISGAU it said, in proud, clear letters.

Not a single one of the officers who stood there waiting had said a word. Everything had taken place precisely according to plan, making it impossible for Bryan to look back and see whether James was lying on the stretcher a couple of meters away.

It must have been quite late in the afternoon. The sun would soon be setting. The street seemed deserted, apart from the SS officers guarding the area in front of the freight station.

So this was their destination for the time being. Freiburg, a town in the Rhine district by the French border in the southwest corner of the German Reich, was only fifty kilometers from the Swiss border and freedom.

In the semidarkness two rows of figures were seated on benches in the back of the truck. Between them, several stretchers lay slantwise across the floor, so tightly packed together that the ends stuck under the feet of the seated figures. Luckily Bryan had been placed under a soldier with short legs whose boots didn't rest so heavily on his frozen shins.

When the last stretcher had been loaded, the accompanying soldiers jumped in and rolled down the tarpaulin while the escort closed the tailgate.

The sudden darkness made it impossible for Bryan to see. The shape beside him was lying quite still. Forty men were breathing heavily and irregularly. There were a few scattered murmurs and grunts. Two guards squeezed down side by side at the end of the bench and talked quietly to each other.

Then Bryan felt the shape beside him move. A tentative hand groped the side of his body and found his chest. There it remained.

Bryan seized it and returned its quiet squeeze.

Gradually, as the silhouettes acquired faces, Bryan realized the truckload of patients had several things in common. But one was more obvious than the rest, a common denominator that now included him and James.

They were all mentally ill.

James had already tried to make him understand this with meaningful glances, pointing out one or two men in particular.

Most of them sat quite still, heads bobbing from side to side as the truck rumbled along. A few sat tensing their necks, eyes fixed on an imaginary point in the air. Others twisted their arms together awkwardly and rocked almost imperceptibly back and forth, alternately clenching and spreading their fingers.

James rolled his eyes and pointed to his open mouth. "They're pumped full of medicine," Bryan deduced in agreement. They, too, had been sedated and the poison was still in their bodies, as exhibited by their slow-motion reflexes and unusually sluggish brain activity. If they'd had a chance to stand up, they would have fallen over.

Bryan began feeling a mixture of relief and renewed anxiety. So the red tag meant they were mentally ill. This had been their objective and therefore they were relieved. But now they'd been lumped together with this group of mentally warped soldiers, and what did the Germans propose to do with them? The master race's care of the incurably ill could easily be accomplished with a syringe, or even more simply with a bullet.

Those were the rumors.

The civilians at the freight goods station had obviously not been meant to see them. And now they lay in darkness, rumbling toward unknown territory. Two soldiers had been set to watch over them. This was the source of their worries.

Bryan tried to smile at James. James showed indifference. He still didn't see any occasion to worry.

At every bend of the road the legs of one of the soldiers swung to and fro above Bryan's feet. The railroad had to bend, twist, and turn itself through the snow-covered terrain alongside fields, drainage trenches, small streams, and natural inclines and slopes in the landscape. Their journey took them around the southern edge of the Schwarzwald and the town of Freiburg. They had passed a lot of small stations and stops on their way that could have been used for unloading if they were going southward. So Bryan had to assume they were heading north or northeast into the Schwarzwald itself.

Most likely the idea was that they were meant to disappear here in some way or other.

Up until now the country had been fairly flat. James rocked forward and back on his own axis, bumping into Bryan as regularly as the tiny jumps of the second hand on a clock. The sound of the engine echoed off the walls of the houses. Graveled surfaces gave way to cobblestones and suddenly, for a matter of seconds, to caressing, lulling asphalt, then churned-up, frozen dirt roads. Not one moment resembled the last, yet time seemed an eternity. Bryan noted his impressions, convinced that the next stop would be their last.

James had dozed off, breathing heavily, leaving Bryan with an uncomfortable feeling of isolation and claustrophobia. Recalling James's promise, he tried to ignore the urge to jump up, and out. An urge that continued to grow as the effect of the medicine wore off.

One of the guards got up, treading on Bryan's thigh with his hobnailed boot. In his effort to control the pain, Bryan didn't notice the guard pushing a patient back toward the bench. But he did hear the tarpaulin rip open as the patient collided with the truck's sideboards, his elbows jutting stiffly backward.

Half the canvas wall suddenly fluttered out into the air and was slung with hollow-sounding cracks against the driver's cab. The soldier who had indirectly caused the situation threw down his weapon, striking James hard and waking him up, while the muzzle pointed straight at Bryan's face.

As the soldier thrust his upper body over the side of the truck, stretching as far into the semidarkness as he could, Bryan reached cautiously for the rifle.

But on meeting James's eyes, he stopped. James shook his head slowly.

The countryside behind the soldier's silhouette was lit up by the reflection of white-clad fields. This was more than enough light for Bryan, whose profession had been to survey landscape, no matter what time of day or night.

Farthest toward the west, in the middle of the flat countryside, there was a distinct gray hilltop that even fledgling navigators would be able to recognize. This naked peak was grooved by verdant, terraced vineyards and had the pompous name of Kaiserstuhl. An outpost of France and a connecting link between the Schwarzwald and the Vosges Mountains, it disappeared into the distance, giving him a landmark. Treetops passed in view alongside the truck. Bryan cautiously propped himself up on his elbows. Small figures were gliding around over the drainage trenches, accompanied by cheerful voices. Children playing winter games and dancing along the frozen canals on their skates. A single glimpse of this reality, and the face of war acquired another new dimension. It had been a long time since Bryan and James had been two Canterbury youngsters who stormed at full speed under the low bridges connecting the cattle paths, bending at the knees and shrieking with delight, gliding crunchily over the ice. What happy, innocent, childish pursuits.

The next swing of the truck knocked Bryan's elbows out from under him, and the treetops disappeared behind the tarpaulin and the soldier's sweaty, self-satisfied face. When the SS youth finally got a firm hold on the tarpaulin, he squeezed himself in between two of the patients and held on to the flap for the rest of the journey. Like a couple of brass weights, the short-legged patient's boots dangled over Bryan's shins at more and more of an angle, indicating that the truck was climbing again.

The heavy vehicle shook as it drove up the stony road, rattling as if they were driving over bare rock.

This was where they were headed. Up into the wilderness.

After another hour's drive the transport came to a halt.

Several men in white were ready to receive them. James's stretcher was pulled out over the edge of the truck before the two of them managed to give each other a farewell squeeze. The two porters who had taken hold of Bryan's stretcher slid on the slippery ground, almost dropping him. In front of them was a dark, pebbled clearing encircled by a narrow border of dead fir trees.

Behind them towered dense formations of snow-crowned pine trees that provided shelter from the worst gusts of wind. The landscape faded away into the valley below in a mist of snow crystals. There was not a single light to reveal any sign of life down in the Promised Land. Bryan assumed Freiburg was now directly south of them.

They had been driven a roundabout way.

The courtyard was partly hidden behind the windbreak. The badly shaken-up passengers were hustled around the stretchers and trudged apathetically behind the soldier in command. Another truck came into view, empty and with the tailgate hanging open. The flock of men who had left it had been lined up farther down the compound, where several three-story buildings came into view. The pale-yellow gleam from the windows shone softly over the yard. Bryan gave a grunt when he saw the Red Cross sign painted on the sloping flat roofs. It resembled an ordinary hospital, apart from the numerous sandbags heaped up against the walls at regular intervals, the barred windows on the second and third stories, and numerous guards with dogs. Seen from the outside, the rectangular boxes were far superior to the hastily assembled reserve hospitals the wounded Royal Air Force men were sent to in ever increasing numbers. "But don't deceive yourself," thought Bryan as he was carried toward the buildings.

Little by little the patients were grouped at one edge of the compound. All in all about sixty or seventy men stood waiting as the stretchers passed by them. Farther ahead the porter carrying James from behind tried to push back the arm he'd let flop over the edge of the swinging stretcher. Against a background of glazed yellowish frost two fingers stuck out from the others in discreet disregard of danger, waving a V-sign back toward Bryan.

Several yellow buildings, slightly staggered in relation to one another, became visible from where they were now assembled. Two of them had their foundations stuck solidly into the rock, whereas the rest were scattered over the tree-encircled plateau that constituted most of the area. The tops of several posts could be seen above a lush undergrowth of holly. They supported the fence between the walls of rock. Farthest away a steel-wire fence cut blatantly through the area, its frost sparkling in the glow of the occasional lights. Down by the gate stood a small group of officers, talking in a cone of light beside a black car with a swastika on the front door and pennants swaggering on the front fenders. An officer stepped out of the group and waved the guards from the nearest building over toward him. On receiving their orders they ran the hundred meters over to the assembly, guns erect and coats flapping, to pass on the commands.

When they began moving this time, the stretchers were at the head of the procession. A few of the silent figures kept standing about apathetically and had to be egged on by the soldiers with threats and shoves. Apart from the dry crunching of hundreds of feet on the frosty snow and the sound of trucks in the distance, the panting of the porters was all that could be heard. From where Bryan was, he could see nine or ten buildings, all in all, several of them connected in pairs by white-painted wooden corridors. It was one of these complexes they were heading for, the farthest of the twin blocks.

Apart from a single wall lamp shining faintly over the entrance, the building lay black and lifeless.

A nurse wearing a cap stepped through the door, shuddered slightly in the wind, and indicated that the procession should turn and follow her over toward two wooden barracks that lay immediately to their left. The porters protested but did as they were told.

The barracks were tall, single-story wooden buildings with golden, frost-rimmed windows under the eaves. Shutters and heavy curtains shielded the windows from the glare of the towering floodlights outside.

The door of the barracks led directly into a room in which dozens of thin, striped mattresses lay side by side in the middle of the floor. The walls were lined with support beams. Weak lightbulbs and hoisted-up parallel bars, rings, and trapezes hung from the ceiling. The far wall of the gymnasium was bare. A single door led into the adjacent building. Four buckets served as latrines. Dark, shabby-looking chairs, each encircled by a small canvas booth, stood at the end where they had entered.

The porters slid Bryan off onto a mattress halfway down the room, stuck his case file underneath it, and disappeared with the stretcher without having made sure their patient was lying properly.

The stream of shuffling, empty-eyed figures into the barracks ceased. James lay only a few mattresses away, following the last arrivals with his eyes. When all of them were either sitting down or lying flat on their backs on the hard beds a nurse clapped her hands and strode down between the rows, repeating the same sentence over and over again. Although Bryan couldn't understand her, he understood his fellow patients' confusion and clumsy attempts to get undressed and pile their clothes beside the mattress. Not all of them did as they had been told and had to be helped roughly by the porters who had been watching the scene, making subdued comments. Neither James nor Bryan reacted, but let porters haul their shirts up over their heads, making their ears smart. Bryan noted with relief that James was not wearing Jill's scarf.

One of the naked men got up, arms hanging limply by his sides, and began peeing mechanically over both the mattress and his neighbor, who made a feeble evasive attempt. The nurse rushed forward and struck him on the neck, instantly interrupting the stream, and led him over to the buckets at the far end of the room.

Bryan counted himself lucky not to have had anything to eat or drink for several days.

The door leading to the back building opened and a trolley was wheeled inside, loaded with blankets.

It remained there for some time.

The floor wasn't cold, but the draft from the entrance gave them goose-flesh. Bryan curled up in order to keep warm.

After a while someone started groaning. Several of the naked men were trembling visibly. The two nurses who had been ordered to watch over them shook their heads in irritation and pointed toward the trolley. Apparently they were supposed to fetch their own blankets. A couple of thin, gnarled men jumped over the mattresses with no sign of embarrassment and snatched a blanket, unaware as to whether it lay at the top of the heap or the bottom.

The rest of the men stayed where they were. Dazed. Their minds clouded over.

Bryan lay there for several hours. The monotonous rhythm of chattering teeth grew louder as the men grew colder. The nurses sat nodding, stealing some sleep on the stools at the far end of the room. They had left the recumbent patients to themselves long ago.

In the feeble light Bryan could scarcely tell James's huddled body from all the others. Then he saw a corner of Jill's scarf sticking out from under the mattress. "For God's sake, leave it there!" he begged silently. Suddenly James shot up in bed and rushed toward the pails. For a few seconds one of them resounded hollowly.

The act itself lasted only a moment, but the reverberations of his upset stomach and chills kept James frozen in his awkward position for some time. Then he snorted in exasperation and fumbled around the buckets without finding paper to dry himself.

Without any further hygienic considerations James rushed over to the trolley, seized a blanket, and ran nimbly back to his mattress. "Why didn't you bring me a blanket, idiot?" Bryan thought, and considered following suit as he glanced over at the dozing, uniformed women beside the end wall.

But he didn't.

Later that night the outside door opened with a crash, immediately followed by a blinding light as the ceiling lights were switched on. Bryan lay motionless. Without hesitation the SS soldiers went straight over to two men who lay huddled in their blankets. They bent over them, found their case notes, and tore off a corner of the front page.

One of the men thus branded lay beside James. The bundle of rags lying on top of him was James's blanket. Bryan doubted whether he himself could have been so cunning.

James had deliberately fished only one blanket out of the pile.

CHAPTER 7

The night inspection had woken the whole room. Even though by then most of them had been dressed in nightshirts and the blankets had at long last been distributed, the moaning increased hour by hour. The effect of the medicine was wearing off.

More and more of them tried to shut out their surroundings by way of rocking movements, awkward contortions, and blank expressions. Bryan had never seen anything like it. For his own part he lay quite still.

Some men he had never seen before switched on the lights and cursorily inspected the crowd of bodies on the floor. One of them was wearing a black, ankle-length coat, buttoned to the neck. When he stamped on the floor everyone looked up. He rapped out an order and a couple of the patients reluctantly got up and tugged at their neighbors' nightshirts until they, too, rose to their feet. Finally only six or seven men remained.

Accompanied by a couple of orderlies, the man in the coat asked one of the recumbent patients a question without receiving any reply. He signaled to his assistants to take hold of the patient under the arms and force him into a standing position. When they let go of him again, he collapsed like a rag doll and struck his neck on the floor between the mattresses with an impotent smack that made Bryan gasp. The nurses glanced up at the officer as they knelt down to help the unconscious man back onto his bed, but he was already striding straight over to Bryan.

When Bryan stared into the pale face that was inspecting him, he chose to get to his feet.

The swaying movements and slight trembling at the knees were genuine enough, since he hadn't stood up for several days. The blood rushed from his brain and made him dizzy. When they let go of him, however, he remained standing. James was the only one of the seven to follow his example.

. . .

During the smarting, painful delousing that followed, Bryan tried to move closer to James, but the women continually slapped their rubber gloves against their rubber aprons, making sure the patients were in constant movement.

James stood in a line alongside a grubby tiled wall, hugging a numbered shirt like all the others and waiting for the next row of showers to become vacant. One of the naked men stood in the bath, head bent back and staring wide-eyed straight up into the shower. He stood like this for a long time and when he began to scream with pain the howls spread from one deranged man to another like a wolves' chorus.

Blows and threats restored order almost as quickly as the commotion had erupted. The man who had started it stood moaning with bloodshot eyes as they beat him, totally unaware of what was going on around him. Then they dragged him by the hair and flung him against the wall. He didn't stop moaning until they pulled the straitjacket over him and hauled him away.

The last Bryan saw of James until they both were in the gym again was as he apathetically let himself be pushed under the ice-cold showers, smiling and humming softly, still hugging his shirt.

Inside the gymnasium they were all equipped with the same-sized shoes and arranged in three rows alongside the ribbed walls facing the middle of the room. A few of them were sorted out immediately and grouped together along the outer wall. Among them Bryan could recognize a couple of the poor fools who had fetched their own blankets during the night. They apparently didn't understand their special status.

In the meantime several tables had been placed in front of the canvas booths. The man in the long coat had discarded his flowing garment and was sitting with other security officers and white-coated representatives of the medical corps. There were no longer any women among them.

One of the men gave a start when his name was called out. A soldier hauled him in front of this court of inquiry. Several names were called without anyone reacting, whereupon a security officer looked over his list and began calling out a number that, as far as Bryan could tell, corresponded to the shirt markings. Bryan wished desperately he could understand what was being said. He listened intensely. As his confusion grew, an officer pointed at him and a soldier dragged him into the line.

James was among the last to be called. According to customary Prussian thoroughness they had apparently been called up in alphabetical order. He, too, had to be pushed into line.

The wounded soldiers were behind the curtains an average of about two or three minutes before they were led out again and placed in a new row against the back wall in the same order as before. They didn't seem to have been harmed, but stood at attention in a ridiculously exaggerated manner with expressionless gray faces.

Soft muttering and rustling sounds could be heard from behind the curtain. Nothing alarming. One of the patients shouted his replies like shrill orders, whereupon a couple of those who were waiting their turn clicked their nonexistent heels and puffed out their chests.

Behind the faded green canvas one of the officers sat behind a flimsy desk reading Bryan's case notes while a doctor looked over his shoulder. The soldier who had led him in pushed Bryan down onto a chair in front of the desk and then hastily withdrew to the other side of the curtain. As the officer ran his finger down the page, the attitude toward Bryan seemed to change slightly. They nodded to him, addressed him respectfully, and nodded again as Bryan tried to control the fear and uneasiness that was about to overcome him. Even though they smiled at him they could become his executioners at a moment's notice.

The questions they asked hung heavily in the air. The security officer drummed his fingers on the edge of the table and glanced up at the doctor, who immediately grasped Bryan's wrist in order to take his pulse. Then he shone a light into Bryan's eyes, slapped him on the side of the head and shone it again. Bryan felt paralyzed and didn't notice the doctor walking around him. The smack of hands being clapped right in front of his face made him blink and hunch his shoulders with such a start that his entire torso shook. However, the observers didn't appear to regard this as anything unusual.

The doctor walked behind the officer who, looking up from his papers, did an about-face, grabbed something from the tabletop, and flung it toward Bryan, all in one movement. He would not have been able to defend himself even if he'd tried. A pain at the bridge of his nose made him open his eyes wide.

Apart from that he kept a straight face.

From the next compartment came the sound of a blow that made the patient cry out, and then another blow that made him stop. The security officer smiled at Bryan again and conferred with the doctor, who spoke so fast that Bryan would not have been able to understand a word even if it had been his mother tongue. The officer shrugged and got up as Bryan was led out to the others.

Here he came to stand just opposite James, who was still waiting in the relatively short line. His dripping-wet shirt still clung to his body. Just under the neckline was a dark shadow. Bryan stiffened. James was wearing Jill's scarf again. Even though this crazy act could prove fatal, James appeared relaxed and calm. But Bryan knew better. Beneath the facade he radiated terror. All his senses were on red alert. Without his talisman he had nothing to cling to.

But it would also be his death if he didn't get rid of it.

"It's okay," Bryan mouthed, but James just shook his head silently and took a step forward like the others.

The chief security officer finally got up from his seat and signaled to the little group of men over in the corner who had helped themselves to blankets during the night to line up beside the curtain nearest the door.

Behind the curtain loud bursts of anger almost raised the roof and the canvas began pulsating as if a fight were going on behind it. The chief security officer's face was bright red when they tore down the curtain and hauled the man who had been questioned across the floor, his feet dragging after him and torment painted all over his face.

Two guards seized his arm. The culprit stared wildly at the apathetic assembly, searching in vain for something to cling to. Bryan looked at him with eyes out of focus. Blood was quietly trickling down the man's forehead. He, too, had been hit by something. Perhaps he'd made the mistake of trying to ward it off.

The senior officer sat down heavily on the corner of the table behind him, smiling cruelly at the guards as they dragged the patient around among the others so they could see him at close quarters. Then he stopped smiling. Breathing deeply in aggressive concentration, he roared his accusation at the rows of men who again began to fidget nervously. The words tumbled out in bursts as the furious man stood with his hands clenched behind his back, rocking back and forth on his toes. There was no mistaking one of the words.

Malingering!

The man stopped trembling when he heard the charge. He let his head fall limply forward, aware of his guilt, unmasked and prepared to suffer the consequences.

Suddenly the officer stopped short in the middle of his outburst of rage. Then, smiling jovially, he spread his arms wide as he appealed gently to his audience. Bryan grasped that he was trying to get other malingerers to own up, if there were any. Nothing would happen to them as long as they stepped forward now, while there was still time.

It was impossible to look over at James as long as this beast was inspecting them. "We're not giving ourselves up, James!" Bryan pleaded silently, mostly to himself.

The officer stood waiting, nodding smilingly at the groups of men for just as long as it took Bryan to say the Lord's Prayer. Then suddenly he stepped behind the accused, drew his pistol, and executed the culprit with a shot to the back of the head before the man could manage to scream.

The rest of the assembly scarcely reacted. Blood welled out of the man's head for a moment and flowed slowly across the floor toward James. Bryan watched imperceptibly. James stood stock-still, white in the face, but no more so than the protracted standing at attention could warrant.

The two guards took hold of the body and dragged it across the floor. One of the white-coated doctors was still shielding his face with his hands in delayed shock. When he came to his senses his protests sounded feeble and remote. The security officer turned on his heel. No report would be written about *that* incident. Protests were out of the question.

Bryan began counting the seconds while James was behind the curtain. When he reached two hundred, James was led out again, remote and paralyzed. The next man in line stood still, ignoring the shouts of the doctor who was holding the curtain open. As the soldiers tried to grab him under his arms he quietly toppled forward. The soldiers took the next one instead and pulled him around the man on the floor. He had rolled onto his side and was sobbing almost deliriously, constantly repeating a name Bryan had heard before. A sweetheart, wife, mother, or daughter?

James had begun humming again, slowly and tonelessly. His skinny, red-eyed neighbor stood ruminating in his straitjacket as urine dripped down his shirt, which grew darker and darker.

Bryan imagined he might have lapped up the shower water too eagerly while staring up into it.

He awoke with a start. Someone had shouted, "Leave me alone!" Could it have been him, since he had understood it? Bryan shuddered at the thought and glanced over at the nurse who had just been standing beside his bed. So he'd only been out for a moment. The nurse poured a glass of water and put two tablets in his neighbor's mouth. She hadn't heard anything. Maybe he'd dreamt it.

By now the whole ward lay quiet. Bryan looked cautiously around, cursing the short second when he and James had become separated on their way from the wooden barracks. Otherwise they would be lying side by side now. This would undoubtedly have felt safer. As it was, Bryan lay in bed number five to the left of the door, while James lay at the far end on the opposite side. Twelve beds on Bryan's side, ten on James's. That was six beds too many in relation to the construction of the ward. Now the beds had scarcely a half meter between them. They were sticking haphazardly out from the wall. Some were in front of a window, others in between, but most of them stood completely at random. It made an extremely disorderly impression.

This pale-green ward with its high ceiling was about twenty meters long and ten meters wide. It constituted Bryan's entire world. Besides the bed, his earthly possessions consisted of a timeworn chair that stood in the central passageway together with twenty-two other such chairs, a hospital shirt, a pair of slippers, and a thin dressing gown.

Apart from four beds already occupied by unconscious, wounded, and bandaged patients, the whole ward was filled with soldiers from the same transport who had been ordered into the bed they happened to be standing next to. A couple of them kept their shoes on in bed and messed up the bedclothes before the nurses had distributed the pills. Each man was fed two white pills followed by a gulp of water from a mug that was passed around and constantly filled up from a white enamel jug.

The nurses had almost completed their round.

The smell of the first meal was indefinable and scarcely appetizing, but extraordinarily tempting nevertheless. Bryan hadn't dared think about food for days, but now his mouth was watering, making the final waiting moments torture.

The lumps on the iron plate looked like celery but were tasteless. Perhaps it was turnip cabbage. Bryan didn't know. His family was used to quite different food.

The men's greedy scraping with their spoons and animal-like chewing spread through the room like wildfire, and Bryan realized that not all their senses were numbed.

The plate over on James's bed was already empty and tipped dangerously over the edge of his bed. His relaxed face and the regular heaving of his chest were clear proof of man's incredible ability to adapt to circumstances. Bryan envied James his peaceful slumber. The dread of revealing himself in his sleep still preoccupied him. A single word and he would end up like that poor soul in the gym who was now lying between the barracks, flung into the snow.

They had seen him when they walked past.

A sweetish smell blended with the blandness of the turnip cabbage and a growing dizziness overwhelmed Bryan's train of thought. The pills were starting to work.

So he was going to sleep, whether he dared to or not.

The man to his right lay on his side, staring at Bryan's pillow with dead eyes. From under the blanket came the sound of a series of pent-up explosions from the gases he was apparently unaware he was releasing.

That was Bryan's final impression before sleep overtook him.

CHAPTER 8

On Heroes Commemoration Day the ward was allowed to hear Hitler's speech. It was the first time this had happened during the two months they'd been there. All the ceiling lights had been switched on and the heating turned up in honor of the occasion. The porters drew cables through the middle of the room to a small loudspeaker on the table beside the end wall.

There was an expectant hum in the room with constant fidgeting, rocking to and fro, prancing back and forth. While the Führer was speaking, most of the nurses listened with folded arms, smiling and visibly moved. Bryan's neighbor to the left had only been conscious for a couple of days and wasn't aware of anything at all, whereas the man on his right stared with eyes wilder than usual and began to clap his hands until an orderly made him stop.

Bryan had received his most recent electroshock treatment only the day before, so it was still difficult to sort out impressions. He was confused by all the commotion. How could anyone understand what the hysterical voice was screaming through that metallic-sounding loudspeaker? In the wake of the treatment even the Sunday *Wünschkonzert's* tribute to lonely housewives, newlyweds, and people celebrating anniversaries sounded like one continuous hodgepodge.

But people loved it and swung their arms and smiled. Operettas, film music, Zarah Leander, and "Es geht alles vorüber." On days like that, one would think the war had never started.

Other days, one was left in no doubt.

The first time they led him out through the striped glass doors into the corridor, Bryan forced himself to believe everything was going to be all right.

Many of them had already been to the examination rooms. And even if they were limp when they returned and often lay for hours without showing any signs of life, they eventually recovered and didn't seem to have suffered any harm.

There were six doors along the corridor, apart from the ward's swinging door that Bryan had only known from the inside. There were exits at both ends, with the nurses' and orderlies' quarters farthest down on the left. Next came the door of the treatment room, and then two more that Bryan presumed led into the doctors' quarters.

Several orderlies and doctors were waiting in the next-to-last room. They bound him roughly with leather straps before he'd quite grasped the situation, gave him an injection, and fastened electrodes to his temples. The electric shock waves paralyzed him instantly and numbed all his senses for several days.

The series of treatments usually consisted of one shock treatment per week for four or five weeks, followed by a rest period. Bryan couldn't tell whether they would repeat the treatment, but it seemed likely. The first patients had in fact started on a new series after a month's pause. During the rest periods they got pills instead. Always the same ones, one or two a day per patient.

Bryan was afraid of how such a treatment might affect him. Pictures he had been clinging to in his head slowly disappeared. The idea of seeing his girlfriend again, of being able to talk to James, or of simply going for a walk unescorted in the gray drizzle outside—everything was blunted and reduced. His memory played tricks on him, so that one day he could recall a forgotten childhood experience in a Dover side street and the next day he couldn't even remember what he looked like.

Escape plans fizzled out even before they were thought through.

Nor did he have much appetite. When Bryan looked at himself in the weekly shower his hip bones seemed to protrude more and more and his chest became disfigured with stuck-out ribs. It wasn't because he didn't like the food. Sometimes it was even quite tasty, with potato pancakes and goulash, soup, or stewed fruit. But when he was finished with a shock treatment and his body was crying out for new energy, the very thought of the breakfast porridge and slice of rye bread and margarine made him want to throw up. So he left his plate untouched and nobody forced him. Usually he could only manage to make himself swallow the sliced bread covered with leftovers from dinner or the occasional slice of sausage and cheese, and then only if he took his time about it.

And there lay James in his corner, passing the time listening and dreaming and fingering Jill's scarf, which was constantly near him. Under the mattress, under the sheet, or under his shirt.

During the first couple of weeks they didn't leave their beds, but as the patients began to be able to find the lavatories down at the end of the passage by themselves, it gradually took longer to get the nursing aides to come with bedpans. Bryan widened his vocabulary with "*Schieber, Schieber*," but the waiting time could be unbearable before the lid clattered out of the utensil washroom and the enamel bedpan was finally slung onto his blanket.

James was the first to get up. Suddenly one morning he tipped his toes over the edge of his mattress and began moving from bed to bed, collecting the breakfast dishes on the trolley. Bryan held his breath. How perfectly he played his part, skipping along in his knee-length socks that had slipped so far down, they barely covered his ankles. His arms stayed pressed against his sides, making all movement awkward, and his rigid neck meant he had to rotate his whole body every time he turned his head.

Bryan was glad to see James getting around. This meant the two would soon be able to make contact.

Only a few days passed before James's neighbor deprived him of this self-appointed job. No sooner had James started moving around the ward than the big pockmarked man was out of bed, standing still and watching him. Then he took James by the shoulder and patted his head a couple of times, after which he led him firmly and authoritatively back to his bed and carefully pressed his head down on his pillow. Ever since then it was Pock Face who assisted the orderlies and tripped around, making the patients comfortable whenever the opportunity arose.

James was the apple of Pock Face's eye and should James drop a pillow during the night, or a crumb on his blanket during dinner, it was he who instantly got out of bed to pick it up.

At first the man had lain opposite Bryan, but on the day James's first neighbor was driven down to the mortuary, Pock Face moved next to him on his own initiative. At first some of the younger nurses had tried to make him return to his proper place, but he had whimpered pitifully and grabbed at their arms with his big hands. When the senior nursing officer finally came he was sleeping soundly in his new bed.

So she let him remain there.

After this thwarted attempt to procure a permanent chore James got up only to go wash himself or use the lavatory.

The first time Bryan got out of bed by himself was a couple of days after a shock treatment.

In the midst of carrying out his customary minimal washing of arms and head, what his mother used to scornfully call a lick and a promise, he'd gotten dizzy and started vomiting uncontrollably, so the washbasin with most of the soapy water tipped over the edge of the bed and the piece of soap, consisting of scouring powder and sawdust, hit the floor and broke. At the same moment one of the most pigheaded of the nurses entered the room. Instead of helping him she cursed about the water that was trickling over the floor. Then she dragged him down to the opposite end of the room farthest from the treatment rooms. Bryan stumbled along, almost falling, delivering blob after blob of vomit onto the newly washed floor.

Light entered the white-tiled room from a big, bolted window that framed some other buildings and the snow-clad rocks behind. Without further ado she locked him in the lavatory. Bryan fell heavily to his knees in front of the toilet bowl and discharged the remains of his giddiness with a hollow groan. When his stomach cramps wore off he sat down on the cold china bowl and looked around.

There were no windows in the lavatory itself, which received plenty of light from above the door. When he'd investigated every flake of paint and every scratch he lay down flat on the floor and looked around as best he could. The partition rested on rusty metal poles cemented into the terrazzo floor. Behind it was another lavatory and then a brick wall. A narrow door on the opposite wall marked the storeroom from which the nursing aides fetched the bedclothes and where the cleaning woman kept her broom and pail. Bryan had seen them carting implements and linen back and forth. Then the room in the corner had to be the showering room, with the door beside the window leading into the utensil washroom.

They didn't fetch him until just before the ward round, patting him on the cheek and smiling at him so effusively that he had to smile back.

After that, Bryan got out of bed several times a day. During the first few days he tried to make contact with James and waited only a moment before following him when he headed for the lavatory, but to no avail. However favorable the opportunity, James hurried in the opposite direction the instant he caught sight of Bryan.

On other occasions, usually after the control check in the middle of the afternoon when it was fairly quiet in the ward, Bryan tried unsuccessfully to exchange glances with James as he toddled quietly about.

In the end James only got out of bed when Bryan was asleep.

He quite simply refused to have anything to do with Bryan.

CHAPTER 9

It was Calendar Man's fault that time didn't take its own course. This was what Bryan called the patient who lay opposite James in the same row as Bryan. It was he who had dangled his short legs over Bryan's stretcher in the truck. A cheerful, silent little man who stayed in bed and whose only pursuit was to scratch the date onto his chart every day. This angered the nurses and for a long time they punished him by cutting his rations and telling tales about him during the ward round, leading the doctors to believe he was completely uncontrollable, so they treated him more harshly than necessary. As a result, after his shock treatment his cramps were sometimes so strong, they made him bend over backward in his bed like a bow.

His salvation arrived in the form of a new load of patients. One day they ambled across the yard and continued into one of the blocks behind it. This group of wounded soldiers was escorted by three young nurses who later replaced some of Calendar Man's worst tormentors. After a few days the thinnest of these young girls, probably younger than either Bryan or James, gave him a small block of coarse gray paper and knocked a headless tack into the wall above the head of his bed so his daily date routine could be seen by anyone passing.

How Calendar Man managed to keep account of the days following a shock treatment, Bryan couldn't understand. He could merely ascertain that the lost time was always miraculously gained again with the greatest accuracy.

Even though it was April, the ward still felt clammy and most of the patients were allowed two woolen blankets at night. Bryan never removed his socks and tried to shield his body as best he could from the draft that sneaked in around the interior bomb shutters of the window and down along the heads of the beds. Many of them had recently caught colds and lay shivering and coughing.

Apparently Pock Face rarely felt the cold and that evening he ambled for the third time over to Bryan to make sure he was tucked in. The wind had dropped a bit and the ward was quiet. Bryan closed his eyes and felt the big hands secure the blanket carefully under him and the pawlike stroking on his forehead. Then he shook Bryan gently by the cheek as if he were a child, until Bryan opened his eyes and smiled back. Suddenly and unexpectedly, Pock Face whispered a few words directly into his ear and for a moment the big man's face was transformed. It had a watchful, attentive expression that instantly took in every detail of Bryan's visage before it clouded over again. Then he turned to Bryan's neighbor, patted him on the cheek, and said: "Gut, guuut!"

Finally he sat down on one of the chairs in the gangway and stared toward James's bed. The two patients lying in the beds beside Pock Face raised their heads, their silhouettes clearly outlined against the window with the moonlight behind. They, too, looked over at James, who lay stretched out flat on his bed.

Bryan scowled over the tip of his nose, his gaze wandering. As far as he could see, the rest of the ward was asleep. Intermittent, whispering sounds echoed toward him and the two shadows lay back down. Then came more whispering and Bryan's mounting uneasiness made sleep impossible.

Was it really a faint whisper he had heard, or was it the shutters vibrating in the wind?

The next morning Pock Face was still sitting on his chair. The patient who shaved them every other day had come scuttling in while they all slept and uttered such a roar of laughter at the sight of the snoring body with its drooping head that the duty nurse came rushing in and chased him back where he came from. She slapped Pock Face on the neck and shook her head when he tried to appease her by charging into the corridor to fetch her apron.

Then, since she'd been woken so thoroughly, she sighed and began the day's work.

Several of the patients were on the mend. Bryan's neighbor no longer lay with the same staring, apathetic look as before, but looked peaceful and was always being patted on the shoulder by the nursing aides with whom he chatted in a jerky fashion. Other patients were no longer bedridden, but mostly sat at the table down at the far end of the ward, leafing through the porters' pulp magazines that were full of love stories and Alpine scenery. Sometimes two of the older porters collected a small crowd when they played a game of Old Maid.

Gradually, as the days grew sunnier around noon, more and more of the patients stood staring out the windows at the men from the other wards who were playing and laughing. They were wounded SS soldiers with common bodily injuries who were playing jacks, ball, or leapfrog. They were soon to be discharged.

If he sat cross-legged up at the head end of his bed and craned his neck, Bryan could follow everything that went on in the yard. He could sit like that for hours, staring at the sky above the watchtowers down by the gate and at the undulating wooded countryside behind.

It was also in this position that he managed to reach the top end of the bedposts, ease up their wooden props, and dump his pills down in the metal tubing that formed the head end of the bed. Ever since he'd finished his shock treatment he had tried to avoid swallowing these pills when they were stuffed in his mouth. Sometimes he swallowed only one, at other times they were half-dissolved before he had a chance to spit them into his hand. But the final result was what he had hoped for. Gradually he began to feel clearer in the head. A longing to escape manifested itself.

Only one patient in his row had seen him deposit the tablets in the bed tubing. It was the man who had been staring up into the stinging jets of water on the first day. In the beginning, this puny man had done so much damage to himself that they kept him in a straitjacket most of the time, doped with medicine. Now, three months later, he always lay quiet as a mouse, his hand under his cheek and legs drawn up under him, staring at the others. Bryan had caught his eye the very second he dumped the pills, and had received an exhilarated smile in return. Later Bryan tripped down along the beds and stopped beside the man's mattress. His features were totally relaxed and his eyes betrayed no sign of recognition as Bryan bent over him.

. . .

With springtime struggling to melt the grayish-brown snow in the court-yard and bring the shadows to life, Bryan investigated every inch of the panorama that lay before him.

Their block was the closest to the boulders, its windows facing due west. The evening sun set directly between the watchtowers and cast dull red rays along the buildings that lay in front. To the extreme left toward the south lay the kitchen, which he could observe more easily from the window in the corridor beside the bathroom. Farther toward the southwest there were small barracks where the guards and security staff had their quarters. From Bryan's own window he could see directly over to the medical staff annex's end wall. Members of the staff often stopped at the entrance, making it possible to follow the young doctors' persistent efforts to seduce the nurses. Apparently they never succeeded, which made the whole scene comical and its protagonists ridiculous but, curiously enough, no more human.

The building to the north lay parallel, though staggered, in relation to theirs and was connected by a corridor. It blocked the view of the gymnasium and the entire area beyond. Some of the wards farther down were also practically hidden by its sharp yellow corner.

Guards with dogs could be seen constantly, day and night, as they patrolled the fence encircling the area. The few civilians who were admitted to the hospital were always accompanied by security officers or SS soldiers.

Fear of being confronted with the family of the soldier whose identity he had assumed was a constant nightmare for Bryan during the first long weeks. But even though the ward was full of men whose recovery might have been speeded up at the sight of a familiar face, no one's family members ever turned up. The men were isolated and no one wished to inform anyone of their existence, let alone their state of health. Why anyone bothered to keep them alive at all was a mystery to him.

Bryan never saw James look out the windows. Since the beginning of April he had seldom been out of bed and was apparently heavily drugged by the medicine he was given.

Three trucks drove out the main gate, which was closed after them. "I should be sitting in one of them, driving like crazy till I was home again," Bryan daydreamed. The motor noise died away quickly behind the ridge and the trucks disappeared down into the valley. Pock Face's neighbor came and stood beside Bryan's bed, looking silently at the guards with his broad face. Meanwhile his leg quivered and his lips moved incessantly. He had carried on this silent conversation with himself since the very first day and Bryan had often seen Pock Face and the broad-faced man's neighbor on the other side put their ears to his mouth with expectant, patient faces. Then they usually shook their heads and giggled like half-witted children.

Bryan laughed as he thought about this and stared directly at the constantly moving lips. The man turned around and looked at him with a loony expression that made his whole face seem even more comical. Bryan had to cover his mouth and suppress his laughter. Then the lips stopped moving for a second and the man smiled at him. The broadest smile he had ever seen.

CHAPTER 10

One morning the sound of waltz music came from the corridor. The barber appeared and shaved their cheeks smoother than ever, even though he had been there the previous day. One of the porters, a veteran of the First World War, rattled his iron hook against the nearest bedpost as usual, the signal for bathtime. Bryan felt confused and disoriented about this change of routine.

Among the patients, he wasn't the only one.

Most of the nursing staff on duty smiled as they handed the patients snow-white, newly washed dressing gowns and told them to get ready quickly. The security officer who had shot the malingerer in the gym stood elegantly, straddling the swinging doors. Inspecting the men, he nodded in an authoritative and almost friendly fashion as they stood lined up in front of their beds. Then their names were called out. Some of them never reacted when this happened. Bryan had decided long ago to be different.

"Arno von der Leyen," barked the security officer. Bryan started. Why should he go first? He hesitated, but yielded when an orderly took his arm.

The security officer clicked his heels and stretched out an arm in a heil as the strange procession filed past him through the swing doors while their names were called. Only the few patients who had just received shock treatment remained behind, among them James.

Bryan glanced around nervously at the head of the procession. Behind him were seventeen or eighteen men who could still be called raving mad. They had been looked after for over three months now. What were they intending to do with them this time? Were they to be moved to other wards or hospitals, or maybe weeded out? And why was he called out before all the others? The security officer who hammered his boots on the stone floor made him uneasy, as did the orderlies and porters who escorted the group on either side. Perhaps it was a good thing James hadn't come with them after all.

The row of men walked past the treatment room, the electroshock room, and the doctors' room and out through the door they had entered the very first day and not been through since. By the time they reached the stairs the group was already showing signs of nervousness and soon a couple of patients were standing along the walls, hugging themselves. They didn't want to go. The orderlies laughed, forced them back into line, and smilingly tried to encourage them.

It was a beautiful day, but it was only the second half of April and at that altitude the dampness was still raw and penetrating. Bryan glanced down at his socks and slippers as he walked, trying imperceptibly to dodge the muddy puddles in the churned-up courtyard. When he saw the group was being led over to the gymnasium, he began feeling panicky.

In the lead was an SS officer who was walking one step ahead of Bryan. His revolver hung heavily and incitingly in his belt, only a few centimeters from Bryan's arm as it swung forward in the goose step. What were his chances of grabbing it? And where should he run if he did? It was over two hundred meters to the fence behind the gym and an even greater number of guards than usual stood chatting not far away.

Then they passed the barracks.

Over behind the gym was a big, open square. Alongside the grass Bryan could now see the houses he had hitherto only been able to imagine. There was a building that lay parallel with the gym, two wards and a complex that resembled an administrative block with small windows and brown double doors. The group came to a halt beside a low wooden corridor that connected the gym and the building behind them, and for a moment the security officer left them alone.

"This will be the last sunrise I'll ever see," thought Bryan, glancing at the nascent light above the tops of the fir trees and then at the row of men standing with their backs to the wall. Standing stiffly at attention with head stretched back, Pock Face towered above them all.

The guy with the broad rubbery face stood between them, muttering the words no one could ever hear. At the sound of more footsteps Bryan froze and his neighbor's lips almost stopped moving.

The first dazzling rays of sunlight swept over the square from behind, adding a touch of grandeur, stylishness, and dignity to the black-and-green uniforms that stepped forward into the light. This was in stark contrast with what Bryan had expected. A carnival of medals, iron crosses, shining diagonal bands, and patent-leather boots banished all thoughts of an execution squad. SS badges and skull and crossbones were everywhere to be seen. All corps, all types, all ages, and all possible kinds of wounds. This was the march of the wounded, an array of bandages, slings, crutches and canes.

The elite soldiers' demonstration that war cannot be won without blood.

The soldiers chattered in small groups and filed slowly toward the flag-pole in the middle of the square. After them followed a rear party of soldiers in wheelchairs pushed by nurses. And finally a few beds with huge wheels rumbled forth on the tiled path with sweating porters as anchormen.

The air was miraculously fresh, but also icy cold in the scanty getup of nightshirts and dressing gowns. Bryan's neighbor's teeth began to chatter. "Don't let this get to you," Bryan told himself as he glanced up at the swastika that had been hoisted in solemn silence, followed by a respectful heil.

They were standing almost at the back of the area's northwest corner. Bryan leaned a bit to one side as if he were about to doze off, and cast a sidelong glance behind the corner of the building. From there he could just make out a small brick building at the edge of the rocks. Presumably the hospital chapel. Down at the opposite end beside the western fence there was another gate, flanked by guards who were standing at attention and staring at the show with arms raised in salute.

With their outstretched arms still pointing up at the flag, they suddenly all burst simultaneously into the "Horst Wessel Song" with such enthusiasm that it made birds flutter up from the bushes.

None of the mental patients joined in. They stood either passively or mumbling to themselves, gazing around in confusion. The echo and force of the many voices filled the square and the air with intoxication and determination and gave the flag an impressive look. Bryan was still petrified by the grotesque beauty of the scene, and not until they unveiled the Führer's portrait did he grasp why they had been assembled there and why they had been shaved a day too early. He closed his eyes and visualized yesterday's scrap of paper hanging above Calendar Man's bed. It had read the nineteenth of April, so today was the twentieth, Hitler's birthday.

The officers held their caps tightly clamped to their sides beneath the elbows. They stood stock-still despite their wounds, looking respectfully at the portrait, which contrasted starkly with the caricatures of Hitler that usually decorated the RAF crews' barracks, defiled by added features, darts, and abusive language.

Some of the veteran warriors were lost in a world of ecstasy and shaded their eyes from the morning light as they stared devotedly up at the flag, dazzled by its beauty and their own sentimental emotions. Bryan checked out the area behind them. Beyond the barbed-wire fence on this long side there was yet another fence made of rough-looking planks intertwined with barbed wire. The stone track they had once driven up hugged the fence for a short while and then presumably continued alongside the boulders and up over the mountain. Bryan turned his head a few degrees and glanced once more to the west and over at the guards, who were now talking together.

This was the direction in which he would escape. Over the first fence and under the next, along the road and its accompanying brook, then down into the valley and over toward the railway line that followed the Rhine all the way to Basel.

If he followed the rails farther southward he would reach the Swiss border sooner or later.

How he would cross it, time would tell.

A sixth sense made Bryan turn his head. He found himself looking straight into Pock Face's eyes, at which point the huge man instantly looked down and kept his eyes on the ground. There had been something very attentive about the gaze he had met. Bryan would have to keep an eye on Pock Face, as discreetly as possible. Then he looked at the fence again.

It wasn't too high, he judged.

If only the flagpole could be tipped over by removing its bottom bolt, it could be leaned over the fence like a bridge. But flakes of rust spreading out over the nuts made him change his mind. If he'd had a wrench he could have done it. It was small things like this that were so important. Insignificant items and events like the chance meeting of a future wife or husband, unexpected incidents in one's childhood, or luck that smiled on one in a propitious second. All the isolated fragments that suddenly emerged and together constituted the future, making it unpredictable.

Just like the random patch of rust on the random bolt.

So he would have to crawl over the fence and count on tearing himself to shreds on the barbed wire that topped it. And then there were the guards. Because it was one thing to climb over unseen, and another to get away afterward. A single stray burst of machine-gun fire in the dark would be enough. There was chance again.

He couldn't leave things to chance if he could at all help it.

The ceremony concluded with a short speech by the chief security officer, delivered with a fervor that no one ever would have credited to such an anemic-looking individual. Finally there was an extended wave of heils, so long as to seem endless. Thereafter the square was slowly emptied of wheelchairs and bedridden patients who lay with a smile on their lips, exuding pride and patriotism. Presumably convinced that they had done their bit and were now safe.

The dark firs behind their block shook gently in the wind. The cold and the few hundred meters' walk over to the building made all Bryan's joints ache. No good came out of trying to make them move faster. "Look after yourself. Take care not to get ill," thought Bryan.

Now he'd found an escape route. If he got sick, he and James wouldn't be able to get away before the next series of electroshocks. So there was some rapid, thorough thinking to be done. And James had to be brought onboard, whether he liked it or not. Without James, no tenable planning.

And without James, no escape, either.

CHAPTER 11

James felt awful when he woke up from the aftermath of the electroshock. It had been like this every time. Most of all he was weak. Every fiber of his body was at low ebb. And then there were the emotions, the sentimentality, the self-pity and confusion. All his mental states were churned up like mud, leaving him in a chronic state of anxiety and melancholy.

Anxiety was a strict master; James had realized this long ago. But as time went by he'd learned to live with it and tame it. And as the war drew nearer and the rumble of bombs over Karlsruhe resounded in the distance, he began to cherish a faint hope that the nightmare would come to an end at some point. Though always on the alert, he tried to enjoy what hours he could. He lay very still, surveying life around him or dreaming himself far away.

In the months that had passed he had learned to get fully into his role. Nobody could suspect him of simulating. They could arouse him from his torpor, no matter when, and receive but an empty stare in return. The nurses didn't have much difficulty with him either, for he ate as he was supposed to and didn't soil his bed. Most important, he took his medicine without showing the slightest reluctance. Which is why he was eternally lethargic, slow-thinking, and, during occasional lucky moments, indifferent as well.

The pills were incredibly effective.

On his first visits to the surgeon lieutenant he had merely nodded when the latter raised his voice. He never made a movement without being ordered to. The senior nursing officer sometimes read aloud from his case history so his borrowed life story slowly grew off the lined yellow pages as James assumed it. If he'd ever had a guilty conscience about throwing the corpse out of the train window, it would have ceased the instant he became acquainted with the true nature of his savior.

James and his victim were roughly the same age. Gerhart Peuckert, as he was called, had risen through the ranks incredibly fast, ending up as a *Standartenführer* in the SS security police—a kind of colonel. Thus, apart from Arno von der Leyen, whose place Bryan had taken, he had the highest rank in the ward. He enjoyed special status. Sometimes he even had the impression that some of the other patients were afraid of him or hated him, and sat on their beds staring at him coldly.

There was no sin this man hadn't committed. Gerhart Peuckert had ruthlessly removed all obstacles in his path in every situation and had dealt out punishment mercilessly to anyone who displeased him. The Eastern Front had suited him admirably. In the end, some of his subordinates had gone berserk and tried to drown him in the same receptacle he had used when he personally tortured Soviet partisans or troublesome civilians.

The attack left him lying in a coma in a field hospital. No one had expected him to recover.

Proceedings against the assailants had been swift, a piano string around their necks. When he woke up nevertheless, it was decided he should be taken home to *Heimatschutz*, in the embrace of the fatherland. It was on this journey that the real Gerhart Peuckert finally paid for his misdeeds and James took his place.

James's case was characteristic for the ward as a whole. He was a high-ranking SS officer, mentally unhinged and too clever a henchman to be abandoned just like that. Normally there was only one SS cure in critical cases such as this: an injection and a coffin. But as long as there was hope that even one of these high-ranking officers in the Führer's most loyal bunch of adherents would recover, all available means were used to bring about that recovery. Until then, the fate of the patients was largely kept a close secret from the outside world. An SS officer could not be brought home insane. It would be demoralizing, a slight to the greatness of the German Reich, and could have unforeseen consequences regarding people's confidence in reports from the front. Furthermore, it would sow doubt in the minds of the populace about their heroes' invulnerability. The officers' families would be disgraced, as the security officers had repeatedly impressed upon the doctors.

Rather a dead officer than a scandal, they might have added.

This circumstance, combined with the fact that the physically wounded

SS officers also constituted an elite, had made the area a strategic target for external as well as internal enemies of the state. The hospital was therefore converted into a fortress so that no unwanted person entered and only healthy patients and their keepers were permitted to leave.

The capacity of the hospital was constantly being stretched by new wounded soldiers, though no longer by mental patients. Perhaps, in view of how the war was progressing, it had been discreetly accepted that the Third Reich wouldn't have time to recycle the latter. After the collapse of the Eastern Front there was no time to waste on trying to heal their minds.

Lately many of the patients had begun showing so many signs of improvement that anyone lagging behind in their recovery would be conspicuous. James stopped humming and hoped to escape the recurring shock treatments. More than anything else, this violent remedy affected his powers of concentration and therefore constituted a threat to his principal occupation: lying flat on his back, eyes closed, visualizing his favorite movies. . . .

"Where's Sergeant Cutter?" shouted Sergeant Higginbotham.

"He's busy," came Victor McLaglen's terse answer from the window. He turned to face Cary Grant—alias Sergeant Cutter—who was busy clobbering the soldiers who tried to rush the stairs.

"Buy a map of a buried treasure—hah! You ought to have your head examined," mocked Douglas Fairbanks Jr., his hands demonstratively on his hips.

Cary "Cutter" Grant socked the whole bunch on the jaw, one by one, and their kilts whirled around their heads as they tumbled backward down the stairs. "We could have left the Army and lived like princes," he sneered, eyes blazing. At the same moment he was torpedoed by a chair. Over him stood a Scot, gaping at the broken chair in his hand. Cutter glared at him unaffected, practically threateningly.

"Hey . . ." he said, pointing at the fleeing figure, "that's the guy who sold me the map!"

Just as Fairbanks Jr. was going to arrest the Scotsman, Grant

raised his hands defensively and, grabbing the Highlander by the
collar, knocked him out with a single blow, then picked him up and
held him out the window with outstretched arms.

"Waitaminute!" thundered Higginbotham, down on the ground.
"Take your hands off that man!"

At this point James always had to be careful not to laugh out loud. Glancing around, he suppressed his laughter as he saw the Scotsman crash to the ground before him and Cary Grant held his arms out in apology.

Gunga Din was one of James's favorite movies. A regular feature in his daydream-film repertoire.

When he "showed" one of his movies he usually started at the beginning and went through the entire film, scene by scene, as well as he could. A sequence that only took an hour in the cinema could easily take him a whole morning or evening. As long as he was engrossed in the film, he was lost to the world. This pastime comforted him whenever sad thoughts or the fear of never seeing his loved ones again became too much for him.

His generous mother had often handed him and his sisters a few coins so they could go sit in the folding chairs at the Sunday movie matinee. They spent a great deal of their childhood in the flickering light of Deanna Durbin, Laurel and Hardy, Nelson Eddy, and Tom Mix while their parents strolled through town exchanging platitudes with other members of the middle-class citizenry.

James could recall his sisters, Elizabeth and Jill, without effort. Under cover of darkness they used to giggle and whisper to each other while the hero kissed the heroine and the rest of the audience howled.

The memories, the movies and the books he had consumed throughout his schooldays, prevented him from going crazy. But the more shock treatment they subjected him to and the more pills he swallowed, the more frequently he got stuck in the middle of a scene, foiled by a sudden hole in his memory.

Right now he couldn't remember what Douglas Fairbanks Jr. and Victor McLaglen were called in the film. But it would surely come back.

It always had before.

James rested his head heavily on the pillow and fingered Jill's scarf under the mattress.

"Herr Standartenführer, don't you think you should try to get up and walk around a bit? You've been snoozing the whole morning. Don't you feel well?"

James opened his eyes and looked straight into the nurse's face. She smiled at him, getting up on tiptoe so she could insert her arm under his pillow and ease it up. For months James had been feeling like answering her or showing faint signs of improvement. Instead he stared at her emptily, his face expressionless.

Her name was Petra and she was the only real human being he had seen there thus far.

Petra had arrived as if sent by providence. The first thing she did was to see that the nurses left Werner Fricke, the man opposite him, in peace with his calendar calculations.

Then she stood up to a couple of the other nurses so that bed-wetting or eating food in an unsuitable manner was no longer punished so severely.

And finally, she took special care of James.

It was obvious he had aroused her sympathy from the first time she saw him. Others in the ward had benefited from her special care too, but so far James had been the only one who could get her to stop at the end of the bed with a sad and vulnerable expression on her face. How can she feel anything for a man like Gerhart Peuckert? James wondered, assuming she was just a naïve and unimaginative young girl who had landed in the nurses' training college at Bad Kreuznach straight from convent school.

She was clearly quite inexperienced in life. Whenever Petra mentioned her mentor and guardian angel, Professor Sauerbruch, to her colleagues, her eyes shone with devotion and her hands worked even more swiftly and surely. And when a patient went amok and cursed everyone to hell, she promptly made the sign of the cross before running to get help.

The most probable explanation for Petra's partiality toward James was that she was a rather diminutive, shy, romantic girl with natural appetites who also thought he was quite handsome with his white teeth and straight shoulders. The war had been going on for nearly five years. She had scarcely been more than sixteen or seventeen when hard and exacting hospital work had become her everyday life. How could she have found an outlet for her dreams and fantasies in the meantime? It was hard to believe she'd ever had the opportunity to love or be loved.

James had nothing against the possibility that he might have stimulated her imagination. She was quite a nice and pretty girl. For the moment he was being cautious and taking advantage of her care. As long as she was there to force some food into him after the shock treatments and close the window if the draft started making his shoulder muscles stiff, he knew his body would not be the first thing to fail him.

"This is no good, Herr Standartenführer," she continued, pushing James's feet over the edge of the bed. "You're not much help. You want to get better, don't you? Then you must get up and walk!"

James stood halfway between the beds and began edging his way to the central corridor. Petra nodded and smiled. It was this form of special treatment James was less keen on. It drew the attention of the other nurses. It gave him a kind of priority status that could lead to reprisals and repercussions in the name of justice.

However, it was not the possible outcome of this situation that James feared the most. More and more he sensed a kind of vigilance and tension in the room. The feeling came over him like a sudden tap on the shoulder. And this day it was there again. James glanced across the corridor through half-closed eyelids.

It was the third time that day that Bryan was staring at him, trying to attract his attention.

"Bryan, stop staring at me, dammit! It's much too obvious!" he thought. Bryan's pleading eyes were fixed on him. Petra took James by the arm, chatting to him as usual about this and that as she led him over to the window beside the trolleys at the opposite end of the room. Behind him James noticed how Bryan was struggling to get up. It was only one day since his last shock treatment, but this didn't hold him back.

The little nurse's stream of words stopped when James began hauling her back toward his bed. He was not going to be trapped in a corner with Bryan. Noticing James's reaction, Bryan let his arms flap down limply by his sides. He leaned back dejectedly in his bed as James marched by with the eager Petra.

"Right now you're weak, Bryan, but tomorrow you'll perk up again," thought James. "I'm not going to feel sorry for you. Just leave me alone. You know that's best! I'll get us out of here, trust me! But not now. They're watching us!" James heard Bryan's bed creak and felt his despairing gaze boring into his back.

The pockmarked man, whose name was Kröner, strode quietly after them and slapped Bryan on the shoulder. "*Gut Junge*, upsy-daisy," he growled, shaking the bars of the next bed's foot end.

"Back to *Gunga Din* . . ." James thought frantically, as he wriggled out of Petra's grasp and back into bed. "What did they call those bloody sergeants? Think carefully, James, you know you know it!"

Kröner sat down heavily, staring at Petra's retreating bottom with its fluttering white bow as she finally continued her rounds. "Lovely bumbum, isn't it, Herr Standartenführer?" he said, addressing James.

Every word was like stinging ice.

The big man folded his legs under him, bumping his knees against the side of the bed until the entire iron frame rattled. James never reacted to his question. Sooner or later he would stop talking.

The men beside Kröner sat straight up in bed like vultures and stared across at Bryan, who was burrowing into the blankets until he finally lay down in the messy pile, exhausted. "Relax, Bryan," James begged silently, "otherwise they're gonna get us!"

CHAPTER 12

The names came to James from the depths of sleep, taking him so much by surprise that he opened his eyes and stared into the ward's semidarkness. The two remaining sergeants in *Gunga Din* were called McChesney and Ballantine.

Heavy breathing and scattered snoring brought him slowly back to reality. A faint beam of light penetrated the bomb shutters. James counted to forty-two. Then the beam came again. The men in the watchtower behind the SS barracks swung the searchlight around another couple of times as part of their routine before creeping back to the shelter of the tower's tar-papered roof. It was raining for the fourth night in a row, and only two nights ago the sound of bombs over Karlsruhe had reverberated along the rocky slopes, causing the guards outside to run around shouting shrill commands.

The patient in bed number 9 had drawn his legs up under him and begun sobbing quietly to himself. He was a *Hauptsturmführer* who had been pinned by a tree trunk for over ten hours during an attack on the Eastern Front, while flamethrowers from his own striking force devastated the countryside. They were the only two in the ward who had been awake that night. Now only James was left.

He breathed heavily and sighed. That afternoon he'd made Petra blush. As usual she and Vonnegut, the porter with the iron hook, sat studying the casualty lists before Vonnegut cast himself over his newspaper's tiny crossword, tapping his pitiful artificial limb on the table in irritation every time he was stuck for a word.

Vonnegut was keeping to himself because there'd been a bad mood in the ward all day.

There was an icy coldness between Petra and the senior nursing officer. First the senior nurse had adjusted the nursing badge on Petra's head scarf and pushed some loose strands of fair hair back into place beneath it. Then Petra had adjusted the nursing officer's party emblem on her right lapel and polished it with her sleeve so the enamel encircling the white text saying *Bund Deutsche Mädel*, shone a bright red.

Toward evening, when Petra should have gone off duty, the nursing officer had sent her replacement over to another ward on the pretext that she was to assist some novices. It was clearly an act of revenge and Petra, her eyes flashing, made threatening gestures at her as soon as she turned her back.

It was difficult to avoid falling for her as she stood there rebelliously in her flat shoes, oatmeal-colored dress, and white apron. James smiled every time she bent down and scratched herself behind her knees where the black woolen stockings irritated her most.

She turned around and caught his gaze as his eyes were dancing over her figure. It was an intimate moment.

That's when she blushed.

Restless movements from Kröner in the next bed usually meant he was about to wake up. "Die in your sleep, you swine!" James whispered inaudibly, and forced himself to go on thinking about Petra. At that moment she was probably asleep in her bed in her attic room above them, dreaming of the way he'd looked at her, just as he was lying there now, thinking about how she'd looked back at him. Perhaps James would have been better off without these fantasies. It was hard to be young and full of erotic stirrings he could never pursue.

Flickering in the darkness through his eyelashes James saw the image of Kröner turned toward him, examining him. James cautiously shut his eyes tight, waiting for the whispering to start again.

The nightmare had first manifested itself late one night, over two months ago. The hard click of the night nurse's heels had woken him. She had just crossed the corridor toward the staff lavatories behind the stairs leading into the yard. Right in front of him a silhouette was bending slightly forward over the head end of the next bed. There was not a sound in the room apart from two quick jerks from the foot end of the bed. Then the shape adjusted James's neighbor's pillow, walked quickly back to the other end of the ward, and lay down in one of the beds.

When Vonnegut tapped the bed ends the following morning he found

James's neighbor dead. He was black in the face, tongue sticking vulgarly and grotesquely from between his jaws. The protruding eyes looked desperate.

Rumor had it that he usually hid remnants of food under his pillow and must have choked on a fish bone. Holst, the surgeon lieutenant, shook his head as he lent an ear to the senior nursing officer, who whispered a few words. Dr. Holst thrust his fists into his coat pockets. He brushed aside a couple of questions from Vonnegut and saw to it that the porters removed the body before the security officer and head doctor had a chance to make trouble for the staff on duty in the ward.

In his drugged and foggy nocturnal state James had witnessed a murder.

Several faces popped up from their beds, ducking from side to side as they watched the nursing helpers change the dead man's bedclothes and leave the bed smooth, fresh, and empty.

At lunchtime a patient got out of his bed, walked toward James, and lay down in the newly made bed. He was the one who had stolen James's idea of helping the nurses on their rounds. There he lay until the helpers brought in dumplings and leg of pork in the enamel food containers. His blubbering and whining were to no avail as the staff pulled him out of the bed. But this had little effect.

Every time they turned their backs he crept back into the bed, pulled the blanket right up to his chin, and lay there, clutching it tightly. Not until he lay stretched out in the bed did he settle down. When this scene had repeated itself a few times the staff gave up and let him stay where he was.

However impossible it was to comprehend, James had just gotten himself an assassin for a neighbor.

James had no idea what was going on. For the first few nights he was too terrified to fall asleep. Whatever this lunatic's motive might have been, if, indeed, there were one, he would be capable of doing it again. So it was safer to sleep during the day and stay awake at night, counting the number of times his neighbor turned around heavily in the creaking bed. If anything happened he would shout for help or get up on the bed to reach the cord that hung from the wall and had been suitably shortened so the patients wouldn't be able to pull it at all hours. Which no one thus far had attempted to do.

On the third night following this episode the ward lay in total darkness.

The light in the corridor had been switched off for once and all the shutters closed. From around him came the sound of snoring and heavy breathing, easing James's anxiety and making him relax. After reenacting one of Pinkerton's exploits he resorted to the last movie he had managed to see in his happy Cambridge days, a magnificent epic by Alexander Korda, and dozed off.

To start with, the hushed, whispered words slid almost imperceptibly into James's dream. Like foreign bodies they blended disturbingly with a love scene and didn't stop when James's eyes flew open with a start. The words were real and they were concrete. Subdued and measured. Not at all those of someone mentally unbalanced. They came from the pockmarked Kröner, the killer lying beside him.

Other voices in the darkness joined in the conversation. There were three altogether: Kröner's and the men in the next two beds.

"I had to make a scene, dammit," came the voice from the farthest bed. "That bitch of a nursing officer caught me reading Vonnegut's magazines."

"That was a stupid thing to do, Dieter!" growled Kröner at James's side.

"What the hell is one supposed to do? If you aren't mad to start with, you go mad from lying here with absolutely nothing to occupy yourself!"

"All right, but from now on, keep away from those magazines. You're not doing that again!"

"Of course not. Do you think I started doing it for fun? Do you think it was funny being stuck in the loony cell for days? I'm not ending up there again. Anyway, they're starting to liquidate those crazies now," he continued. "What else can they do?"

"What the hell are they screaming for? I thought it was only Stuka pilots who went that crazy," whispered Horst Lankau, the broad-faced man in the middle.

James felt his heart pounding and his head growing light from lack of oxygen as he fought to control his agitation and follow the conversation at the same time. His temples throbbed as he slowly inhaled through his teeth so his breathing wouldn't drown out the quiet whispering beside him. Apart from the circumstances, the conversation was quite normal. None of the three had ever been the slightest bit mentally deranged.

Not until morning did James fully realize how shaky the situation could be for himself and Bryan if they were not the only ones who were feigning illness.

The greatest problem was that Bryan knew nothing. If he kept on trying to make contact, it could be the death of them.

James would have to avoid him at any price, ignore any attempts to make contact and anything else that might connect the two of them.

What Bryan would do about it was up to him. They knew each other so well that presumably Bryan would eventually realize James would only act like that if he felt he had to.

Bryan would have to learn to be on his guard. He would, indeed.

Kröner's manner of speech was cultivated. Behind the enormous, gnarled figure and the pockmarked face was an able-minded, well-educated, and entirely self-centered man. It was he who was in charge and made sure they stopped talking if there was an unexpected movement or strange sound. Kröner was always on the alert and in constant activity, while the other two—the broad-faced man and his skinny companion, Dieter Schmidt— slept most of the day so they could keep awake for the nightly discussions.

Everything Kröner did had one simple purpose: to survive in that hospital until the war was over. In the daytime he was friends with everyone, patting them on the cheek and running errands for the staff. At night he was capable of murdering anyone he thought stood between him and his goal. He had already murdered once.

During a night like this the whispering could last a couple of hours. The nightly control had been intensified somewhat since the affair with the fish bone and the night nurse could be expected to turn up in the ward at irregular intervals. She would wave the beam of a dynamo lamp to and fro over their faces. And the ward was always as silent as the grave.

But Kröner lay there ready, waiting just a moment to make sure the room was perfectly still again after the beam danced out of the room and the slight noise from the twisting finger movements that powered the little dynamo had disappeared in the direction of the nurses' guardroom.

The whispering didn't start up again until he gave the sign. And James pricked up his ears.

Kröner had strangled the man simply to be closer to his confederates so they could talk. As long as James constituted no threat to them, he had nothing to fear.

He would even have been able to sleep peacefully, if it weren't for the stories the malingerers told.

CHAPTER 13

For the most part the accounts were horrifyingly detailed. Night after night the malingerers feasted on tales of their atrocities and tried to outdo one another. Each of them usually began relating a piece of the mosaic with a "Can you remember . . ." that gradually revealed how they had landed beside him, and why they intended to remain there at any price until they could slip away or the war came to an end.

More often than not, James was shocked.

When these monsters finally quit talking, their stories morphed into nightmarish dreams with a form, color, smell, and wealth of detail that usually ended with his waking up bathed in sweat.

Throughout 1942 and 1943 Obersturmbannführer Wilfried Kröner had been ordered to make sure his SS Wehrmacht support troops for the security police, the SD, kept close on the heels of the Waffen-SS armored divisions operating on the Eastern Front. Here he learned that every will can be broken, and that made him love his job.

"Before we came to the Eastern Front we'd heard how stubborn the Soviet supporters could be when interrogated." Kröner paused. "But when the first ten partisans finished screaming, then it was time for ten more, right? One of them would always say something in order to get into heaven a little less agonizingly."

The silhouette in the bed beside James spoke about hangings in which the delinquents were hoisted up slowly until their toes just reached the ground, and tried to describe the tingling sensation he'd felt when the ground was frozen and the condemned's toes danced feverishly over the mirror-smooth ice. He related with satisfaction the time he'd managed to fling the rope so precisely over the gallows that two equally heavy partisans could be hanged at each end. "Naturally, if they wriggled too much it wouldn't work every time, so we had to resort to more traditional methods," he added. "But otherwise one was encouraged to show a little imagination. It inspired respect. You could say the partisans spoke their minds more freely during my interrogations. . . ." Kröner glanced around to see if there was any movement in the ward. James shut his eyes instantly when Pock Face turned around and stared at him. "If they spoke at all," he added.

James felt nauseous.

In many respects those had been rewarding times for Kröner. During one interrogation a stubborn little lieutenant in the Soviet Army had broken down despite his iron will and obstinacy, and had pulled a leather purse from his riding breeches. It hadn't helped him, since they beat him to death anyway, but the purse was interesting.

Rings and German marks, silver and gold amulets, and a few rubles poured out onto the table. Kröner's aide-de-camp estimated there were two thousand marks when the time came to share the spoils. That made four hundred for each of the officers on Kröner's staff and eight hundred for himself. They called it recovered spoils of war and took care in the future to search all the prisoners personally before they were brought for interrogation, or "liquidation," as Kröner laconically termed the summary executions. Pock Face laughed as he related the time his subordinates had caught him in the process of plundering a prisoner without intending to share with them. "They threatened to rat on me, the ridiculous beasts! They were just as guilty! Everyone pocketed something if they could get away with it." The two listeners laughed quietly with legs drawn up beneath them, even though they had heard the story before. Then, in a low, confidential voice Kröner said, "But one has to take care of oneself! So I got rid of all three of them so they couldn't try any more stunts. I was questioned when two of the bodies were found, but of course they couldn't prove anything. They reckoned the third man had deserted. All very admirable. And this meant that in the future I wouldn't have to share with anyone, would I?"

The man in the middle bed raised himself on his elbows. "Ah, but you shared with me, nonetheless," he said. His face was absolutely the broadest James had ever seen, full of small transverse wrinkles that turned into a smile for no apparent reason or, more rarely, showed a tinge of anxiety. The dark eyebrows shot up and down, inspiring confidence.

A fatal misjudgment.

The first time Kröner and this Horst Lankau had come across each other was in the winter of 1943, more specifically two weeks before Christmas. Kröner had been on a raid in the southern sector of the Eastern Front. The objective was to mop up after a recent attack.

The villages were devastated, but not crushed. Behind the bombarded plank walls and screened by bunches of straw, families were still sitting, making soup from the last bones of their slain animals. Kröner had them all hauled out and shot. "Onward!" he commanded the SS soldiers. It wasn't potential partisans he was after, but Soviet officers who had something to tell and perhaps also a few valuables to be stolen.

On the outskirts of the fourth village a detachment of SS soldiers dragged a man out from among the burning huts and threw him in front of Kröner's staff car. The cur got up immediately, brushed the snow off his face, and sneered at his captors. He stared fearlessly at their leader. "Order them to go," he said with a broad Prussian accent, waving SS men away with a deprecatingly cold-blooded look. "I have important things to tell!"

Kröner found such contempt for death irritating and ordered him to kneel down, tightening a leather-gloved finger on the trigger as he aimed at the defiant face. Without the slightest hesitation the man in the shabby peasant clothes reported that he was a German deserter, a *Standartenführer* in a mountain commando division, and a damned good soldier who'd been decorated many times and definitely not one to be shot without a court-martial.

Kröner's rising curiosity saved the wretch's life. Triumph was already painted on his broad face when he said his name was Horst Lankau and that he had a proposal to make.

Horst Lankau's military past was murky. James concluded that he'd already joined the military before war broke out. He was a seasoned soldier and had apparently been destined for a glorious, if traditional, career.

But even the most illustrious traditions were quickly affected by the war on the Eastern Front.

Originally Lankau's mountain division, one of the trump cards of the offensive, had been deployed in order to capture Soviet staff officers at the enemy's rear. Whereupon they were to leave it to the SD, or occasionally the Gestapo, to extract what they could from them. This is what Horst Lankau had been doing for some months. A dirty, dangerous job.

One lucky day they had picked up a major general whose possessions included a tiny box containing thirty small diamonds, clear as glass and worth a fortune.

These thirty small stones made him decide to survive the war, whatever the price.

Kröner laughed with recognition when Lankau came to the point in the story where he said, almost apologetically, that the theft had been discovered by his own men.

"I gathered them around the bonfire and gave them an extra ration of ersatz coffee, the trustful idiots." While they were slurping their coffee, Lankau blew all his elite soldiers and their prisoners into unrecognizable bits with a single hand grenade. Both he and Kröner laughed when he reached the climax of his story. After that Horst Lankau had sought refuge among Soviet peasants, with whom he traded small change for safety. He and the war would just have to get along without each other, he'd reckoned.

And then Kröner had come into the picture and made things complicated.

He'd enticed his captor, undaunted. "I'll pay for my life with half the diamonds. If you want them all, you can shoot me now though you won't get them and you won't find them, either. But you can have half if you hand over your pistol and take me to your quarters. When the time comes, you'll report that you've liberated me from Soviet partisans. Until then you'll let me remain in your quarters without my having to have any contact with the other officers. I'll tell you later what's going to happen after that."

He and Kröner haggled over the division of the diamonds, but it ended up with Lankau having his way. Fifteen each, and Lankau was to be quartered in Kröner's camp with a loaded pistol in his pocket.

Kröner made a final attempt: "I want a diamond for every week I take care of your board and lodging." The broad face broke into an even broader smile. Kröner realized it was a refusal. He would have to get rid of Lankau as quickly as possible so he wouldn't attract unwanted attention.

Lankau was by his savior's side constantly during the three days Kröner was on Christmas leave outside the camp. Kröner wasn't sure whether it was the hand permanently planted in the pocket with the pistol or Lankau's eternally foolish-looking, almost pious facial expression that made him uneasy. But he began respecting the man's cold-blooded endurance. Gradually he began to realize that together they'd be able to achieve results that would be impossible to achieve separately.

On the third day they traveled to Kirovograd, where most of the soldiers went when the food in the field kitchen became too monotonous or life at the front too depressing.

Kröner often sat there half dozing with his elbows on the oaken tables of the pub, amusing himself by picking out patrons he could start a fight with or, better still, who would pay him for not being beaten to a pulp.

It was there that Lankau initiated Kröner into the plans he had hatched during the months of dreary idleness in the Soviet village.

"I want to go back to Germany as soon as possible and now I know how," he said quietly, straight in Kröner's ear. "One of these days you'll report to headquarters that you have liberated me from captivity, just as we've agreed. Then you'll procure me a doctor's certificate saying that I've been so badly tortured by the partisans that I've gone raving mad. When I'm sitting in the hospital train on its way west, you'll get two more of my diamonds."

The idea appealed to Kröner. He could get rid of Lankau and benefit from it at the same time. It could be a kind of dress rehearsal for what he himself could do if life at the front became too risky.

Dress rehearsal or not, it was not to be. Behind the officers' pub there were four small outhouses to supplement the ones indoors. Kröner had always preferred shitting in the fresh air.

He swayed as he buttoned up his fly, relieved, and smiled at the thought of the two extra diamonds as he opened the door wide. In front of him stood a shape almost completely engulfed by darkness that made no signs of letting him pass. A stupid thing to do, thought Kröner, for someone so small in stature and puny to look at.

"*Heil Hitler, Herr Obersturmbannführer*," piped the man without budging. Just as Kröner had clenched his fist and was about to knock the obstacle out of his way, the officer stepped back into the feeble light illuminating the wall of the backyard.

"Obersturmbannführer Kröner, have you time to talk for a moment?" asked the stranger. "I have a proposal to make to you."

. . .

After a few sentences, the officer had Kröner's undivided attention. He looked around, took the *Hauptsturmführer* under the arm, and led him out to the street where Lankau was standing, and into his car, which he'd parked at the end of the nearest side street.

The sinewy little man's name was Dieter Schmidt. He had been ordered by his superior to make contact with Wilfried Kröner. His superior didn't wish to disclose his identity but added that Kröner wouldn't find it very difficult to find out if he absolutely wanted to.

"It's safer for everyone that we don't all know each other's identity in the event that anything should go wrong," Dieter Schmidt said, glancing at Horst Lankau, who made no signs of introducing himself. "Since it is my superior's plan, and until things get going he is the only one who would be incriminated, he asks that the gentlemen respect his desire for anonymity."

The thin man undid the top buttons of his coat and looked them both in the eyes for a long time before he continued.

Dieter Schmidt came from an SS Wehrmacht armored division, this was obvious. But originally he had been a *Sturmbannführer* and vice commandant of a concentration camp. This was something very few people knew.

Some months previously he and his commandant, who was responsible for the concentration camp and a few smaller work camps belonging to it, had been forcibly removed from their posts, demoted one grade, and transferred to administrative duty in the SS Wehrmacht on the Eastern Front, a practical alternative to dishonor and execution. But the longer they remained on Soviet soil, the more they realized they would probably never leave it again. The Germans fought like devils to hold their positions, but there was no longer any indication that they would be able to stop the massive Soviet Army. Despite the fact that Dieter Schmidt's and his superior's job consisted mainly of administration and office work, the distance from the front could be covered in less than half an hour by Soviet armored cars.

In short, their lives were in constant danger. Every day their typewriter tapping was accompanied by the thunder of cannons. Only fourteen of the original twenty-four superior staff officers remained.

Such was life on the Eastern Front. Everyone knew that.

"Our little game in the concentration camp probably wasn't that unique, but we didn't know that then," Dieter Schmidt explained. "We had a daily budget for running costs that had to be kept. For example, we had 1,100 marks a day for the prisoners' food. So we cheated central administration and skipped food distribution roughly every fifth day. The prison mob didn't make a fuss. We called it collective hunger punishment and referred to offenses that had never taken place. Of course a few thousand of them gave up the ghost because of it, but nobody complained about *that*.

"Then there was the income from hiring out slave laborers, though we seldom kept precise accounts, and finally we lowered the hiring fees a bit, which definitely increased our turnover. The factory owners and the other employers never complained. The cooperation was exemplary.

"During the late summer we estimated our total earnings at over a million marks. It was a fantastic business until a *kapo*—one of those pathetic concentration camp prisoners turned guard—inadvertently knocked down an official from Berlin during inspection, smashing his glasses. The *kapo* instantly fell to his knees and begged for his life, as though it were something they could be bothered to deprive him of. He wept and begged and clutched the official, who desperately tried to wrench himself free with the result that the man simply held him tighter. Finally the *kapo* screamed that he could tell him all about the running of the camp, if only his life were spared.

"Naturally, what he knew was very limited, but before we could pull him away and take care of him he managed to shout out that the food rations had been fiddled with. And by then it was too late.

"As a result of the audit, everything we'd put to the side was discovered and confiscated. For over a month we sat in the jail in Lublin, waiting for our death sentences to be carried out. Apart from the course the war was taking, we don't know what it was that altered our sentences, but someone had changed his mind and we landed on the Eastern Front."

James gradually sorted out all this information in his mind, bit by bit. Small fragments of information here, a tale there, and endless bragging made up the story of the malingerers next to him.

Dieter Schmidt, the thin one who lay farthest away from him, often spoke very quietly and many things were difficult to understand. In an extreme situation like that, it was hard to determine whether he was subdued by nature or if it was due to the fear of discovery. But it was obvious that the longer the bouts of electroshock, the more hazy he became, whereas neither Kröner nor Lankau seemed to react much to the treatments and exchanged stories undaunted.

James prayed that sooner or later a nurse would hear them. Then the three fiends would be exposed and his nightmare would come to an end.

Until then he would simply have to make sure none of them became suspicious of him.

While the malingerers' story was certainly horrifying, it was also fascinating. Like the movies and novels James reenacted in his mind, it absorbed him more and more.

To him, the scenes seemed large as life.

Dieter Schmidt always referred to his anonymous superior as the Mailman, a nickname that came from his habit of using bits of human skin when writing messages of congratulation. "Isn't it the wish of everyone in the camp to be sent away from here?" Schmidt's superior had asked.

He described the Mailman as cheerful and inventive, as someone who had made their life in the concentration camp comparable to conditions at home in every respect.

But after they were demoted and transferred, it was the end of their little game and their time of plenty. The means had become fewer, the responsibility someone else's, and the supervision of their work was officious, distrustful, and thorough.

And yet their chance had come in the form of a fantastic coincidence.

"One day, when several sections of the front had collapsed—which in Berlin they preferred to call 'front contraction'—the Mailman got an idea," said Schmidt. "You know how everyone's always screaming for reinforcements and fresh supplies in a situation like that.

"Obergruppenführer Hoth, general of the 4th Panzer Army, was furious that day. He insisted that a whole freight train with spare parts for armored vehicles had disappeared and ordered our unit to recover these parts immediately.

"Three days before Kiev was conquered by the Russians we did in fact find the freight cars in a corner of the city's switchyard. Hoth was happy and ordered the Mailman to personally supervise their immediate transportation to Vinnitsa, where damaged military equipment was waiting for spare parts.

"In Vinnitsa hundreds of heavy wooden cases containing bits of motors, caterpillar treads, axles, and smaller spare parts were unloaded into a warehouse. It was almost dark at the back of this enormous warehouse, where thousands of cases were already stacked in complete disorder. There were countless objects and materials sticking out everywhere that attracted our attention and made us curious. The Mailman and I, we were thunderstruck by the sight. It seemed a huge amount of war spoils were being stored here, waiting to be taken back to the fatherland when there was a freight train available.

"It didn't take long before we found out our hunch was right. Throughout all of 1943 any object valued at over 3,000 Reichsmarks that had been stolen from neighboring churches, official offices, museums, or private collections had been stored here. Now, as the fronts drew nearer, it was clear that this enormous booty was going to be evacuated as soon as possible. And that's when the Mailman got the fantastic idea of taking a couple of hundred cases and stacking them on their own, about fifty meters farther to the back of the warehouse.

"Then one could always wait and see what happened."

The Mailman and Dieter Schmidt were thrilled when they returned to the warehouse five days later. Their trick had worked. All the cases had already been removed.

Except for the ones they had set aside.

Now they had to get busy. When the transport reached Berlin the fact that a couple of hundred cases were missing would be discovered during the unloading and counting. "And that's why I've been ordered to try to contact you, Herr Obersturmbannführer Kröner," Dieter Schmidt explained as they were sitting in the car behind the pub in Kirovograd. "We need the help of a superior associated with the SD. Nobody around here wants to mix themselves up in the security police's business. Aside from that, units that work with the security police have a number of advantages, such as mobility and determination. We came to the conclusion that you might be the right man for us.

"You, Herr Obersturmbannführer, work on the same section of the front as us. We know you have displayed exceptional initiative in a number of cases. You're talented and imaginative, but what struck us first and foremost was your total lack of scruples. You must excuse me for making myself so plain, but there is no time for the usual niceties."

They began planning.

Kröner was to see to it that Russian slave workers were transferred to Vinnitsa. Then Lankau was to have them load the relics, icons, altar silver, and other valuables onto a freight car the Mailman had had sidetracked a few hundred meters from the warehouse. The freight car was to be used for "collecting spare parts." No one would miss it.

The subsequent removal of the slave workers could safely be left to Kröner and Lankau.

Dieter Schmidt would then see to it that the freight car was furnished with false transport papers ordering it immediately to a village in the heart of Germany, where it was to stay locked up on a siding and unnoticed until after the war.

Not until the goods were on their way was Kröner to report to headquarters about Lankau's "liberation" from the Russian "partisans." Then he was to be declared mentally disturbed and sent back to Germany, precisely as in the original plan.

After some initial doubts, Dieter Schmidt was even enthusiastic about the insanity aspect. Of course, there was the risk of being discovered or done away with. He himself had given the order for hundreds of mental cases to be liquidated when he'd been helping run the concentration camp. But the degree of madness was the decisive factor. One had to make sure the condition wasn't diagnosed as incurable and then there would be a fair chance of success.

What alternative was there, anyway? During recent weeks the war had become hell on Earth. Resistance had been incessant and terribly effective. The war could not be won. It was a question of survival at any price, and it would be of considerable advantage to be as far away as possible if their swindle was discovered.

The idea of feigning madness fit like a glove. Why should anyone suspect some shell-shock victims, thousands of kilometers from the front, of having stolen several tons of valuables? Dieter Schmidt was confident. They had to simulate mental illness. All of them! Schmidt himself, Kröner, Lankau, and the Mailman.

The plan worked like a charm. Apart from the enormous profit they expected to make, each had his own particular motives for getting away.

"Operation Insanity" would be put into action when the Mailman sent out the code word, "*Heimatschutz.*" As soon as they received the code, Kröner would see to it that all the inhabitants of a couple of Ukrainian villages were wiped out and pretend that Lankau had been found there and liberated.

Afterward, Kröner was to contact Dieter Schmidt, supposedly to agitate for special treatment of SD auxiliary troops in the difficult and acute supply situation.

During this meeting they had to find a way to be alone in the afternoon when the Soviet artillery were usually hammering the Germans' rear. As soon as the bombardment drew nearer they would seek cover and blow up Schmidt's quarters. It would look as if a stray Soviet shell had hit it. Later, when they were dug out of the ruins, Kröner and Schmidt would be found totally paralyzed by shell shock. They would remain in that condition until the war was over.

The Mailman would make his own preparations. "I'll show up when the time comes," he'd told them. It took a while, but Dieter Schmidt succeeded in convincing Kröner and Lankau that the Mailman was not someone who let his friends down.

CHAPTER 14

The previous night was the third time in barely a week that James had slept badly. His whole body was clammy.

"I'll get us out of this, Bryan, I promise you!" he told himself. He shook his head to banish the remaining dream images, and in the process banged the back of his head on the bars. The sudden pain made him open his eyes wide. Pock Face was already awake, lying on his side and propped up on his doubled-up pillow. He was looking straight at James, who instantly reacted with his toneless humming. Feeling Kröner's cold gaze upon him, he turned around and blinked at the strips of morning light that cast a red gleam through tiny gaps in the bomb shutters. It reminded him of mornings on the cliffs at Dover, many years ago.

Bryan's family had a house in Dover where James loved to go. Even in midweek the entire Young family would impulsively jump in the car and drive the twenty-five kilometers through the beautiful countryside out to the coast. The house stood ready all year round, ever since Mr. Young's bachelor days. The caretaker couple saw to that.

Mr. Young loved the sea, the wind, and the view.

There was rarely a weekend visit where James didn't accompany them.

According to James's mother, Dover wasn't a town you stayed in, it was a town you drove through. Still, to her it also represented something unknown and venturesome. She was anxious by nature, which was why James had never told his parents about their experiments with smoke- and stink bombs or about his and Bryan's splendid inventions that included a raft made of herring barrels and a giant catapult made of braided bicycle inner tubes.

If Mrs. Teasdale had known her son could fire a brick with such velocity and precision that it could penetrate a sack of corn at fifty meters, she would scarcely have been overjoyed.

For the boys, Dover was a true oasis. "There go Mr. Young's sons!" people used to say when they strolled along the seafront promenade.

It had always pleased them to be taken for brothers and they usually reacted by slinging their arms around each other's shoulders and singing their battle song at the top of their lungs. It was a banal ditty that one of Elizabeth's suitors had heard in a movie he and Bryan never managed to see:

I don't know what they have to say
it makes no difference anyway.
Whatever it is, I'm against it

The song continued in a similar style, listing various scenarios that always ended with the contrary refrain, "I'm against it!" They bawled it, singing these lines again and again, driving everyone in the neighborhood crazy. The song had another verse or two.

But they never learned them.

During their beloved teacher Mr. Denham's excellent history lessons the boys had been initiated in the exploits of courageous men and women. Cromwell, Thomas Becket, Queen Victoria, and Mary Stuart were conjured up. Knights in armor thundered past the teacher's desk.

This was the boys' favorite class.

It was here, inspired by Jules Verne, that the boys penetrated the Earth's core, dove into the ocean, and flew in strange, wonderful machines.

As soon as one of them made a brief sketch, the other caught on immediately. They elaborated on each other's ideas, hour after hour, without saying a word.

During this delightful time they invented a gigantic drill that could bore out a mine shaft or a tunnel to France, and an automobile that could transport whole towns to places where the weather was good.

In the boys' eyes all these things could be done. The question was why on Earth it hadn't happened long ago. So they tried it themselves.

Once, during an autumn storm, Mr. Denham had measured a wind force of twenty-seven yards per second. Bryan and James had looked dumbfounded at the little anemometer. Ninety kilometers per hour!

It was an enormous figure.

On the way home from school they'd sat awhile on the curb in front of the corn exchange, not even noticing the passersby.

At a speed of ninety kilometers one could fly to France in half an hour, if there were favorable conditions. Being blown across the ice in an iceboat would probably take twice that long.

Before the day was over they'd outlined the venture that was to shape their destinies. They would sew together a balloon, so the wind's fascinating energy could be put to the test.

They wanted to fly.

During the weekends they stole sailcloth, piece by piece, from building sites down by Dover harbor. Mr. Young unknowingly provided the transport home to Canterbury. The space under the backseat was very roomy.

The lads worked on the balloon in the Young family's old shed for nearly a year. No one was to know, and it had to be done quickly. Fate would catch up with them after the holidays, for they were to leave King's College in Canterbury and continue their schooling at Eton.

Then the weekends in Dover would be few and far between.

On the third day of the holidays they put the finishing touches on their work.

It was Jill who inadvertently came to solve the problem of getting the balloon transported back to Dover, where the cliff and the wind awaited them.

On the tenth of July, 1934, Jill would be eighteen. In her part of the country it had become the fashion for girls her age, from better-class homes, to begin preparing themselves for matrimony, which had been conventional for daughters of the servant class for centuries. Before the wedding it was customary to collect silverware and china.

According to Jill and her friends it was essential to have a glass case in which to keep such treasures. She had seen an ad in the newspaper: "Glass case for sale. Possibly in exchange for a lady's bicycle of reputable make and in good condition. Enquiries to Briggs & Co." The boys got excited when she read out the address.

They were going to Dover.

It was Mrs. Teasdale's bicycle that was to be sacrificed. They packed it in the balloon cloth.

When they reached their destination, the boys hid the cloth under a loading ramp while Mr. Teasdale and his daughter took care of their errand.

The glass case had already been sold. Jill was inconsolable. On the way home James had to pat her hand several times. "Want to borrow my hanky?" he finally offered. Jill looked incredulously at the remains that were stuck to it. Then she burst into laughter. "Seems like you have more use for mine, little brother."

James could still recall her dimples.

The scarf she'd handed him was blue, with a border Jill had embroidered herself.

Bryan had been amazed to see James tying this talisman around his neck every morning.

The boys waited two weeks for the wind to blow. Finally the day came. The wind had risen. They'd stuffed their beds with pillows and blankets. It was so windy on the top of the cliffs that the seagulls could scarcely control their aggressive downward swoops toward them. The boys put their arms around each other's shoulders as they paused to gaze out toward the Promised Land on the other side of the channel.

The wind direction was perfect.

They had fetched the wicker trunk, full of firewood, that they'd hidden the previous autumn among the trees on the slope behind the cliffs. They lashed the trunk, their magnificent gondola, under the open end of the balloon with five strong ropes. Then they arranged the wood under the tree whose crown the sailcloth was decorating. By dawn the fire had been crackling brightly for several hours under the expanding balloon.

The sun rose in a clear sky before the sailcloth was two-thirds full, and they now could just make out the outline of the European continent. Down along the row of bathing cabins on the public beach some boardinghouse guests were already wading about at the water's edge.

James never forgot their voices.

James made several mistakes during the critical minutes before their voyage was to begin. As soon as the morning bathers turned up he insisted they launch themselves before they were discovered. Bryan protested. The balloon wasn't full enough yet. "Trust me," James said. "It'll go according to plan!"

He felt sure of himself when the wind finally lifted the balloon the first inch. The cloth above them looked impressive. Oval, swollen, and huge. Then he released the final mooring line and threw a couple of logs overboard.

The balloon's giant silhouette swayed for a moment over the edge. Bryan looked up, frightened, and pointed at some of the seams that were letting warm air out in puffs. "Let's do it another day," he said, but James shook his head and gazed out toward Cap Gris Nez. The next second, as though possessed by the devil, James flung the rest of the wood, their food supplies, and extra clothes onto the plateau.

As the basket ascended gracefully the balloon flattened out, stretching like a sail in the unpredictable gusts of wind. At this point Bryan jumped to safety while James watched him, dumbfounded.

Then the balloon was snatched out over the edge.

Later, observers down in the town said the balloon had been instantly thrown against the cliff in the turbulence and with a tearing sound had caught itself on a jagged bit of rock.

"Dumb bastard!" James screamed up to Bryan, who'd stuck his ashen face cautiously over the edge of the cliff. The sagging dream above James's head emitted a series of exhausted and ominous noises. The gusts of wind kept scraping the balloon against the rocks so that it gradually fell apart. No one had missed this stolen property because the sailcloth had gotten moldy.

After that James gave up his ranting. Above him Bryan reluctantly stuck his feet out over the edge of the cliff and began to crawl down. There had been no accidents on that part of the cliff in recent years, but the western cliff had cost many a life in the course of time and both boys knew that. Some said the victims were as flat as dried cod when they'd been gathered up.

The sailcloth slipped yet another couple of meters with a noise like the crack of a whip, the loose ends like rags flapping in the wind. Bryan silently peed in his pants without interrupting his dangerous rescue operation. The cascade passed unhindered out his trouser leg and into the wind.

At the very top of the balloon was a brass ring through which the ropes—that had originally fastened a sail to a capstan bar—had been passed. Into this hole they'd bound a rope that was still hanging loosely in the middle of the balloon. As soon as their mission was accomplished they would grab the end of this rope and let the air out of the balloon so their descent was fully under control.

While Bryan was hanging on to the chalky, porous side of the cliff, feverishly searching for the brass ring, James started humming their favorite tune.

With a sudden jerk the balloon tore apart some more.

Down below him James's song struck the wall of the cliff with rhythmic thuds.

I don't know what they have to say
it makes no difference anyway.
Whatever it is, I'm against it . . .

James didn't remember much of what happened after that. With tears in his eyes Bryan managed to seize the rope end, pull it up, and ease it down again in its full length. James's trousers also had dark stains around the fly when they finally lay on the edge of the cliff. Bryan looked at his friend for some time as he tried to recover his breath.

James was still singing.

Memories of this episode had visited James often. During "Operation Supercharge" in the African desert, on night flights, in their rooms at Trinity College during the arduous years at Cambridge.

James attempted to return to the reality of the German ward. It wasn't easy. The first clinking sounds rose from the floor below. The air was heavy with reeking smells of the previous night. He turned his head cautiously and glanced over at Bryan. The curtains behind him were flapping a trifle, even though the shutters were closed. Only the puny, red-eyed man was awake in Bryan's row. Looking straight at James, he smiled searchingly. When James failed to react he pulled the blanket over his face and settled down.

"I'll get you out of here, Bryan!" was James's constant silent mantra as the ward's torpor and the stifling aftereffects of the electroshock gradually made him doze off.

CHAPTER 15

Then came the heat. And with the heat, all the changes.

The nurses exchanged their knee stockings for small, white ankle socks.

The smells in the ward grew stronger. Every time the swinging door was pushed, air that was heavy with moisture streamed into the ward from the lavatories and washroom at the end of the room. This caused Vonnegut to send for an SS private who'd been a carpenter, who planed one of the windows so enthusiastically that fresh air streamed into the room and diluted all the smells, whether the window was wide open or shut.

All the other windows were screwed firmly into their frames.

The period of constant bird twittering under the eaves a floor and a half above them had already passed. Long streaks of indeterminable filth on the windowpanes still bore witness thereof.

Vonnegut had stopped looking through the casualty lists in the newspapers. All too often he'd suddenly sat stock-still, mumbling to himself. Now he settled for laughing over "Süss, the Jew" and other small newspaper satires, or solving the crossword before anyone else.

Several of the patients were so noticeably better that it couldn't be more than a matter of weeks before they'd be sent back to their units.

All forms of sick leave had been canceled indefinitely for patients belonging to groups Z15,1; L15,1; vU15,1; and vU15,3. All these categories were represented in their ward. They comprised most kinds of mental illness of either a temporary or chronic nature. In times of peace, such illnesses would mean automatic exemption or light duties. No one ever told them what the individual designations actually stood for, and as time went by, no one took notice of these categories anyway. All that remained of the letter/number combinations was the nickname the nurses had given the ward.

They called it the Alphabet House.

The main object of the hospital treatment was to make lower-ranking officers well enough to know in which direction to order their companies to point their weapons, and make higher-ranking officers capable of assessing why they should point them at all.

But something more was expected of this special ward.

The army surgeon, Manfried Thieringer, had already had to report twice to the local gauleiter, who, as representative of the authorities in Berlin, had been ordered to achieve some real results. He'd been told the welfare of certain officers was being closely monitored by the Supreme Command and that he could be made personally responsible if these excellent soldiers did not get well at a reasonable rate.

Manfried Thieringer loved to repeat these reminders to his subordinates and twirled his mustache as he inspected these so-called excellent patients who could still scarcely distinguish their own slippers from their neighbor's. "But a cure is a cure," he remarked. No matter what even Himmler himself said.

James's powers of concentration deteriorated week by week.

The first to disappear were all the details that spiced his flights of fancy and gave the characters in his stories personality and life. Then chunks of the plot vanished, making the deterioration of his mind evident.

James had considered not taking the pills countless times. These preparations that dulled him, yet made life easier to endure. If he threw them on the floor he'd run considerable risk of being discovered. The daily cleaning was adequate, if not thorough. If he were caught taking them out to the lavatory, there could be consequences that were not unpredictable. There weren't many other possibilities.

And then of course there was Petra.

When it came down to it, Sister Petra was the real reason why he made no attempt to avoid swallowing the pills when she placed them carefully on his tongue and put her face close to his.

Her breath was sweetly feminine.

Inevitably she disturbed his thoughts. She was his enemy, but also his benefactor and savior. So he had to swallow the pills in order not to get her into trouble.

As long as things were as they were, escape was out of the question. The risk that the malingerers might discover something was always present.

James felt pinned down. Discovery would mean instant death. Kröner, Lankau, and Schmidt had already struck twice. The first time was when Kröner strangled James's neighbor in order to take over his bed.

The second time had been less than a week ago.

A new patient had been transferred from a normal ward with a hole in his leg and a short circuit in his brain. He'd lain sighing all day long on his bed beside Calendar Man.

There had been reports on Vonnegut's radio of such serious developments on the Western Front that the one-armed orderly had rushed into the ward in order to pass on his information to the junior resident doctor, who immediately flung his papers onto the nearest bed and followed Vonnegut back to the guardroom. Later in the day came the rumors. During the course of the evening the rumors had solidified into verified reports and reached the ward in the form of the nurses' chatter and the porters' mumbling.

"They've landed in France!" Vonnegut finally shouted. That gave James a start. The thought of Allied troops now fighting a few hundred kilometers away from them, with the sole object of advancing closer and closer, made him feel like weeping. "That'd be something for you to know, Bryan!" he thought. "Maybe it would make you relax."

As James was about to turn his face to the wall, the new patient diagonally opposite him began to laugh. Finally his hysterical laughter made the bed shake next to James. It was Kröner's. The latter pushed his blanket down over his shins, got up slowly, and stared across at the presumptuous man. James felt Kröner's eyes on him, causing a flash of heat to rise inside him and recede again more quickly than it came. The laughter stopped by itself but Kröner didn't lie down again.

During the next couple of days the malingerers took turns monitoring the new arrival. When he was fed, when he sat on the bedpan, when they changed him and wiped his body with alcohol. They watched over him in all ways possible. The whispering in the dark ceased, making the nights unpredictable. On the fourth night Lankau got up and walked over and killed the new arrival almost noiselessly. The muffled snap of the neck vertebrae was fainter than when the idiot patient at the other end of the room cracked his knuckles. Then they dragged him down to the window the SS soldier had planed so nicely and pushed him out, headfirst.

It took less than three minutes from the moment the guards outside started shouting until one of the security officers stood in the ward. All the lights were switched on. The officer rushed furiously to and fro between the window and the duty nurse, who stood wringing her hands. His anger knew no bounds. The window was to be nailed down immediately and whoever had made it openable would be called to account.

Then the officer walked up and down the rows of beds, inspecting each patient in turn. James stared him straight in the face, visibly shocked as he had reason to be, and made the officer pause for a moment.

The chief security officer entered the ward with sleep in his eyes, closely followed by two weary SS officers who could hardly stand on their feet. The army surgeon turned up too, but didn't react to the accusations awaiting him. "The window will be nailed up tomorrow," he said curtly, then turned his back on his interrogators and strolled back to his quarters.

Just before the light was switched off, Bryan woke up from his stupor following the morning's shock treatment and looked around dully. James closed his eyes instantly.

Later that night the whispering started up as before, bringing with it the familiar state of uneasiness. The malingerers exchanged remarks briefly. Kröner had recognized the dead man and had all too clearly seen himself be recognized. He praised Lankau but added dryly that in the future they'd better find other methods if new "problems" turned up in the ward.

"But why?" Lankau asked. "So what if they've nailed the window shut? What should prevent a suicidal patient from flinging himself out of a closed window?" he chuckled. But Kröner didn't laugh.

This was a worrisome development. Bryan would resume his small signs and attempts to contact James before long.

Schmidt and Lankau would continue to sleep well through the daytime, but Kröner showed no signs of letting himself be caught off guard.

This was something Bryan would have to realize.

CHAPTER 16

The nurses had been smiling at Bryan all morning.

Pock Face nodded eagerly as he passed by with his overloaded linen trolley and pointed toward the swing door. A group of nurses, of whom Bryan recognized only a couple, walked stiffly up to him and promptly began singing right in his face. Their enthusiasm and volume were worthy of a Wagnerian choir. Nice, it wasn't.

Bryan drew back, hoping they'd go away. Instead, one of the older ones bent over the bed, pressing the palms of her hands to her bosom. She sang like a baritone. Bryan was afraid she might leap right into bed with him. A couple of patients clapped and the chief nursing officer handed him a small package beautifully wrapped in tissue paper. She waved impatiently behind her and a paltry brown object appeared in a nursing aide's outstretched hands. As far as Bryan could tell by the frayed border and wavy surface, the object was a piece of cake adorned with a tiny swastika. Everyone around him was beaming. Later the head doctor arrived, looked covetously at the cake, and gave Bryan a friendly smile for the first time. His teeth were rotten.

Bryan lay back in his bed, staring uneasily at the dry piece of pastry. He was the focal point of another man's birthday. The first to be celebrated in the ward.

It hadn't been long since James's twenty-second birthday, which had passed by in silence for obvious reasons. Bryan had tried to give him a little nod, but James had just lain there, staring into thin air.

James had been lying like this most of the time for the past couple of months. It was becoming more and more difficult to imagine how he was going to help carry out their escape plans.

It was understandable if James succumbed to melancholy on his birthday. But what about the other days? Why did James isolate himself like that? How much longer was Bryan going to have to wait?

Bryan nibbled gingerly at the cake and gave a bit to his neighbor, who smacked his heels together as usual and devoured it as if it had been an order. It could only be a matter of days before the man would be sent back to hell. The fool was looking forward to it and he stood most of the day with his back to the ward, staring out the window at the undulating green landscape beyond the watchtowers.

A sound of rumbling came from the north as Pock Face and his broad-faced companion were wheeling the food trolleys into the room. It didn't last long, but it was enough to make an experienced Royal Air Force officer take notice. Bryan glanced at James, who was lying with his hands behind his neck.

The muffled sounds came from quite a distance. Baden-Baden, some people whispered. Others mentioned Strasbourg. Finally Vonnegut pointed out the window with his iron hook and shouted the names of both towns at a cleaning woman who was lying in the middle of the floor, scrubbing between the chairs as if nothing in the world had anything to do with her.

Suddenly the noise became much louder and several of the patients stood up and watched the flashes from the antiaircraft guns become brighter as daylight dwindled. Strasbourg burned the whole night, casting a faint aura of reddish-yellow light into the summer night.

"They're getting closer," thought Bryan, and prayed for his friends in the air, for himself, and for James. "Next time it may be Freiburg. Then we'll make our move, James!"

One of the patients, who had been lying like a stalk of limp asparagus, began waltzing around, closely followed by a thin, stiff-necked fellow patient who preferred to turn his whole body rather than just his head. These Siamese twins had been standing at Calendar Man's window all morning, gazing patiently and wordlessly across the valley as if something more were under way. When the blaze over Strasbourg was at its peak and the explosions echoed faintly from the mountain ridge, the thin man took the other one under the arm and rested his head gently on his shoulder.

Down at the other end of the ward Calendar Man returned from one of his rare visits to the lavatory to find the Siamese twins with their heads stuck between the window bars. Growling, he tried in vain to drag the thin man away from his turf by the knees.

Bryan noticed them and began leaning against the window as well. The twins had heard correctly. There was in fact something in the air. The quiet hum bounced off the mountain and was sucked up by the trees. They're headed south. To Italy, maybe, Bryan thought, staring across at James.

A few seconds later the twins gave a start. The dull explosions came from behind, washed over the hospital, and struck the wall of rock eight or nine hundred meters away, to return as hollow echoes that could hardly be distinguished from one another. The planes must have come from the west in a line south of them. The formations may have moved in over Colmar, or else the wind had been playing ball with the sound and tricked Bryan.

At any rate the bombardment of Freiburg was now a fact.

"*Schnell, schnell,*" the nurses urged, without displaying outward signs of surprise or fear, let alone panic. They let the few unconscious patients remain where they were. The rest were down the stairs in a couple of minutes.

From outside came the sound of air-raid sirens, hasty crunching steps, and banging doors. A guard stood at the entrance to the yard, pointing his weapon so no one could be in doubt that they were to walk past him and follow the steel banister down into the Alphabet House basement. The mentally disturbed men kept pushing from behind. The explosions and turbulent atmosphere conjured up the experiences that had driven them insane.

The basement was divided into two sections. On the left, a number of cells were furnished with gray steel doors from which came a constant stream of laments and muffled screams. A single door on the right led into a room half the size of their own ward. With no chance of moving back toward James, Bryan was propelled forward until he found himself squeezed up in the far corner while scores of patients from other wards pushed in through the narrow door opening.

James stood under one of the faint, flickering ceiling lamps in the middle of the room, gazing emptily into space with Pock Face's arm resting on his shoulder. Several of the patients with physical wounds from the neighboring block were in pain, due in part to their upright position, and were trying to procure enough space to enable them to squat on the floor or at least avoid being shoved.

The staff was busy calming the most agitated cases and making sure no one was trampled on. A young orderly gazed despondently into the air, breathing heavily and oblivious of the sweat trickling down his face. Perhaps he had some relatives in the thick of the bombardment.

Bryan rocked backward and forward, humming as James had done at first. With every movement he managed to create a slight opening in front of him into which he could step without protests from those around him. "Keep going, air-raid siren, keep going," Bryan said to himself, rocking and humming as he edged his way slowly toward James. The ceiling light had stopped flickering. The noises from outside merged into one.

A patient seized Bryan's shirt and began to spit a lot of nonsensical abuse at him. His eyes were heavy and his grip limp. Bryan couldn't comprehend how he had the energy to be so aggressive. He twisted the man's thumb out of joint and glanced over at James.

The look that met him was one he had never seen in James's face before. It was neither hateful nor angry, but dismissive, threatening, murderous.

Bryan suddenly stopped humming and snorted heavily. James looked away. Then Bryan took another couple of steps forward and the look immediately returned. Pock Face glanced down over Bryan's neck and his eyes followed the direction in which Bryan's nose was pointing. Bryan had no idea if he'd managed to look away in time.

Until he was lying in his bed once more he couldn't shake the feeling of constantly being watched.

The time spent in the basement had given him a lot to think about. Like the screams coming from the small cells alongside the passage, which everyone could hear but no one paid any attention to, even as they left the air-raid shelter again. Who could become like that? What had happened to them? Was it possible, after all, that Dr. Holst and Manfried Thieringer didn't really know the number of shocks a human brain could stand over the course of time? Or was this the punishment that awaited James and

Bryan if they were found out? Would they become like those wretches in the cellar?

And then there were the looks that James and Pock Face gave him.

In the evening Pock Face and his broad-faced companion were as smiling and solicitous as ever when they dealt out the plates and cutlery. Even though the latter almost always slept most of the day, he nevertheless toddled around the corridors at mealtimes and fetched the food pails from the kitchen a couple of blocks away. Everyone smiled happily at the two of them as they struggled past with their heavy burden.

That evening, Pock Face winked to his partner. It was scarcely visible, but Bryan saw it. At the same moment he turned to look at Bryan. Bryan was caught off guard as he stared at Pock Face, but had the resourcefulness to let the spit that had assembled in front of his tongue slide out of his open mouth, filling the cracks in his lips and the cleft in his chin with foamy saliva.

Then the giant straightened the plate in front of him and ladled another spoonful of sliced sausage up beside the chunks of bread. The lucky patient tried ungratefully to avoid this extra ration, but Pock Face didn't notice. He saw only the saliva on Bryan's chin.

Bryan had learned a few words of German since he'd landed in the hospital, even though their meaning was not always clear. But with the help of guesswork, tone, and emphasis and the facial expressions of the speakers, he managed to figure out what mental state his fellow patients were in, and to a certain extent the doctors' expectations regarding his recovery.

This insight demanded great concentration, which was not Bryan's strongest point during the shock-treatment phase. When the first few days of dullness had passed, the surrounding world reappeared in a series of distorted, slow-motion images.

Bryan knew he had to avoid looking at Pock Face. If his suspicions were correct, there were things going on in the ward that he did not yet understand, things he had to watch out for. Pock Face would often bend over him while he was dozing. The big man kept changing his tone of voice and he scared Bryan out of his wits with his friendly chatter and jovial smile. Bryan didn't understand a thing. "Make sure you don't give yourself away," he admonished himself when he felt the giant's breath on his face. "Pull yourself together!" he scolded, struggling to shake off his stupor.

The atmosphere in the hospital had changed since the bombardment of Freiburg. Several of the young orderlies had been sent to the front or to help with reconstruction work in the surrounding towns. The workload in the wards had therefore increased as the number of wounded arriving through the gates began to far exceed the number that were driven out again. It had become necessary to incorporate the gym as an emergency ward. It could only be a matter of time before it was the Alphabet House's turn. The wounded always came first.

Worry was reflected in the faces of the personnel. Many of them had lost members of their family during the bombardment. Little Petra crossed herself fifteen times a day and seldom said a word to anyone but James. The smiles and the little kindnesses were now few and far between.

Everyone just did his or her duty.

CHAPTER 17

The sixth time Bryan walked back and forth between the lavatories, it became too much for the nurse they called Sister Lili. Even though everyone knew patients were unusually thirsty and restless on the second day after shock treatment, there were other things to be done than continually letting an agitated, thirsty patient pass by.

Bryan's mouth was irritatingly dry again before the nursing staff had finished changing the bed linen. He watched the rapid, skillful movements of the nursing aides' hands, twisting in and out of the blanket covers and pillowcases as they made the beds. He laid his head back heavily on the clinical-smelling linen. His mouth encapsulated his tongue firmly while the sweetish taste spread from inside his cheeks. Even though he bit his cheek, there came not so much as a single drop of saliva.

There were bursts of irritation from the thin Siamese twin's bed, making Bryan raise his head. Pock Face had wanted to give the thin man some water, but he didn't like anyone touching his bed besides his Siamese counterpart, and was trying to brush Pock Face off. Bryan regarded the scene impassively and tried once more to swallow at the sight of the glass of water Pock Face was pressing against the tightly clenched lips of the thin twin. Full of promise, its clear contents sloshed over the side every time he tried to avoid it like some naughty boy. Bryan stuck his arm up and waved until the giant finally stopped his teasing and turned to him. A big smile spread over his lips as he stalked over to Bryan with his arm and the glass stretched out before him.

The water was infinitely refreshing. Having watched Bryan empty the glass so eagerly, Kröner was about to go back to the trolley and fill it up when he bumped heavily into the bed as he turned around. The pills rattled so loudly in the bedpost that Bryan thought everyone would stop what they were doing and look at him accusingly. Instantly his mouth became dry again. Pock Face turned slowly toward him and stared at the bed. He knocked his knee gently against the end of the bed frame, but the pills didn't rattle. Then Bryan began to cough so violently that a nursing aide came rushing over to thump him on the back. Pock Face watched for a moment, then reluctantly fetched another glass of water at the nursing aide's request.

Bryan dared hardly move the rest of the day, even though he had a feeling the tablets had fallen to the bottom of the bedpost and would scarcely make any more noise.

Apparently the giant was the only one to have heard anything.

At midnight clouds were hiding the moon and Bryan figured it was time to get rid of the pills. There was no one moving in the ward, no shadows behind the swing door. When he felt convinced he was the only one awake he got out of bed and raised the head end by its right leg. The plug in the bottom of the leg had never been out since leaving the manufacturer. Bryan twisted it so hard that he rubbed the skin off his fingertips. He had to keep on changing hands and try to avoid panting. Bryan was so tired when he finally managed to pull the plug out that he was hardly conscious of his triumph.

In a fraction of a second he sensed catastrophe and clutched hold of the open end of the tubing as the pills gushed out like corn from a silo. A couple of them danced across the floor. Bryan opened his eyes wide in the feeble light.

One of the pills landed in the middle gangway; a couple of others lay under beds. Bryan cautiously edged his hand free until the remaining pills formed a neat pile under the bedpost, ready to be gathered up. Bryan held his shirt in front of him and scooped the pills into its fold as he groped around feverishly on his knees, trying desperately to clear the white devils off the floor. When he was quite sure there were none left, he turned around and rammed the plug in as hard as he could. Outdoors a heavy cloud thinned out in the middle, leaving a hole in the night sky through which moonbeams suddenly lit up the whole room. Over behind the bed ends on the opposite side of the corridor a figure slowly raised itself up and began staring at him. Bryan drew himself all the way under the bed.

It was Pock Face, he was sure.

The moonlight shone gently and coolly in between the forest of bed legs, so that scores of sharply demarcated shadows swept diagonally across the floor of the ward. Among them crept a tiny, elongated shadow the thickness of a knitting needle. It was yet another pill that had slid treacherously across the gangway and come to rest under the head end of Pock Face's bed.

The big man's bed creaked. He had no intention of lying down.

When the sky clouded over again Bryan cautiously stretched upward. In one quick movement he pulled his blanket onto the floor and got halfway up so Pock Face couldn't quite make out whether he'd been about to get out of bed.

His eyes followed Bryan with unveiled attention as he headed for the lavatory. Bryan looked straight ahead, concentrating on his upturned shirt-tails and taking care not to fall over anything.

Only after the third flush did the last pills disappear in the foaming eddies of the toilet bowl.

The ward was lit by moonlight again. Pock Face was sitting with his legs swinging to and fro over the edge of the bed, his big fists grasping the edge firmly so he could push himself up quickly. His torso was bent slightly forward, eyes squinting and on the alert. It was obvious the giant wouldn't let Bryan pass so easily. For a moment he seemed normal.

The feeling of having been found out made Bryan stop his shuffling. He stood at the head of the bed, his lower jaw hanging and his tongue protruding. Pock Face seemed to be watching him tirelessly, scarcely blinking. Then Bryan suddenly took an irrational step forward, leaning over so that he bumped into the curved, brown steel tubing that topped the bed. Their faces were now so close that their breath intermingled. Bryan leaned his head to one side as if about to fall asleep, then cautiously thrust his foot forward to the spot under the bed where he'd seen the last, treacherous little tablet. Just as he'd finally located the pill and was carefully curving his toes around it, Pock Face flew forward with a jerk and their foreheads crashed together with a brutal crack. Bryan was taken completely unawares and tumbled over backward, banging his head against the floor. When he opened his eyes the pain was almost unbearable.

In falling he'd almost bitten his tongue in half.

Bryan slid slowly and totally silently backward over the floor on his shirttails, away from the eyes that pursued him. When he lay in bed once more, heart hammering and trying to convince himself that everything would be all right again, Pock Face finally backed off and glided back to his bed, unaware of the nasty injury he had caused.

During the next hour Bryan's tongue swelled up and began to throb violently. The very real pain came out in a series of groans that were too subdued to wake anyone up.

When he finally got himself under control and felt sleep coming mercifully to his rescue, he remembered the pill.

It was still lying on the floor.

For a long time he lay staring up at the ceiling, considering whether or not to crawl over and look for it.

But then he heard the whispering.

CHAPTER 18

Little Sister Petra got a fright when she saw Bryan.

After a whole night of pain and misery his bed was soaked with sweat and his forehead swollen from the blow from Pock Face's skull. His lips and jaw throbbed. There were spots of blood on his shirt collar and on the pillow. He hadn't slept. Even when the whispering had stopped again and only the fearful emptiness remained, his body had not claimed its right to sleep. He'd been much too worked up, now that the realization had come to him.

The discovery was terrifying. Apart from him and James there were three others in the ward who were simulating madness. They were clever, resourceful, observant, and unpredictable, and he didn't doubt for a moment they were also dangerous. Besides this, there could be other things he knew nothing about. This was Bryan's greatest fear. The unknown factors.

There was no doubt now that Pock Face had his eye on Bryan. However, the question was: What had he already observed? James had been trying for some time to warn him about the malingerers. Bryan knew that now. His mind was tortured by the thought of how powerless James must have felt. What he must have had to endure during the past weeks and months because of him! Bryan wished desperately that he'd taken more heed of his signals. "I won't make it difficult for you anymore, James" was his unspoken promise. He prayed that James would realize this now. Last night's episode could not have escaped his attention.

The invisible bond between them was again united.

Several of the patients twitched nervously when one of the new nurses shoved the swing door open with a bang and began shrieking something about Hitler and the word "*Wolfsschanze*."

Bryan followed her with his eyes all the way down the gangway past

Petra, who crossed herself, and Vonnegut, who merely stared vacantly. Bryan hoped it meant Hitler was dead. Dr. Holst watched her and listened to what she had to say. Her stammering and excitement didn't seem to make much of an impression on him. James, on the other hand, sat half up in bed for once, listening to what was being said with a slightly too attentive expression. In the next bed Pock Face was looking at James.

Then Dr. Holst turned abruptly toward the beds behind him, leaving the nurse, Hitler, and Wolfsschanze to take care of themselves. The daily running of the hospital took precedence. Bryan could see James had been taken so much by surprise by the way the report ended so suddenly that he could scarcely manage to resume his customary apathy. Pock Face, on the other hand, just smiled and loosened his blanket to make it easier for the doctor when it was his turn.

Although Dr. Holst had not reacted, something serious must have happened. The general atmosphere was electric, the outdoor activities completely different from usual, and a security officer appeared in the ward for the first time in several weeks.

They had never seen him before. He was practically a boy, not even as old as Bryan, he reckoned. As the youth strode along the beds, he greeted each patient briefly, arm half-outstretched, and nodded if the greeting was reciprocated. He looked each patient straight in the eyes. Next he inspected the corridor leading to the lavatories and shower room with slow, measured steps, and doors were flung open, resounding hollowly. The presence of the black-coated figure seemed not to make the slightest impression on anyone. Even the malingerers looked him straight in the face as he greeted them, and the broad-faced man smiled more than ever, stretching his arm out and heiling so forcefully that it gave everyone a start.

His thin fellow conspirator in the next bed was not quite so perky. The narrow face smiled, to be sure, but he raised his arm only halfway. In doing so his blanket fell partly to the floor. Just under the bed lay the pill Bryan had lost in the collision with Pock Face. Bryan saw it instantly and tried to resist the swallowing reflex that accompanies sudden alarm.

If the security officer discovered it, he naturally wouldn't know where it had come from. But if he were questioned closely, what would the malingerer beside him say? And what wouldn't Pock Face be able to conclude from the events of the previous night? It took Bryan only a second to establish that this insignificant tablet had pushed him much, much closer to his downfall. The pill would be picked up sooner or later and he wasn't going to be the one to do it. Ten wild horses couldn't make him risk trying.

The man beside the thinner of the Siamese twins had been badly burned in the face. He'd already been lying in the ward when they arrived. All the bandages had now been removed and the mutilated skin had begun to resume a more normal, pale hue. He was one of the many who had been trapped in a burning armored vehicle, the only difference being that he'd survived. A painful survival that had left him silent and completely confused. The security officer saw the arm he had tried to raise stiffly in salute and stepped in between the beds to help him.

In the process, the toe of his shoe struck the pill, which shot over toward the outer wall and ricocheted farther into the room with an almost inaudible tick-tick-tick. Bryan gasped. The danger seemed to have been momentarily averted. But two minutes later the officer trod on the pill over by the entrance doors. The crunching sound brought him to a halt.

One of the nurses rushed into the room when she heard the security officer yell and found him kneeling on the floor as he calmly and cautiously poked at the white powder. Then he handed her a pinch of the white substance and got her to taste it. To judge from her facial expression and gesticulations Bryan presumed she was trying to belittle the matter, at the same time protesting her innocence or ignorance. The young security officer asked her some questions to which she shook her head as her face imperceptibly began to change color. After a few minutes' interrogation her gaze began to falter and she looked very much as if she wished she were somewhere far, far away.

Then the officer bent down so the end of the bed obstructed Bryan's view, though he could hear him make some indefinable sounds. The next moment he reappeared between the beds, stretched out flat with his cheek pressed to the floor, crawling forward like a bloodhound. After a brief search he had found two more pills. Bryan was horror-struck.

Everyone was summoned. The nurses on day duty and the night shift that was still half-asleep after their rude awakening; the porters, whose basic job was to wheel the patients to shock treatment and back again; the orderlies, including Vonnegut; the nursing aides; the cleaning staff; Surgeon Lieutenant Holst; and finally, Army Surgeon Thieringer. No one could provide a reasonable explanation of what had happened. It was easy to see that the more statements the security officer had to listen to, the more convinced he became that something was utterly wrong.

The head security officer who had interrogated them in the gymnasium was summoned and the situation explained to him. Of the many furious words he spat out Bryan understood only one.

"Simulation."

In next to no time, a thorough investigation had been initiated. Several SS soldiers removed their jackets and were all over the ward, on their knees, on their stomachs, on tiptoe. Every centimeter was examined. Not a single likely hiding place was overlooked. The bedside cupboards were emptied, newspapers leafed through, clothes and bedclothes felt, mattresses lifted, windowsills and shutters checked. Only the few patients who couldn't stand up were allowed to remain in bed. The rest stood against the end wall with bare legs, watching in wonderment. James drew his scarf out from under the mattress when no one was looking and tied it around his neck under his collar.

Morose and unhappy about not being able to control the situation, Army Surgeon Thieringer tried to keep everyone calm. But he fell silent when they loosened the plug in one of the bed frames and dozens of pills rattled to the floor.

Everything in the ward that could move, froze instantly. The SS sergeant in command immediately signaled for all the plugs to be removed from the beds. The security officer asked Vonnegut a question. As if he'd been compelled to inform on one of his own children, he slowly raised his iron hook and reluctantly pointed toward the middle of the group standing beside the end wall. The thinnest of the Siamese twins promptly cried out, shaking all over as he fell to his knees in front of the security officer.

As the remaining bed plugs were being pulled out Bryan prayed fervently that not a single, insignificant little pill had remained in his bed frame from the previous night. Not until later, when the ward was quiet again and the thin twin had been led away sobbing, did it dawn on Bryan that he was responsible for the man's misfortune. He now also knew with certainty that out of the ward's original twenty-two patients, at least six had been simulating madness. An incredible figure that could be even higher. The thin Siamese twin had never given him cause for suspicion. On the contrary, during the foregoing months the man had presented the perfect picture of a mentally deranged patient who was recovering infinitely slowly, but steadily. From the first time Bryan had seen him in the truck he'd played his part meticulously, down to the last detail.

His other Siamese half sat on the edge of his bed as usual, tranquilly picking his nose. It would be incredible if he, too, were simulating. He displayed not the slightest trace of anxiety or grief about what had just occurred. The only thing that made him react was if his index finger hit pay dirt.

Not even later, when the thin twin was returned to the ward, bruised and pale, did it have any appreciable effect on his "twin brother." He simply smiled and went on picking. Bryan, on the other hand, couldn't believe his eyes. How the skinny one had managed to avoid disaster he had no idea, but it made him uneasy.

All the others were seemingly well satisfied with how things had turned out. The doctors smiled and the nurses actually became friendly. They'd been under enormous pressure.

The following morning they fetched the thin twin again. He'd been trembling like an aspen leaf all night and must have anticipated what was going to happen.

At noon the young security officer entered the ward with an SS private. A few orders were given and the patients began moving toward the windows opposite Bryan's row of beds. No one protested. Bryan was one of the last to follow them, thereby coming to stand in the second row, from where it was impossible to catch a glimpse of what was going on without standing on tiptoe. Even then, what he could see between the window bars was limited, so he carefully thrust his head forward, resting it on the shoulder in front of him.

There was a relatively clear view along the edge of rock that ran a couple meters from the wall of the hospital block up to the chapel about a hundred meters farther on. The only thing that interrupted the narrow, naked border of rock was a single pole that seemed to mark a hole that had once been bored.

It was to this pole they bound the thin twin, and it was at this pole they shot him before the eyes of the patients with whom he had shared space, air, and life itself for over half a year. The instant the shot rang out Bryan turned his head away. Instead he looked at James, who stood farther away in the front row, with Pock Face towering next to him. The start James gave upon hearing the sound could hardly be mistaken, and for a few seconds his eyes were much too attentive, feverishly nailed to the figure buckled over in its final death throes. It wasn't the execution or James's reaction that called forth the cold sweat on Bryan's forehead, but the way Pock Face nodded to the broad-faced man as he stared intensely at James.

It took some time before they tied the next one to the pole and shot him. Who the sinner was, Bryan didn't know. It was not anyone from the Alphabet House, but there was no doubt he'd been caught in an attempt to avoid his military duty. Such offenses were punished severely and without mercy, and that was what they wanted everyone to know.

The sight of the thin twin's lifeless, drooping head had not made any impression on the other twin, who obviously hadn't grasped what had happened. No one made any attempt to comfort him. No one questioned him. After the sentence had been executed, they removed the unfortunate twin's bed, washed the floor in the entire ward, served ersatz coffee, and had Vonnegut bring in the loudspeaker so violins and kettledrums could soothe their minds.

When it came down to it, the men in the ward were there to receive treatment.

CHAPTER 19

Sounds of shooting could be heard in the area almost every week since the day the executions had taken place. The three malingerers no longer whispered at night and James lay in his corner almost constantly, reacting only when food was wheeled into the ward. But otherwise life continued as usual.

Of the simulants, it was obvious Pock Face was especially on his guard. His customary solicitude for his fellow patients was still manifest. But whereas previously he'd had a glint in his eye and a word for everyone on his route, his eyes were now watchful and his words sparse. Bryan knew what he was thinking, and thought the same: Who else might be an imposter?

Pock Face had his eye on James, first and foremost. Some evenings Bryan could catch all three of them sitting in a row, scrutinizing James. They were clearly keeping watch. Two of them couldn't concentrate very long, however, and after a few minutes their eyes were wandering in and out of focus. They let the pills take over. Pock Face, on the other hand, was able to keep himself awake for hours.

At first Bryan thought the malingerers were going to leave James in peace. What had they to fear from someone who by now lay most of the day as if unconscious? Bryan didn't realize everything wasn't as it should be until one day when Calendar Man pointed at James and began shouting and flapping his arms. Sister Lili came rushing in and immediately started thumping James on the back. He was extremely pale, trying to suppress a fit of coughing.

At lunchtime the next day the incident repeated itself.

During the days that followed, Bryan sat up in bed instead of sitting on the edge beside his bed table as he usually did at mealtime. From there he could follow James's attempts to swallow his lumps of food. While the clatter of plates, noisy chewing, and contented burps filled the room, James sat motionless, staring at his plate as if trying to muster some appetite. Finally, before the plates were collected, James's shoulders dropped as if he was sighing, and he swallowed a couple of spoonfuls.

Then he immediately began to cough.

After this sequence of events had repeated itself for six days running, Bryan got out of bed while lunch was being brought in and strutted down to Vonnegut's table, humming softly, his plate held high in front of him. Had Vonnegut or Sister Lili been there, he would have been ordered back to bed straightaway. But a little earlier a patient had become very violent during shock treatment, giving the orderlies and nurses plenty to do before the afternoon rounds. Bryan put the plate down on the edge of Vonnegut's table and began to ease the food into his mouth. His tongue was still considerably thicker than normal, but healing well. The malingerers watched his controlled swallowing movements with interest and glanced alternately at him and over at the rigid figure in the corner. James didn't look up, even though he was probably well aware that Bryan was observing him.

James ate another spoonful, followed by one more. There were only a few meters between Bryan and James. Bryan pressed the edge of the deep plate, judging its resistance and weight.

Then he hit the plate so it shot out over the edge of the table straight toward the bedpost beside James's foot, precisely as James's coughing fit began. The loud noise made everyone stop gorging themselves for a moment. Bryan dashed apologetically after the runaway plate.

He stopped abruptly when he reached James and laughed tonelessly straight in his face as he pointed down at the mess on the floor and the overturned plate. James's gaze didn't shift from his own plate. Among the chunks of pork and gray, overcooked celery root lay something indefinable that resembled human excrement.

Starting to hum again, Bryan leaned playfully forward and poked at it with his spoon. It was difficult to suppress the wave of nausea than came over him. True enough, in the middle of James' food lay a human stool.

Pock Face laughed outright as his broad-faced accomplice rushed forward and snatched the plate away from James. Then, after scraping the mess on the floor onto it, he hurried out to the lavatory.

How the excrement had gotten into the food was a mystery to Bryan. But two things were certain. The malingerers were responsible, and they intended to keep it to themselves.

They had been harassing James like this for several days. It was an ill-matched and merciless open war with the sole object of getting James to give himself away. And perhaps they'd succeeded. James had reacted. He wouldn't eat.

For the whole afternoon James was allowed to sit undisturbed on the edge of his bed.

There was nothing Bryan could do for him.

A couple of bomb shutters rattled against a window and woke Bryan up so suddenly that the echo in the room scarcely had time to die away before he was wide-awake. A panzer officer lay in the bed beside him, panting heavily. Farther down the row, the man who had stared straight up into the shower was leaning against the head of his bed, staring vacantly at the row opposite him.

The room was still softly illuminated by the summery night sky. The silhouettes of the malingerers towered in the darkness across from him and gave Bryan the shivers. All three were standing around James's bed. One of them at the head end, one in the middle, and one at the foot end. Now and then an arm was raised to administer a blow. There were no screams to reveal how James was taking the beating. Only groans could be heard later that night after they'd finally left him in peace.

"You're not touching him again!" Bryan threatened silently through clenched teeth when he saw James hobble out to the bathroom the next day.

But they dealt with him as it suited them. So far they hadn't bruised his face, yet night after night the sound of muffled blows came from the far corner.

Bryan felt desperate. He feared for James's life. Several times he was on the verge of screaming out, pulling the emergency cord for the night nurse, or throwing himself between James and his tormentors. But years of war had created rules for survival that under normal conditions would appear absurd and irrational. In the midst of his helplessness Bryan knew helplessness was the one state he could abandon himself to.

. . .

James endured his final round of punishment the night before Sister Petra found him lying unconscious in a pool of blood the following morning. Her shocked and confused reaction was a clear indication of the gravity of the matter. Both Holst and a surgical doctor were summoned. "You must be able to see that the hole in his head didn't happen by itself, for God's sake!" Bryan hissed silently as they examined the edge of the bed, the head and foot ends, and the floor for possible explanations as to how the injuries had come about. "Traitor," he accused himself, and prayed James's life would be spared.

There was a brief investigation despite the doctors' reluctance. The young security officer inspected the deep wound thoroughly and felt James's forehead as if he himself were a qualified doctor, then examined every inch of the bed. Next he inspected the floor, walls, and bedposts. Finding nothing, he walked from bed to bed, stripping the blankets off the patients to see if they had anything to hide. "Please let there be marks on their hands or blood on their nightshirts," Bryan pleaded. James was white as a sheet and must have lost a lot of blood. But the security officer found nothing. Then he hassled the nurses, who were having a hard time finding out who was to do what, and paced back and forth with clicking boots until Sister Petra arrived with the necessary medical paraphernalia.

They inserted a needle in the bend of James's elbow before Bryan managed to grasp the seriousness of what was happening. At that distance the bottle hanging above James looked black as coal.

"Oh, no, now you're gonna die!" Bryan's mind screamed as he tried to recall what James had said on the hospital train about blood transfusions and blood types. It seemed ages ago. "You do what you like, Bryan, but I'm going to tattoo A+," James had said, thereby sealing his fate. Now the blood plasma was flowing treacherously down the plastic tube from the bottle. They were in the process of mixing two different blood types in one battered body.

Bryan was convinced that the malingerers had not intended to kill James. Not that they couldn't do so if they wanted. A dead Mr. Nobody constituted no danger. But Gerhart Peuckert was not Mr. Nobody. He was a *Standartenführer* in the SS security police. And if they found he had been beaten to death or had ended his days in a way that was unnatural, no stone would be left unturned when the investigations and interrogations got under way.

The malingerers had hoped to gain certainty and control. So far they'd achieved neither.

Later on, James was undressed, prior to being washed. He was deathly pale. Bryan sighed with relief when he noticed he wasn't wearing his scarf. This was the only mitigating circumstance. The three men followed closely what was going on. The more bruises and severe blood effusions that appeared, the more the three bastards huddled in the safety of their beds.

All of Sister Petra's repeated attempts to dig deeper into the cause of this strange catastrophe were immediately thwarted with authoritative grumpiness by her superior. Little Petra spread unrest. Sister Lili, on the other hand, always set out to normalize conditions in the ward as quickly as possible. Apparently she had adopted the pragmatic attitude that any suspicion of criminality would incriminate her. Investigations and interrogations might lead to mistrust, and mistrust, in turn, to her transfer. A field hospital on the Eastern Front could be the consequence.

Obviously Sister Lili was not lacking in imagination.

Therefore, despite Petra's disapproval, she became solely responsible for looking after James the next couple of days. The patient was unwell, so the patient got his blood plasma. Two bottles in all. Thus they let more than a liter of the wrong type of blood trickle into James's body.

And he was still alive.

CHAPTER 20

As the days dragged on, Bryan gradually realized the nightmare was by no means over.

The first warning came when he woke up one morning and saw Petra sitting on the edge of James's bed, body trembling as she pressed his head tightly to her breast. She was caressing him as if he were crying.

Later that week James vomited while he was sitting straight up in bed. The same evening Bryan ventured past his friend's bed while Pock Face and his broad-faced companion were out fetching the food buckets. The third malingerer appeared to be sleeping heavily.

Again James's face was very, very pale. His skin was like parchment and the arteries in his temples shone bluish.

"See to it that you get well, James!" Bryan whispered, glancing around. "Our troops will be here soon. A month or two and we'll be free, you just wait and see." The words had no visible effect. James smiled, pursing his lips as if he were about to shush Bryan. Then he formed some words. Bryan had to put his ear close to the dry lips in order to understand them. "Keep away!" was all he whispered.

As Bryan backed away from James, the third simulant flapped his blanket.

The Allies bombed Karlsruhe again, sending a massive stream of refugees into the hinterland and the Schwarzwald's protective idyll.

Toward the end of September several things happened that caused Bryan to rethink his precautionary measures, perhaps for the last time.

One bright morning, when the autumn light was penetrating the bomb shutters in all its clarity, they found James on the verge of bleeding to death again. All his bandages had been ripped off and the wounds in his head that had almost healed were gaping open. James's skin color merged with that of the sheet. His hands were almost black with coagulated blood. In their blind faith that James had inflicted these wounds on himself, the medical staff bandaged his hands so that he couldn't try it again.

And then they gave him another blood transfusion.

Bryan was at his wits' end when he saw the glass bottle swinging over James's bed once more.

Bryan and the malingerers kept an eye on one another in a state of armed neutrality. One day during one of these balancing acts, James drifted into such a deep state of unconsciousness that Dr. Holst employed the word "coma." Shaking his head, he turned with a smile to say good-bye to Bryan's neighbor and the patient opposite, both of whom had obtained their green discharge stamps.

It was the first time Bryan had seen anyone in the ward dressed in something other than a hospital shirt. Since the very first day they had all literally gone around bare-assed in a getup that reached to their knees and was fastened at the neck. Occasionally, very occasionally, they'd been given underpants.

The two officers beamed, having regained their full authority and dignity in their newly pressed riding breeches and high, erect caps, their baubles dangling on their stiff jackets. Dr. Holst shook hands with them both and the nurses curtsied. The same nurses who only a few days previously had slapped them if they wouldn't file past naked after their bath. When Bryan's neighbor tried to shake Vonnegut's hand, the latter became so embarrassed that he extended his iron hook instead of his sound left hand.

How the doctors could distinguish between the well and ill was hard to fathom. In any case, these two had been pronounced well enough to become cannon fodder.

Both men were proud as peacocks and naïvely merry. They mentioned Arnhem.

Apparently it was there they were going.

When Bryan's neighbor said good-bye and looked him straight in the eyes, Bryan could scarcely associate him with the patient who had been breathing heavily at his side, night and day, for over eight months.

. . .

The mood in the ward was divided after the first reports of a German victory at Arnhem arrived. Those patients who could expect to be discharged shortly straightened their backs and missed no opportunity to prove they were feeling much better. The rest became even more ill, screamed more frequently at night, rocked to and fro more than ever, displayed strange new twitches and grimaces, and resumed their piggish eating habits.

The malingerers reacted as well.

Pock Face intensified his voluntary service to the point where the orderlies had to take over his job, lest he come to scald someone or knock the doctors to the floor while barging around on his many chores. His broadfaced confederate performed the same piece of playacting every day and heiled at Vonnegut and his fellow patients constantly. At night he could suddenly get the night nurse to storm into the ward in response to one of his attacks of gaiety, expressed by raucous singing accompanied by a rhythmic banging on his bed bars.

Like the thin malingerer, Bryan huddled in his bed, pulling the blanket over his head and remaining silent. His obvious high rank and great responsibility, his frailty and doubtful signs of improvement, were Bryan's life insurance and guarantee not to end up at the front like his two neighbors. Perhaps no one had any idea where they should send him.

Bryan was not concerned about himself. Only about James and what the malingerers had in mind to do with him.

He had regained consciousness as a shadow of his former self, mentally passive and physically starved. It would be some time before he'd be able to get out of bed again.

And by now, thoughts of escape and how it could be accomplished had been uppermost in Bryan's mind for more than four months.

Clothing was the first problem. Apart from the nightshirt, Bryan possessed nothing but a pair of socks that were replaced every third day by a pair that was even more washed-out than the previous one. Since he'd begun going to the bathroom by himself, he had also been given a dressing gown. It was supposed to protect him against the biting gusts of wind.

But now the dressing gown was gone. One of the orderlies had been gazing at it covetously for a long time. His slippers had disappeared ages ago.

The distance to the Swiss border was manageable, scarcely more than fifty or sixty kilometers. There was still a summer sky above that painted the landscape in clear, sharp contours. But it was cold at night.

Several weeks ago the west wind had blown up and carried new sounds with it. The occasional whistle and deep rumble of a train came like an echo of salvation. "We're on the edge of the mountains, James!" he thought. "The railway line can't be far away. We could jump on the train and ride down to the border. We've done it before. We can do it again. It would get us all the way to Basel, James! We're jumping on that train!"

But James himself was a problem.

The blue rings under his eyes seemed permanent.

Sister Petra's expression became more and more grave.

One night it dawned on Bryan that he'd have to escape alone. He'd woken with a start caused by an inescapable suspicion that he'd been talking in his sleep. Pock Face was standing beside his bed, looking at him. There was a brooding mistrust in his eyes.

Escape could be delayed no longer.

In certain risky moments he had toyed with the idea of knocking down an orderly and stealing his clothes. There was also the possibility that a doctor might leave his civilian clothes in the ward or in one of the offices. But daydream and reality never came seriously to grips with each other. Bryan's daily sphere of activity wasn't large. He had a thorough knowledge of only the ward, the consultation room, the electroshock room, the lavatories, and the bathroom. None of these presented any possibilities.

The solution came when one of the patients peed up against the bathroom door and shouted and screamed until they gave him a shot to calm him down. While Vonnegut was on his knees wiping up the mess, Bryan shuffled sideways out to the lavatory, wagging his head from side to side.

The door opposite the lavatory was wide open. Bryan sat down heavily on the seat, leaving the wooden door ajar. He had never seen inside the storeroom before.

It was actually just a big cupboard with cleaning rags, soap flakes, and brooms and pails stacked on shelves or deposited on the floor.

A narrow ray of light illuminated the room from the side. Vonnegut was still at work on the floor outside, expressing audibly how far away he wished both himself and everyone else. A few steps and Bryan was over by the cupboard. He inspected the doorframe. It was half-rotten. The lock barely held in the brittle wood. The metal fittings had lost their grip long ago. The door opened inward and only needed a firm push on the handle along with the pressure of a knee. A worn, old pair of overalls hung on a porcelain hook on the back of the door.

Bryan gasped when Vonnegut shoved the storeroom door open. With a firm grip on his wrist, Bryan was led back to his bed, holding his breath with his heart pounding.

By the time the moon disappeared and left the ward in total darkness, Bryan had gone through in his head again and again what he'd seen in the storeroom. He'd left his bed and scuttled out to the lavatory four times during the evening. Frequent attacks of diarrhea were not unusual in the ward. The increasingly poor quality of the food had its effect.

The first time Bryan went to the lavatory he'd forced his way into the storeroom and removed the two top shelves.

There was a small window in the storeroom. Situated above the top shelf, it was not easy to reach, but just large enough. And, unlike the small slits up by the ceiling in the bathroom and lavatories, it was not furnished with bars.

The window clasps could be unfastened without a sound.

Bryan quickly made up his mind. He would make his attempt the next time or the time after. He would put on the overalls, climb up onto the shelf, crawl out through the window, and count on surviving the fall to the ground. Then he would make for the open square and climb over the barbed wire. It was a plan with all odds against it. A desperate undertaking like most of the missions he and James had survived. And now James was once again lying lifeless in the ward. Reality was a harsh master. The thought of having to live the rest of his life with a guilty conscience tormented him.

But what could he do?

It took three more trips to the toilet before Bryan remained in the storeroom. On his second visit he was disturbed by the little man with the bloodshot eyes. They flushed with their respective chains and tottered back to their warm nests, elbow to elbow.

Not until the third time did Bryan feel safe enough to put on the overalls. They provided scant protection against the cold.

The shelf creaked threateningly as Bryan pushed off and grabbed the windowframe. The window was rather narrower than he'd expected. Not a sound was to be heard from the ward.

He squeezed out through the window to the point where he was about to tip over. Despite the darkness, the abyss beneath him stood out in terrifying detail. The jump was suicidal.

Parachute jumping and simulated plane crashes had made Bryan better prepared than most. But with a six-meter free fall, the chances of not being injured were devastatingly slim. There were no mitigating circumstances in regard to the dark chasm. If the fall killed him, it would happen quickly and mercifully. If, on the other hand, he was wounded and caught, the security police would be sure to take terrible revenge.

The kitchen building that leaned snugly against the wall of rock was dark and peaceful. Familiar sounds floated alongside the wall and portended the guards' regular night rounds. Breath escaped their mouths in steamy puffs of semirepressed laughter and rose up to Bryan, perched above.

One of them started laughing loudly as they passed the building. Just as the mirthful roar reached him, a creaking sound came from behind and the shelf detached itself from the storeroom wall.

Only faint oaths escaped Bryan's lips. He tried in vain to gain a foothold in order to push himself out as he clung to the brick wall with his elbows.

He was clammy with sweat in spite of the cold. The guards had not yet quite disappeared behind the square, but the dogs were diverted by their masters' merriment and danced around playfully.

In a moment they would be back.

The crash from inside the storeroom was indefinable. He was still trying desperately to force himself the last bit forward and out the window when an iron grip locked his ankles from behind.

It was too late.

CHAPTER 21

James was still plagued by the nausea and discomfort caused by the blood transfusions. With it came anxiety. Voices merged and confused him. His strength had deserted him.

Unconsciousness had stolen his time and his daydreaming suffered.

The aftermath of all the shock treatments, the heavy-handed care, and the blood transfusions played tricks on James's memory. Most of the movies and books had vanished or merged into one. Only the greatest literary and film classics remained. And, of course, the fear.

James felt terrible. He felt sick in body and soul. Exhausted, alone, and drained of tears. Around him lurked impotence and madness. Dejected faces, suppressed mania, and weird, depressed behavior. Then there were his oppressors, and finally—Bryan.

James let things be, now that the malingerers had selected a new victim, and pretended most of the time to be lost to the world.

He didn't find this difficult.

It was the malingerers who had stopped Bryan's escape attempt. "Take him alive," Kröner had growled as they grabbed him. "Wash the blood off the storeroom wall and replace the shelf." It was remarkable how promptly they'd obeyed. In the ward, only the remaining Siamese twin appeared uneasy, his gaze dancing from the floor to the bell cord over his head. Kröner hissed at him like a wildcat until the twin started squeaking and curled up under his blanket in the fetal position.

Bryan let them escort him back to the ward without a struggle. His hands were bleeding. The malingerers bent over him, raining questions down on him as the first faint rays of morning light penetrated the shutters. Were there any others faking it? Had he any coconspirators? How much did he know?

But Bryan remained silent, leaving the malingerers in doubt. Was he indeed simulating? Had he been trying to escape, or commit suicide?

Bryan survived the next morning's trials as well. But his desperation was obvious.

The cleaning woman had discovered marks on the wall. She sounded the alarm and shook the loose shelf without making any appreciable impression on the ward nurse.

The morning ablutions were over long ago. The malingerers had scowled at Bryan with an odd mixture of relief and malice as he went out to the bathroom, stiff in all his limbs, and removed every trace of the previous night from his arms, hands, shirt, and body.

But he hadn't been able to remove the scratches on his fingertips he'd received while struggling to squeeze through the window. One of the orderlies noticed the little cuts on his fingers and confided his suspicions to his replacement as he pointed at Bryan.

And James saw that Bryan was aware of it.

The security officer finally turned up later that morning. As he was inspecting them one by one, the orderly pulled Bryan's hands out and thrust them accusingly toward the officer. Bryan just smiled and nodded. Countless tiny wooden splinters stuck out of the bloody fingertips. They looked like porcupine needles. The orderly frowned and shook Bryan's arms like the neck of a naughty puppy. Then Bryan pulled his hands free and struck them several times against the bomb shutter behind him as he closed his eyes in euphoria.

The officer's authority manifested itself so audibly that it gave everyone a start. He grabbed Bryan's shirt angrily and forced him to the floor. "I'll teach you to make fun of us!" he spat, forcing Bryan to stand up. He stood with drooping shoulders, face-to-face with his fate.

James knew he was fighting for his life.

In a feverish struggle against time, Bryan had managed to drive the splinters into his fingertips prior to inspection by rubbing them against the rough bomb shutters. At first the malingerers had found it amusing. But they weren't laughing now.

The officer investigated every centimeter of Bryan's body. The nightshirt was crumpled and grayish, still a bit damp after his thorough morning bath.

The orderly shrugged his shoulders. "It looks like he didn't take it off before his bath," he said.

Instead of letting go of the shirt, the officer pulled it farther up. Softly, almost caressingly, he took hold of Bryan's testicles and looked him kindly in the face. "Were you feeling a bit homesick, Herr Oberführer? Don't worry, you can confide in me. No harm will come to you." He stood still for a moment, looking Bryan in the eyes without loosening his grip.

"And of course you don't understand what I'm saying, do you, Herr Oberführer?" The pain reflected in Bryan's face as the officer started squeezing couldn't hide his helplessness and confusion from James. The questions were just as incomprehensible to Bryan as to the crazy Arno von der Leyen he was presumed to be. In moments like this, being able to understand was not nearly as important as not being able to. His passivity irritated the officer. But it also made him unsure of himself.

At the fifth question he squeezed so hard that Bryan's screams were stifled by his vomit. Uttering gurgling sounds he fell clumsily backward, crashing his abdomen into the side of the bed and striking his head against the bomb shutter. The officer instinctively released his hold and stepped aside in order not to mess up his uniform. Then he yelled until a nurse came rushing in to wipe up the floor around his boots.

Some vomit landed on the neighboring bed. One of the patients got up and walked past the soiled bed, pointing the whole time at the wall.

James didn't know much about the patient. His name was Peter Stich and he always had red eyes.

Now he was also the one who saved Bryan's life.

The security officer was about to knock his hand away when he looked to see where the finger was pointing. Behind Bryan, who was still drooping beside the window, the bomb shutter had slid half open. Long brown lines were seeping into the grain of the wood along the edge of the shutter frame. The officer went closer, felt along the rough wood, and looked again at Bryan's fingers. He turned abruptly on his heel and charged out of the room, knocking the red-eyed man over.

Then they gave Bryan a shot to calm him down and replaced the shutter cover.

The shelf in the storeroom was never replaced.

. . .

For a while the nightly whispering increased.

The gnomelike Dieter Schmidt was convinced that Oberführer Arno von der Leyen knew all about them and their plans for the future. He demanded they take action.

But the pock-faced Kröner insisted that in the future they should avoid scenes in the ward. Their situation would soon change. The fortunes of war were on the side of the Allies. The war could be over before they knew it.

If Arno von der Leyen were found liquidated, the interrogations would never cease. Both he and Lankau knew what it was like to be interrogated. No one would be able to keep quiet and no one would be let off.

Themselves included.

"If you want to find out something, poke him in the eyes a little, pinch his uvula, or press hard inside his auditory canal," he recited. "But be sure you don't make any marks that are visible, and that he doesn't make any noise. Understood?"

During the nights that followed, Bryan wept and his throat rattled. But they never got him to say anything. The malingerers were perplexed. James could do nothing. But their cat-and-mouse game would come to an end. This he knew from his own experience.

Kröner stuck out his lower lip and looked from Bryan to James. "Mad or not, as long as they understand we'll kill them if they don't behave, I couldn't care less about what else they don't understand!"

The skinny Schmidt shook his head. "Arno von der Leyen knows everything, believe me. The Mailman will want him liquidated. That's what I'm trying to tell you!"

"Really? And how's that to be done?" Kröner inquired sarcastically. "By telepathy?" He wasn't smiling. The Mailman was like a phantom with all the odds on his side. "Don't you think he's hightailed it long ago? Don't you think he's forgotten all about his faithful little squire? And what would that make you, Herr Haupsturmführer? Aren't you just a fool, you little Jew-plunderer? Isn't that what we all are?"

"Wait and see!" There was a special glint in Dieter Schmidt's eyes.

. . .

"*David Copperfield*! Today I'll take *David Copperfield*." James leaned his head back on the pillow. The room was quiet. Ever since childhood, James had regarded this book as Dickens's greatest. Victor Hugo, Swift, Defoe, Émile Zola, Stevenson, Kipling, and Alexandre Dumas had also chiseled their works into James's memory. But above them all sparkled Charles Dickens and *David Copperfield*.

He recalled the comforting tale during the afternoon peace and quiet when the nurses had plenty to do.

And these re-creations demanded peace and quiet. Confusion and diffuse thought processes had become his worst opponents. The pills, that disgusting chlorine compound, were gradually muddling his memory more than the shock treatments.

Already as he began the story, James realized he couldn't complete it. The names in *David Copperfield* had vanished. "Who was Copperfield's second wife, his childhood friend?" James pondered for some time. "The first wife's name was Dora. Was the other one Emily? No, that wasn't right. Was she called Elizabeth? Rubbish!"

James was interrupted in the middle of this unhappy realization and the growing anxiety over his memory having suffered permanent damage. Two orderlies clapped their hands, turned up the charts, and pulled out the case notes. "You patients are leaving! Collect your things, you're going upstairs!"

Following this announcement the men were herded outside into the passageway and new ones were led into the ward in their place. Sister Petra smiled at James. She blushed a trifle.

It was Vonnegut's job to lead the way. It was a terrible constellation, seven men in all. The three tormentors, himself and Bryan, Red-Eye, and Calendar Man. Five malingerers in one and the same room.

"You gentlemen are on the mend, according to the professor," said Vonnegut, although doubt was painted on his face. "You're being separated from the others. Then you'll be sure to recover, he says. There's a room that's become vacant upstairs. It's quite empty.

"They've all been sent to the front!"

CHAPTER 22

The first thing that happened was that Calendar Man stuck his little date pad up on the wall behind him. It said October 6, 1944.

The room was far smaller than the ward. Sounds were muffled, the insanity of the lower floor rendered invisible.

James's bed stood in majestic solitude against the short-end wall. The view from his window was seductive. To the right of him lurked Dieter Schmidt and his broad-faced confederate, Horst Lankau, with Werner Fricke, the Calendar Man, in between. The door at the far end of the room rattled in the draft.

James regarded Bryan's placement between the red-eyed man and Kröner listlessly. When he returned from shock treatment in a few hours' time, unconscious and dulled, Bryan, like James himself, would be at the mercy of the malingerers. The days ahead might take years to live through. Every joint in James's body protested. His internal organs were at low ebb. He was emptied and weak.

"I'll get you out of here, Bryan," he thought apathetically.

But in the meantime he'd have to get well.

Kröner had already waved a warning hand several times in response to Horst Lankau's talkativeness. James noted for the first time that Kröner could sweat. The man's gaze searched the room minutely. It was as though he felt spied upon.

It wasn't until after the evening rounds that Kröner dared voice himself freely. They weren't being monitored by sound sensors.

Army Surgeon Thieringer was apparently satisfied with his treatment results. From now on their care would be intensified. Perhaps it was only a question of months before they again would be considered fit enough to serve the Führer.

"Thieringer doesn't suspect anything," Kröner began softly, looking at Lankau and Schmidt in turn. "But prospects aren't good. We'll be back at our old posts before we know it. How do you suppose that'll be? Does the Mailman have a solution to that problem as well, little Schmidty?"

"As for myself, I'm making goddamn sure I'm not sent to the front. You can too!" Lankau growled, dropping his voice. "We have worse problems, in my opinion!" He got up and calmly faced Calendar Man.

"Up you go, Fricke. You're lying over here," he said, slapping his bed. At first, Calendar Man didn't take the broad-faced Lankau seriously and made no attempt to move. After the third slap Lankau clenched his first and held it threateningly in front of Calendar Man. "Next time it won't be with the flat of my hand, understand? It'll be with this! Are you gonna move now?"

"How do you think the nurses will feel about all this shifting around? Are you deciding which is your own bed now?" Kröner looked weary.

"They won't notice it as long as the right case notes are in the right pocket. That's all!" Lankau turned up the case-note holders and turned toward Dieter Schmidt, who was once again his neighbor. "So we're a happy little family once more, you gnome! And you're going to answer our questions, comrade, so spit it out: Where's the Mailman, and what the hell do you know about his plans? After that, you can tell me what we're going to do about *those* two bastards!" The broad-faced man pointed at Bryan's empty bed and jerked his thumb in the direction of James without taking his eyes off Dieter Schmidt. "Those two devils know too much. They're our biggest problem right now." He glanced briefly at James, who lay with his eyes closed, breathing lightly. "What would happen if that stupid von der Leyen tried to run away again? You think the Mailman can tell me that, too?"

"Naturally." Dieter Schmidt stared at him coldly.

"Then I think you should bloody well tell us!"

Footsteps in the corridor warned Lankau. All of them were lying apathetically when Sister Petra looked in on them. She didn't appear to notice Lankau's new place. She only had eyes for James.

. . .

That night the malingerers continued bickering about the Mailman and the valuables in the freight car. And about Bryan.

Things had taken a turn for the worse. James could scarcely move. His nausea seemed to be chronic and he'd begun feeling feverish. Bryan had never been away so long for treatment. Everyone in the ward was worried, though the reasons were totally different.

On the one hand, James wished fervently that Bryan would return soon, safe and sound. Normally a shock treatment only took this long if the patient got cramps. Then it could easily take a couple of hours longer. But on the other hand Bryan might have been moved to another ward. And even though that meant separation and uncertainty, it would definitely be best for Bryan in the long run.

As the hours passed, the malingerers became more and more intent on doing away with Arno von der Leyen as soon as he was brought back. Their whispering got on James's nerves. He, too, was the object of their quiet discussions, but for the time being they seemed confident that he was under control. Red-Eye and Calendar Man they ignored entirely.

For once, Kröner was the most cautious. Lankau suggested tying a sheet around Bryan's neck and throwing him out the window. Kröner grunted and shook his head. It was only a few hours since they'd been moved. A "suicide" in this little ward would be risky business.

"Then we'll only be six when it comes to the interrogation," he finally said. "Are you two really sure you can manage being cross-examined?"

Then Kröner stiffened. The answer came from an unexpected quarter.

"I can!" The voice in the dark was new, authoritative, and icy cold. Its effect practically lit up the room. "Whether you others can is probably more doubtful." The words came from the insignificant, sharp-featured man with bloodshot eyes, Peter Stich.

"It's a pleasure to meet you gentlemen after such a long, one-sided acquaintanceship." The sounds coming from Kröner's and Lankau's beds indicated they were probably already sitting up. James didn't take his eyes off Stich. "Stay where you are, Herr Sturmbannführer!" Addressed by his well-deserved title, Dieter Schmidt stopped in his tracks in front of James's bed. "You have done excellently. I'm very satisfied with your loyalty and silence. You've brought us a long way toward our goal. Now go back to your bed. As for you, gentlemen," he said, taking note of the attention he was attracting, "having got thus far, let me introduce myself. As you have doubtlessly already figured out, I am the one who's been haunting your thoughts for such a long time as the 'Mailman.'"

The effect of the words was unexpectedly slight. The muttering from Horst Lankau's bed was instantly interrupted by Kröner. "Well, well, how about that! What an exclusive little society we're becoming." Kröner nodded to Red-Eye with no trace of astonishment. "The leader himself has shed his skin. And an interesting disguise, too, one might add. Highly effective!"

"And so it shall continue." The Mailman silenced Kröner's irony. "But as you say: an exclusive society. Do I need remind you that the man you gentlemen are thinking of dispatching to the next world is the highest-ranking officer in the ward? Naturally I share your opinion, gentlemen. Arno von der Leyen does not behave as a madman should. In fact, I, too, am pretty convinced he's just as healthy as you gentlemen and me. I've seen him doing things he shouldn't. Hiding pills, for example! But there's another snag about this von der Leyen we need to bear in mind. I doubt whether you gentlemen are as familiar with Oberführer von der Leyen's merits as I."

Lankau snorted. "He's a wimp, he is! One of those good boys who stands by while we others go into action and then takes all the credit." Lankau's ridicule applied to anyone with a higher rank than his. Here in the ward Arno von der Leyen was the only one. "He was easy to catch, the wimp. Like a flustered lap dog!"

"Possibly. But you should realize he's also an opportunist with a history. Apart from being a natural ass licker, he's utterly loyal. A true Nazi. And not least of all he's one of Hitler's confidants. One of the Berlin saints. But despite all the outward glamour, I think you should be damned glad he was so easy for you to catch, Herr Standartenführer Lankau. Because the Arno von der Leyen I know is not merely a wunderkind but also an extremely efficient killer." Red-Eye looked around slowly, nodding affirmatively. Lankau's expression was doubtful and disapproving. "Yes, indeed, my dear *Standartenführer*. How do you imagine that kid has gotten as far as he has? I can assure you Arno von der Leyen had scarcely begun growing down on his chin before he earned himself a worthy place among our Führer's body-guards. With death's-head and everything. It's not everyone who gets as far at so young an age. The epitome of youth, indeed! But also a war hero. There's blood on his medals, as there should be. He's being given special treatment because of his status. Without him, I doubt any of us would have ended up here. We're the ones who are the small fry and he's the one who's important. We are merely his roommates, his backdrop! Do you understand that, gentlemen?"

James was terrified by the Mailman's cold, monotonous voice. During the months of silence this man had been assessing both his enemies and his friends. He was their puppeteer. James shuddered at the thought of how he might have given himself away to him.

"But it's not only Arno von der Leyen's history and merits I'm familiar with," the Mailman emphasized. "I also saw his face once, though it's a long time ago. At the time I scarcely noticed him.

"And now comes the interesting part: I cannot connect the Arno von der Leyen I saw with the man lying over there. I'm not even certain I've ever seen that face before we arrived in this hospital! I have my doubts, you see."

He shushed Kröner, who was about to interrupt. James was trembling all over. The sheet was already clammy with sweat. The situation could scarcely be worse. Bryan's identity was getting shaky and even Kröner could be made to shut up.

The fact that Kröner let this happen was disquieting in itself.

"We must think rationally and take all possibilities into consideration. And now you must listen extra-carefully, gentlemen. For which is worse? That he commits suicide with our modest help and thereby departs from our lives, possibly meaning torture for us as a consequence, or that one day he is revealed as a deceiver, a malingerer? If we let him live and he is the real Arno von der Leyen, then everything is fine, apart from the fact that he knows too much about our plans, thanks to the great need of you gentle-men to whisper at night. And should he not be Arno von der Leyen, he would still know too much. If it turns out one day he's faking it, the security people would almost certainly suspect us as well. They would dig into our past. That's why I had to come to his rescue with the bomb shutter! I'm certain he would have avenged himself on you gentlemen for spoiling his escape if he'd been found out. There, too, our fates could inadvertently have been linked to his." He glanced around. His audience looked grim. "Yes, indeed. It's definitely a dilemma worth thinking over.

"I've been studying him since the day we arrived. I consider him to be unstable, young, and confused. It's hard to determine whether he's Arno von der Leyen or not. But if he's not the real thing, I don't think he'll be able to carry out his deception to the bitter end." He scrutinized each of them in turn. "For me, pain is a titillating dance of new sensations, I might add. A way of investigating the outer elements of the body. But not everyone need see things the way I do." Dieter Schmidt shrugged. He was pale. The Mailman concluded with "Am I right?"

It was clear that Dieter Schmidt's respect for the Mailman was not shared by Lankau. Kröner accepted the situation. "Shut up, Lankau! We know what's on your mind," Kröner admonished, as Lankau's grumbling increased. "From now on we stand together! Got it?"

"Then let us agree," said the Mailman dispassionately, "that Herr Standartenführer Lankau, man of action that he is, would also be the right man to dispatch the so-called von der Leyen from this miserable world."

Practically all the plans were ready for Bryan's liquidation by the time he was brought back to the room. "You can't use *his* sheet, Lankau! They'll see it when they put him to bed. Use yours, if you insist on getting ready now," Kröner spluttered. "You can always switch it later."

"Let's wait until he returns. Then we can take his sheet, anyway." The Mailman smiled across at James. "Isn't that true, Herr Standartenführer Peuckert?" James didn't react, but continued staring into space as his blood turned to ice in his veins.

"I don't like him seeing what we do." Lankau looked hatefully at James.

Red-Eye nodded. "I know, but he won't report us. I don't know why, but he won't. You gentlemen have gotten him well under control."

James looked out toward the fir trees and began counting them unconsciously. When he finished he counted them again. The calm he was so badly in need of was not forthcoming.

As anticipated, Bryan had gotten cramps following his shock treatment. He had been under observation all night. It would take a long time before he could defend himself. James was at his wits' end. Exhausted and hard-pressed in both mind and body.

While the nursing aides were dealing out lunch rations farther down the hallway, Lankau wrung out Bryan's sheet in the washbasin. It was now as thin and taut as a length of hemp rope and lay ready under Bryan's blanket, fastened at one end to the head of the bed.

The nurses had already made up his bed. They would leave Arno von der Leyen unattended until he woke up.

"Is that the right way to do it? Suicide, that is? Shouldn't we just toss him out?" Lankau asked uneasily. "It would look like an attempt to escape. It's not far to the firs on the other side of the fence. With a good jump from the windowsill it would be possible to land over there."

"And . . . ?" The Mailman didn't seem to want an answer.

"And then his 'jump' would fail, of course!"

The Mailman sucked in his cheeks. "In other words, there will have been an escape attempt in our ward and we'll have the investigations again. Not to mention them bolting the windows. Then that route would be barred for us should the situation demand it. And what if he were to survive the fall? Nope, we'll hang him when it gets dark."

James was the only one who didn't have a bell cord over his bed. His placement in the middle of a six-man ward was merely temporary. It was a depressing situation. If he tried to foil their plans he would end up like Bryan. And right now he had trouble enough just remaining conscious.

The help would have to come from without. He'd have to see to that.

But if the makeshift rope were discovered, investigations would be put into effect immediately and Red-Eye's prophecy brought to fulfillment in all its horror. Only Sister Petra could avert a complete catastrophe and cast suspicion in the right direction.

But Petra no longer came every day.

That day it began growing dark already in the middle of the afternoon, as if symbolizing Bryan's vanishing existence.

Petra entered the ward quite without warning. Kröner was clearly taken by surprise when the ceiling light was switched on. She filled her jug with tap water from the washbasin and walked past every bed, filling up the glasses on the bed tables.

When she reached James, he tried to force himself up in bed for a moment. "My goodness, Herr Peuckert!" she exclaimed, pressing him back gently. James positioned his head so her head blocked the others' vision. But the words wouldn't come. His desperate eyes and uncontrolled movements were new to her and incomprehensible.

So she fetched the senior nursing officer.

This person of authority, who was seldom caught displaying signs of sensitivity either to the staff or patients, studied James attentively. Bending over him, her face shone with realization. Shaking her head indulgently, she scurried past the anxious Petra and over to the window, where she drew the curtain a trifle over the anti-bomb shutters. Thus a tiny patch of grayish light that had been dancing on James's cheek was extinguished. Feeling momentarily pleased with herself after this little operation, the head nurse turned to Bryan and patted him surprisingly hard on the cheek.

Bryan grunted distantly and drew his head away from the direction of the blow. "He'll wake up soon," she said, heading out of the room without looking to see if Petra was following. "About time, too!" were her final words.

Petra bent over James and stroked his hair gently. He emitted a faint, unintelligible whisper. Petra's eyes smiled. The whistling sounds made her lips part with delight.

Then the senior nursing officer called for her.

The following seconds seemed like infinity.

"Well, buddy." Lankau smiled at Calendar Man. "Now we're going to have some fun. Come over here!" he called, tightening the sheet around his victim's neck so the knot covered the pulsating carotid artery as planned. It would be a short, efficient fall, designed to break the neck.

The malingerers knew what they were doing. James lay in his bed hyperventilating while Calendar Man grinned like a child at play. He raised Bryan up onto his shoulder as instructed by Lankau. He patted Bryan's naked buttocks and wriggled with glee while the broad-faced man laughed and flung open the window behind Bryan's bed. The other malingerers merely looked on languidly.

Calendar Man's pats, grunts, and rough movements made Bryan open his eyes. Bewildered by his position and the cold, hard edge of the window-sill beneath him, he raised his head and began squealing senselessly like a stuck pig.

"Take hold of his arms, dammit!" sputtered Kröner, jumping out of bed and striking Bryan a hard blow on the shoulder. Calendar Man suddenly stopped and let go, confused about the abrupt, serious turn the game had taken. He twisted around and began to whine, slapping the back of his hand feebly and reluctantly against Lankau's and Kröner's bodies as the two stood on either side of Bryan, struggling with him. The despairing figure now had one leg out the window, the other hooked firmly over the window-sill.

The Mailman didn't move from his bed, but the skinny man shot up and ran with all his hate and fury headfirst into Bryan's diaphragm. The effect was unintentional. With a roar, Bryan jerked forward so violently that it sounded like a hammer blow when his forehead struck the top of the puny man's head. Dieter Schmidt toppled over without a sound.

"Stop!" shouted the Mailman, and ordered the malingerers back to their beds. He had heard the running footsteps in the corridor before they had.

The two porters came to an abrupt halt when they found Bryan on the floor. Madness radiated from his eyes and his groans were half-stifled on account of the tight sheet.

"He's completely out of his mind! You hold him down," one of them admonished as he closed the window. "I'll fetch the straitjacket."

But then the air-raid sirens started wailing.

CHAPTER 23

The evacuation to the cellar took place in great haste, giving the porters other things to think about. As the days passed, Bryan became more and more convinced they had never reported the episode, and thanked God they hadn't got as far as putting him in a straitjacket. Then he would have been an easy victim.

The bombardment of Freiburg had not caused any damage in the immediate vicinity.

Some small barracks were being erected over by the square, presumably to relieve pressure on the wards. Any thoughts of escaping by that route were thereby eliminated. Moreover, all the fences had been furnished with porcelain insulators and warning signs. But apart from that, and the strained expressions on the nursing staff's faces, things were pretty much as usual for everyone. Except for Bryan himself.

He didn't sleep the next two days and nights. Despite his terrible experience and the complications following the recent shock treatment he felt strong and determined. Even though the malingerers kept a constant eye on him and spoke to him nastily and threateningly, Bryan felt neither anxious nor helpless in the midst of a hopeless situation.

Red-Eye smiled at him sympathetically and kindly as he lay on his side in the adjacent bed hour after hour, watching him with a combination of curiosity and merriment. When Bryan tried to recall the episode it seemed to him it had been Red-Eye who had stepped in and saved his life. The echo of the man's cries still rang in the back of his head.

It was the second time Red-Eye had come to his rescue. During the ward round Bryan noted his name. Peter Stich. Bryan smiled back at him as though they were bound by a mutually comforting and promising alliance.

. . .

Little Petra looked in on James constantly. Bryan rarely caught his eye and had the feeling he wasn't well. And yet Petra seemed quite satisfied.

On the ward round the following day the doctors talked at the foot of James's bed for some time. Afterward he was taken to a room a bit farther down the hall for some rounds of consultation and examination.

That evening the army surgeon performed the unusual act of giving James a warm handshake. Petra stood beside him, tripping almost playfully and smiling shyly with folded arms. They spoke to him in a normal fashion and although he didn't reply, he looked them in the eye as if he understood.

Bryan was glad to see this development. His confidence that James could soon be included in an escape plan began to grow.

On the following evening the malingerers' discussion was orderly and officious. Even the Mailman offered his opinions dispassionately as he lay staring up at the ceiling. To Bryan it seemed he was making fun of the others. Bryan assumed they were leaving the Mailman in peace because of his mental illness and brutish behavior. Every time Bryan looked at James, he seemed to be expressing displeasure.

Bryan didn't attach any particular importance to it.

One of the new nurses switched on the light, immediately causing the room's inhabitants to stop whispering. Thereafter she held the door open for a new officer, followed by Army Surgeon Thieringer, who was smiling broadly. The young officer spoke briefly to the ward's patients and shook hands with both the nurses and Thieringer. Then he clicked his heels and heiled respectfully, whereupon they all left the room again.

The episode apparently made an impression on the malingerers, who went on whispering quietly, the sound of which, surprisingly, almost lulled Bryan to sleep.

The young officer had arrived at the same time as him. Now he'd apparently recovered sufficiently to be sent back to the battlefield, more alive than dead, more well than sick. A good example to all of them.

His thoughts merged and the voices gradually disappeared. All Bryan's lifelines had been severed. The bell cord above him had been torn off. James had no cord at all. The young officer heiled a final time at the threshold of dreamland.

And then Bryan fell asleep.

Every metallic sound contains its own message. When a wing is ripped off a B-17 bomber it sounds different from when the fuselage splits open. A heavy hammer on a small nail sounds different from a small hammer on a large nail. The sound is transmitted in its entirety to the metal and tells its story in the resulting sound. But this sound was difficult to decipher. It was metallic and melodic, but new. Bryan's eyelids were so heavy that he had to do without an answer a bit longer. A whitish glow told him it was daytime again and he had survived the night. The room seemed different.

As the mysterious, sharp sound gradually acquired character, Bryan began imagining a pumping, clattering science-fiction machine. Like an invention of H. G. Wells or one of the diabolical cosmic machines he had inspected with boyish curiosity in traveling entertainers' caravans and market squares for the price of a single penny.

Bryan opened his eyes. The room seemed unfamiliar.

There was one bed beside his, the only other one in the room. On the edge of the other bed hung a glass bottle connected to a rubber tube through which small yellowish-white drops trickled constantly. The bottle was a quarter full. Someone was breathing irregularly under the blanket. He didn't recognize the face that was half-covered by a mask.

The oxygen flask that was connected to the mask stood on the other side of the bed. A kind of ventilator fan emitted regular puffs of warmish, damp air from a green-painted shelf above the bed. Its blade was crooked. This was where the unfamiliar metallic sounds were coming from.

The entire room seemed to be separated from the reality of the rest of the hospital, devoid of the vile odors, noises, and insane behavior.

Bryan looked around. The two of them were alone in the room. A carpet lay on the floor. Unlike the rest of the hospital, the walls were draped with pictures. Engravings with religious motifs contrasted with framed photographs of pretentious young specimens of the Third Reich in imaginative, proud poses.

.   .   .

The transfer to the new location was a mystery to Bryan. Obviously they'd given him the bed of the newly discharged officer. But why him? Had they suspected something and removed him from his oppressors? Or did they intend to place him under special observation?

The room lay opposite the one he'd come from. He recognized the nursing staff.

Sister Petra's face revealed nothing that could make him uneasy. She was happy and attentive as usual, smiling and patting his cheek and chattering endlessly in a respectful and cheerful tone that could indicate they deemed him well on the way to recovery. Bryan made a decision. She should see signs of progress. This would give him increased mobility.

But it mustn't happen too suddenly.

On one of his visits to the lavatory another new world opened to him. The corridor that also led past the room in which James lay was about three meters wide. There wasn't much distance between the doors, suggesting there were only a few beds in each room. Their room was the one nearest the end of the building. After this there was a small room and then a two-man room. Farther down came the examination room, the lavatories, and the shower. This was the extent of his world. He didn't go all the way to the end of the corridor. On the other side of the hallway was yet another room the size of the one in which James lay.

A time-honored allocation of roles was apparently taking place in the ward Bryan had left. Kröner had reassumed his role of volunteer orderly and no one seemed to protest. He could thereby walk freely about in all the rooms as though it were his job.

Bryan would have preferred it had been someone else.

CHAPTER 24

Petra Wagner was distantly related to Gauleiter Wagner in Baden. A fact she had never needed to reveal, since it was such a common surname.

In the time she'd been stationed there she'd grown fond of the district and the Schwarzwald. She had adjusted to the clinic, even though the brusque, militant tone was alien to her at first. The few friends the hard work permitted her were all at the hospital, and thanks to the peaceful hours in the nurses' block with lace-making and girlish gossip, she seldom felt the grim presence of war.

Unlike her, nearly all her girlfriends were distressed over sweethearts in the war or grieving over dead or missing or injured loved ones. They lived with the accompanying hate and fear. But although Petra displayed no outward signs of grief, this didn't mean she didn't have a life. It was just different.

Many atrocities took place at the hospital that upset Petra. Experiments with new types of medicine, hasty decisions, strange diagnoses, and undisguised favoritism. There was only one kind of order in a military hospital, which was military rank and the military code. And even though it plagued her, the execution of deserters and malingerers and the sporadic mercy killings were an integral part of that order. A reality with which she had hitherto avoided any direct confrontation, even though at one point she had nursed one of the wretched victims of this system.

Petra was still astonished that the patient they'd called the Siamese twin had been able to get away with his simulating for such a long time. She had never once suspected him, as he wandered around like a little monkey, holding his twin by the hand. Since then, this disclosure and the episode with the pills had made her view her surroundings with new eyes.

The ward was for the mentally disturbed. Most of them were seriously ill and presumably would never recover. The oppressive shock-treatment sessions seemed haphazard, and their effect questionable. The few patients who had been discharged since her arrival faced an uncertain fate. They were weak, their reactions sluggish, and their treatment incomplete. In reality, they were much too vulnerable to be discharged. She knew the army surgeon was of the same opinion, but they had to respect the fact that new arrivals needed their beds.

And soon they were going to discharge several in her section.

Some of the patients didn't react when spoken to, like Werner Fricke, who went around in his own world and understood nothing but his date pad. Not even the renowned Arno von der Leyen appeared to understand what she said, but Gerhart Peuckert understood everything. She was sure of this, even though she had yet to make contact with him.

Many of the symptoms Gerhart Peuckert displayed could not be explained solely by the ravages of shell shock. Some of his reactions were reminiscent of the suffering she had confronted in the medical ward. His physical condition appeared unduly weak and feeble in relation to the others, and he displayed irrational reactions as if he were in anaphylactic shock. The doctors dismissed it, which worried her even more and made her feel powerless.

He was the most handsome man she had ever seen. She couldn't believe he was the kind of fiend described in his dossier. Either it was exaggerated, or his papers had been exchanged with someone else's.

That much she knew about human nature.

Nevertheless, she was unable to understand what had made Peuckert inflict such severe wounds on himself. The many bruises and the enormous loss of blood aroused her suspicions. But the human mechanism of self-torture could be inscrutable. Angst had deep roots and provided its own kind of sustenance when one least expected it. She had seen it so often. How someone could almost bite off his own tongue as Arno von der Leyen had done seemed incomprehensible. Yet things like this happened. So why not Gerhart? Therefore it was comforting that he'd been a bit better recently, even though he was still weak.

When he reacted to her tenderness with his first attempts to form words, she decided to try to dispel Gerhart Peuckert's anxiety so he wouldn't suffer the same fate as so many others.

If it were up to her, he would stay in the hospital until the war ended.

Munich, Karlsruhe, Mannheim, and dozens of other German cities were now under intense bombardment. Nancy had been occupied. Even Freiburg had been attacked. The Americans were pushing forward; the Allies were poised to enter German territory. And when it was all over she hoped Gerhart Peuckert would still be alive.

Both for his sake and her own.

"New directives from Berlin. The Wehrmacht medical authorities' Supreme Command has finally summarized the conclusions of their hearing in August." The sleeves of Army Surgeon Manfried Thieringer's white coat were folded up to expose his slender wrists. "They are demanding tighter control with regard to simulating," he continued. "The reserve hospital in Ensen has already reacted by discharging all debatable cases for service at the front." He looked slowly around the little room. It had been his decision to use the old conference room for treating patients as the pressure on the wards became too great. The barracks buildings could no longer keep up with demand. The fighting on the Eastern Front and the latest battle at Aachen had given them much too much to do. But now it would be possible to get back to normal again.

The directive from Berlin would make more room for them.

Dr. Holst's eyes looked small behind his thick glasses. "The reserve hospital in Ensen basically treats only war neurotics. Why does this concern us?"

"It concerns us, Dr. Holst, because if we don't do as they do, our results will seem poor in comparison. Then they'll ask us to give the remaining ones a lethal injection or massive quantities of their beloved chloral hydrate, carbromal, and barbital. And after that we can report for service at the front, can't we?" Thieringer scrutinized his lieutenant surgeon. "Do you realize how privileged we are, Dr. Holst? If Goebbels's wife hadn't begged her husband to see that the hospitals treated their patients better, our most important task today would be liquidating the mentally ill. More mercy killings, right? 'Cause of death: influenza.' Can you see it? At least now the only ones who give us problems are the few crybabies who land in the basement." He shook his head. "Nope, we'll do what's expected of us. We'll start to discharge gradually. Otherwise that'll be the end of the experiments at the Alphabet House, Dr. Holst. No more of your dubious chlorine-preparation trials and that sort of thing. No more measuring the effects of different types of shock treatment. Our relatively comfortable life here is over!" Dr. Holst looked down. "No, we were lucky Frau Goebbels got her husband to protect our elite soldiers. That gave us something to work with, didn't it? So we could help maintain the German people's illusion of the infallibility of the SS Corps!"

Manfried Thieringer looked over at Petra and the other nurses in the ward. Until now he hadn't deigned to cast them a glance. But this look meant they should pay attention to his closing remarks. He seized a pile of case files.

"This means we must cut down on the dosages in Ward Nine. All insulin therapy is to cease as of today. We'll take Wilfried Kröner and Dieter Schmidt completely off chemo-psychotherapy by December. I think we can soon give up on Werner Fricke. We won't make him much more sensible. He's from a well-to-do family, isn't he?" No one answered. The army surgeon kept turning the pages. "We'll have to keep Gerhart Peuckert under observation a little while longer, but he seems to be recovering." Petra clasped her hands together.

"And then of course there's Arno von der Leyen," he continued. "We've been told he's to receive an important visitor from Berlin around Christmas. We'll need to concentrate all our efforts on his convalescence. I've heard rumors that he attempted suicide. Can anyone here confirm this?"

The nurses looked at one another and shook their heads in silence.

"Under no circumstances can we take any chances. I've been allocated two patients about to be discharged from the medical ward who will be receiving final treatment in this section. They'll be able to stand guard and make sure there are no more suicide attempts. We can keep them for three months. That ought to be sufficient, don't you think?"

"Are they to stand guard around the clock?" As usual, the senior nursing officer wanted to make sure her staff wasn't forced to take on any further night watches.

Thieringer shook his head. "Devers and Leyen are to sleep at night. You must see to that."

"What about Arno von der Leyen's roommate?" Dr. Holst queried uncertainly.

"Gruppenführer Devers is unlikely to recover. The gas has done too much damage to his lungs and brain. We have to do our best, but he must continue getting the full dose. He has powerful friends, understand?"

"Is he the right person? To share a room with Arno von der Leyen, I mean? I just thought . . ." Dr. Holst scarcely knew how to put it. Thieringer's look made him shift in his chair. "He just lies there . . ."

"Yes, I think it's an excellent idea. By the way, I must emphasize that neither Horst Lankau nor any of the other patients from Ward Three are to enter Arno von der Leyen and Gruppenführer Devers's room."

"Wilfried gives us a hand with several jobs. Does this also apply to him?" wondered Sister Lili.

"Kröner?" Manfried Thieringer stuck out his lower lip and shook his head. "No, I don't think it should. He's showing good progress. On the other hand, I don't think Standartenführer Lankau's behavioral pattern is improving. He seems unstable. We must do our best to make sure he is kept calm and doesn't disturb his fellow patients until we discharge him."

Since Gerhart Peuckert's situation had already been discussed, Petra had only a single question: "How are we to treat Gruppenführer Devers's guest, Professor? Can we give her something to eat, since she comes so often?"

"How often is that?"

"Several times a week. Almost every day, I think."

"You can give her the option, yes. Ask her. She could be a diversion for Arno von der Leyen." Looking pleased, he glanced at his subordinate. "Yes, that would be an excellent idea. I'll speak to her about it myself when I meet her."

Petra had envied Gruppenführer Devers's wife from the first time she saw her. Not for her physiognomy or because life for her appeared relatively undemanding, but solely because of her clothing. Whenever Frau Devers walked past, upright and proud, she nodded amiably. Sister Petra only had eyes for her stockings and dress. "Bamberg silk, all of it," she told the other nurses when they were up in their rooms. None of them had ever worn anything like that.

Petra had managed to briefly touch Gisela Devers's dress as she sat reading beside her husband's bed. The material was wonderfully smooth, almost cool.

Arno von der Leyen was looking at Gruppenführer Devers's wife constantly. Petra had noticed that. Secretly she thanked God that Gerhart didn't have the same scenery.

The two newly appointed guards were pale-looking young ones. Like so many others, their eyes reflected great affliction. Their freshly ironed SS Rottenführer uniforms were sparklingly new, but their badges and insignia were worn and bore witness to quite an amount of active duty. The badges for their division consisted of two crossed hand grenades. Petra had seen them before. They were scarcely becoming.

Gisela Devers's presence made the two young guards stand at attention and look alert. She was the elegant wife of a superior officer in the SS and the only relative in that section of the hospital to have been cleared for visiting.

But as soon as she had walked past them, they began chatting together, smiling. They treated all the others with indifference, including the doctors. They knew their job and carried it out efficiently, without grumbling. As long as they did so, they were safe. Better eighteen hours on duty every single day than just one hour at the front.

Petra had to agree with Thieringer. Horst Lankau was not the same as before. His ruddy, weather-beaten, and jovial broad face was no longer smiling. The other patients seemed to be afraid of him. The army surgeon had also been right about his having been in Devers and ward hero Arno von der Leyen's room a number of times without having had any business there.

After Lankau had been forbidden to leave his room, his fury knew no bounds. His protests became surprisingly colorful and graphic until he was finally given a shot to calm down.

Since then he had regained some of his previous charm.

Thus a great deal had taken place. Wilfried Kröner was getting much better and he now wandered freely around the entire Alphabet House. To everyone's great amusement he carried the laundry down to the basement and pushed the canteen trolleys around on all the floors. Apart from his muscle spasms that mostly caused incontinence and occasional speech-impeding twitches, his behavior seemed to indicate the treatment was basically drawing to a close.

The strange Peter Stich, with his sardonic smile, had quit staring up into the shower when he took a bath. Instead he'd begun picking his nose so violently that it looked as if he thought it would relieve the headaches from which he clearly suffered. Sometimes blood poured out of him during fits like this. Petra hated it. It made a mess and put the nursing aides in a bad mood. There was also the squelching sound of the vehement digging in his nostrils.

It made her nauseous.

The guards had acquired another object of their vigilance. An *Obergruppenführer* with a nervous breakdown had been admitted to the room next to Arno von der Leyen. Even though the porters described him in detail, no one apart from a couple of the doctors and Manfried Thieringer knew the general's true identity. Petra knew only that he was a well-groomed, middle-aged gentleman who seemed completely out of his mind.

No one was allowed to enter his room without the army surgeon being present. It was said he was simply to be given peace and quiet to regain his strength. It would cause quite a scandal if word got out that one of the pillars of the Third Reich was lying there.

Gisela Devers had used her cunning in an attempt to obtain permission to visit the *Obergruppenführer,* but in vain. Some suggested it was in this way she had attained her present position. Petra doubted it. Her handbag was furnished with a label from I. G. Farben. It was also said she was related to the owners, to which both her clothes and her marriage lent credence. This was a reasonable explanation as to why she was allowed to enter the section so freely.

CHAPTER 25

Suddenly Lankau stopped annoying Bryan.

Out in the hallway it was the guards who ruled. Why they had been posted there he didn't know, but the single patient in the next room was not just anybody.

The two SS guards looked to be even younger than Bryan and their eyes were colder than a corpse.

A couple of times a day they opened the door of the room wide in order to air out the corridor. At times like this Pock Face often passed by, chatting with folks.

Bryan wasn't fooled by his attempt at a gentle facade. Beneath the surface lurked an alarming and callous determination.

The combination was frightening.

Upon entering their room he always began by straightening his neighbor's pillow and stroking his cheek a bit. Whereupon he usually turned slowly to Bryan with a grim expression on his face and deliberately traced a forefinger across his throat. Then he patted the unconscious man on the cheek again and continued on his rounds with a quiet smile on his kindly face.

The thin man also studied him briefly while the door was open. That was all the guards would permit.

They despised his manner.

At night Bryan was alone. A mere groan from his senseless neighbor was enough to make him jerk upright in bed.

They usually left his pills on the bedside table so he could take them himself. He couldn't go to the toilet after the onset of darkness; the door to the hallway was locked. His room had no washbasin, either. After a couple of attempts, he abandoned trying to get rid of the pills by dissolving them in urine in his chamber pot. So he waited until the ward was perfectly quiet, whereupon he went over to his neighbor, pulled his mask aside, and crushed the pills into his mouth. He coughed a bit when Bryan pressed the glass of water to his lips, but after a while the swallowing movements always started.

The nurses gave his neighbor medicine as well. Bryan didn't know whether it was supposed to make him go on sleeping or wake him up, but naturally he was worried, lest the combination should prove fatal. But nothing happened. His breathing just became calmer and smoother.

If the malingerers were still after him, they would have to strike at night. This meant that in order to watch out for himself, Bryan's nights had to become days, and his days, nights.

He would fight back. If he screamed loudly, the duty room was close enough for help to reach him in time.

He would scream loud enough to wake both the dead and the man beside him.

And then Gisela Devers had stepped into the room and disturbed his rest.

A dangerous but impressive interruption.

Her presence brought back memories of parties his family had given in Dover when summer was drawing to a close and the upper-middle-class families were about to disperse in all directions to their winter domiciles. This was where Bryan learned about the intoxicating scent of women.

Frau Devers was only a few years older than him. Her posture was perfect and her clothes fit well, accentuating the curves of her body. At first sight of her, Bryan kept his eyes half-closed.

He was spellbound by the graceful profile and the short, soft hairs on her neck that escaped the upswept hair. He inhaled her perfume and felt his desire growing. The scent was mild and ethereal, like an armful of fresh fruit.

She had sat down, her skirt following the curves of her thighs.

No one took further notice of Bryan. He was not expected to regain his usual level of activity until the fourth day. So he could lie gazing at Gisela Devers in the comfortable dozing between wakefulness and sleep.

On about the third evening, Gisela's body began trembling as though she were about to burst into tears. She bent over her husband's bed, head hanging down over the book that lay in her lap. It was a sad sight. Bryan understood her.

And then the trembling stopped for a moment before returning in strange, suppressed laughter that slowly spread to her entire body. Her sudden laughter made Bryan forget himself and laugh too.

Gisela turned around abruptly. She had completely forgotten Bryan's presence and had never really looked at him. His eyes were glistening with mirth.

And this gleaming luster made her freeze on the spot.

During the following days Gisela moved closer and closer to Bryan's bed. She was apparently fascinated by his distant silence. Bryan had never heard so much German. She was very particular, choosing her words carefully and speaking slowly as if she realized special tactics were needed to break through Bryan's barriers.

And she succeeded. The constantly repeated words gradually became meaningful. Finally he began to indicate that he understood her. This amused her. And if he nodded eagerly, she took his hand and patted it. Later she began stroking it gently even when he didn't nod.

She was enthralling.

The thin man had been irritating the guards long enough with his curiosity. He'd ignored their orders once too often on his eternal rounds in the ward. Without warning, one of the guards took firm hold of him from behind while the other stuck his fingers so deep inside the skinny throat that only guttural sounds came out after the vomit. Then they kicked him to the floor and ordered him to wipe up the vomit with his sleeves. During the afternoon inspection Bryan could clearly hear the senior nurse scolding him for the mess.

Gisela looked puzzled when the guards began to laugh.

The young Frau Devers didn't understand much of what was going on in the ward. Instead she talked enthusiastically about herself most of the time, as far as Bryan could tell. He desired her intensely even though he didn't doubt for a moment she would denounce him if she knew the truth about him. He was just as captivated by her as she was by Arno von der Leyen.

In spite of the deceit, it was delicious when she slid her hand under the bed covers and whispered strange, gentle words in his ear.

On a day when Bryan least expected Frau Devers to make advances, Sister Petra had stood in the doorway for a surprisingly long time, chattering away as she cast stolen glances at Gisela's black dress.

Frau Devers had merely given Petra a friendly nod without going out of her way to acknowledge her existence, let alone show any interest in her.

Just as Petra was called away by shouts from the guardroom, Gisela Devers turned toward Bryan. Her lips were parted. She let the book on her lap fall to the floor and carefully pushed the door closed. For a while she leaned up against the doorframe, looking him deep in the eyes. She bent back one leg, thrust out her knee, and began breathing so deeply that it was audible.

A fit of shivering drained the tension from Bryan's body, leaving him hot and vulnerable. Then she took a step forward and stood so close to him that all he could see were the folds of her dress following the contours of her thighs. She leaned toward him, resting one knee on the edge of the bed. Bryan rose to meet her just as she put her arm around his neck. Her clothing was smooth, supple, and cool. Her skin was moist.

These embraces were repeated, though only over a short period. The rhythm of the ward was constantly changing. Peace was difficult to come by. And they both had reason to be careful.

Eventually they could make do by merely looking at each other for hours on end. Only seldom did their bodies give way. Her voice alone was like making love. All other women were blotted out.

On one of these days her customary chatter became spiced with a new undertone. Concrete and direct.

Bryan's inner alarm was slow in reacting. At first he thought she was saying Gruppenführer Devers would soon be having visitors.

Then it dawned on him that she was referring to him, Arno von der

Leyen. That she admired him and felt convinced he would be home by Christmas. That he would soon be receiving distinguished visitors from Berlin.

And that she would miss him.

She glanced contemptuously over at her husband.

This was terrible news, if he had understood her correctly.

It became more difficult for Bryan to keep track of the days after he'd been moved to the new room, and he hated himself for being so slipshod. When he'd heard the violent reverberations from the last big raid on Karlsruhe, he reckoned it to be the fifth of November—two days before his birthday. That must have been about two weeks ago.

The fighting on the other side of the Rhine could no longer be ignored, but in which direction the fortunes of war were going, he couldn't know. On the other hand it was obvious the patients in the hospital risked being moved if the Allied advance became a threat to the region.

This, combined with the fact that he could expect a visit from Berlin at any time, made finding an escape plan particularly urgent.

This time it had to succeed.

Every night as he kept his lone vigil he busied himself with these plans and thought about James.

Several problems had to be sorted out. Clothing and footwear. How to get past all the watchful eyes. How to get out of, and away from, the building. The dog patrols and the new electric fence. The rocky mountainside in the dark. Having to navigate roads in the valley where military preparedness was now at its peak. The cold from the damp earth and the streams. The more than ten kilometers of flat vineyards before reaching the Rhine. The uncertainty as to whether they were still harvesting grapes so late in the year.

And then there were the villages below, and all the possible surprise encounters and strange activities of small communities. All this had to be overcome.

Bryan knew he could no longer head south. The concentration of troops along the Swiss border had to be the greatest in the world. Instead he would have to flee via the shorter route toward the west by attempting to cross the railway that ran through the Rhine Valley on the edge of the mountains. Finally, he would try to reach the river.

Judging by the increasing din of war during recent weeks, the Allied troops must be just on the other side of the Rhine. But how would he get that far?

Right now, this mighty river that Bryan had so often used as a landmark on his raids was probably the world's most heavily guarded waterway. Anyone caught there wouldn't need to speculate about the consequences. So close to the front line, every suspicious civilian would be taken for a deserter and promptly shot.

And when the Rhine finally lay in front of him, how should he cross it? How wide was it, in fact, and how deep? How strong was the current?

The final question he asked himself wasn't pleasant either: What if he *did* manage to cross it? Wouldn't his own side open fire instantly? Wouldn't they shoot at anything that moved?

All in all, the odds were not good. As a child Bryan had learned from his stepfather that stupid people don't appreciate the importance of reckoning with the odds. These people repeatedly came to prefer dreams, fantasies, and illusions that were never realized, rather than steering their life in a safer—if more commonplace—direction. In this way they were often rendered incapable of making any decisions at all. The odds they disregarded forced them down blind alleys that gave them poor opportunities and turned them into losers.

And yet, in the given situation and despite his good upbringing, Bryan chose to disregard the odds. Another important aspect of his upbringing outweighed the gloomy outlook.

It was the eternal truth that problems exist only to be solved.

Naturally he was unfamiliar with the surrounding countryside, and his poor knowledge of the language was just as incontestable. But this was the very terminology of escape, as it were. Since he could no longer stay where he was, he'd have to do his best, and do it soon.

If and when the moment finally arrived, it was of the utmost importance to reach the Rhine before daybreak.

The question was whether James would follow him.

. . .

Bryan would have given his right arm for a walk around the buildings or a better view from his window.

The electric fence constituted the first obstacle. He would encounter that fence even if he chose to make for the craggy rocks. And even if he succeeded in getting over the rocks by some other route, he would be forced to creep all the way around the hospital site in order to get down to the road going west.

The easiest way was through the gate. Bryan ruled that out. It was also the easiest way of getting killed.

The next possibility was to dig his way out. But all the sections of the hospital facing the open countryside were dotted with barracks. He wouldn't be able to dig there in peace. As far as Bryan could tell, the remainder of the fence was on rocky ground.

So he would have to get over the fence without touching it.

The recollection of the cold march back from the square on Hitler's birthday, past all the big fir trees that leaned over the fence on the eastern side, was still vivid in his mind. Just one little stroll out there and he'd know for sure whether a jump of that distance was too far.

There was actually another way of finding this out. If only he could get into James's room, he'd easily be able to judge the distance across to the fir trees from the window.

Bryan nodded resolutely. That's what he'd have to do.

In any case, James would have to be drawn into the plan at the first given opportunity.

Caught unawares, Gisela grabbed her handbag and rushed out into the corridor. She'd heard the door creak the second before she'd kissed Bryan. Now Kröner was smiling in the doorway as she sidled past him with an indignant look. He had been watching, and he had seen their embrace. Bryan and Kröner exchanged icy looks. The rude awakening from a realm of silk and soft forms to the confrontation with Pock Face's smile instantly sent intense mixed sensations of warmth and hate through him.

Kröner was still laughing when Bryan rose threateningly from his bed. Pock Face retreated to the hallway and glided away with his hand in front of his face, still chuckling. The guards were startled to see Bryan follow after him, but their vigilance ceased the moment Kröner evaded his stubborn pursuer by entering the lavatory and locking the door. Bryan wasn't sure what he was doing, or why. Kröner was still laughing behind the door. And what could he do about it? Wait an eternity and jump him when he finally came out?

Even though this appealed to him more and more, there was little point in it.

The guards began talking in quiet tones. Things on the ward were proceeding at their usual slow rate. Next to the lavatory door, behind which Kröner had gradually quieted down, the door to the shower room stood ajar. As did another door a couple of meters farther along the hall. Bryan had never considered this last, pale-green surface as being a door, merely a section of wall before the glass door leading to the back stairs.

The guards didn't react in the slightest when he went over and opened it. Bryan immediately knew why.

It was merely another lavatory.

That same evening Kröner was still cackling as he went around with the assistant nurses and the food trolley. With eyebrows raised in merriment, he approached Bryan and whispered some words with satanic solemnity. Bryan didn't understand their meaning. *"Bald, Herr Leyen! Sehr bald . . . Sehr, sehr bald!"*

One of the escape problems was now solved. There was a window in the newly discovered lavatory. Its thin iron frame was bolted so it couldn't be opened, but the view from it was promising.

The lavatory itself was incorporated in the back-stair extension. From there one had a completely clear view along the facade, past the showers, lavatories, examination room, the two-man room, the mysterious single room, and all the way over to the corner of the building where Bryan's own room lay. A magnificent view, with drainpipes every three or four meters. Especially interesting was the drainpipe outside the room that only the army surgeon used, because it was anchored so solidly. This drainpipe ran down into a small niche at the foot of the building that housed garbage cans and surplus materials. Above, however, it was attached to the top floor, just outside a bay window in the pitched roof.

This attic window was open so that sunlight lit up the shelves inside with their piles of linen.

Bryan would go upward, not downward.

Gisela Devers didn't come to their room in the days that followed.

Bryan missed her presence with a mixture of pain and sweetness.

After two nightmarish nights and two very lonely days she suddenly turned up again. On the third morning she sat with her husband, reading, as if nothing had happened. During the few hours she was there she didn't say a word and made no overtures. Just as she was about to leave, she sat down for a moment beside Bryan's bed. She patted his hand dispassionately and nodded proudly at him. In a few phrases she made it clear that she had heard the Führer was in the vicinity. Warming to the subject, she mentioned an offensive in the Ardennes, sounding very optimistic, and smiled when she spoke his name.

Then she winked at him. The hero Arno von der Leyen would soon be receiving a visitor. If not the Führer himself, then someone close to him.

The look of veneration Gisela Devers gave Bryan when she left remained imprinted in his memory.

CHAPTER 26

Just keep sleeping, kiddo," Bryan thought to himself. Herr Devers was a heavy man and it was difficult to haul him out of bed. The blanket on his own bed was turned back, ready to receive his roommate. Then he put Devers's dressing gown in the empty bed and molded it carefully into the shape of a reclining body, pulled the blanket up over it, put on his own dressing gown, and left the room after having made sure there was no one in the hallway who didn't have any business there.

It was just before seven in the evening. Their overcooked dinner had been rapidly consumed. A number of emergency drills had put the staff into a flurry most of the day. At first Bryan thought it was for real, that they were all about to be evacuated. Then self-reproach gave way to curses as he realized a chance to escape had been lost.

But the nursing aides smiled, and even Vonnegut stuck his head into his room and grinned. The night medicine had already been distributed, several hours earlier than usual.

The time had come.

The guards in the hall almost laughed as he stood in the corridor, scratching his neck and looking lost. Suddenly his face brightened and he walked over to the seven-man room with an indifferent shrug.

Instead of stopping him, they looked almost as relieved as he did.

The malingerers were already lying flat in their beds, except Kröner, who propped himself up on his elbows the moment Bryan entered and gave him a derisive look. James now lay between him and Red-Eye in Bryan's old bed.

An unfamiliar, passive face peeped up over the blanket in the bed at the end wall and followed Kröner's movements across the floor. The broad-faced man grunted and awakened when Kröner shook him. James woke up as well.

The look James sent Bryan signaled another form of apathy than mere lassitude.

It was all Bryan needed to know.

James wouldn't be able to come with him.

Then Bryan strode in between Kröner's and James's beds and looked out the window. The fir trees on the southern part of the rock face were at least six meters from the house wall. But just outside this window, and a bit farther along the building, the distance was much less.

The branches were dark green, full of sap, supple, and dense. There was plenty to grab hold of, as long as the angle of the fall was correct.

From his bed on the floor below, Bryan had watched the bases of these giant shadows dance tantalizingly in front of his eyes every single day. Tiny fragments of a quiet, normal existence, swaying lazily out there behind the windows. Unapproachable and alluring.

And now he finally had a complete picture of them.

Lankau and Kröner were standing between the beds behind Bryan, blocking his path. Kröner was just as calmly expectant as Lankau was quivering with impatience. Jill's scarf decorated Pock Face's neck coquettishly beneath his crooked smile. Kröner stroked the scarf with the back of his hand and grinned diabolically the instant he saw Bryan had noticed it. The malingerers had wrested James's last remnant of security from him. Bryan looked down at James as Red-Eye regarded them with interest from the adjoining bed, the picture of innocence.

James didn't even blink when Bryan gave him an oblique smile.

Then Bryan raised his shirt, bent over, and bared his naked bottom. Both Kröner and Lankau kept laughing until Bryan bent down still farther and blew a long and offensive fart directly in their faces. Pock Face stopped momentarily and backed off slightly, but the roar from Lankau behind him was too much and Kröner burst into laughter again when Bryan glanced over his shoulder with an elfish, naïve expression.

Bryan gave James a last look. It was hard to see if it was acknowledged. James's face was pale. The torment in it made Bryan look away again. Then, pausing a moment, he stepped so close to Kröner that their foreheads met, and belched straight in his face.

The pocked face changed color in a flash. Kröner's momentary confusion left him vulnerable to the blow that hit him squarely on the cheekbone, so he staggered backward in surprise, straight into Lankau's arms. The two malingerers couldn't contain their fury and both of them flew at Bryan without heeding the red-eyed man's protests.

But Bryan had gotten what he was after.

Lankau had scarcely tightened his grip before Bryan began screaming with abandon, loud enough to wake his ancestors from the grave. Everyone in the room became wide-awake witnesses to the three tumbling figures, as well as the guards who came storming in from the hallway like dark shadows and instantly fell upon the brawling men. Both Pock Face and the broad-faced man were out of control. One of the guards tore Bryan away from them as Lankau's blows rained down impotently on the guard.

Suddenly everything was quiet, except for Bryan, who was sitting on the floor, sobbing. Red-Eye had heaved his bell cord, then fallen back against the pillow with a sigh of resignation and irritation upon hearing the shouts of the orderlies, who were already on their way down the hall.

Bryan glanced at James for the last time as he backed out the door, still sobbing, but James had already turned onto his side and withdrawn into the blanket's embrace.

Bryan crossed the corridor in a few quick steps after slamming the door behind him. By the time the nurses reached the swing door from the stairs he'd stopped his whimpering. He was now in the middle room where the mysterious, important patient lay.

The single room was in complete darkness.

Bryan stood stock-still, growing accustomed to the dark. Presumably they'd be giving Kröner and Lankau a sedative now. Under no circumstances would the nursing staff leave James's room for the next five or ten minutes.

He heard the sound of the door to his own room being opened on the other side of the wall. The guards' voices were clear and sounded relieved. They'd already determined that Bryan was back in bed.

That meant Herr Devers, Bryan's unconscious neighbor, hadn't turned over in Bryan's bed. The dose of sleeping pills had been sufficient.

Gradually he discerned the contours of someone staring at him out of the darkness.

The man's lack of expression worried Bryan. Like so much else in the ward, his failure to react didn't make sense. Bryan put his fingers to his lips and squatted beside the bed. The sick man was now breathing quicker and more heavily, as if summoning up a scream. The febrile breathing became deeper and deeper. His lower lip quivered.

Then Bryan pulled the pillow away from the man's elbows and pushed him back in the bed. He didn't even seem surprised when Bryan raised the pillow, placed it over his face and began pressing.

It was like watching their caretaker in Dover take hold of a dove and slowly squeeze the life out of it. The man offered no resistance whatsoever, didn't even squirm. The soft, defenseless body seemed abandoned and so alone.

Thin arms raised a trifle, breaking Bryan's will to continue. He pulled the pillow aside and gazed into the frightened eyes that had just seen death recede.

Feeling just as relieved, Bryan stroked him gently on the cheek and smiled. He received a meek glint in return.

The obligatory dressing gown was hanging on a hook. Bryan put it on over his own, tying the belt tightly around his waist. While it was tempting, he dared not switch on the light to inspect the rest of the room for useful objects.

The window opened the wrong way and blocked his access to the drainpipe. The patient gurgled imperceptibly as Bryan lifted the window off its frame and carefully placed it behind the curtain by the washbasin.

The tumult in the ward had now ceased completely. The staff was no longer shouting. The guards' laughter in the corridor sounded subdued. They'd done their duty.

As far as they knew.

Bryan reckoned he had at least seven or eight hours before his escape would be discovered, if everything in the ward went as usual from now on.

But before he was done thinking this, his body stiffened.

Something inexplicable, practically intuitive, had made him let go of the curtain before stepping onto the windowsill. It may merely have been the sound of a key jingling in a trouser pocket.

Before whoever it was took proper hold of the door handle, Bryan threw himself backward toward the door, twisting his ankle in the process. It started throbbing as he stared around wildly.

A small beam of light danced into the room and across his toes. One of the guards stuck his dark face inside the room less than ten centimeters away. The light coming from behind gave him a satanic halo. The slightest sound or movement and Bryan was finished. The solitary patient still lay in the bed with his head pressed deeply into the pillow, smiling vaguely. The window curtain was flapping a bit. The fresh air seemed treacherously out of place and, to his horror, Bryan saw the beam of light catch the foot of the windowframe behind the curtain. The guard muttered something and gradually opened the door until he was accustomed enough to the dark to see the recumbent shape. Then he stopped. Bryan's ankle was now aching so much that he was about to fall on his side. Perhaps it was the best thing that could happen, that he simply fell. Could he still hope to get away with it? Bryan dismissed the thought and regained his balance. They would find a dressing gown in Devers's bed, and Devers lying in Arno von der Leyen's. Bryan would be wearing two dressing gowns.

It would be hard to explain away.

The *Obergruppenführer* suddenly sat up in bed. He seemed completely attentive. "*Gute Nacht*," he said softly, so well articulated that even Bryan could understand it. "*Gute Nacht!*" the guard replied, shutting the door so quietly that it all seemed quite human.

The evening was damp and the wintry night air already had a bite to it. There wasn't a soul to be seen in the square below. The drainpipe seemed firm, but was smoother than Bryan had counted on.

And his ankle hurt, so his few hoists up to the bay window were harder and more exhausting than he'd expected. It was only a hand's breadth from the roof gutter to the window, but the window was closed. Bryan pushed at it carefully. The steamed-up pane sat loose in its frame but stubbornly refused to give way, wasting time. So he aimed a hard blow at it, and the splintering glass tore a penny-sized gash in his hand. The topmost window latch was far too high. Bryan took a firm hold on the frame and pulled it off. The topmost pane flew out, all in one piece, and smashed to bits on one of the garbage bins ten meters below. To Bryan, the sharp tinkle of shattering glass sounded as if the sky were falling.

But he was the only one who noticed.

In spite of his luck, however, he was now back to square one. The savage irony of fate had sneered at him once more. For even though the window-frame was no longer a problem, he'd have to find another way into the building. A massive piece of furniture had been placed in front of the bay window since he'd viewed it from below, two days ago.

Much too massive.

The prospect of having to climb down again made him begin desperately to investigate the possibilities and pitfalls of the slate roof. It was smooth and shiny and reflected the faint light from the lampposts behind the kitchen area in a series of flickering mirages. Several attic windows in iron frames also appeared in the black surface.

More and more flashes to the north-northwest indicated delayed, muffled explosions. The fighting on the other side of the Rhine had increased greatly during the past hour. Strasbourg appeared to be giving way under Allied pressure.

From the bay window a couple of meters away came the sound of women's voices. Bryan presumed he was just outside the nurses' quarters. Also from the attic window behind him faint noises began indicating that nurses on the early evening shift were retiring to their night quarters. He could be discovered at any moment if just one of the inhabitants wished to air out her room or see where the rumbles and flashes of light were coming from. All it would take was a quick glance along the roof. Despite the cold, Bryan began to sweat so much that his hands gradually lost their grip on the windowframe. He'd have to find another way into the building at once. In a few moments the guards would be coming around the corner.

Hanging there like that, he would not be difficult to spot.

Bryan examined the roof for a second time. Joint by joint, roof tile by roof tile. His hopes were suddenly renewed when an iron frame appeared out of the darkness. It was almost hidden by the roof of the bay window just above him. He'd be able to get inside that window if he could just gain a foothold in the attic's gutter.

The first grasp upward was the worst. The surface was cold as hell and slimy with decaying leaves. Just as Bryan slithered a step backward toward the abyss and was leaning feverishly parallel with the slope of the roof, he heard the menacing bark that always signaled the arrival of the guards and their dogs.

They normally came in pairs, but this time two couples had apparently run into each other and decided to have a chat immediately below Bryan's precarious perch.

The old men mumbled to one another, mechanically reaching to their breast pockets for cigarettes. The cone of light from the lampposts above bore witness to their merriment. Their guns hung heavily on their shoulders as the dogs tugged at their leashes, eager to be off. It wasn't until Bryan nearly lost his grip again and thrust his foot heavily against the side of the bay that the animals sensed something.

Several lumps of slimy leaf mold flew out over the gutter and splattered on the garbage cans. This immediately made two of the dogs bark. The men glanced around in confusion. Then they shook their heads, reluctantly stubbed out their cigarettes, and went their separate ways.

The moment their voices died away Bryan pushed himself up toward the roof. A couple of seconds more and he would have gotten a cramp in his leg.

The attic room had nothing really to offer. Stacks of old beds and disintegrating mattresses had found their final resting place on the dusty planks. Musty wood shavings and rags had created a paradise for scampering mice. Here they could reproduce in peace. Had Bryan not been forced to leave tracks revealing the route by which he'd disappeared, he might have been able to wait up there for several days in case the weather grew milder, making escape less risky.

As things were, he had to be on his way immediately, but first he needed something to put on his feet. Unfortunately no footwear was to be found.

The stairs leading down to the floor below ended at a door. It may have been locked once, but now only dampness and dirt resisted his shove. The room he entered was devoid of activity. The bombardment sounded different here. The entire pitched roof vibrated. The chaotic imminence of destruction felt grim and disheartening.

The corridor outside the room was narrow and stretched through the entire building, with several doors on either side. Bryan stood in the dim light in the middle of the passageway, feeling his entire body break into a cold sweat. Here was a man in a dressing gown in the women's quarters. No one could be in any doubt that he was a patient who'd gone astray.

The attic room he hadn't been able to enter from the roof had to be behind one of the three doors straight in front of him. Sounds coming from inside the door on the right, and the distance between it and the next two doors, told him where the bathroom and lavatories must be. Thus the door in the middle had to be the room above the examination room on the floor below, and the one on the left had to be the door to the attic room.

Behind the lavatory door Bryan heard a chain being pulled and a nose being blown. He disappeared into the attic room just as the woman entered the hallway, taking tiny, weary steps. As she passed the next door she knocked on it and shouted something. Within a second the passage was a confusion of footsteps and scattered talk.

Flashes of light pulsating against the night sky could be seen through the sliver of window space above the massive cupboard. Echoes of truck motors starting up came from down in the yard.

It was more hectic activity than normal for that time of night.

Bryan looked around. Piles of neatly folded linen appeared in the flashes that accompanied each detonation. No shoes. Only linen. Even a shirt or some underwear would have been enough.

But there was nothing there he could use.

Gradually the activity in the hallway slackened off and gave way to the sound of humming chatter inside the rooms. The unidentifiable shadows he saw through the keyhole disappeared. Bryan's chances were now greatly reduced. He could run upstairs again onto the roof in his present getup and try to make it over to the fir trees. It was a long drop. Or he could try to get into one of the rooms on the other side of the corridor without being noticed. Here he might find some clothes, as well as less risky access to the trees. Both possibilities made him shudder. "If you were here, James, you'd know what to do!" he thought.

His stomach was churning.

A thundering inferno of simultaneous crashes made the windowpanes vibrate and voices rise inside the rooms. Several doors on the opposite side of the corridor were thrown open and the girls flew across the passage into the rooms facing west, where there was a clear view. Bryan opened the door without pausing to think and rushed across the passage. Several young nurses were running around farther down. Another series of booms were flung toward the building. No one noticed him disappear into the nearest attic room.

The room was small and dark, the bed recently evacuated. A dark, almost indigo-colored blackout curtain covered the window. Bryan found some of what he was looking for in the cupboard beside the door. A faded shirt, long woolen socks, and some voluminous long underwear. He opened the window without hesitation and threw all the garments toward the nearest fir tree. It was illuminated in flashes, like from fireworks on New Year's Eve. The socks immediately rebounded off the branches and disappeared on the wrong side of the fence.

Before Bryan jumped, the thought struck him that the room's inhabitant might discover the open window behind the closed curtains.

When Bryan flung his arms around the damp branches that whipped against him mercilessly, the sudden impact reopened the wound in his hand. It had been a dreadful jump. Without warning he slid a couple of meters downward while the needles tore silently across his face. For a moment he hung motionless, half-impaled on a number of branches, until he slid farther down in fits and starts and finally fell into thin air.

Despite a blow to the neck, he raised his head from the ground and looked up. Just a meter to one side, and he would have hit a sharp boulder. The underwear and shirt had landed beside him. Just behind him the fence shimmered grayishly. Only faint streaks of light signified any sign of life in the building beyond the fence.

Not a soul was to be seen, apart from inside a window on the third floor where Bryan thought he could make out a silhouette. It was blurred, but familiar.

CHAPTER 27

It was some time before he recovered sufficient strength to put on the stolen articles of clothing. He regretted losing the socks. His feet already burned with the cold. He would be able to increase his pace and get warm again as soon as he got off the rocky ground onto something softer. Although his ankle still felt swollen and sprained, it didn't hurt. In this case the cold helped.

There was plenty of activity in the area.

Trucks were streaming back and forth along the narrow roads heading west from the villages in the hinterland, forcing Bryan to run along the edge of the ditches.

The first part of the way he followed a stream, treacherously dark and cold as inverted hell. It was the only place Bryan felt sure the dogs wouldn't be able to track him.

Knowing this made it worth the suffering.

The air above echoed with the continual commands of soldiers, coming from indeterminate directions. The deep growl of guns could be heard from the north-northwest. The night air had a life of its own.

Several rooftops announced the presence of a village and forced Bryan back toward the mountainside. On a night like this everyone was awake. Every single explosion could mean someone's son, husband, or father wouldn't be coming home.

This was the kind of night where one learned to pray.

A big town lay on the other side of the village, and behind it vineyards stretched right to the Rhine. The idyllic luxuriance of this Rhineland landscape was marred only by its lifeline, a broad concrete road running through the valley.

This was the terrain he was going to have to deal with.

There were a few buildings scattered along the roads leading out of the town. There were restless cattle in their stalls, washing left on the line, shovels ready to dig rows of potatoes. This all bore witness to the fact that life would continue, undaunted, tomorrow and the day after. Then came some new buildings, deserted hovels, dilapidated sheds, and more ditches.

Behind him the impact of cannon fire echoed softly from the Schwarzwald. He had never been so close to ground fighting before. Gun positions entrenched on his side of the Rhine were trying in vain to retaliate. Bryan didn't see a single shell drop in spite of the fact that the entire area seemed like the gaping jaws of adversity and death.

And he'd reached only the outpost of the inferno.

It was on the other side of the river that unreality, the incarnate confrontation with reason and humanity, was spawned.

Finally Bryan reached the road.

Crossing it unseen seemed practically impossible. The road was wet and reflected the narrow slits of car headlights. He would stand out much too clearly on this long, straight stretch of concrete. The danger of being discovered seemed imminent even though the lights alongside the road were not functioning.

Truck after truck was transporting troops and supplies to and from the front. A few hundred meters before him several motorcycle dispatch riders in long coats were trying to slow down the traffic. Behind them an enormous sign had been torn down and lay twisted on the right-hand side of the road. It had indicated the access road from the mountains a few kilometers farther on.

Bryan could see dim lights crossing beneath the main road where the dispatch riders were standing, and he made for the wrecked sign. If vehicles could pass under the motorway, so could he.

Most of the time the viaduct lay in darkness. Only occasionally was it illuminated by overloaded vans and private cars that were evacuating civilians from the villages close to the Rhine. Muffled voices rose from below. Suspecting something might be wrong, he retreated toward the motorway. People in scanty garments were scattered along the smaller road, clutching themselves and shuddering in front of their houses as they watched what was going on.

Confused by the flashes of simultaneous explosions that lit up the sky as if dawn had broken, one of the flatbed-truck drivers overlooked the dispatch riders' request to slow down. The screech of brakes as he caught sight of the twisted road sign at the very last moment sent the dispatch riders diving for the sides of the motorway, shouting so loudly that Bryan could hear the panic in their voices. Just as the driver was over the viaduct his brakes jammed, forcing the truck diagonally along the road. Then, propelled by the inertia of its heavy load, it slid sideways, smashed into the sign, and finally came to a halt against the crash barrier. The trucks behind it were so close that it was completely impossible for the truck to back up. The ensuing jam stopped the traffic for a moment, and with it, the sporadic illumination of the motorway.

Bryan looked toward the south. In a few seconds the temporary halt in the traffic would be over and the entire motorway in front of him would be blocked by moving vehicles. Then he'd be stuck where he was. All was clear to the north at the moment. Elated by his luck, Bryan took advantage of the short traffic jam and hobbled determinedly across the motorway and disappeared on the other side.

In the fraction of a second when he looked back to make sure that neither the villagers nor the dispatch riders had seen him, he thought he saw other shadows that had also crossed the road.

The grapes had long since been harvested. The soil between the vines had been churned up to reveal countless severed branches sticking up treacherously, turning every step into a balancing act if his feet were not to be torn to shreds. Bryan would have given anything for a pair of shoes.

The cold penetrated his body. His toes had ceased to protest. Like his sprained ankle, they had been engulfed in his general state of pain.

On the other side of the river the rattle of small arms could be heard during a brief, unexplainable pause in the bombardment to the north. When this, too, ceased for a moment, Bryan heard rustling in the bushes behind him. He straightened up quickly and used all his senses to scan the half-naked, withering vines. Less than ten rows away he saw the gray, unfamiliar shadows moving again.

So he quickened his pace.

The fields came to an end farther on, where the shadow of a waving windbreak rose up, seemingly impenetrable and infinitely thick. Bryan sensed he was approaching the river. The plopping sounds became more and more audible. The ground beneath him was slippery and he had to fling out his arms to keep his balance. A frightened bird flapped up in front of him, making him stop. He heard a faint sucking sound from behind, like a delayed echo of his groping steps. He turned around and crouched down.

He was not alone.

His pursuer stood less than ten paces away, hands on his hips. Bryan couldn't see the face but recognized the silhouette. His blood ran cold.

It was Lankau.

He had no intention of letting Bryan escape.

The broad-faced man stood silently and made no attempt to approach, although he could have reached Bryan in a few steps. His attitude was respectful, but it was more than that. It was comfortably expectant. Bryan pricked his ears. The undergrowth behind him rustled.

He had never seen anything like it. The vegetation from there to the Rhine was a combination of marsh and jungle. A completely interwoven botanical masterpiece of running water and forest. A perfect place to disappear on a perfect night. This was clearly something his pursuer had counted on.

They sized each other up for some time. It seemed longer than reasonable, considering the seriousness of the situation, until Bryan realized that Lankau had all the time in the world. He glanced over his shoulder once more. Again the undergrowth rustled. Then it dawned on him. Someone else was about to jump him from inside the thicket. Instead of seeking cover, Bryan made off southward along the boundary of the vineyard. Lankau was taken by surprise and had to leap over several rows of vines before he reached the spot Bryan had just left.

The head start Bryan had was suddenly quite sizable. As soon as there was an opening in the undergrowth he dove into the strange scrub, where he sank to the waist in water. Though slippery, the bottom was firm. The question was whether they could cut him off from the other side, and perhaps even more relevant, whether the bottom would continue to bear him. The thought of a long, drawn-out death in the mire made him take an extra time-consuming moment to feel the ground with his toes every time he took a step.

Behind him came the sound of excited voices. So Lankau was indeed not alone. They had lost track of him for the moment and Bryan tried to propel himself forward in the water without making any sudden sounds. He wouldn't be able to endure the coldness of the water much longer. His body would soon be cooled down to the point where his organs would cease to function.

One of the men uttered a hollow, piercing yell from the depths of the undergrowth behind him. So they, too, were now standing in the cold water.

The crack of machine-gun fire that previously had come from in front was no longer clearly audible in the brush. The Germans' light defense was mobile and the dike beside the Rhine was not under direct fire just then.

On a summer's day it would be wonderful there. Birds and flowers and colors everywhere. But right now it was a disaster area.

Bryan dragged himself over a muddy bank where some rotten branches had wedged themselves and set new roots.

Time was beginning to run out. Probably about six or seven hours had passed. It could be three o'clock in the morning, or even four.

Bryan prayed it wasn't five. Then there would only be two hours of darkness left.

A motor vehicle rumbled past, right in front of him, as though it were flying through the air. He was very close to the dike now.

The sounds had changed and were far more distinct than before. To reach the dike, it was two or three hundred meters at the most. Bryan was tense and uneasy as to how he was going to get over the dike to the riverbed, and troubled by the thought of the seething cauldron of troops forced up against the wall on the river's far bank. Summoning all his senses, he cautiously made his way into the last stretch of marsh.

The air around him suddenly darkened in a commotion of flapping wings and shrill bird cries. The stench hit him instantly. It was acrid and rotten. One of the many hundred water birds was unable to fly and began pecking at him. He stood completely still in the pale moonlight and saw the flock rise and gradually assemble again in the treetops. All the birds sat with their beaks pointing upward as if expecting an enemy from above. The treetops were their fortress and the liana-like growths that swayed exotically from the branches were their shields. It was like being in a primeval forest.

Everyone around must have heard the infernal din, yet Bryan noticed nothing irregular in his vicinity. He stood quietly, listening for some time before proceeding. As he took the first step toward the nearest clump of rushes, Dieter Schmidt attacked him head-on out of nowhere. The wiry man reached instantly for Bryan's throat as he tried unsuccessfully to kick him in the groin through the water. His body worked mechanically, without hesitation. They tumbled over, sending the birds soaring into the air again. Bryan rolled onto his side, forcing a muddy piece of broken-off branch into Schmidt's ear. He roared with pain and kicked his feet so violently against the bottom that both men were ejected out of the water at the same time. Furious at having lost his grip, the thin man staggered in front of him, slapping the water with the flat of his hand like a malicious, provocative child as he slowly approached. Bryan glanced desperately over his shoulder. Lankau was nowhere to be seen.

As Schmidt sprang forward again like a rabies-crazed animal, Bryan grabbed a floating branch and lashed out at his face. The man neither cried out nor slowed down as the branch went sideways through his mouth and halfway out his left cheek. Then Bryan jumped to one side to get a firmer foothold and two more rapid steps sideways enabled him to take stock of his position. The skinny man bared his teeth, standing to his knees in water. He stood for a moment, collecting himself. The branch moved in and out of his bulging cheek at every breath, making him look ridiculous in spite of the deadly seriousness of the situation. Like Bryan, his body was covered only by a soaking-wet gray dressing gown. His legs were naked, with no covering of fat, and just as blue black as the water he was standing in. They'd been quick off the mark, he and the broad-faced man. It was hard not to admire their efficiency and determination.

And now Bryan had to break the fanatical willpower that had driven them to this spot with the sole object of killing him.

A shout from Lankau came from not very far away. Bryan's eyes narrowed and he bared his teeth like a cornered animal, causing the thin man to instantly rush forward with outstretched hands. Bryan was no longer afraid. In his sudden leap, Schmidt momentarily lost his foothold in the smooth water, making him lean forward in an attempt to regain his balance. That's when Bryan's precise kick landed on his larynx.

Hardly any gurgles escaped the quivering figure as it fell over backward. Not even as Bryan pressed the man under the water with all his might.

Just as the skinny man was about to lose his hold on life, Lankau appeared out of the thicket, jumping clumsily through the muck with knees held high. The machine guns began ticking again. This time they were quite close. Lankau and Bryan stood face-to-face, silent and determined in the calf-high water.

Lankau was still as a statue. He held a knife in his left hand with its long, ragged edge pointing into the air. Bryan knew those knives. A perfectly ordinary piece of cutlery from the hospital kitchen. How the broad-faced man had managed to get hold of it was puzzling. But how he'd managed to get it sharpened was really a mystery.

It was pointed like an awl.

Lankau stood sizing him up for some time and began speaking to him quietly. It was clear that he had respect for his adversary. But not the kind that would weaken his resolve.

The fight was unavoidable and unequal.

If nothing happened soon, they'd both be frozen stiff. Neither wished to lose the initiative and neither wished to take it. But then an almost inaudible sound from the forest mobilized Bryan's senses. The thin man's body turned at a right angle and lay on its side in the water as his last breath left him. The bubbles were silent and reminded Bryan that the water was his ally. He had the water, the darkness, and the difference in age on his side.

All the other advantages were Lankau's.

A web of remarkable liana vines rustled above Bryan's head. Long, thin roots in the tangled branches. Lifelines searching downward for nourishment and a foothold. Right in front of his face they had twisted into a spongy Gordian knot. The soft ground delayed Bryan's takeoff, but it affected Lankau's forward leap as well.

Bryan was above his assailant in only three grasps up the vine, ready to fall on him. Lankau's neck made a cracking sound as Bryan's full weight crashed into the man's raised head. Lankau's entire body collapsed like a rag doll. Bryan felt no resistance. Only passive, soft flesh that slid under the water and remained there.

The fight was over before it had begun. Bryan took a couple of steps backward and let himself tumble heavily onto the slope as he watched the eddies of water gradually subside above Lankau's body. The surrounding landscape was slowly taking on more detail. It was scarcely an hour till sunrise. His mind went blank for a couple of seconds. When he began wondering why there were no more bubbles rising from Lankau's body, it was too late.

The broad-faced man had already opened his eyes before he popped up to the surface. His eyelashes were muddied and the expression on the mask-like face was maniacal.

The knife was still in his hand and his grip was firm. Bryan was on his feet before Lankau managed to complete his deadly mission.

In a weary reflex Bryan struck out with his left arm and received a deep and painful cut from Lankau's knife. With the knife buried to the handle just above the elbow, Bryan withdrew his arm so violently that Lankau stumbled forward. It was the broad-faced man's own massive weight that did the work when Bryan stuck his fingers in his eyes.

The scream of pain came instantly. Lankau fell backward onto the bank, pressing his hands to his face. He lay defenseless in the mud, kicking his legs and howling, half-covered by the filthy, churned-up water. A burst of machine-gun fire came from quite close by. Bryan made his way up the embankment without looking back, leaving his enemy to his fate.

Not until he'd passed the last windbreak before the dike did he throw himself to his knees, exhausted. He drew the knife out cautiously. The wound beside his elbow wasn't bleeding as much as he'd feared. It had been a clean and lucky stab.

For lack of anything better he tore some strips off his outer dressing gown for a temporary bandage. It was damned cold. So cold that the perilous waters flowing past him didn't seem so forbidding. He simply couldn't be any colder than he was. And yet the view that met him on the edge of the dike was both frightful and baffling.

Farther down the bank of the dike an armored vehicle was approaching. Several barrier gates were standing open alongside the wheel tracks, allowing free passage for the convoys heading northward with their supplies.

Bryan pressed himself flat to the ground. He had to get away. There was no cover on the dike. On the other side of the waterway he could just make out the dark shoreline that stretched a few hundred meters to the north, whereupon it disappeared into a wider body of water. So he was lying by a long shoal, covered with vegetation, which divided the Rhine in two.

This lucky coincidence meant Bryan could take on the current in two rounds. A short pause on the shoal would allow him to catch his breath. By the time the truck's headlights lit up the piles of peat a few meters from him, he'd already rolled the rest of the way down into the water that was to lead him back to life.

Bryan had been mistaken. The water was colder than death. So cold that his dressing gown was an advantage, despite its weight and resistance. His body was nearing a critical state of hypothermia. Bryan knew the danger signals. He'd seen severely chilled paratroopers plop defenselessly to the ground, unable to brace themselves for the impact. That kind of cold came stealthily and relentlessly, regardless of the will to live.

The organism simply came to a halt.

And then there was the current. Though impossible, it felt as if the melted-ice-water season was in full swing. Since he could do little else, Bryan let himself drift with the current. He saw the shoal glide backward past him and disappear.

The Rhine was broad here. Bryan couldn't tell how wide, since he was lying so low in the water, but at least wide enough to make it impossible for his alternately floating, swimming figure to be spotted from either shore in the semidarkness. Unless he was caught in the beams of light that swept over the river from time to time.

Two dead bodies popped up, seemingly out of nowhere, and lay still in the middle of the river. Bloated as they were, they must have been in the water for some time. One soldier's face was already splitting open in spite of the cold. The other corpse lay so low in the water that Bryan could scarcely see it.

The exchange of fire on the western bank was now almost constant. Bryan held on to the second body as he tried to determine whether there were any signs of life on the shore. His body temperature was so low that he would have to make for the shore within a few minutes, whatever the cost. The first bridge rose a few hundred meters in front of him. Faint lights farther northward indicated another high bridge. Between them the engineer corps could have handily laid out a number of pontoon bridges. The need for lifelines over the river was considerable that night.

Flashes from mortar shelling came almost without pause and the din made the air quiver. Occasionally Bryan heard screams.

The dead soldier rolled onto his back, pitching gently as Bryan let go of him. Only then did Bryan see why he hadn't floated farther downriver. Thin, parallel, vertical stripes slowly appeared out of the darkness of the water, tracing a pattern. The corpse had been caught in a grating. It may have been a coincidence, but in that spot it seemed as if the grating ran lengthwise along the entire river, dividing it in two. As the day grew lighter, more and more tiny ripples appeared on the surface around snagged branches and rubbish.

The grating meant he would be visible from the shore during the brief moment it would take to crawl over it. The eastern shore was calm, but the western shore could easily be harboring his assassin. Bryan had only his sight to rely on. No human sounds would be able to penetrate the cacophony of artillery fire.

Bryan took firm hold of the barrier on the far side of the eroded spikes and plopped down backward on the redeeming side. Breathing heavily, he clung to the grating and inspected the shore.

He would attempt to reach land precisely at that spot. Clumps of trees were waving in the breeze. The vegetation seemed dense and protective. There he would try to get warm before proceeding farther.

Only an animal would have sensed the danger. Bryan was as unprepared for the iron grip on his arm as an old man struck with a sudden heart attack.

The feeling that something had risen from the dead in order to take possession of him was nothing compared with what Bryan felt when he looked into Lankau's half-obliterated, bestial face. Bryan could only utter a choked scream. The grip on his neck drew him down until the water closed over him. So this was where he was to end his life. His adversary willed it so.

In a last feeble, stubborn attempt, Bryan found his footing on the grating's crossbar and pushed. Lankau had no intention of letting go and bellowed with pain when his underarm got stuck in the mesh that separated them. It was Bryan's salvation.

The shots from the shore came from behind and made the broad-faced man roar even louder. Then he grew silent and relaxed his grip. Finally he let go. He looked quite mortal and vulnerable as he clung to the spikes, watching Bryan swim toward land. The burst of gunfire ceased as suddenly as it had begun.

The German soldiers on the shore had other things to do.

Still some way from shore, Bryan had to give up. His limbs could function no longer. The current in the shallow water was not strong enough to keep him afloat. Bryan had to let his legs drop, even though the shore of salvation was right in front of him. Another couple of eddies of the current swept him around in the water. And then he sank.

Bryan later recalled that he'd begun to laugh. Then, just before the water engulfed him, his feet touched bottom.

His final wading steps ashore were accompanied by the cool embrace of daylight. Now the rattle of small arms was coming from the south. Despite the sporadic density of the vegetation, the shore bore witness to the fact that the night's skirmishes had taken their toll. Bryan shuddered when he saw the uniform.

The countryside was flat. The American soldier had been taken unawares by the sudden clearing in the thicket. He still looked surprised. Bryan lay down next to the corpse and rubbed his frostbitten blue fingers.

The soldier's clothing would provide his body with some encouraging warmth.

Bryan looked around. The shoal in the middle of the river lay far behind, with several barges decorating its point. Another barge was tethered a bit farther up the river's western shore. It was heavily loaded with manure. The stench reached all the way down to him, reminding him of tranquil days gone by. Then explosions to the north brought him back to reality.

Lankau's broad face was just a speck out in the river.

CHAPTER 28

Can you tell me about this *Obergruppenführer* again? Was he being guarded? Was he locked up? Was he insane? Do you know anything for sure?" The intelligence officer named Wilkens had bright-yellow fingertips. He lit yet another cigarette. Presumably his colleagues had warned him. Bryan Underwood Scott Young was not particularly communicative.

Bryan wrinkled his nose as the smoke reached his nostrils. "I don't know, sir! I think he was mad. But I don't know. I'm not a doctor."

"You spent over ten months in that hospital. You must have formed an opinion as to who was ill and who was not."

"Do you really think so?" Bryan closed his eyes again. He was tired. Captain Wilkens had asked him the same questions over and over again. He was seeking simple explanations. Again he inhaled deeply and studied Bryan a long while before exhaling. With the cigarette stuck between the base of his fingers, he suddenly raised his hand and waved it abruptly at Bryan as if to draw some kind of response. The ash landed on the edge of Bryan's bed. "I've stated several times that the general was insane! I think he was, in any case." Bryan looked down at the floor and continued tone-lessly. "Yes, I'm convinced he was."

"How's it going here?" The army surgeon had entered the room without anyone noticing. "We must be making progress, Mr. Young." Bryan shrugged his shoulders. Wilkens leaned back in his chair. His irritation at being interrupted was well concealed.

"I don't like having to talk. My tongue still feels wrong."

"Not so strange, is it?" The army surgeon smiled and nodded at the captain, who was already gathering up his notes.

Bryan laid his head back on the pillow. Since the American infantrymen had picked him up nearly three weeks earlier he'd had enough of his native tongue. He had been questioned for an eternity. The many months in linguistic isolation had made him overly sensitive to questions. The answers seemed of no consequence.

Even though the doctors had assured him repeatedly that he would suffer no permanent harm from his stay in the mental hospital, he knew it couldn't be true. Perhaps the scars on his body would diminish, perhaps his incomprehensible moodiness would gradually fade away and his brain tissue be restored after the shock treatment. Maybe his constant fear of losing his life would release its nightmarish grip on him. But the real wound, the feeling of having let someone down, became deeper every day. They couldn't heal that, nor did they even try.

The nights were long.

Even when he was still in the American field hospital in Strasbourg there were reports that the center of Freiburg had been reduced to rubble. "In less than twenty minutes," it was proudly stated. Since then, James had been on his mind day and night.

He and James had been listed as missing ever since they were shot down. For months their families had been inconsolable. His most difficult task would be having to look the Teasdales in the face. They would never see their son again. Bryan felt sure of it. Everything else seemed uncertain.

"Wait and see. Your tongue won't give you any more problems. It's just a matter of training. But it would probably go a bit quicker if you spoke a little more during these sessions. You must force yourself to talk, Mr. Young. It's the only thing that will help." Snow flurries had given way to rain and the fogged-up windows made it impossible for the doctor to see out. He often stood with his back to Bryan, wiping off the windowpane as he spoke.

"You have been recommended for a medal for bravery. I hear you intend to refuse it. Is that so?"

"Yes."

"Is it that story about your friend that still haunts you?"

"Yes."

"Don't you realize you'll have to cooperate with the intelligence officers if you expect to have a chance of seeing your friend again?"

Bryan frowned.

"All right, then. But I have decided to keep you at the hospital a while longer. Your body wounds will probably be healed within a couple of weeks. I'm convinced the tendons in your arm aren't so badly damaged after all.

All in all, your wounds are healing very well." The surgeon general's somewhat superficial smile made his bushy eyebrows meet. "But your mind has to have a chance to keep pace with it, am I right?"

"Then send me home."

"But if we did that, we wouldn't get answers to our questions, would we, Mr. Young? Besides, it's pretty early yet, wouldn't you say?"

"Maybe . . ." Bryan looked toward the window. The panes were misted up again. "But I haven't any more to say. I've told you everything I know."

A tall young girl turned away from the bed opposite, where her badly wounded brother lay. An ordinary Welsh girl with thick hair tied in a bun in the back. She inspired confidence and calm. Her smile reflected optimism.

A few days after New Year they began to indicate that Bryan would soon be sent home. Christmas had been lonely. The desire to recover in the company of his loved ones had become urgent.

The Welsh girl was the only person he would miss.

The questioning ceased two weeks into the New Year. Bryan was allowed to get out of bed. He had nothing more to tell them.

Intelligence Officer Wilkens's final visit was on a Tuesday. The previous evening he had told Bryan he could expect to be discharged at 1200 hours the following day, January 16, 1945, and that he would be expected to report to base in Gravely at 1400 hours on the second of February. The remaining instructions would be sent direct from Castle Hill House to his home in Canterbury.

Bryan answered the questions mechanically. The thought of having to fly again didn't appeal to him at all. He doubted whether he could.

"We want to make sure of the hospital's position just once more, Mr. Young."

"Why? I've told you at least ten times." Bryan looked around. The officer was puffing on a stub of cigarette so close to his fingernails that Bryan turned his back on him, feeling nauseated, and stepped out into the corridor. Here there was plenty of activity. It was hard to say where there were more patients, in the rooms or in the corridors. A broad staircase led directly to the floor below, where there was yet another row of beds, packed so close together that it was almost impossible to tell one from the other.

"Why do we want to know this, Mr. Young?" Wilkens followed behind Bryan. "Because we'd like to feel completely certain that we've wiped out that viper's nest!"

"What's that supposed to mean?" Bryan spun around and was caught by the cold eyes that met him.

"By that I mean, yesterday Freiburg im Breisgau was bombed by 107 B-17s. They dropped 269 tons of bombs, which doesn't mean a thing to me, but apparently it's a lot. And while we're at it, Mr. Young, I can also tell you that a couple of these tons were earmarked for your old hospital. So I don't think we need be afraid of that loony bin hatching any more pigs for front-line slaughter, do we?"

Later, even Bryan himself couldn't say whether or not it had been deliberate. All the young Welsh girl could relate was that Bryan had simply fallen backward down the stairs at that precise moment. The doctors thought he'd broken a bone for every stair he hit.

In his dossier it was reported to have been an accident.

PART II

PART II

PROLOGUE 1972

The traffic had been streaming westward for over half an hour. Down in the utility room the radio was already at full blast and the maid was having a hard time humming in tune. For the past hour the room had been baking hot. The sun was merciless that summer.

She studied herself in the mirror once more.

The morning had been full of ups and downs. For some time her husband had been regarding her with the kind of wistfulness that some psychologists thought might be the beginning of a midlife crisis. But she knew better. Mirrors didn't lie. She was looking older.

Carefully she stretched the corner of her mouth outward with her fingertip. The skin was supple, but the effect insufficient. Once again she moistened her lips and tilted her head.

Time had passed. It was simple as that.

She had gotten up alone that morning. The figure in the bed behind her had lain there, staring into the corners of the room for a long time. She knew those moods and the periods with sleepless nights and recurring nightmares.

And it had been another long night.

He didn't come down until after breakfast. He stood there for a moment, as if deliberating. The gentle eyes were confused, not yet awake. His smile came quietly and apologetically. "I have to go now," he said.

For a while the drawing room felt much too big.

When the telephone rang she took it reluctantly. "Laureen speaking," she said, fingering her neck as if she were standing face-to-face with her sister-in-law.

Her hair sat tight and immaculate.

CHAPTER 29

No, I can't say when Mr. Scott will be here. Yes, that's correct, he's usually here before ten." The secretary replaced the receiver and smiled apologetically at the two men who had been sitting there, staring patiently into space since 9:29. Now they began looking at their watches. Rolex, the secretary noted as she glanced at the younger man's wide trouser legs. Quite the dandy, she thought.

A tiny red lamp finally flashed on the intercom in front of her.

"Mr. Scott is ready to receive you now." Her boss had parked in the basement beside Kennington Road and chosen to walk up the back stairs. There must have been a traffic jam on Brook Drive again.

Mr. Scott's guests were given an extremely formal welcome. He didn't know them and hadn't asked them to come. It was a busy week, as usual. Naturally the work burden reflected his company's success, but it was also making him pretty fed up. He hadn't slept enough all week.

"You must excuse me, gentlemen, but the traffic on the M2 is just crazy today."

"You drive in from the east," the older man said, smiling, "so perhaps you're still living in Canterbury?"

Mr. Scott looked questioningly at his visitor and screwed up his eyes. He glanced at his desk calendar again and studied the names: Managing Director Clarence W. Lester and Junior Partner W. W. Lester, Wyscombe & Lester & Sons, Coventry. "That's right, I do, in fact. I've never lived anywhere else." The smile made his eyes close still further. Many people found the deep wrinkles around his eyes attractive. "Perhaps we've met before, Mr. Lester?"

"Oh, yes. Indeed. Though it was many years ago and under quite different circumstances."

Mr. Scott raised a finger. "But you're not from Canterbury yourself, I can hear. May I guess? Wolverhampton?"

"You're very close. I was born in Shrewsbury and spent my younger days in Sheffield."

"And now you're in Coventry, I see," he said, after another peek at his desk calendar. "Have we done business before, Mr. Lester?"

"No, we haven't. That is to say, sooner or later all English pharmaceutical companies run into difficulties with one of your licenses. But no, we haven't had the pleasure of meeting one another on business terms before now."

"Rotary? Sports federation? Eton? Cambridge?"

The younger of the two men straightened his attaché case and smiled. Mr. Lester shook his head. "Well, we're not here to talk about old times, Mr. Scott, so I think I'd better raise the veil. I know you're a busy man. You see, we met each other long ago. True enough, it was under different names then. Naturally that confuses the issue."

"I see. Yes, it's true I've changed my name. My mother and stepfather were divorced. I don't think about it anymore. My name was Young then. Bryan Underwood Scott Young, and now it's just plain Scott. What about you?"

"Lester is my wife's name. She thought my own name sounded provincial. But I took revenge on her by keeping my family name as a middle name. Wilkens, sir."

Bryan took his time studying the elderly gentleman. Even though Bryan's own features had become chiseled in the course of time, he nevertheless imagined himself more or less imperishable. On the other hand it was difficult to recognize the stern Captain Wilkens's sharp features in this round, almost bald head.

"I'm older than you, Mr. Scott." He smoothed back his few gray hairs and nodded. "But you're in remarkably good shape. You got over your nasty fall, I see."

"Yes, I did." In time Bryan Underwood Scott had become known as a block of ice who always seemed self-assured, never took his eyes off an opponent, and always settled disagreements with well-founded rebuttals. Historical consideration and appeals to friendship were unknown concepts.

After qualifying as a doctor he had set himself up as a specialist in gastric disorders, and in recent years had steadily cut down on both his research and his work as a sports doctor as he became more and more a businessman. His inveterate determination and lack of sentimentality had had its price. But never financially. At the time of his mother's death four years ago he already had so much money that the six million pounds she'd left to be divided between him and his brothers and sisters hardly made a difference.

The key word was licenses. The right to produce pharmaceuticals, surgical instruments, components for scanners, and spare parts for Japanese and American monitors. All in the service of health. A seemingly limitless field where financial resources apparently were not subjected to the usual British moderation.

Many uncomfortable business situations had arisen during this period, but nothing could compare with his total unpreparedness as he once again sat face-to-face with Captain Wilkens. A man for whom he'd had no reason to harbor warm feelings.

"Of course I remember you, Captain Wilkens."

"Other circumstances. Other times." Clarence W. Lester folded his arms across his chest and leaned back in the conference chair. "It was a hard time for all of us." He raised his eyebrows. "Did you ever find out what had happened to your mate, Mr. Scott?"

"No."

"And I suppose you've exhausted all possibilities?"

Bryan nodded and looked toward the door. The Teasdale case had been shelved even before the Germans capitulated. Not until eight months later did Intelligence reluctantly admit that the Gestapo archives were in the possession of the Russians, and that the fate of SS officer Gerhart Peuckert would therefore remain unknown. Bryan could do nothing. James Teasdale was merely one of many. Not even his father's political influence and numerous contacts had brought anything new to light. Since then, Bryan had tried in vain to buy information. Gradually his bad conscience had lost intensity. And now twenty-eight years had elapsed.

Wilkens attempted a look of commiseration.

It was only a few steps to the door. Bryan deliberated as to whether he should take those steps and slam the door behind him. The feeling of nausea that had come over him was overwhelming. The nightmares had returned.

"I told my son this very morning what an effort you made to obtain information about your friend. Have you been in Germany since?"

"No, I haven't."

"That's remarkable, considering your business, Mr. Scott." Bryan didn't react. "I say, I hope you're not annoyed by my digging up the past." Wilkens seemed as if he already knew the answer, but he was mistaken. The meeting was over before the grandfather clock in the reception room had struck the half hour. The two of them had wanted permission to produce generic drugs on Bryan's license. They didn't get it. Only a few insignificant promises were made. A single order had been sent to be evaluated by Ken Fowles, Mr. Scott's assistant. The father and son appeared crestfallen.

They had been expecting more.

By now, smoking a filterless Pall Mall was a rare event for Bryan.

Despite the heat he turned up the collar of his cotton coat. Leaning against the wall, he looked over at the newsstand. The stream of people from Elephant & Castle Station was increasing steadily. Lunch hour was over.

"I won't be coming back today, Mrs. Shuster," he'd told his secretary.

This was unusual. Already now Laureen would be suspecting something was wrong. Even though his wife had never shown any particular interest in his changing moods and impulses, she had an inexplicable ability to sense when problems threatened to intrude on the safety of their home turf. And Mrs. Shuster wasn't the type who could hide her surprise when Laureen acted on her intuition and phoned the office. Bryan's wife was a woman of many talents, which is why she could take credit for a major part of Bryan's success. Without her, he would have drowned in moral qualms and self-pity.

She was a fairly ordinary, average girl from Wales who had smiled at him once and had continued to do so, even though he hadn't smiled in return.

She'd taken special care of him after his fall down the stairs at the British field hospital. The girl's name was Laureen Moore. Her hair was thick and gathered in a bun at the neck. For a long time he'd wondered what was inside it. Sometimes he thought it was a small ball of curly wool. Other times, a scrap of electric cable.

The war had taken eight members of her close family. One brother died in her arms at the hospital while Bryan was looking on. Cousins, two brothers, an uncle, and then her father. Sadness still crept into her voice when she spoke of him. She was familiar with grief and left Bryan in peace with his. An important part of her was the realization that life had to be lived and the past respected.

Bryan loved her for this and much else.

But the price had been that Bryan was left alone with his past, his nightmares, his experiences, and his grief. They never visited the Teasdales. Though they lived only a few streets away, Bryan never spoke of the Teasdale family and its fate. Thus Laureen's innermost thoughts and feelings remained her own, just as Bryan's did.

But when it came to the outside world, she was extremely capable of organizing it for them both.

"Why do you worry about rich people's diarrhea and intestinal disorders if it doesn't interest you, Bryan?" she'd said years ago, thus initiating a new epoch in their lives. "They're always bound to hate you for depriving them of their expensive chocolate, cigars, and whisky-and-sodas," she'd said simply, accepting with a laugh that they might have to live modestly from then on. Less than a week later Bryan had put his practice up for sale.

At first he couldn't make a living from his research, but Laureen never complained. Perhaps the knowledge that Bryan's mother would be able to support them if necessary had been in the back of her mind. But without Laureen, the future would have been another.

And when success finally came, it really came.

"Oh, Dad!" his daughter had groaned when he finally established himself in London. "An office in Lambeth? It's not exactly a district where people just drop by. Why not Tudor Street or Chancery Lane?" Ann was a charming, straightforward girl, whose great interest in athletics—and especially its long-limbed exponents of the opposite sex—had in some inscrutable way come to mean that for some years, along with his research and his business, he also applied his expertise in the service of sport.

Diets and the treatment of acute gastric trouble were his domain. When problems originated in the abdominal region, sports people went to him and not to their sports federation or Harley Street specialists.

A good life, all in all.

Bryan lit another Pall Mall and recalled Wilkens's yellow fingers during the interrogations. He had not been a smoker himself in those days. He took a deep puff. Wilkens's arrival on precisely that day had been quite an extraordinary coincidence.

He allowed himself confrontations with the past only a few times a year, at most. He was still feeling the effects of the previous night's nightmare. Even though the dreams were always different, the essence was always the same: He had failed James! The shame followed him around for days afterward. If he were at work, he usually walked the few hundred meters from the office over to the Imperial War Museum and drowned himself in its impressions. Here he found a colossal accumulation of misery and hardship that made personal sorrows seen unforgivably small. Centuries of blunders and thousands of years of spilled blood were symbolized by the monumental boasting of these buildings.

But this time he didn't feel like going.

Delegates from the National Olympic Committee had phoned him at home in Canterbury the previous evening and asked if he would act as consultant for the medical team at the Games in Munich.

This was what had prompted the nightmare. For years he had turned down all invitations that involved traveling to Germany. He had pushed aside everything that might dig up old, unhappy episodes. All his investigations had arrived at the same conclusion: It was pointless. James was dead.

Why continue to torture himself?

And then came this invitation, the nightmare, and Wilkens's visit—all within hours of one another. The committee had given him eight days to think it over. There was just about a month until the Games opened. He'd had more time to think it over four years previously, when he'd been asked to join the group as consultant for acute gastric infections at the Mexico Olympics.

Harper Road, Great Suffolk Street, The Cut. Everywhere the city was a whirlwind of activity, teeming with life.

Bryan noticed none of it.

. . .

"Bryan, are you telling me you've been shuffling around in this weather in that getup, in Southwark besides, because you had to make up your mind whether or not to go to Munich? What for? You could have done that at home." Laureen's teacup was about to overflow. "You know I'd try to persuade you not to go. But I guess you can't get out of it, can you?"

"I guess not."

"I've had enough of that kind of nonsense since Mexico."

"Nonsense?" He looked at her. She'd been to the hairdresser's.

"Too hot, too many people. That idiotic schedule!" She noticed how he was looking at her. Bryan looked away again.

"It's not hot in Germany."

"No, Bryan, but on the other hand there's so much else. It's so German!" Laureen's tea was spilling into the saucer.

They had always shared a reluctance to travel. Laureen because she was afraid of the unknown, and Bryan because he feared being reminded of the all-too-well-known. So if they finally did travel, it was usually in isolated, English-speaking business environments.

If Laureen couldn't prevent Bryan from traveling, she usually arranged to go with him and get it over with as quickly as possible, in a well-organized manner. That's how it had been with many of Bryan's business trips, and that's how it was to be this time.

The next day she produced their itinerary and tickets with her customary lack of enthusiasm. Her surprise was minimal when Bryan told her he'd decided to turn down the National Olympic Committee's invitation after all. He didn't want to go to Munich.

His sleep that night was more troubled than it had been for years.

CHAPTER 30

The next morning Laureen was already in full swing.

Ecstatic about having got out of the trip, she rushed around the house doing measurements for new curtains for their silver wedding anniversary in the fall. Bryan had already slipped away to the office. A couple of hours later they contacted him again. He gesticulated toward Mrs. Shuster, who immediately got up and silently shut his office door. It was unusual for the committee to inquire more than once.

"I'm sorry, but at the moment we are in the midst of a Europe-wide launch of a new fast-acting painkiller for gastric ulcers. I have to help draw up our sales strategy and select who we'll be working with."

That's how the conversation ended. Basically what he said was correct. He was in fact busy planning a new sales drive and needed new agents. But Bryan had never had anything to do with the interviewing of new salesmen or distributors.

In this case, however, he felt obliged to make an exception, simply to convert the white lie into truth.

Ken Fowles, who was responsible for logistics, had selected only ten out of fifty potential distributors for an interview. This would be boiled down to four, each covering a specific geographical area.

In Bryan's eyes all the prospective distributors were equally good, and only rarely did he say anything during the interviews.

Even though courtesy demanded Fowles ask his boss for his comments, there was no doubt it was he who would make the final decisions.

On the second day an applicant by the name of Keith Welles turned up. A cheerful, slightly sickly man who, despite the seriousness of the situation, allowed himself to take the interview with a sense of humor. He'd waited most of the day and was the very last interviewee. It was clear that the ruddy-faced man would not be Ken Fowles's choice. His prospective territory—Scandinavia, Germany, Austria, and Holland—was far too important a market to be placed in the hands of anyone Fowles was not on the same wavelength with.

"And what went so wrong with your previous sales district?" Bryan asked, before his assistant could.

Welles looked Bryan straight in the face. He seemed to have expected the question, though not from that quarter. "There were many reasons. When you're a foreigner residing in Hamburg, your products need to be better than anyone else's. If not, the Germans prefer to deal with a foreigner living in Bonn, or better still, with a German residing abroad. That's just how the system works."

"And your products were no better than all the others?"

"Better?" He shrugged and looked away. "They were like most products. My field has been too limited the last couple of years to accommodate great new discoveries and miracles."

"Psychotropic drugs?"

"Yes. Neuroleptic." Welles's wry smile made Ken Fowles shift impatiently in his chair. "And fashions change. Those types of chlorpromazine drugs are not exactly alpha and omega in the treatment of psychoses anymore. I was caught napping. In the end my stock was too large, my outstanding accounts even bigger, and chances of selling the product extremely slim."

Bryan remembered the drug when Welles named it. He knew many names for it, like Largactil and Prozil. But their common ingredient was in fact chlorpromazine. Several of the guinea-pig patients in the Alphabet House had faded away before his eyes under the influence of a medication that was very similar. Even though he'd managed to avoid taking it during most of the ten months he spent at the SS hospital, the aftereffects of this drug's precursor had nevertheless become part of Bryan's everyday self for many years afterward. The very thought of it could still make him sweat, become dry in the mouth, and feel restless.

"You're Canadian, Mr. Welles?" he finally managed to ask.

"Fraserville, beside the St. Lawrence River. German mother, English father, French-speaking population."

"A good starting point for a career in Europe. And yet you don't cover France. Why not?"

"Too difficult! My wife would like to see me from time to time, Mr. Scott. She's wiser than I am."

"And she's the reason you landed in Hamburg rather than Bonn?"

Fowles kept glancing at his watch. He tried to smile. Welles's story was completely irrelevant to the case at hand.

"I took part in the 1943 Salerno Bay landings in Italy under McCreery's 10th British Army. As a trained pharmacist I was an obvious choice for the medical corps. I was with them the whole way and wound up in Germany."

"And there she stood, waiting at the border." Fowles smiled until Bryan stopped him with a glance.

"Certainly not. We met for the first time a year after the capitulation. I was attached to the reconstruction program." Bryan let him speak. With this account, a number of previously unconsidered angles had presented themselves.

Welles had been enlisted in Dempsey's 2nd British Army when they liberated the Bergen-Belsen concentration camp. He had been promoted twice and at the hearings preceding the Nuremberg trials had occasionally testified about the Nazis' concentration-camp medical experiments. Finally he had been assigned the task of inspecting the Nazi hospitals as part of a team of experts set up by British Intelligence.

There had been hundreds of field hospitals spread all over the country. The great majority were deserted, their purpose no longer relevant. A few had been converted into local hospitals and private clinics. And then there were places like the mental hospital in Hadamar, where they'd found patients in mass graves. The disfigured, the crippled, the hideous, and the insane.

It had been a harrowing time for the inspection team, even in the case of ordinary patients with body wounds. The consequences of the Nazi view of human nature also applied to their own ranks. During the last months of the war it was not unusual for the food to be so lacking in fat that the patients suffered irreparable damage to their nervous systems. Of the hospitals they visited, only a few in southern Germany and Berlin itself were what could be described as acceptable. Otherwise conditions had been completely miserable.

After some months on the job Welles felt emotionally drained. In the end he no longer cared where he was, whom he was with, or what he drank. He stopped thinking of going home.

The notion of a mother country no longer held any meaning for him.

Welles's final stationing was in connection with the hospital at Bad Kreuznach, where he met a young nurse with an incredible zest for life and a wonderful laugh that made him wake up. Bryan could remember having had a similar experience.

They'd fallen in love and after a couple of years had moved to Hamburg, where his wife's family lived, and where people didn't give her quite as strange looks because she'd married someone attached to the occupation forces.

Welles built up a firm in Hamburg that prospered for a number of years. They now had three children. All in all he was satisfied.

His account made a great impression on Bryan.

Later in the evening Fowles gave Bryan a list of the agents he had selected. Welles's name was not among them. He had been assessed and found wanting. Too old, too jovial, too Canadian, and he snuffled when he spoke.

Bryan was simply supposed to sign Fowles's rejection.

The letter lay on Bryan's desk all evening and all night. It was also the first thing he saw the following morning.

Nobody could have detected the slightest disappointment or surprise in Welles's voice when Bryan phoned him. "It'll all work out, don't you think, Mr. Scott?" he said. "But I'm thankful you found time to tell me yourself."

"Naturally we'll refund your travel expenses, Mr. Welles, but I may be able to help you just the same. How much longer will you be at your hotel?"

"I'm leaving for the airport in two hours' time."

"Can we meet before you leave?"

The standard of the boardinghouse in Bayswater was far lower than what Bryan considered suitable for his own employees. Although the fashionable avenue had more hotels than the city had banks, Keith Welles had succeeded in finding the crummiest of them all. The stairs themselves left no doubt that this humble dwelling's days of glory were ancient history.

Welles had already poured himself a drink when Bryan arrived. Feeling himself unobserved, disappointment was written all over his face. Not until Bryan spoke did he assume his cheerful mask. Much too relaxed, much too harmonious.

He was clumsy and unshaven, but Bryan liked him and needed him.

"I've found you a job, Mr. Welles. Insofar as you and your family are still able to move to Bonn, the job is yours from the middle of next month. You are to function as an English-speaking pharmacist in the management of one of our subcontractors' subsuppliers. You are precisely the man the company has been looking for. The job includes a staff house near the Rhine, a couple of kilometers out of town. Suitable salary and pension. Wasn't that what you were looking for?"

Welles knew the company. He was clearly confused and astonished, without realizing he'd dropped his mask. He wasn't used to coming by things so easily.

"You can do something for me in return, Mr. Welles."

"As long as it isn't illegal or involves my having to sing," he said, attempting to sound cheerful as he knitted his brow.

"When you were talking about your inspection of the German hospitals after the war, you mentioned you'd been visiting mental hospitals, and that you'd also been on a tour of inspection in southern Germany. Isn't that so?"

"Yes, on several occasions."

"Also in the vicinity of Freiburg?"

"Freiburg im Breisgau? Yes, I was all over Baden Württemberg."

"I am especially interested in knowing something about a sanitarium—a hospital, rather—near a small town called Herbolzheim, north of Freiburg on the outskirts of the Schwarzwald. The hospital was solely for SS soldiers. There was also a psychiatric ward. Does that mean anything to you?"

"There are many sanitariums in Freiburg. There were then, too."

"Yes, but north of Freiburg. It was a big one. Up in the mountains. A whole hospital with at least ten large buildings."

"You don't know what it was called?"

"Some called it the Alphabet House, that's all I know. Only SS soldiers were admitted."

"I'm afraid I'll have to disappoint you, Mr. Scott. Scores of reserve hospitals were built during the war. It's also many years ago. Sometimes I inspected several hospitals and clinics during the course of one day. It's probably too long ago. I just can't remember much from that time anymore."

"But you could try just the same, couldn't you?" Bryan leaned forward, looking him straight in the eyes. The look that met him was alert and intelligent. "You go back to Germany, talk to your family, and spend a couple of days sorting out your affairs. Then you go to Freiburg and investigate some things for me for a couple of weeks, if it proves necessary. You'll have time before you begin your new job. In the meantime I'll pay all your expenses generously." Bryan nodded. "That's how you can repay me."

"What am I supposed to be looking for? Am I simply to find that hospital you just mentioned?"

"No, the hospital was destroyed at the beginning of 1945. I'm looking for a man I met there."

"At the hospital?"

"That's right. The same hospital that I was in, though I managed to escape on November 23, 1944. I'll explain the circumstances later. But this man remained at the hospital and I lost track of him. I'd like to know what happened. He was admitted under the name of Gerhart Peuckert. During the next couple of days I'll supply you with all the information you'll need, such as rank, appearance, and other particulars."

"Do you know if he's still alive?"

"I assume he's dead. He was probably at the hospital when we bombed it."

"And the usual intelligence sources and archives? Have all the possibilities been investigated?"

"You can be damned sure they have! No stone unturned."

Even though Bryan didn't tell him more than necessary on this occasion, a somewhat puzzled Keith Welles agreed to take on the job. He had the time and could hardly refuse. But despite Bryan's minute description of the place and the other patients and staff, including names and physical characteristics, Welles's first report didn't succeeded in uncovering any clues about Gerhart Peuckert's fate. Nearly thirty years had elapsed. He complained that the task was almost impossible. The hospital and the man they were looking for had disappeared without a trace. Moreover, any patient lying in a mental hospital during the last days of the Third Reich would in all probability have been liquidated. Mercy killing was the state's safest form of treatment for that type of patient.

Bryan was overcome with disappointment. The coincidence during recent weeks of the meetings with Welles and Wilkens and the invitation to the Olympic Games had instilled in him the hope of resolving the case and finally gaining peace of mind.

"Couldn't you come over for a couple of days, Mr. Scott?" Welles appealed. "I'm sure it would be a great help."

On the third day Bryan phoned the National Olympic Committee and explained he had some business to do in southern Germany. If they would place a flat in the Olympic City at his disposal, they could consult him if there were any acute problems. The committee agreed. This time England was going to do better than the five gold medals, five silver medals, and three bronze medals in Mexico.

No matter what the cost.

Laureen was displeased. Not because Bryan was going to travel, but because she only got to know about it on the eve of his departure.

"Couldn't you at least have told me yesterday? You realize I can't possibly go with you now, Bryan. If you're expecting me to tell my sister-in-law that she can just stay at home in Penarth, I can assure you it's too late now! Bridget is waiting on the platform in Cardiff at this very moment."

Laureen looked at her watch in despair and sighed deeply as her shoulders slumped. Bryan avoided her gaze. He knew what she was thinking. It had been difficult enough arranging her sister-in-law's visit. To cancel it would be the end of the world.

But that's how he'd wanted it.

CHAPTER 31

It was a smiling Keith Welles who strode across the road. Traffic had come to a complete standstill. The classic description of German order and efficiency didn't exactly fit with the sight that met Bryan at Munich's airport. The heat struck him in the face. Cars were packed so close together that it wasn't even possible to open the trunk.

"Chaos, total chaos." Welles grinned as he tugged him along the traffic lanes. Only the buses were moving. Everyone was out to watch the opening of the Games. Everyone except Bryan.

The city itself was about to boil over. A magical thrill of color and festivity. The stronghold of culture. Musicians, artists, and dancers were assembled. Every street corner reflected countless days of preparation. It was both big business and no business. And Bryan was feeling extremely strange.

He felt as if he were in a vacuum in this mixed crowd of Germans and foreigners, all strolling around, safe and smiling. It was possible to banish the ghost of the past for only moments at a time. Then the voices rose again and brought back memories of the tone and aggressiveness of the language that years ago would have made Bryan shudder. Letting Welles guide him forward, he stared at the numerous young people who were enjoying the outdoor pleasures of café life and speaking the native language so naturally, sweetly, and melodiously, without the savage, threatening undertones of the past. He also surveyed the stream of old women and men in whose faces he saw the dreadful mark of Cain.

And then he knew he had returned.

It took Welles two whole steins of beer to familiarize Bryan with his fruitless reconnoitering. The crowded, easygoing atmosphere of the outdoor café couldn't hide his shame. He raised his hand deprecatingly when the waiter came around a third time. "I know that if I kept on forever, sooner or later I'd probably stumble across a clue that could be traced to someone who had been at the sanitarium in Freiburg. But I honestly think it could take years. I'm not a professional, you see. The question is whether I'm the right person to undertake the task." Welles pursed his lips. "I haven't sufficient time, we know that. There are far too many treatment centers, far too many archives, far too many case histories, and far too great distances. And then there's the Wall. Who says the decisive clue is to be found in Western Germany? If it's in Eastern Germany, we'd have visa problems among other things, and that, too, takes time and still more time." He smiled and then frowned. "What you really need is a huge system of nosy sleuths and archivists."

"That's been tried."

"Then why do it again now?"

Bryan regarded Welles at length. Unfortunately he was right. Everything pointed to his being unable to get to the bottom of James's enigmatic fate. It was also true that he could have entrusted the job to a professional. The fact was that Bryan hadn't intended to delve further into the past until providence sent him the unshaven man who was sitting in front of him.

He had always assumed James was dead. And now he had to attempt to find out, once and for all.

"I'm getting the feeling I ought to use the carrot-and-stick method. I'd be terribly sorry if you gave up in advance. So sorry, in fact, that it might affect your new position in Bonn."

The reaction in Welles's eyes said this would be a bad idea. At any rate, fruitless.

"But I'm a man of my word, Mr. Welles, and you don't owe me anything. You can hear that I'm desperate. We're venturing into an area that should probably never have been investigated. I'm seriously afraid I'm doing myself a disservice with all this. But you see, the man we're looking for was my best friend. He was English and his real name was James Teasdale. I left him behind at that hospital and I haven't seen him since. If I never learn more about his fate, the uncertainty will haunt me the rest of my life because I'll never find the strength to try again."

The adjoining tables were emptying as they were talking. Even the impatient waiters had given up trying to make them order more or leave so new customers could get at the all-too-few tables. The broadcast of the opening of the Games was already in full swing. Welles was studying Bryan with interest. "Give me another two weeks, until the Games are over," Bryan finally said. "Concentrate on the area around Freiburg. If we don't get a bite, I'll have to find some other way. I'll give you an extra five thousand pounds. Will you do that for me?"

From inside the restaurant came the sound of fanfares and the roar of thousands of spectators—a round of cheering that echoed simultaneously from all the windows along the street. A beam of light from the beer glass Welles had been constantly fingering caught his serious expression and gave birth to a small laugh line in the corners of his mouth. He quietly extended his hand.

"Then you're going to have to call me Keith!"

Despite the heat and the potential danger to health that always arises when thousands of people are crowded together, Bryan didn't have much to do in the Olympic City. There were no acute gastric cases. The only contact Bryan had had so far with the English group was over the telephone. On checking in, he'd received his admittance card to the stadiums and the usual invitations to various receptions and evening parties. But although time seemed to drag along, he never felt the need for company. As in the calm eye of a hurricane, Bryan dozed through events upon which the whole world was focused. "I envy you," said Keith Welles when he phoned in his morning report. "I don't envy you," Laureen lied in their daily chat.

The Olympic City was a seething cauldron. Everyone seemed to be constantly moving from one place to another. No one noticed Bryan. The few hours outside his hotel were spent in town—lunching in department-store cafeterias, visiting museums, sitting on benches in green parks that were wilting in an eternal summer that refused to loosen its grip.

The waiting was unbearable. Even books gave him no relief. The temptation to investigate Munich's numerous pharmaceutical firms wasn't strong enough.

Everything revolved around James.

"It may be that I'm getting too old," Bryan reflected, staring at the TV he hadn't turned on in the far corner of his hotel room. There would be other Olympic Games. If he wanted to attend them in the future he'd be glad to pay for it.

On the tenth day, Welles phoned him. He sounded different.

"I may have something for you, Bryan." The words almost knocked him over. Bryan held his breath. "Don't expect too much, but I think I've found your Calendar Man."

"Where are you?"

"I'm in Stuttgart, but he's in Karlsruhe. Can we meet there?"

"I'll have to rent a car. Can I pick you up on the way?" Bryan didn't expect an answer as he sat rocking to and fro, legs crossed. It felt as if he were getting diarrhea. "I just have to report that I'm leaving the area. I could meet you in three hours."

It was clear that Welles didn't relish speed. The big car was silent. It wasn't a love of speed that made Bryan always rent Jaguars—rather a case of national pride. But it could drive fast. Much too fast for Welles's taste. He leaned in toward the middle of the car and tried to avoid looking at the road. "I decided I was looking for a true eccentric whose calling in life was to keep an exact account of the years, months, weeks, and days. Then it was just a question of whether this Werner Fricke was still alive. If so, he was bound to turn up if I phoned enough places. It may sound simple, but I've been doing nothing else for days. Maybe a professional would have tackled it differently, but I phoned all the hospitals and treatment clinics I could find. At least fifty, before I found him."

"And Gerhart Peuckert? What about him?" Bryan fixed his gaze on the road far ahead and clutched the steering wheel.

"I'm sorry, Bryan, but up to now, nobody has known anything about him."

"Don't worry, I'm not expecting too much at once. You've done a good piece of work, Keith. One step at a time, right?" Bryan tried to smile. "I'm looking forward to seeing him again. So good old Calendar Man is alive. . . ." Bryan stared into space. "If he's alive there's hope for James, too."

.   .   .

"You can ask him questions, if you like, but I can't promise he'll answer." Like the rest of the clinic, the head doctor's office was light and painted colorfully. It was an expensive place, not for just anyone. "Werner Fricke's family has already been informed about your visit. They have no objections," Dr. Würtz continued in her heavy accent, without a smile. "Perhaps Mr. Welles could be your interpreter, Mr. Scott."

"May we see his case notes?"

"You're a doctor, Mr. Scott. Would you allow that?"

"Probably not."

"You can see his identity card. It will give you his most important data."

Bryan asked Welles to skip all the psychiatric terms. Fricke was ill and was being treated as such. It was his history at the hospital that was of interest, not whether Fricke had a chance of being normal again.

All the notes originated in March 1945. Not a word about where he had come from, or what had precipitated his illness. Freiburg was not even mentioned. Werner Fricke had simply turned up out of nowhere at a clinic outside Karlsruhe on March 3, 1945. Having been reported missing for over a year, he'd been transferred from an interim SS camp in Tübingen. There was nothing about the history of his illness. His Army records revealed nothing about the year that had been torn from the almanac of Calendar Man's life.

Werner Fricke's temporary quarters in Tübingen had been evacuated during the Allied advance and all the patients transferred to Karlsruhe. When the clinic was privatized in the beginning of the sixties, most of the patients had to let themselves be transferred. Now he was the only original patient left. Calendar Man's family had had the means to keep him where he was.

The list of the other patients from that time was fairly short. Bryan couldn't recognize a single name.

Calendar Man was obviously the only one from the Alphabet House.

Bryan's sudden burst of emotion took him unawares. The intervening years vanished at the sight of this short-legged, stocky body and the gentle eyes. All other feelings were quelled by a surprising tenderness. "Ahhh!" the man exclaimed, raising his bushy snow-white eyebrows as Bryan stepped between him and the television. Bryan nodded at Calendar Man and felt the tears welling up inside him. "That's what he says to everyone," Dr. Würtz interjected.

Decades of inactivity may have crumpled the body, but had not destroyed this man's dignity. Despite the sleeveless shirt and trousers with open fly, it was still an SS officer sitting in front of him, looking at him curiously in the eyes. Bryan's experiences in the hospital in Freiburg came strikingly alive. Here sat Calendar Man in the flesh, watching the Olympic Games in Munich on a tiny black-and-white screen. The date on the calendar pad hanging above the screen was, of course, correct.

Montag, the fourth of September, 1972.

"What shall I say to him?" asked Welles, squatting down beside the other two.

"I don't know. Ask him about all the names I gave you. About Sister Petra and Vonnegut. And ask him whether he can remember Arno von der Leyen, the man he was about to hurl out the window."

Their farewells had been brief. Even before they'd left the room Werner Fricke had lapsed back into his passive viewing of the 200-meter-sprint finalists who were about to kick off from the starting blocks.

"I know you're disappointed, Bryan, but I don't think it's any use. I've already made so many inquiries about Vonnegut. I don't think I'll find him alive, if I can find him at all. You have to realize the name is not uncommon."

"And Fricke's only reaction was to Vonnegut?"

"Yes. Apart from the chocolate I gave him, naturally. I don't think you should make too much out of it."

Keith Welles waited a long time for Bryan to speak. The parking lot had almost emptied while they sat in the Jaguar. Several people had peered in at them with surprised looks. Bryan sat motionless.

"So, what now?" Welles was the first to break the silence when the last car had left the lot.

"Yes, what now?" The answer was so inaudible it was ambiguous.

"There are still ten days left before I have to start work, Bryan. I'll willingly give you five days extra. A lot can still happen." Welles had to force himself to sound optimistic.

"You have to go back to Stuttgart, Keith, don't you?"

"Yes. My notes, my car, and my luggage are all there."

"Would you mind too much if I asked you to rent a car for the return trip? I'll pay you, of course."

"Okay. But why, Bryan?"

"I'm wondering if I should drive to Freiburg. Right now."

The man Bryan knew as Calendar Man sat on a chair in a small room in a private clinic in Karlsruhe, rocking quietly to and fro. Reality, for him, was limited. The television was already switched off. It was growing dark. His lips moved slightly out of rhythm with his rocking. There was no one to hear him.

Sixty kilometers to the south Bryan had had enough of the traffic and turned off the Autobahn. There were two possibilities. Either he took the beautiful route along the Rhine or else the main road at the foot of the Schwarzwald.

He took the main road.

He couldn't face the thought of passing the spot where he'd fled like a madman from Lankau and Schmidt.

Not now.

CHAPTER 32

Before Bryan had completely recalled where he was, an unfamiliar sound rose from a deep rumbling to a brittle contralto. The trams had already welcomed him to the streets of Freiburg the previous evening and now they were bidding him good morning.

The ceiling light in his room was still on. He lay on the bed with all his clothes on. And he was still tired.

An unpleasant feeling like final-exam fever crept over Bryan before he even opened his eyes. Perhaps it would have been different if he'd had Laureen in bed beside him. He had a lonely task ahead of him.

"Hotel Roseneck" was the name on the sign. "Urachstrasse 1" had been added onto the business card with which the receptionist had furnished him. Bryan had no idea where in the town he had found lodgings.

"Is there a telephone?" he'd asked the previous evening. The clerk had replied tersely, pointing at a pay phone opposite the steep flight of stairs.

"Could you give me some small change?" was Bryan's final question.

"Yes, early tomorrow morning!" came the answer. So he hadn't phoned Laureen yet.

Now the streets awaited him. As did the mountains and the train station. Freiburg had a hypnotic effect on him. He'd clung to his fantasies during his months in the hospital outside the town. Fantasies about his life at home in Canterbury, about freedom, and about this town, so close by.

And here he was.

The hotel lay on a corner facing a small oasis of whispering trees. The entrance to this pitted building with its ornate porch and dangling, wrought-iron lamps was in a small passageway leading to the little park. Urachstrasse was not a smart address but it was convenient, since it was a side street to

Günthertalstrasse, which plowed its way via Kaiser Joseph Strasse through the town gate, Martinstor, and into the heart of the city.

Feeling unprepared, listless, and unable to concentrate, he wandered randomly into the city's bustle of walkers, joggers, cyclists, and motorists—people in a hurry or waiting at tram stops. It felt like he was among fellow actors on a movie set—a diverse crowd that included everything from fat, graying housewives to smiling boys with hands buried deep in their pockets.

A prosperous city.

Perhaps he had expected to see the buildings still scarred from the bombardments. Maybe he'd believed the nerves of the town's past had been severed. But in fact Freiburg was lively and enchanting. Restored, rebuilt, varied, and inviting.

The department stores were filled with goods that people obviously could afford. This irritated Bryan. The debt to the past was still too great for frivolity, the costs not visible enough.

In the middle of the entrance to a department store a crowd of women were grabbing clothes out of a bin that threatened to topple over. Summer shorts for next year. Fair price guaranteed. An elderly, swarthy man was hopping on one leg as he pulled a pair of shorts over his long, crumpled trousers to see if they fit. This was a glimpse of the new peacetime.

Bryan kept wandering aimlessly.

Bertoldstrasse led to the train station. The tram tracks in the cobbled street shone in the clear sunlight and carried four lines up over the railway bridge, draped from twin towers in the distance.

The crowds of people on the railway platforms were fairly orderly. A tour guide was trying to keep his flock together with admonitions that streamed endlessly from his ruddy-faced mouth. All the women were wearing backpacks, showing bare legs beneath their shorts. "Laureen would be staring," Bryan thought.

An alien world. He scanned the seven railway lines and seven platforms without recognizing anything. The platform where he'd spent anxious hours in the icy frost almost thirty years ago seemed to have disappeared without a trace. Presumably obliterated by his buddies in the RAF.

His eye glided southward under the bridge toward where the town pe-
tered out. A massive, dark, and strikingly different building stood far off in
the background. Bryan gasped.

So the old railway's superstructure was still standing.

The distance from the train tracks to the wall of massive bricks was scarcely
four meters. Bryan remembered it as having been at least twice as much.
This was the platform on which he'd lain. Bryan closed his eyes and could
clearly see James's silhouette lying a couple of meters farther up the platform. Where were they now, those lifeless figures that had been lying on
stretchers, shivering? Were they buried long ago, or at home with their
loved ones, absorbed in a no-man's-land of oblivion?

The range of hills in the distance was soft and faded green, spatial and
layered like the scenery in a puppet theater. A rusty track switch pointed
toward the hills, recalling the time he saw a railway worker running down
these tracks, clutching an iron rod. The soldiers with their dangling gas
masks, the happy, relaxed youths on their way home on leave—they, too,
emerged from the capricious labyrinth of remembrance. The old freight
cars, the building's indestructibility, the colors, and the silence—just as they
were then, when the snow softly covered the platform. It all served to stim-
ulate the part of Bryan's mind that was usually almost impossible to reach.

Then he collapsed and wept.

He let Hotel Roseneck's porter see to his needs the rest of the day. A
neighboring café supplied him with nondescript ham-and-faded-lettuce
sandwiches. The hotel had no restaurant of its own. The porter had a
hard time smiling, despite a generous tip. Bryan didn't manage to phone
home that evening, either. He had no appetite, no needs. It was all simply
a question of whether he'd be able to pull himself together and get up the
next day.

And the next day came. Several of the children stared at the Jaguar as Bryan
passed Waldkirch to be swallowed up by the Schwarzwald's foothills, over
which Hünersedel's peak towered. Had he driven west around the mountains he would most certainly have been distracted by details instead of

concentrating on his goal: to find out where the hospital had been. Bryan's experience told him that he would best accomplish this from above, where the Ortoschwanden Plateau would presumably provide an open view downward toward the west.

The rocks and tree formations seemed endless, even through the window of a fast-moving vehicle. Countless paths and waterfalls underlined the uselessness of searching at random. Bryan looked for a landmark.

His fixed point was Kaiserstuhl, the lush mountain swathed in vineyards in the middle of the flat wine-growing country. Now he had to find the same angle from which he first sighted the mountain from under the German truck's flapping tarpaulin.

It took a long time, but Bryan found the spot. And it wasn't surprising that the tarpaulin had flapped up precisely there. A constant, mild breeze swept up through the valley before him, exuding humus vapors and ozone. There lay Kaiserstuhl. The stream formed by the narrow draining canals cut downward across the landscape a few hundred meters farther on.

To the south was a minor road that ran northwest down through the hills. Over on the opposite ridge, there was only forest as far as the eye could see. Ditches lined the road and behind them flowed the small streams through which he had fled.

It was a moving sight. Grandiose, beautiful—and what he'd been looking for.

After hiking along the forest trails for a while the woods became dense. Bryan looked around, trying to recall the terrain. There was no trace of what he was looking for. The trees here were younger and only half as high as those he had just passed. Not a single sign or relic to bear witness to the presence of the large buildings and all the activity that had once filled the area. The underbrush was thick. Only a small game trail indicated the presence of life other than botanical. Bryan pulled his socks up over his trouser cuffs and fought his way into the scrub, half stooping, half stumbling. Some old, solitary fir trees towered above him in the middle of a small opening. Then straight in front of him, less than ten meters away, the moss-covered rock rose a couple of meters above the ground. Bryan squatted down and looked around slowly.

Everything was gone, and yet this was where it all had stood. The kitchen building, the nurses' quarters, the security guards' barracks, five several-story buildings, the chapel, gymnasium, garages, the execution pole.

And now it was completely razed.

As he drove back down, villages popped up and acquired names. He slowed the car during the last few kilometers before the swamp. In flashes he sensed the coldness of naked feet, the rumbling of guns, and the anguish. And suddenly it lay before him, Europe's last primeval forest, Taubergiessen. The wilderness in which he had nearly lost his life. And the slopes, the mire, the sandbar in the river, the thicket on the opposite shore. It was all there. Except for the explosions, the corpses, and the broad-faced man and his thin accomplice.

These were all long gone.

Even the distances had vanished, shrunk. But the atmosphere was intact in spite of the grapes ready for harvesting and birds that brought the mild autumn over the countryside.

It was here he knew he had killed a man.

The town drifted past Bryan like fog. The morning's events ought to have satisfied years of pent-up need. In the wake of his abrupt decision to go to Freiburg, a sudden flood of expectations had arisen as well as the hope of finding peace of mind. Now he had to face the facts. It was not so easy. The past was an entity unto itself and the images inside him would never fade, no matter how much they were distorted by the march of time. Further progress would be difficult.

There were hardly any people on the streets of Freiburg. Everyone in the post office was acting strangely. The woman who showed him to the long-distance phone booth looked clearly distressed. Several people waiting at the counter were staring into thin air. Bryan let the telephone ring for quite a while. Sometimes Laureen took a long time putting down her crossword puzzle.

"Yes?" was all she said, when she finally answered.

"Laureen? Is that you?"

"Bryan!" Bryan immediately noted the rage in her voice. "Why the

bloody hell haven't you phoned? You must damned well be able to understand how worried I've been!"

She hadn't sworn in years. "I haven't been able to call, Laureen."

"Has something happened to you, Bryan? Have you gotten mixed up in
something?"

"What do you mean? What should I have gotten mixed up in? I've just
been busy, Laureen."

"Where are you, Bryan?" The question came precise and matter-of-fact.
"You're not in Munich, are you?"

"No, not just now. I went to Freiburg yesterday."

"On business?"

"Yes, possibly."

For a moment it was quiet at the other end, but not time enough for
Bryan to gauge the consequences of his lie.

"How can it be that you don't know why I've been worried?" The voice
was quiet, she was trying to control herself. "Everyone knows! You don't
even have to open the newspaper, Bryan. It's on the front page all over the
world!"

"I don't know what you're talking about. Have we been cheated out of a
gold medal, or something?"

"Would you care to know?" The tone was curt. Laureen didn't wait for
an answer. "Yesterday lots of Israeli athletes were taken hostage in their
Olympic quarters. It was the Palestinians. We've all been following it. It
was repulsive and disgusting, and now they're dead. All the hostages and
all the terrorists." Bryan was incapable of cutting in, even when she paused.
He was speechless. "Everyone's talking about it, can't you understand? The
whole world is grieving! How come you know nothing about it, Bryan?
What's going on?"

Bryan tried to keep a hold on reality. He felt limp. Perhaps now was the
time to tell Laureen about his real purpose for being in Germany and
Freiburg. As wife and friend, Laureen had taken Bryan as he was, without
any prying or mistrust. She knew he had been a pilot and that he had been
shot down over Germany. That was all she knew. And now that was long
ago.

She wouldn't be able to understand his need to seek out the past, even
if she knew the story about James. What was done could not be undone.

That was how she looked at things.

Perhaps he'd tell her everything when he got home.

And so the portentous moment passed.

He said nothing.

"Phone me when you're yourself again," she said quietly.

As Bryan followed Bertoldstrasse back over the railway lines, he again began succumbing to lethargy and flights of fancy. A brief conversation with Keith Welles hadn't shed any new light. Calendar Man was turning over the pages of his date pad in a blind alley.

The inner city neighborhoods gave room to breathe. The lakeside park beside Ensisheimer Strasse was almost devoid of people. The boats were moored. Only the benches bore any sign of life, overflowing with old men engrossed in their newspapers. A fleeting glance at one of the front pages would have instantly told him something was wrong. So that was what he had sensed in the post office. People were in shock. "*16 tote!*" it said in bold type. "*Alle Geiseln als Leichen gefunden!*" *Das Bild* had presumably always known how to make itself easily understood. Words like "*Blutbad*" demanded no great knowledge of languages.

Bryan didn't find the events in Munich unnatural, considering the past. Just an example of what happens when hate breeds hate in a predictable chain of unpredictability. Today the citizens of Munich were bearing the mask of sorrow, along with the rest of the world. In another time the same faces had borne the mask of terror.

Bryan drifted through sprawling new residential districts to the outskirts of town. He finally awoke from his aimless wandering and self-castigating thoughts and stopped in the middle of the sidewalk. On the other side of the street an unattractive sign merged with its surroundings.

"Pension Gisela" was written on the facade. "Gisela." An insignificant name on an insignificant street. He stood stock-still.

This new possible angle took him completely by surprise.

For years he'd retained romantic memories of Gisela Devers, the only person from those days he occasionally tried to remember.

Bryan trembled in anticipation. Despite the slim odds of anything turning up, Bryan trusted his premonitions.

Gisela would be the next key with which he'd attempt to unlock the vault of oblivion.

Devers was not such an unusual name. At Bryan's hotel they'd shown remarkable helpfulness by lending him the regional phone book and even placing a cup of tea beside the pay phone. His stack of pfennig had diminished considerably during the past two hours. Now that people were home from work, he got hold of nearly everyone he phoned. The majority didn't speak English. No one knew a Gisela Devers who was around fifty years old.

"Perhaps she's no longer alive. Maybe she doesn't live in Freiburg or have a phone." The desk clerk tried to comfort him, almost kindly. Even if he was right, the comfort soon proved superfluous. A few minutes later, after the pile of pfennig had been replenished, a quiet voice sent his heart racing.

"My mother's name was Gisela Devers and she would soon have been fifty-seven, yes," the young woman replied. Her English was correct, though clumsy. Bryan had interrupted her evening routine.

Her name was Mariann G. Devers. Considering the name, she probably lived alone. "Why do you ask? Did you know her?" She asked more out of politeness than curiosity.

"Is she dead?"

"Yes, she's been dead for more than ten years now."

"I'm sorry to hear that." Bryan was silent for a moment. His sympathy was genuine. "Then I won't intrude."

"I don't think my mother ever told me she was acquainted with an Englishman. Where did you know her from?"

"I met her here in Freiburg." His disappointment was tangible. It was not only about James. Gisela Devers was dead. The past was imploding. He would never see her again. Surprisingly enough, he was disheartened. He could still remember the painfully straight stocking seams on her lovely legs. She had been beautiful and she had kissed him fervently in the antechamber of horror.

"When was that? When did you last speak with her?"

"Listen, maybe you have a photo of your mother. I would so much like to see a picture of her. Your mother and I were once very close, you see."

. . .

Mariann Devers was somewhat older than Bryan had imagined. At any rate older than her mother had been when Bryan met her. She was quite a different woman. She wore no makeup and was by no means as beautiful as her tall, lithe, stylishly dressed mother. But there was a resemblance about the cheekbones.

The flat was like a shoe box. Its gay colors and numerous posters on the walls were well suited to Mariann Devers's spontaneous manner and her strange style of dress. She seemed like someone who was poor but used to a better life. The flowers Bryan brought immediately found their niche.

"So you were born during the war? Then you must have already been alive when I met your mother."

"I was born in 1942."

"In 1942? Were you really?"

"And you saw my father, you say?" Mariann Devers casually adjusted her dark hair and the numerous scarves around her neck.

"Yes."

"Tell me about him."

The more Mariann Devers seemed to grasp, the more Bryan embroidered the truth. She knew so little about her father.

"I know my father was killed during a bombing attack. Maybe it was in the sanitarium you're telling me about. I don't know. Mother said it made no difference where it happened."

"Did she live here, in town? For some reason I thought she might have. She didn't come from here, as far as I know."

"No. But many people moved after the war. They had to."

"Had to? What do you mean, Miss Devers?"

"Court cases, confiscations. My mother's family lost everything. Your fellow countrymen saw to that." The undertone lacked bitterness, but hit home nevertheless.

"How did she manage, then? Did she have an education?"

"For the first few years she didn't manage at all. She never used to talk about it. I don't know where she lived or what she lived on. I was living with my mother's cousin in Bad Godesberg. I was nearly seven before she brought me here."

"And then she got a job here in Freiburg?"

"No, she got herself a new husband." The blow she dealt the tabletop to emphasize the word "husband" wasn't hard, but effective. It was clear that Mariann Devers would have found a different way out of the situation. The smile she gave behind her thick, flowing bangs was a bitter one.

"Was she married here in Freiburg?"

"She was, unfortunately, yes! It was here she was married and it was here she died. After a wretched life, if you ask me. Full of disappointments and mental torture. She married for money and status, so she got what she deserved. Her own family became poor after the war and she couldn't take it. But the way he treated her was disgusting."

"And he treated you the same way?"

"Fuck him!" Mariann Devers's vehemence astounded Bryan. "He's never been able to get to me, the shit! I'd like to see him try!"

The photo album was brown and stiff and worn. It was full of pictures of landscapes in which a young girl—scarcely older than Bryan's own daughter—ran around and posed with a twinkle in her eye, first half-hidden behind tree trunks, then sprawling in an alpine meadow. They were photographs from Gisela Devers's happiest summer, she'd told her daughter.

The young girl displayed the carefree attitude of youth to the album's very last page. Mariann Devers pointed at her father with obvious pride. He was a handsome man in uniform to whom Gisela Devers was clinging in enviable harmony. That was long ago.

"You take after both your parents a great deal, Miss Devers, do you know that?"

"Yes, I know, Mr. Scott. And I also know I've got to get up early in the morning. I don't want to be impolite, but you've seen what you came for, haven't you?"

"Yes, thank you. I have, Miss Devers. And I apologize if I've kept you up. You don't happen to have a late photo of your mother, do you? I'd hate to leave without asking you. I have so many different images in my mind, you understand."

She shrugged, knelt down, and reached under the plain bed. The dust that covered the wicker basket she dragged forth revealed her lack of interest in housekeeping. A huge jumble of photos appeared. Almost ten years of different hairstyles, poses, and clothes. Rapid transformations, great changes of fortune.

"Here she is," she said simply, handing him a faded photograph. It could have been anyone. Mariann looked over his shoulder. Presumably she hadn't seen it for years and probably there'd been no occasion to. Gisela Devers's face was quite close to the camera. Her features were out of focus; the photo was taken in a moment of playfulness. She was shouting something to the photographer, her hands spread out. Everyone around her was smiling at her, apart from the little girl who was lying on her tummy on the grass, looking at her mother from behind. She had been a lovely child, Mariann Devers. Above her stood a man with his arms folded. He was the only one who was looking away from the scene. He seemed uninterested in the others. Not even the little girl seemed to concern him. An apparently handsome man whose bearing bore witness to a person of position and self-assurance. Several scratches across his face rendered the photograph unclear. And yet Bryan began feeling uncomfortable. Not at the thought of the young girl's attempt to revenge herself by scratching her stepfather's face out of the family photo. It was something else. A kind of presence that was almost familiar.

Mariann Devers apologized, asserting that unfortunately she didn't have a better picture. It was all she had managed to get out of her mother's husband when her mother finally found peace.

"But your stepfather was well known here in town, wasn't he?" She nodded noncommittally. "So don't you think any official photos were ever taken? I can hardly recognize your mother in this picture."

"There are lots of official photos. Plenty. But Mother was never with him. He was ashamed of her. She drank, you see." Mariann Devers sat down on the arm of his chair and pursed her lips. There were holes under the arms of her blouse. Once more Bryan felt a growing, inexplicable uneasiness. There was something ominous in the air. It was the photo he'd just seen.

And he also felt guilty for having intruded. His hostess adjusted her clothing and straightened her back. "Were you in love with my mother?" she asked suddenly.

"Maybe. . . ." The young woman beside him bit her upper lip. Once again Bryan felt obliged to ask himself the same question. "I don't know," he finally said after a while. "Your father was very ill. It was difficult to identify one's feelings under those strange circumstances. But she was very beautiful. I might well have fallen in love, if I wasn't already."

"What circumstances are we talking about?" Mariann Devers's eyes were locked on him.

"It's actually terribly difficult to explain, Miss Devers, but you might say they were pretty unusual, considering I was here in this country and there was a war on."

"My mother couldn't possibly have been interested in you." She laughed. The absurdity of it had just struck her. "I don't know anyone who was such a confirmed Nazi as my mother. She loved all the paraphernalia. I don't think a single day went by without her dreaming of the Third Reich. The uniforms, the marches, the parades. She loved it. And you were a Brit. Should she have been interested in you? It sounds very strange."

"Your mother didn't know I was British. No one in the hospital knew."

"So you were a spy, then? Maybe you fell down from the sky dressed as Father Christmas?" She laughed. The truth didn't interest her much. "Do you know what? Come to think of it, I might have another photo, since you're so fascinated. From my school graduation. Mother's standing in the background, but it's better than the other one."

This time she had to turn the wicker basket upside down. The picture was framed, but the glass was broken. There were still fragments along the edge and in the bottom of the basket. This was another Mariann Devers from the woman who was sitting in front of him. Her hair was smooth and the bell-bottoms had been replaced by a white dress that scarcely revealed she was a woman. But she looked proud and she was the focal point.

Her mother was standing in the picture, looking at her. She seemed cold and subdued. And she looked run-down. The years had not treated her kindly, even when one saw her from a distance.

Then came the shock. Not because of the merciless workings of time, nor the suffering and disappointment mirrored in the woman's eyes, but because of the man who was standing behind her, hands resting heavily on her shoulders. It was the man whose face Mariann had tried to scratch out of the other photo.

"Her husband?" Mariann Devers noticed Bryan's hand was trembling as he pointed at the photograph.

"Her husband and tormentor, yes! You can tell by looking at her, can't you? She wasn't happy."

"And her husband, is he still alive?"

"Still alive? No one can get rid of him. Yes, he's alive. In the best of health, one might add. Well known in town. New wife. Money in the bank. Piles of it in fact, the bastard!"

The stab of pain in Bryan's chest came stealthily. He swallowed a couple of times, forgetting to breathe. "May I ask you for a glass of water, Miss Devers?"

"Do you feel ill?"

"No, no! It's nothing."

Bryan refused Mariann Devers when she politely offered to let him stay awhile longer, even though he was still pale. He had to get some fresh air.

"And your stepfather, Miss Devers . . ." She was helping him on with his coat, but stopped in the middle of his sentence.

"I'd appreciate it if you didn't call him that."

"Did he take his wife's last name, or have you just kept your mother's maiden name?"

"Good God, my mother kept her own name and he kept his. His name is what it's always been: Hans Schmidt. Original, isn't it? 'Herr Direktor Hans Schmidt,' as he likes to call himself."

Original, indeed. Bryan was surprised by the name's anonymity. "Not very characteristic," he thought. It may have surprised Mariann Devers when he asked for his address, but he got it.

The house was not enormous, but of a standard that required a practiced eye to appreciate. No detail had been overlooked, nor was anything exaggerated. A beautiful, discreet work of architecture. The utilization of materials bore witness to taste, a sense of quality, and the presence of resources. A palace in harmony with the palatial side street. A small brass plate indicated the house's owner. It simply said HANS SCHMIDT. "Liar!" thought Bryan, and felt like scratching the engraving. It sent shivers down his spine to think that here was the man who had taken possession of the romantic flirt of his youth, the beautiful Gisela Devers, and destroyed her life.

Up on the second floor a light was still burning in the southern corner of the house. A shadow was outlined so faintly behind the curtain that it could be the curtain itself, blowing in the breeze. But it could also be the outline of Gisela Devers's oppressor. A silhouette from the past. Swine and businessman Hans Schmidt, alias the pock-faced pig, Obersturmbann-führer Wilfried Kröner.

Activity in the neighborhood the next morning soon quieted down. Since the light of day Bryan had been watching the businessmen marching out to their BMWs and Mercedes. The sight was familiar to Bryan. There were really only two things that distinguished the scene from his own, back home. The make of car and the wives. The wives in England also waved good-bye, but in Canterbury an upper-class lady of the house would rather lose access to the bank box than display herself the way these women in Freiburg did. Laureen was always impeccably dressed before she emerged from the house. But here the sight was the same in all the doorways. Irre-spective of the house size or the price of the husband's suit, wives were standing everywhere in kimonos with their hair in curlers.

But in Kröner's house nothing happened.

Bryan kept being struck by the thought that he ought to have been better equipped. Perhaps even armed. The possibility of a confrontation with the most calculating tormentor of a bygone age brought out the unre-strained aggression of his younger days. All Kröner's atrocities leapt vividly to mind. The sadistic face whispered to him of weapons, violence, revenge, and still more revenge. And somewhere else in Bryan's mind other pictures took shape. Glimpses of James, moments of hope, anxiety that demanded caution.

Not until ten o'clock was there any movement behind the shade of the awnings. An elderly woman stepped out onto the garden path and began shaking out a rug.

Bryan emerged from his hiding place and made straight for her.

She looked afraid when Bryan addressed her in English. Then she shook her head and made as if to hurry indoors again. Smiling, Bryan unbuttoned his coat and fanned his face. The sun was already gathering strength, too warm for a coat. That, at least, she could understand. She looked sternly at him again and then shook her head, this time less antagonistically. "I speak no English, *leider nicht.*"

"Herr Schmidt?" Bryan spread out his arms questioningly.

Again the woman shook her head. Then suddenly she let out a stream of German and broken English. Neither the mister nor missus was home, that much Bryan understood. But they would be coming. Later.

Today, perhaps.

CHAPTER 33

That same morning Bridget had been impossible. "You're going through menopause, dear." Laureen tried as gently as possible to get her sister-in-law to face the facts.

She had enough to think about herself.

The days in Canterbury without Bryan had been critical. Not that his absence in itself mattered. The house was her domain and there was nothing there that she found particularly burdensome. It was Bridget who made his absence stand out. Bryan had only to cast a glance at his brother-in-law's wife and she'd settle down. But without this decorum, Laureen's brother's wife was unbearable.

"Your wretched brother's a wimp!" she could suddenly exclaim, flinging her fork down on her plate. As long as Bridget was visiting, Laureen could only use her everyday tableware.

"Don't upset yourself . . ." Laureen seldom got any further before her sister-in-law burst into tears, began sweating and getting swollen in the face, and continued talking nonstop. Nevertheless it was difficult to avoid being affected by Bridget's complaints about her husband's infidelity and her displeasure about the way her body was changing.

"Just wait," she wept, "it can happen to you, too!"

Laureen nodded neutrally.

Bryan and Laureen were not such exotic types. Both of them knew that. The need for constant erotic variation was not a big issue.

But her intuition told her something was wrong.

Through the years Laureen had learned that the first stage in every business project was to gather information about the market, competitors, costs, and needs. It was the same in the case of her and Bryan's little private matter.

She thought she knew the need. She would have to barter her way to the rest.

Bryan's secretary, Mrs. Shuster, gave Laureen a mystified look as she passed by with an authoritative nod and disappeared in the direction of Ken Fowles's office. Never before had Mrs. Scott come to the Lambeth office in her husband's absence.

"As far as I know, I can't see what Mr. Scott would be doing in Freiburg, Mrs. Scott." Ken Fowles looked at her attentively. "What makes you ask? I phoned him on Monday and he was still in Munich."

"And since then? When did you last speak to him, Ken?"

"I haven't had any reason to contact him since then."

"And who are we working with in Germany? Can you tell me that?" The question made Ken Fowles tilt his head in puzzlement. He understood neither her interest nor her unusually friendly tone.

"But we haven't any permanent business connections in Germany. Not yet, that is. It's no more than a couple of weeks since we started serious negotiations regarding the new gastric ulcer medicine. We employed a salesman recently who is to build up our domain in northern Europe."

"And who was this lucky man?"

"Peter Manner from Gesellschaft Heinz W. Binken & Breumann. But they haven't established themselves in Germany yet."

"Why not?"

"Why not? Because Binken & Breumann is a Liechtenstein company and Peter Manner is as English as you or I and is currently in Portsmouth."

"I just have to do something for Bryan, Lizzie," said Laureen, striding past Mrs. Shuster again. The air in Bryan's massive office was heavy and sweetish. Bryan's desk was his archive, and it was extensive. Every pile represented a success. In certain piles a lifetime of research lay ready to be revealed. This was the sorting station of the very best laboratory research. Mrs. Shuster looked on disapprovingly from her office as she leaned uncomfortably over the sharp edge of her desk.

All the drawers were locked. Laureen had no need to worry about them. None of the piles on the desk mentioned anything about Freiburg, let alone Germany. Bryan's conservative tastes were in evidence on the walls above the room's heavy furniture. Not even a calendar was allowed to disturb the office's neatness. There were a few paintings, none of which were less than two hundred years old, and brass light fixtures to illuminate them. Otherwise there was nothing. No bulletin boards, no appointment planners, no notes on the flip-over pad. Only a single small object was allowed to intrude on the efficient, slightly old-fashioned, diligent executive office atmosphere—a little spike of the type used to skewer unpaid bills. The kind of small murderous weapon that Laureen hadn't allowed Bryan to place on the desk at home but now reared up between three telephones, not even a quarter full of notes.

Laureen knew that it was Bryan's idea bank. A random thought, a bright colleague's brainstorm, a vision—and each idea subsequently articulated with neat handwriting and impaled on that little spike. There wasn't much there to get her hopes up at the moment—only five notes—but the one at the bottom aroused her interest. It read: "Keith Welles! £2,000 transferred to Commerzbank, Hamburg." Laureen stared at it for a moment and strode out to the secretary's office.

"Oh, Lizzie, would you be good enough to tell me what this is all about?" She placed the note in front of the secretary, who screwed up her eyes and frowned at the note.

"It's in Mr. Scott's handwriting."

"Yes. I can see that quite well, Lizzie, but what does it mean?"

"That he's transferred two thousand pounds to Keith Welles, apparently."

"Who is this Keith Welles, Lizzie?"

"I think Ken Fowles would be better able to answer that, but he's just left."

"Then do your best, Lizzie, dear. Tell me what you know."

"But he was only one of many. I seem to remember he was the last of the applicants whom Mr. Scott and Mr. Fowles interviewed about a month ago. Just let me look at Mr. Scott's appointment calendar."

Mrs. Shuster had the habit of humming when she was given a task. Laureen didn't understand how Bryan could stand it. He didn't notice it, he said. "She's not the sharpest tool in the shed," Laureen thought, assessing the secretary's other virtues.

"Yes, here it is. Week thirty-three. Mr. Welles was indeed the last to be interviewed."

"And what was the purpose of the interview?"

"To find new agents for the gastric ulcer medicine. But Keith Welles was not employed."

"Then why should he have two thousand pounds?"

"I don't know. To cover his traveling expenses, I suppose. He flew over from Germany and spent the night at a hotel." Lizzie Shuster was not used to being cross-examined. Being bombarded with questions made her unsure of herself. The two women had never really hit it off since she'd joined the firm seven years ago. Even in everyday situations, when she merely had to put Laureen through to her husband, one could imagine icicles forming on the telephone line. Until now Laureen had never attempted a smile. When it finally came, it was much too radiant.

"Oh, Lizzie. Please, won't you give me Keith Welles's phone number?"

"Keith Welles's number? I don't know. . . . I guess I can find it. But wouldn't it be more natural if you phoned your husband in Munich and got it from him?"

Again Laureen smiled, camouflaging her I'm-your-employer's-wife look that could make even Ken Fowles do as he was told.

Mrs. Shuster received no thanks as Laureen folded the note and left the office without turning around.

Keith Welles's daughter spoke better English than his tired wife, who had taken the phone. No, her father wasn't at home. He was in Munich, or else he was just about to leave. She didn't really know. Laureen waited patiently as the telephone clicked regular signals indicating the expensive rate, until the girl finally returned with the number of Welles's hotel.

Two minutes later she'd asked the desk clerk the same question. He was very sorry. Mr. Welles had unfortunately just left the reception counter. He could make out the taxi as it was moving off.

"I have a problem," Laureen said slowly, "and perhaps you can help me. Keith Welles has my husband's telephone number in Freiburg. I'm quite sure he has phoned my husband several times from your hotel. My husband's name is Bryan Underwood Scott. Can you help me? Isn't there some kind of list of the calls made from the hotel?"

"We have telephones with direct lines, madam. We don't list the calls.

But maybe our bartender knows something. Mr. Welles spoke to him a few times, I think. Our bartender is also Canadian, you see. Just a moment, madam, I'll ask him."

Laureen heard an almost inaudible murmur of voices in the background that was interrupted several times by metallic clinking and brief conversation. Apparently, new guests were arriving. For a couple of minutes there was total silence apart from the ticking of the line. Bridget stood with her coat on, tripping impatiently beside Laureen as she pointed at her watch. From the street outside came the beeping of the taxi.

Laureen waved deprecatingly with her free hand, staring at a point in space as she clutched the receiver. "Many thanks! That was very kind of you," she merely said, and smiled.

A few hours later, when the taxi driver deposited their luggage outside Hotel Colombi in Rotteckring, the more fashionable part of Freiburg, Bridget looked self-consciously at the chalk-white facade, then the gleaming picture windows and the park across the street. Their tribulations since arriving at EuroAirport Basel–Mulhouse–Freiburg, where they hadn't received their hotel reservation confirmation until they had taken the bus to the Freiburg railway station, were already forgotten. She bent calmly over one of the numerous white flower boxes that decorated the hotel courtyard and carefully ran her finger along the edge, after which she inspected her fingertip. An ordinary housewife from Wales, in action.

"Don't you think they mine coal in this town, Laureen?" she exclaimed.

CHAPTER 34

All the pent-up rage he'd been unable to come to terms with for years flowed through every breath Bryan took as he waited the entire morning in front of Kröner's house. Sometimes when a car appeared he felt an uncontrollable urge to throw himself upon the occupants like a wild animal. But they were never the ones he was waiting for. At other anxious moments he kept watch to see if Kröner's domestic help had noticed he was still standing on the pavement opposite his house.

The house seemed quite dead.

His bitterness about Pock Face having succeeded in living a comfortable, untroubled life all these years set off some crazy notions in his head. "I'll ruin him," he thought. "I'll strip him of everything: his house, his wife, his domestic help, and his false name. I'll haunt him until he begs me to stop! He must atone for his crime. He'll come to regret what he's done.

"But first he has to tell me about James!"

The car arrived noiselessly. Bryan saw no sign of movement behind the toned windows. It was up the driveway in no time. Three men got out, laughing and arguing as they hitched up their trousers and straightened their clothes. Bryan didn't manage to see their faces before they went inside, but he heard Kröner's voice. Affable, deep, and ingratiating, as always. Authoritative, masculine, hair-raisingly recognizable.

Bryan gave himself an additional two hours. If Kröner hadn't shown himself by then, he would go straight up to the house and ring the bell.

But that didn't prove necessary.

Yet another car drew up to the house. It was somewhat smaller than Kröner's. After a moment's hesitation a little face popped out by the rear door. The boy was almost white-haired. His short legs stepped very gingerly onto the gravel path. A slim young woman staggered behind him, heavily laden with plastic bags. The boy laughed as his mother nudged him with her knee.

After a few minutes the men who had arrived first left the villa again. Standing in the driveway, they said a cheerful good-bye to the young woman who'd come to the doorway, holding the boy by the hand.

Kröner came last. He picked the boy up and pulled him close. The youngster sat on his arm for a moment, hugging Kröner's face like a little monkey. These mutual embraces took Bryan's breath away. Then Kröner kissed the young woman in anything but a fatherly fashion and put his hat on.

Before Bryan managed to take stock of the situation, all the men had driven off in Kröner's Audi. It all happened so suddenly that Bryan never managed to consider how to react. The long waiting time had made him stiff all over. The Audi had reached the bottom of the road before Bryan climbed into his Jaguar.

And by then much too much time had elapsed.

They slipped out of sight at the very first traffic light. A pedestrian waved his fist threateningly as Bryan's tires burned rubber and sent pigeons' wings flapping. Most of the streets were thick with traffic. The week was drawing to a close and many families were heading to the countryside for the weekend.

He drove around the area aimlessly, and half an hour later miraculously caught sight of the car again.

It was parked less than five meters away on the other side of the street. Kröner and one of the men from that morning had returned to the car and were standing beside it, talking cordially.

Several passersby smiled at Kröner, and each time he raised his hat and nodded almost imperceptibly. He was obviously well liked and respected.

The man standing beside Kröner was a prototype of the well-mannered sort who is usually destined for a high position in the civil service. He was better-looking than Kröner, but it was Kröner who stole the picture despite his pockmarked face and much-too-amiable smile. He was full of life and extremely conscious of it. In the hospital Bryan had never quite been able to determine his age. Now it was easier. He was certainly less than sixty, but looked like someone of fifty.

He still had many good years left.

Suddenly Kröner turned and stared straight over toward him. So suddenly that Bryan couldn't manage to look down. Pock Face spread his arms and clapped his hands enthusiastically, whereupon he laid one hand on his companion's shoulder and pointed out the source of his enthusiasm with descriptive gestures. Bryan pressed himself back into his seat so his face was behind the windowframe.

It was Bryan's Jaguar that had caught Kröner's fancy. He looked as if he might come over for a closer look as soon as there was a pause in the traffic. Bryan glanced feverishly over his shoulder. As soon as the stream of cars abated, he immediately pulled out onto the street and disappeared before their eyes. In the rearview mirror he could see the two men standing in the middle of the road, shaking their heads.

He saw the Volkswagen as soon as he got to Bertoldstrasse. It had obviously once been decorated with a full spectrum of psychedelic colors. Faint motifs could still be seen. Now it was more or less black, having been hastily painted over. The paint job wasn't shiny.

The message in the back window was clear enough. A reasonable price and a very long telephone number. It was parked in front of a low, yellowish building with a flat roof. The name "Roxy" was extravagantly displayed on a sign on the otherwise bare facade. The bodega's windows consisted of transparent bricks. Had it not been for the dark door and the signs advertising Lasser Bier and Bitburger Pils, the dirty glass blocks would have covered the entire front of the building. This authentic horror of a *Bierstube* had survived the ruthless trend toward so-called urban harmonization.

The room was surprisingly light inside. The car's owner was easy to spot. Among the quiet hangovers and fleshy, red-veined faces a single antiquated hippie stood out from the rest. He was the only one who noticed Bryan enter. Bryan nodded in the direction of the crocheted vest's orgy of colors and the tie-dyed, too-tight T-shirt.

He tossed his long hair behind his back at least twenty times as they negotiated. The price was reasonable but the hippie insisted on pointless dickering. After this had gone on long enough, Bryan slammed the money down on the table and asked for the car's registration papers. He would see to all the formalities later. If he kept the car at all.

And if he didn't, he would park it where it was now, with the key in the ignition and the papers in the glove compartment. In that event, the guy could just have it back.

Thus Bryan parked his new anonymous find opposite Kröner's villa at precisely one in the afternoon, when most people in the neighborhood had presumably returned home for lunch. This time less than five minutes elapsed before Kröner stepped out of his villa. Looking serious and concentrated, he was preparing for the second act of his working day.

During the next few hours Bryan got a good impression of Kröner's activities and numerous enterprises. Six visits to various addresses. All in the best part of town and all accomplished in less than ten minutes. Every time Kröner left, he was holding a small stack of letters. By now, Bryan knew the procedure.

He, too, had many enterprises that needed attending to.

Everywhere he went, Kröner appeared relaxed and at home. He shopped at the supermarket, visited Sparda Bank and the post office, and occasionally stopped his car to exchange greetings with passersby through his rolled-down window.

Apparently he knew everyone in town and everyone knew him.

In one of the more outlying districts Pock Face stopped in front of a large villa covered with Boston ivy. He straightened his clothes and disappeared into the house at a leisurely pace that distinguished this call from the others. Despite the Volkswagen's protests, Bryan put the car into a grinding reverse gear and backed past the villa's column-flanked driveway.

The cracked enamel plate was almost impossible to read, its ornate Gothic letters half eroded by the march of time. But it was no ordinary sign. It read: KURANSTALT ST. URSULA DES LANDGEBIETES FREIBURG IM BREISGAU.

A chaos of conceptions flashed through Bryan's mind as he waited for Pock Face outside this compact mausoleum in all its pompous, crumbling lavishness.

There could be countless reasons why Kröner was visiting a sanitarium. He could have relatives there. He could be ill himself, even though he didn't look it. His visit could be of a local political nature. But there might just as well be other reasons that weren't quite so straightforward.

Bryan hardly dared think this thought to the end. On the opposite side of the road stood a building, its brass-ornamented door garlanded by a couple of shrubs in earthenware pots. It turned out to be a cross between a beer hall and an upper-class restaurant. Except for over in the corner by the telephone cubicles, the view of the clinic was fairly good.

Bryan's first call made him wonder. Even if Laureen was not at home to take the telephone herself, it should be possible to leave a message with their domestic helper, Mrs. Armstrong. And if she wasn't there, why couldn't he at least leave a message on the answering machine? Bryan cursed. It was Laureen herself who had insisted on buying this electronic wonder that she'd irreverently placed atop a noble heirloom she derisively termed "the most expensive bit of walnut ever to stand on English soil." If it had to stand there, why didn't she at least use it? "My God," he thought, and phoned again. Laureen could be unpredictable when they weren't quite on the same wavelength. Maybe she'd accompanied Bridget back to Cardiff.

The third call was more rewarding. Keith Welles was there, precisely as arranged. He'd been patiently waiting to hear from Bryan.

"I don't expect it's anything in particular," he began without enthusiasm, "but in fact there is a Gerhart Peuckert in a nursing home in Haguenau."

"Good Lord, Keith! Where's Haguenau?" Bryan drummed his fingers on the shelf in the telephone cubicle. Another of the guests was standing behind him impatiently. Bryan turned around and shook his head. He wasn't giving up his place to anyone.

"Well, that's just it," Welles continued reluctantly. "Haguenau is just thirty or forty kilometers from Baden-Baden, where I am now. But . . ."

"Then go there!"

"But you see, it's just that Haguenau is in France."

"In France?" Bryan tried to think of some logical connection. It wasn't easy.

"Have you spoken to the director?"

"I haven't spoken to anyone. It's Friday, you know. There's no one to speak to."

"Then drive over there. But do me a favor first."

"I will if I can. It's still Friday afternoon."

"I want you to phone Kuranstalt St. Ursula, here in Freiburg."

"But I've already done that several weeks ago. It was one of the first private hospitals I called."

"Yes, and you drew a blank, I gather. But I must have an introduction to the sanitarium. I saw one of the men entering who we've been looking for."

"You're kidding! Who?"

"Kröner. The man I call Pock Face."

"Incredible! Wilfried Kröner, you say?" Welles paused briefly. "I wanted to ask you if it's all right if I stop already on Monday. I'd like to be at home with my family for a couple of days before I start in Bonn."

"Then we have to hurry, Keith. I have a feeling we're onto something. Do me the favor of phoning St. Ursula and say you have a representative in town who you'd very much like to send over to them. Tell them he has a present for them."

Bryan gave him the phone number and kept the receiver to his ear while his hand rested on the contact-breaker. The line behind him had thinned out, but a man who had hitherto been waiting patiently gave him an angry look when the phone rang five minutes later. Keith Welles said regretfully that they didn't wish to see any representatives at the clinic on such short notice. Moreover, they were not usually available on weekends. Hospital administrators deserved days off too, the director had admonished.

That was her professional way to end the conversation.

Bryan was frustrated. His ideas as to why Kröner might be visiting the sanitarium were mounting up. He would stop at nothing to get inside. But he would prefer not to be noticed as long as his and Welles's primitive investigations were incomplete. The few determined steps Kröner had taken toward the Jaguar a couple of hours ago still felt like an extremely unpleasant incident. He had no wish to get any closer to his old tormentor. Not yet.

The beer hall's regulars had already begun their weekend. They appeared to be upper-class folks who had just come from work, presumably in this fashionable neighborhood. Through the small, tinted windowpanes he was able to see the entrance to the building. Kröner hadn't left yet. Bryan phoned the sanitarium less than an hour after his last conversation with Welles. He moved way into a corner behind the telephone cubicle and took a deep breath. It was difficult to deaden the noise from the bar. He looked at his watch. It was half past four.

The director of Kuranstalt St. Ursula seemed taken aback when he introduced himself in English.

"I don't understand, Frau Rehmann," Bryan continued, hugging the receiver when she refused to talk to him. "You say you have just spoken to my superior, but there must be some mistake. You must be referring to someone else." From her silence Bryan could tell he'd gotten her attention. "You see, I'm phoning from the medical faculty at Oxford, where I'm the dean. My name is John MacReedy. I'm phoning on behalf of a research group of administrative psychiatric head doctors who are presently attending a conference in Baden-Baden. They are going on an excursion to Freiburg tomorrow, and in this connection one of our conference participants, Mr. Bryan Underwood Scott, has asked me to inquire if he might pay your clinic a visit sometime tomorrow, preferably in the morning. A brief visit, of course."

"Tomorrow?" The question and the brusque tone of voice distracted Bryan from his unaccustomed playacting. He had to wait a moment before he could again muster MacReedy's affected tone of voice. A couple of new guests threw open the door of the beer hall. They were in a boisterous, expectant mood. Bryan hoped his hand over the receiver modulated the background noise sufficiently. Frau Rehmann would probably find it odd to hear people plainly speaking German in the famous town of Oxford.

"Yes, I know it's on unsatisfactorily short notice, Frau Rehmann," he continued, "but the fault is entirely mine. Mr. Underwood Scott asked me to convey his request several weeks ago, but I've been so busy that it unfortunately slipped my mind. Perhaps you can help me out of my embarrassing situation."

"I'm sorry, Mr. MacReedy, but I can't help you. Besides, a visit on a Saturday would be out of the question. We, too, need the few work breaks we can get."

The refusal was absolutely final. Some newly arrived bar guests stopped as they were hanging up their coats and looked at Bryan in bewilderment when he slammed down the receiver and began cursing softly in his corner—ready to do battle, yet totally unarmed.

So he would simply have to plunge straight into the lion's den and see what came out of it. Tomorrow he would present himself, unannounced, as the Bryan Underwood Scott of whom Mr. MacReedy had spoken so warmly. He would have to count on the director being home in her staff quarters, which, according to the floor plan at the entrance, was in the west wing of the villa.

It had begun getting dark a long time ago.

The elm trees along the avenue outside the sanitarium had begun swaying in the evening breeze when Kröner's silhouette finally appeared in the dull glow of the wrought-iron lights in the main entrance.

After jesting a bit with a woman in the doorway he took a stoop-shouldered man by the arm and accompanied him down the driveway, chatting quietly. Bryan slipped out of the beer hall and moved behind one of the elms, his heart beating rapidly.

The two men passed by quite close to him. Kröner's solicitude for the man was almost touching. A member of the family, perhaps, but hardly Pock Face's father. He wasn't old enough, even though with his delicate build, lined face, and almost snow-white beard, his age seemed indeterminate.

The old man said nothing. He looked ill and tired. To Bryan it seemed he was someone who was beginning to lose heart. So this old man was the reason for Kröner's visit, and now he was going home with Kröner for the weekend.

Therefore Bryan was surprised to see the two men walk past Kröner's car and continue beneath the whispering trees toward the center of town.

For a while the two men chatted quietly beside the tram stop. A crowd of exuberant youths on their way to the first party of the weekend came and stood beside them, shoving one another playfully and laughing so loud that the neighboring house facades' echo laughed back. Bryan crossed over to the tram stop and stood unnoticed, shielded by the youthful mob. He was less than two meters from Kröner and the old man. They were still talking softly, but the old man's voice was hoarse and before every other word he tried in vain to clear his throat.

Then the tram came.

Without turning to face his companion Kröner disappeared in the direction from which they had come. Bryan watched Pock Face for a moment, uncertain what to do, then decided to follow the old man onto the tram. Looking around calmly, the stoop-shouldered man caught sight of an empty seat beside a dark-complexioned young man.

Then he took up position beside the seat without sitting down. Before the next stop he stood directly facing the young man. As they looked at each other the young man's face changed almost imperceptibly. Then quite without warning the young man got up and walked quickly past the old man without touching him and down to the rear exit, where he remained standing, breathing heavily.

As the tram car pitched to and fro, the old man sat down heavily on the double seat, clearing his throat a couple of times. He stared out the window.

They had to change trams once before they reached the old man's destination in the center of town, where he finally alighted and strolled on past the brightly lit shop windows.

After pausing awhile in front of a pastry boutique's enticing assortment, the old man succumbed to temptation, giving Bryan time to think rationally. He had to choose between keeping guard in front of Kröner's house or following the old man. He glanced at his watch. There were still forty-five minutes before Keith Welles was due to report on his visit to Haguenau. From where he stood now, it couldn't be more than a ten-minute walk to the hotel.

When the old man left the shop, smiling contentedly, Bryan followed him.

The small paper bag dangled from the man's feeble wrist all the way to Holzmarkt. In the middle of this elegant square he stopped to speak to some other passersby, then cleared his throat and finally disappeared into a building, timeworn yet attractive, that stood a short way down a small side street called Luisenstrasse.

Bryan had to wait almost ten minutes before a light was lit on the third floor. An elderly woman went over to the windows to open the curtains. Some big potted plants made this a slow and laborious procedure. The massive building seemed to have only one flat on each floor. They must have been enormous. The rest of the building lay in darkness. In a room with a chandelier that shone cold and brightly and made him think of an old-fashioned dining room, an elderly man with a beard stepped behind the woman and rested his hands gently on her shoulders.

Bryan looked down at the narrow brass plate between the carved wooden doorframe and the phone booth. The plaque simply read: HERMANN MÜLLER INVEST.

CHAPTER 35

H ey, Laureen, have you seen how that gentleman over there is looking at me?"

"Who, Bridget? I can't see anyone." Laureen looked around Hotel Colombi's restaurant. About a hundred people had gathered to enjoy the short interval at the start of the evening as the waiters were preparing to serve dinner. Oblivious to the sound of clanking crockery and the babble of numerous languages, her thoughts were solely about Bryan and whatever had made her take the drastic step of going to Freiburg. Her feeling of unease returned instinctively.

She couldn't recall ever having felt like this before.

"Down there! Behind the empty table with the lilac tablecloth. He's looking at us now. He's wearing a checkered jacket. Look!"

"Oh, yes. Now I can see him."

"Good-looking man, isn't he?"

"Sure, I suppose so." Her sister-in-law's infatuation made Laureen wonder. "Good-looking" wasn't exactly how she'd describe him.

"Exciting, isn't it?"

Bridget placed her arms on the table and leaned forward. Tiny, fine wrinkles grew awkwardly around her mouth, revealing her arousal. She tossed her head slightly, as if to restore a lock of hair to its rightful place, though the half canister of hair spray she'd just spewed into their double room ensured that this movement was merely an affected reflex.

Laureen's plan was to get up early the next day, Saturday, and keep a constant watch on Bryan's hotel until he left it. Then she would sneak after him and see what happened. While the thought of observing her husband unnoticed presented a challenge, Bridget's presence presented a problem. Laureen couldn't possibly drag her along.

"Why don't you raise your glass to him, Bridget?"

Her sister-in-law blushed instantly and came down to earth. "Laureen!" she exclaimed. "You, my own sister-in-law. Whatever are you thinking?"

"Well, not the same as you. But does it matter?"

"Good Lord, whatever would he think?"

"Who?"

"The man over there!" Bridget blushed again.

"Probably the same as you, Bridget, dear." Laureen noticed that Bridget was unable to blush anymore. Almost, but not quite.

The next morning Laureen got up at a quarter past four. She had slept poorly, twisting and turning in an endless embrace with her pillow in order to get a grasp on her dreams. The bed beside the window was untouched. Laureen could already hear her sister-in-law's qualms of conscience and her plentiful assurances and pleas for understanding.

There had been a heavy morning dew. No trams or taxis were in sight and the town had still to awaken, so Laureen was practically the only living soul on the stretch of road between her hotel and Bryan's.

Nonetheless, she hadn't long to wait before things began to happen. Had she thought of it before, she would have hidden behind one of the chestnut trees that lined the entranceway to his hotel. From there she could have kept an eye on the recessed hotel portal and at the same time been able to see Bryan, should he decide to walk around the back of the hotel when he left. From where she was standing now on Urachstrasse, if he decided to go behind the hotel he would easily be able to disappear without her noticing.

She had scarcely become conscious of the problem before it was solved. The sound of crunching steps came from the pebbles on the passageway at the entrance and suddenly Bryan was out onto the street. Laureen stood quite unprotected. She was the only other human being in the vicinity. Before turning her back to the street, she caught a glimpse of Bryan's worried face as he turned up his collar. He was far away in his own thoughts and hadn't spotted her. For him, that was unusual.

Bryan walked briskly downtown. He was elegantly dressed. Laureen tiptoed after him over the cobblestones, praying that more people would soon turn up and that the sidewalk would become more suitable for high heels.

The figure a hundred meters in front of her seemed younger than the man she'd been living with for nearly a lifetime. He exuded a kind of fitness and youthful detachment that bore witness to the fact that he was presently disconnected from his normal daily sphere. He seemed like a stranger wandering through a distant city at this unholy hour when most people were submerged in their deepest sleep.

Some roadwork lay at a Saturday standstill. Bryan strode over it, disregarding the gravel that scuffed up his Lloyd shoes. Hesitating, Laureen lost sight of him. She stared around in confusion. Trams couldn't be as noiseless as that, but Bryan was gone.

"Oh, hell!" she thought. She felt ridiculous in her amateurish attempt to carry out a task as simple as shadowing the only person on the street. She'd traveled a long way to achieve this miserable outcome.

Then she made up her mind and began walking more rapidly downtown.

Her relief was enormous when she spotted Bryan striding with measured steps a couple hundred meters ahead of her. There were more people now, but Laureen felt they were all looking at her as she rushed down the street at breakneck speed with tiny steps, impeded by high heels, aching ankles, her clothing, her age, and her being out of shape.

She almost caught up with him near the center of town. But just as she was beginning to feel she had things under control, he sprinted over to a tram in the middle of the street and jumped onto one of the cars. Although Laureen had heard the tram coming behind her, she'd paid it no heed.

And now she couldn't reach it in time.

The very worst swearwords and phrases from her childhood began slowly to reemerge. She looked herself over. Why on Earth was she stumbling around on high heels with a dangling handbag full of lipstick and other stuff she couldn't possibly have use for on this mission? Whatever had she been thinking when she got dressed that morning? Putting on a tight skirt and a light-colored coat! Could it be she had the notion in the back of her mind that she ought to be well dressed in the event of a confrontation?

She nodded at this explanation and at her own folly.

She stood gaping at the tram as it rumbled away at a leisurely pace.

Perhaps it had been an advantage not to bring Bridget along after all. "Then Bryan would have been bound to have caught sight of us and everything would be over by now," Laureen thought as she retraced the exact same steps she had taken barely an hour before.

The tram stopped on the other side of the canal to allow the first early risers to get off and on. Then she saw Bryan again. He'd only taken the tram for a single stop.

This time she took no notice of the surprised glances. She hitched up her skirt and rushed off.

From a long distance it is almost impossible to see into which side street a car or a person turns. Distances in towns or on streets can be deceptive. More and more streets can keep turning up in a landscape that seems quite compact and fathomable.

Laureen had been sure the first time Bryan made a turn, but she had problems the second time. So she had to approach the next few street corners with caution in order to peep around them unnoticed. A couple of pedestrians looked at her, wondering about her strange behavior.

On the corner of Luisenstrasse and Holzmarkt, Laureen once more caught sight of Bryan. He was leaning against a wall a bit farther down the street, staring up at some big, barred windows. The staid building was classical in style but had been neglected. He was taking his time. And he was smoking.

As the town gradually woke up to a Saturday of hectic activity, waves of uneasiness once more surged over Laureen. Bryan was almost certainly up to something he hadn't wished to share with her.

By now the situation seemed so confusing and meaningless that, had it not been for the fact that Laureen knew her husband so well, she might easily have imagined there was another woman involved.

She could see Bridget's face before her and shook her head.

"We know nothing about our fellow human beings, and we know nothing about ourselves!" Laureen could clearly hear her daughter chanting this piece of homespun philosophy. But the problem was that it was nonsense. She'd always known that. It was simply a question of daring to look one's own and one's fellow human beings straight in the face.

If you weren't willing to do that from the start, you were in for a nasty surprise.

Right now Laureen had to accept the possibility that she hadn't been open enough in her view of her husband. Of course Bryan was capable of deceiving her, and he could also behave in ways Laureen knew nothing about. At any rate he'd never stood in front of *her* window for hours on end in the days he'd been courting her.

Still she felt that this was about something else. Something more complicated.

Normally someone like Bryan would always go about things directly when given a specific task.

And now he just stood there, waiting and smoking. Put on the defensive.

Occasionally the noise from the main street wafted down on the morning breeze. After several deliberations Laureen left her post. She had to be better equipped if she wanted to continue shadowing Bryan. And that meant different clothes and shoes. It seemed very unlikely that he had any intention of budging for quite a while.

It was only a few hundred paces down to the main street.

Having putting on her newly purchased jeans, she noticed a pair of running shoes in one of the special-offer boxes that littered the main entrance of the department store. Just as she was putting them on she saw her husband walk by on the opposite sidewalk.

Their glances met superficially. Laureen bit her lower lip and was just about to wave at him self-consciously like an awkward schoolgirl when he looked away and walked on.

He hadn't registered anything.

It was not until she reached the ring road that she was close enough to him again to feel sure he wouldn't slip away. He stopped in the middle of the pedestrian bridge and looked toward the park on the opposite side. The Stadtpark, as far as Laureen knew. She put down her huge plastic bag containing her skirt and coat and laced up her shoes. They were comfortable and they supported her ankles, but they were new. Before the end of the day her toes would be studded with blisters.

And then Bryan caught sight of the woman.

CHAPTER 36

He had begun to freeze.

Even though it was yet another morning with clear skies and late summer temperatures, the street was like an icy, windswept sluice.

Bryan had been in a kind of a dream for a couple of hours, trying to get a grip on the situation.

His phone conversation with Keith Welles the evening before had been a terrible disappointment. The Gerhart Peuckert he had seen in Haguenau was not James. If Welles had possessed sufficient presence of mind from the start, he would have investigated the man's age before taking the trouble to travel to France. When he finally reached his goal, a single glance at the patient had been sufficient. The Gerhart Peuckert in Haguenau was completely gray-haired and over seventy. With eyes that were brown and lively. It was a glaring mistake that had set back their investigation a whole day.

Now it was Saturday and Bryan was sure Welles wouldn't get much further. So from now on it was up to him.

The first item on the day's agenda was to have been a visit to the sanitarium. But he'd spent a sleepless, restless night, and before he knew it he was standing in front of the old man's house on Luisenstrasse without really knowing why. It was a pointless exercise. He was merely whiling away the time with occupational therapy. Perhaps he should have picked up his car, which he'd left at the sanitarium, or stood on guard outside Kröner's house, but this was how it had turned out.

There had been too many impressions. The sight of the delicate boy in Kröner's arms troubled him. What did Bryan actually know about the man? Why was Kröner in Freiburg? What had happened since their time in the hospital?

A string of questions remained unanswered. There had been no sign of life in the old man's house. The tatty curtains had not been drawn back. No one came and no one left, and it was now ten o'clock. So he finally decided to leave.

There were still some hours left before he was to visit the sanitarium.

The main street seemed very much itself—the sounds pleasant and comforting. The women had their husbands with them and the shops had opened, luring customers with baskets of special offers and garish, meaningless lighting. It was a typical morning atmosphere.

Colors were clear, pristine, and subtle.

In front of the department store, where a couple of days previously he'd watched an immigrant pull shorts over his cheap trousers, a woman was trying on one of the day's bargains. She stuck her feet hurriedly into a pair of shoes, stamping ritually on the ground to check their fit in much the same way as one judges a new car by kicking the tire. When she glanced up briefly she reminded him slightly of Laureen. Bryan had often been out shopping with her, sitting in the sultry heat in his overcoat while she tried something on. But this woman was in a hurry. Laureen never was.

He wished it could have been her.

The cathedral at Münsterplatz was a hodgepodge of three hundred years of architecture. A Gothic masterpiece that had walled in the joys and sorrows of the town for nearly eight centuries. A unique assembly point for the townspeople and a choice target for the Allied bombers when they were trying to destroy Freiburg's very spirit and backbone thirty years ago.

This time the town center seemed smaller. From the marketplace atmosphere of the cathedral square to the hectic Leopoldring and on to Stadtgarten, which leaned comfortably into the ridge of hills to the east, took less than two minutes on foot.

The concrete pillars of the long pedestrian bridge somehow fit flawlessly into the colorful setting of the park below. Above the narrow bridge, swaying, orange-striped gondolas on the aerial cable lift made their way up to the top of Schlossberg. Halfway up the hill an imposing, idyllic restaurant temporarily brought time to a halt. From there, the view down over the town and countryside, and farther toward Emmendingen and the mountain behind, had to be magnificent.

Bryan stopped for a moment to look around as he crossed the bridge above Leopoldring. Whether it was true or not, it felt as if Freiburg were repulsing him. It wouldn't have him. It didn't even notice him. The cathedral bells were chiming perpetually, as they had done in the days he'd been less than twenty-five kilometers away, fighting to preserve his sanity and his life.

Now it bore the message of peace.

People passed by without noticing him. Traffic rumbled busily beneath him. Apart from the tall woman who was leaning against the railing a bit farther on and gazing at Schlossberg with a big plastic bag at her feet, he was the only one who hadn't been engulfed by the town.

A noisy mob of cheerful children approached, supplemented by a group of chattering parents. Within a few seconds they were down in the park, on their way to the foot of the aerial cable lift. Even before the young parents had finished passing by, Bryan heard the sound of brisk steps and heels clicking hard against the surface of the bridge.

The woman was small and erect and wore a beige turtleneck sweater that framed her blond hair.

This was the second time that day when a woman had reminded Bryan of someone. But in this case the association was hazy.

She was not exactly young. Her clothing—a shiny black raincoat and long skirt of multicolored India cotton—made it difficult to determine her age.

This was the first thing that caught his eye, and then her rapid pace.

Bryan turned to face her, then studied her carefully.

She was one of those women one always seems to have seen somewhere before. It could have been anywhere: in the bus twenty minutes earlier, at the university twenty years ago, on the movie screen, in a moment's glimpse of fascination at a train station. The result was usually the same.

One never found out where, and definitely not who.

After she walked past him, he followed her, at a leisurely pace and at a distance. She slowed down when she reached the park. When she passed the gondola ticket office window she stood still for a moment, watching the hooting, expectant children. The gentle way in which she came to a halt was part of the total picture he was trying to recall. Bryan discarded a number of possibilities. Then she took a path in among the trees. It was the third or fourth time Bryan had been there but he didn't feel he knew the area very well. The woman turned left around the lake and disappeared in the direction of Jakob something-or-other Strasse.

When Bryan got past the trees she was gone. The grassy lawn in front of him was a turmoil of activity. He stopped next to a crowd of people who were watching a group of street entertainers, and looked around intently. The picture of the woman that was taking form almost imperceptibly in his mind's eye was beginning to disturb him.

He half ran a bit farther until he reached the deserted far corner of the park, then stopped and looked around for her in all directions.

The rustling noise behind him took him by surprise. The woman's face was livid as she stepped out of the undergrowth at the foot of the trees. She walked straight up to him, sized him up for a moment, and came to a halt just a couple of steps in front of him. "*Warum folgen Sie mir nach? Haben Sie nichts besser zu tun?*" she said.

But Bryan didn't answer. He couldn't.

Before him stood Petra.

For a moment he thought he was going to faint.

"I'm sorry!" he said. She was startled to hear his English. For a couple of seconds he stopped breathing and his pulse almost disappeared. The blood drained from his face, leaving his skin pallid. He swallowed a number of times in order to stave off a sudden feeling of nausea.

She was different, but her troubled face was painfully unchanged. It was precisely the small, fine characteristics and movements that never changed. The hard life that had apparently worn her out and turned her into an ordinary middle-aged woman had not been able to remove these, in spite of everything.

What an incredible coincidence. Cold shivers ran down his spine. The past became all too present as a totality of repressed impressions was reconstructed with unbelievable precision. Suddenly he could even remember her voice.

"Well, shall we call it a day?" she said. She turned on her heel without waiting for an answer and strode rapidly away.

It slipped out before he could think: "Petra!" he called out softly.

The woman stopped in midstep.

Her face displayed disbelief as she faced him again. "Who are you? How do you know my name? Tell me." She studied him closely. For a long while and in silence.

Bryan's pulse was hammering with excitement. Here was someone who presumably might be able to unveil James's fate.

The woman frowned slightly as if a thought had struck her, only to shake her head dismissively. "I don't know any Englishmen. So I don't know you, either. Are you going to give me an explanation?"

"You recognize me, I can tell!"

"I may have seen you before, yes. But I've seen so many people. I don't know any English people, in any case."

"Look at me, Petra! You know me, but it's been many years since you last saw me. You've never heard me speak. Besides, I speak English because I *am* English. You just didn't know it at the time." For every word Bryan uttered, the woman's face became more naked and recognizable. Her skin color showed signs of growing agitation. "I haven't come in order to annoy you, Petra, believe me! I had no idea you were still here, in Freiburg. It was a coincidence that I saw you up on the bridge. I didn't recognize you straightaway, either. You merely seemed familiar. It made me curious."

"Who are you? Where have we met?" She took a step backward as though the truth might be more than she could bear.

"In the SS hospital. Here in Freiburg. I was a patient there in 1944. You knew me under the name of Arno von der Leyen."

If Bryan hadn't sprung forward, she would have fallen. Halfway to the ground she worked herself free of his grasp and staggered backward. She scanned him briefly from top to toe and almost collapsed again. She put her hand to her breast, taking deep gasps of breath.

"I'm sorry! I didn't want to frighten you." Bryan looked at her, spellbound at the coincidence, and let her calm down a bit. "I've come to Freiburg to find Gerhart Peuckert. Can you help me?" Bryan spread out his arms. The air between them was palpable.

"Gerhart Peuckert?" She took a final deep breath and then collected herself for a moment as she looked down at the ground. When their eyes met again she had a bit more color in her cheeks. "Gerhart Peuckert, you say? I believe he is dead."

CHAPTER 37

The clear sky outside had clouded over momentarily. The light in the room was gray and barren. Wilfried Kröner still had the receiver in his hand. He'd been sitting like that for more than two minutes. The conversation with Petra Wagner had stunned him. She had been upset and incoherent, but what she'd had to report was unbelievable.

Then he straightened up and made a few notes on the pad beside him before dialing a number.

"Hermann Müller Invest," came the expressionless voice.

"It's me." The man at the other end of the line was silent. "We've got a problem on our hands."

"Well?"

"I've just spoken to Petra Wagner."

"Is she being difficult again?"

"Good Lord, no. She's as gentle as a lamb." Kröner pulled out the drawer of his desk and coaxed a pill from a small china bowl. "It's just that she met Arno von der Leyen here in Freiburg today."

There was a long silence at the other end. "Well, I'll be damned!" the man finally said. "Arno von der Leyen? Here in Freiburg?"

"Yes, in the Stadtgarten. They met by accident, she says."

"Are you sure?"

"That it was by accident? That's what she says."

"Well, and then what happened?"

"He introduced himself. She insists she's quite sure. It's him! Petra could recognize him when he told her who he was. She was very upset."

"I can damned well believe it!" Again there was silence at the other end.

Kröner clutched his midriff. It was acting up for the first time in several weeks. "The man's a killer," he said.

The old man seemed distant and cleared his throat softly. "Yes, he was a good man, poor Dieter Schmidt. He sure took care of him." Then he laughed dryly.

Kröner found this uncalled-for. "Petra also had some other disturbing news," he continued.

"He's presumably after us now. It that it?"

"He's looking for Gerhart Peuckert."

"Looking for Gerhart Peuckert? Indeed. And what does he know about him?"

"Apparently only what Petra told him."

"Then I certainly hope for her sake that she didn't say too much."

"Only that Gerhart is dead. It seemed to shock him." Kröner put his hand to his cheek. This was a situation he definitely could have done without. For the first time in many years he felt vulnerable.

They would have to get rid of Arno von der Leyen.

"And then he wanted to know where he was buried," he said at length.

"And she couldn't tell him, I would imagine." The old man was about to laugh, but had to clear his throat instead. The sound was dry and hollow.

"She told him she'd try to find out and let him know. They're to meet in the wine bar in Hotel Rappens at two o'clock. She made it clear that she doubted whether she could help him." Kröner could practically hear the wheels turning in the old man's head. "What do you think? Should we go there?"

"No!" came the instant reply. "Phone and tell her she's to let Arno von der Leyen know Gerhart Peuckert is buried in the memorial grove beside the panorama view on the Burghaldering, up beside the colonnade."

"But there's no such memorial grove."

"No, there isn't, Wilfried. But who would know that? What doesn't exist can materialize, can't it? And tell Petra Wagner that Arno von der Leyen can take the gondola up there. Have her tell him it takes only a couple of minutes from the Stadtgarten beside Karlsplatz. And finally, Wilfried, ask her to tell him that he can't get in before three o'clock."

"And what then? That can't be sufficient."

"Of course not. I've been considering whether we shouldn't try and get hold of Lankau. He seems to be the one best suited for the job, don't you think? It can be so nice and secluded up there on Schlossberg."

Kröner drew out yet another pill from the drawer. In a year's time

Kröner's son was to start school. The other parents would tell their children to play with him. He would have an easy time of it, and that's what Kröner wanted. After the war, life had treated him mercifully. And he wanted it to continue. He wasn't prepared to give up anything. "There's something else I don't like about the situation," he added.

"And that is . . . ?"

"He made Petra believe he was English. He spoke only English to her."

"She said that?" The old man paused for a moment. "And what then?"

"Yes, and what then? Who is he anyway? Is he here alone? Why is he looking for Gerhart Peuckert? Why does Arno von der Leyen make himself out to be English? I don't like it. There are too many unknowns in this story."

"Leave the unknowns to me, Wilfried. Isn't that my specialty? Haven't I always said there was something fishy about the man? Didn't I already tell you at the time that I suspected he wasn't the person he made himself out to be? I did, indeed! And now you can see for yourself! Unknowns are my trademark, you know that." He attempted a laugh, but it was stifled by his cough. "I practically live off unknowns. Would we have been where we are today if it weren't for my ability to make use of unknowns?" he said with difficulty.

"Then what's Arno von der Leyen's trademark? With what he learned from our nightly chats in the hospital, he's got to know what he's after."

"Nonsense, Kröner!" Peter Stich's voice hardened. "He'd have shown up years ago if he suspected we were here, but he doesn't. Our names are not the same. You mustn't forget the passage of time. It's a far cry from that red-eyed patient in the hospital to old, white-bearded Hermann Müller. But get rid of him we must, that's obvious. Now, take it easy and phone Petra Wagner, and in the meantime I'll find Horst Lankau."

Lankau was furious when he finally got to the flat on Luisenstrasse. He was oddly dressed. His pullover sat crooked, as if his golf bag were still slung over his shoulder. He didn't even shake hands. "Hasn't it dawned on you yet?" he blurted out. Kröner gave him a worried look. This time his incredibly broad face was entirely copper red. He had put on a lot of weight in recent years, forcing his blood pressure to dangerous heights. Andrea Stich took his coat and disappeared into the hallway. The light in the big flat was blinding, even though the sun was above the building. The old man stroked his beard once or twice and pointed amiably toward the corner sofa, where Kröner was already sitting.

"I play golf on Saturday, damn it! Freiburger Golf Club is my sanctuary! And I always have lunch with my opponent at the Colombi between the ninth and the tenth hole, don't I?" Lankau didn't expect an answer. "And that time when my daughter was in labor I didn't want to be disturbed either. You know that, damn it all! Why the hell are you disturbing me now?" He sat down heavily. "Make it brief!" he snapped.

"Calm down, Horst, we've got some interesting news to tell you." Peter Stich cleared his throat another couple of times and briefly explained the situation to the hefty, irritable man. Lankau's broad face was soon drained of every trace of color. He was speechless. He clasped his chubby hands and leaned forward. He was still a giant.

"So that's how it is, Horst! If you want to keep your little sanctuary on the golf course—or any other kind of sanctuary, for that matter—I'm afraid you're going to have to phone your golf partner and tell him he'll have to pop the ball into the last nine holes by himself this afternoon. You can tell him you have unexpected visitors from the old days, can't you?" Again the old man had to clear his throat instead of laughing.

"We'll have to drop everything else immediately," said Kröner, trying to ignore Lankau's rebellious glare. In the old days their order of rank had been clearer. "Until this is all over I'd suggest our families go away for a couple of days."

Lankau frowned, which made his injured eye close completely. That was the calling card Arno von der Leyen had left him the last time they met. "You think the swine knows where we live?" He turned toward Kröner, sticking out his bottom lip. Kröner felt certain Lankau was worrying more about his possessions than his family. The result was the same in any case. Lankau kept listening.

"I'm convinced that Arno von der Leyen is well prepared, and that he's planning his next move right now. Stich doesn't agree with me. He believes in coincidences."

"I don't know what I'm going to do, myself," said Stich. "But whatever steps you take with regard to your families is up to you. So long as you do it discreetly. Besides, I don't think I'll get Andrea to move from here, will I, Andrea?" The small figure shook her head silently and put the cups on the table.

Kröner looked at her. For him, she was an appendix to her husband—not an independent person, but unpolished and crude. Unlike Kröner's present wife, who was the embodiment of innocence, Andrea Stich had tried a bit of everything. A long life with her husband had made her immune to worries and pain. A concentration-camp commandant's wife's heart couldn't remain innocent indefinitely. If her husband had an enemy, he would have to be gotten rid of. It was as simple as that. She didn't question that kind of thing. It was for the men to deal with. In the meantime she would look after the home and herself. But Kröner couldn't involve his own family in this game. He neither could nor would. Lankau sat muttering to himself for a while. Then he leaned forward.

"And now I'm supposed to kill him! Isn't that what you're saying? Well, I'll be happy to. I've been waiting for this opportunity for years. But couldn't you have chosen a better place than Schlossberg for that kind of thing?"

"You just take it easy, Lankau. It's an excellent place. At three o'clock in the afternoon all the schoolchildren will have left. At that time of day, in the middle of September, there won't be a single onlooker in the colonnade. You'll be able to get your revenge in peace." The old man dipped another cookie in his coffee. It was a Saturday privilege that his doctor would have castigated him for. Kröner knew this from his own son. Diabetic patients had a habit of breaking the rules. "In the meantime you'll see that both your families go away for the weekend, won't you, Wilfried? And I suggest we meet at five o'clock at Dattler's when it's all over. Then we can get rid of the body together. I'll find a solution to that little problem, don't worry. But until then we have some things to do. First and foremost, yet another little job for you, my dear Wilfried."

Kröner looked at him absentmindedly. He had been wondering what he was going to say to his wife. She would ask questions. Peter Stich placed his hand on top of his.

"But before you do anything else, Wilfried, you must pay Erich Blumenfeld a visit."

CHAPTER 38

Feelings of joy and sorrow, tension and relief, anxiety and sadness kept on sweeping over him in unpredictable and self-contradictory waves. The one moment he stopped breathing; the next moment he was gasping for breath.

His tears blurred the contours of the surroundings.

James hadn't made it. It didn't come as a surprise, but as an accusation. The feeling of having let James down was no longer merely latent.

"Have you seen the grave?" Welles inquired at the other end of the line. Bryan could all but see his incredulous face.

"No, not yet."

"Are you sure he's dead?"

"The nurse thought so, yes."

"But you haven't seen the grave yet! Shall I carry on until Monday as we agreed?"

"Do as you like, Keith. I think we've reached our goal."

"You *think* so." Keith accentuated Bryan's reservation. "You're not certain?"

Bryan sighed. "Certain?" He rubbed the back of his neck. "Yes, I suppose I am. I'll let you know when I know more."

One of the waitresses gave Bryan an indignant look. The pay phone was their greatest obstacle between the kitchen and the cafeteria. They all nodded toward a notice printed on the wall above the telephone. Bryan couldn't understand what it said, but presumed it referred customers to one of the phone booths he'd seen on the ground floor of the department store. Bryan shrugged his shoulders every time they edged past him with overfilled trays, shaking their heads. It had been his third phone call. Or rather his third attempt.

After several tries he could only conclude that Laureen was not at home in Canterbury. There was a good chance of her having accompanied Bridget back to Cardiff.

The next call was to Munich. They hadn't had need for him in the Olympic City. The exchange of words was brief. They spoke solely of England's victory in the women's pentathlon. Apparently this triumph overshadowed everything else. Mary Peters had exceeded the magical 4,800 by one single point. It was sensational. The world record was within reach. Despite pauses in the conversation, neither party found occasion to touch upon the tragic events of recent days. The desecration of the Games had been discussed, screamed, and written to death even before the victims had been buried. But in sports, the show must go on.

His heart was hammering at a dangerous pace when he finally reached Hotel Rappens's entrance on Münsterplatz. The bar was almost full. Bryan saw nothing and no one else but Petra. She was sitting by the door facing the square in her overcoat, sipping a large glass of draft beer. The froth on the uppermost part of the glass had already solidified. She must have been waiting for some time. So his being early didn't matter.

It was ten minutes to two.

Before the hour struck she had deprived him of his last hope. The realization made Bryan's lips tremble. Petra kept her eyes on the table and shook her head slightly. Then she looked at him and put her hand on his arm.

The taxi driver had to ask three times before he understood where Bryan wanted to go. Bryan was already regretting not having stayed with Petra so they could try to come to terms with their common past. But he had no choice.

He simply had to get out of there.

She had confirmed that Gerhart Peuckert was dead. Once again the shock was instantaneous. James had been buried in the common grave of a memorial grove—another shock that took Bryan unawares. Many people had been killed in the raid on January 15, 1945, and many had been buried without having been identified—a fact that dawned on him only now. James had been laid to rest without a name, without a stone to mark his grave. That was what was worst of all.

The conversations with Captain Wilkens, who had guided the Allied bombers to the hospital, came back all too vividly now.

Painfully vividly.

When Bryan finally reached the Kuranstalt St. Ursula where he'd parked the mutilated Volkswagen, his mind was in complete turmoil.

Everyone reacts differently to having his or her patience put to the test under pressure. Bryan remembered clearly how James always became sleepy in such situations and instantly looked around for someplace to stretch out. That's how it had been prior to taking off on a raid, and that's how it had been on exam days at Eton and Cambridge. A gruff exam leader had often had to shake some life into James before he could sit down and face the examiners.

This was an enviable talent, and a blessing.

But it had never been like that for Bryan. Waiting made him restless. It made him get up from his chair, then sit down again. Constantly. He had to wriggle his feet, run out into the fresh air, hurriedly scan the syllabus again, dream of freedom. Do *something*.

This feeling overpowered him now for the first time in ages. The waiting fever had taken possession of him. There was an hour before he could go up Schlossberg to see his best friend's grave. An hour where agitation and irrationality would reign. He was under pressure, and he was impatient.

He looked at his wreck of a Volkswagen again. It stood out somewhat from the other cars on the street. Although hard to imagine, it was filthier than ever. There wasn't a square centimeter that wasn't covered with dust. It was no longer black, but gray.

His intention had been to drive the Volkswagen over to the little bodega by the railway bridge and park it there so its previous owner could fetch it again, as they'd agreed.

Bryan folded his arms on the roof of the car, not noticing how black his underarms were getting, and looked over at Kuranstalt St. Ursula.

Like all institutions housing psychological deviants, St. Ursula naturally had its secrets. His hope had been that James was one of them. But that was not the case, he knew now. However, the pock-faced murderer, Kröner, was part of that place. An unknown part. He could be anything at all.

The Volkswagen rocked slightly when he struck the roof. He'd made a quick decision.

The waiting fever had had its effect.

. . .

Several minutes passed before the director, Frau Rehmann, appeared in the administration unit. Until then an unwilling orderly had tried to turn him away. But the bouquet Bryan thrust toward him confused him and cleared the path into Frau Rehmann's front office. Bryan glanced at the bouquet, already wilting from the heat, and congratulated himself on his resourcefulness.

It had been intended for James's grave.

The front office was neat and tidy. Not a piece of paper to be seen. Bryan nodded appreciatively. The only decorative object in the whole room was the framed photo of a young woman looking over the head of a dark-haired boy. Therefore Bryan assumed that Frau Rehmann's secretary was a man, and expected the worst of her.

And he was right, though only partially.

Frau Rehmann was just as impregnable in reality as on the telephone. It had been her firm intention all along to throw Bryan out. But as she was about to guide him out again, Bryan's sudden presentation of the bouquet pacified her long enough for him to sit down on the edge of the secretary's desk and flash her a broad, authoritative smile.

It was a question of negotiation. Bryan was an expert at this even when, as now, he hadn't the slightest idea of his goal, let alone his motive.

"Frau Rehmann, do forgive me! I must simply have misunderstood Mr. MacReedy. There was a message left at my hotel saying that the morning hours wouldn't suit you, so I took it to mean I should come in the afternoon, instead. Shall I go again?"

"Yes, please, Mr. Scott. I would appreciate that."

"Of course it's sad, now that I'm here. The commission will be very disappointed."

"Commission?"

"Yes. Naturally we know your clinic is run according to the best management principles. Yet I'm sure you'll agree with me, Frau Rehmann, that there isn't a single administrative enclave that wouldn't benefit from the available funds."

"Available funds? I don't know that you're talking about, Mr. Scott. What is this commission you're referring to?"

"Did I say commission? Well, maybe that's putting it a bit strongly, insofar as it hasn't been set up yet. Let's call it a commission committee. That's probably a more appropriate term."

Frau Rehmann nodded. "I see. A commission committee." The director was noticeably curious beneath her well-polished, authoritative veneer. "And that's the committee you're a member of, Mr. Scott?"

"A member? Well, you could call me a kind of chairman. We committee members are all more or less equal. No, perhaps we should call me the spokesman."

"Yes, we can do that, if you find it a better term, Mr. Scott."

Bryan felt manic. The seduction of this bony woman in front of him was therapeutic in itself. He glanced at his watch. It was half past two. Now he wouldn't have time to park the Volkswagen outside the hippie's bar.

"Yes, it's a matter of EEC funds that are in the developmental phase at present but that we venture to presume are in the offing. All private clinics like yours may come into consideration regarding some quite substantial funding, Frau Rehmann."

"Aha, the EEC!" she said, thoughtfully. "Yes, I think I've read something about it somewhere. . . ." Frau Rehmann was a terrible actress. "You say it's in the committee stage? When will the commission be set up, Mr. Scott? I mean, when will you come to a decision regarding the distribution and size of the funding?"

"Uh, I'm afraid that's very difficult to determine. It depends partly on the individual countries' membership after the New Year and partly on our present work. Obstacles are always cropping up. Destructive and delaying obstacles, small stupid details. Like this business with MacReedy, for example. He bungled it, didn't he?" Still sitting, Bryan leaned toward her so that his face just reached the height of her square shoulders. "Tell me, Frau Rehmann, you don't mean to say that all this is new to you? The thought just struck me."

"Yes, I must confess it is." Frau Rehmann laughed a bit awkwardly. Now Bryan knew he had her.

Frau Rehmann was both accommodating and instructive as she showed him around the clinic. Bryan nodded with polite interest and posed few questions, which seemed to suit his guide admirably. Despite Bryan's expert knowledge, most of Frau Rehmann's copious psychiatric terminology went over his head. His thoughts were elsewhere.

It was a modern establishment. Light and friendly, with subdued colors and a smiling staff. In one wing practically all the patients were sitting in the lounge. Everywhere the Olympic Games finals resounded over the television.

The great majority of patients in the first ward seemed to be suffering from senile dementia. They were sitting passively in a drug-induced stupor, the saliva flowing unimpeded down their chests. Some others were constantly digging around discreetly in their crotch.

There were remarkably few women.

Although Frau Rehmann appeared to be taken aback, Bryan insisted on being allowed to take a peek into all the rooms.

"Frau Rehmann, I've never seen a higher standard. That's why I'm still curious. Can your entire institution really be like that?" The director smiled. She was half a head taller than all the men they had encountered on their rounds. Most of this difference in height was due to her unusually long legs, and even more so to a hairstyle that was constantly threatening to topple over. She reached up and touched this enormous superstructure every time Bryan complimented her. Now she did it again.

It was already three o'clock when they passed the counter in the front hall on their way to the other wing. An immense, indefinable exotic plant stood on each side of the entrance, stretching its leaves toward the skylight in the roof. Besides being decorative, the purpose of the plants was to mitigate the sight of two abominable, freestanding clothes racks where Bryan had been instructed to hang his coat upon arrival.

Behind these gigantic plants and behind these clothes racks, a large figure with a scarred face had withdrawn, unnoticed. He was breathing between his teeth, quiet and controlled. The sight of Frau Rehmann's companion made him clench his fists.

It wasn't until they reached the last room that Frau Rehmann's attention was deflected from showing Bryan around. There had already been several attempts to call her on the intercom, but with no apparent effect.

Bryan looked about. The interior was the same as in the previous ward.

But here, however, the condition of the patients had changed. A world of difference from the quiet death of geriatric psychosis.

Cold shivers ran down Bryan's spine. More than anything else, this ward reminded him of the time he spent in the SS hospital's psychiatric ward. The inarticulate forms of speech and body language. The underlying apathy and a feeling of things having been hushed up.

Although Bryan hadn't seen any really young patients anywhere, the average age here was scarcely more than forty-five. At first glance some of the patients seemed to be fairly healthy, politely acknowledging the director's curt nod—so curt that her hair scarcely concurred with the nod.

And there were other patients whose entire body language bore the mark of schizophrenia. Lethargic, contradictory facial movements and deep, disquieting eyes.

They were all staring at the television set from their respective places. Most of them were sitting in a row of oak architect-designed armchairs, some on colorful sofas, and a few in large, high-backed armchairs that faced away from the entrance doors.

As Bryan looked the TV viewers over, he noticed a new and more serious expression on Frau Rehmann's face as she stood beside the intercom. Then she said a couple of words, made straight for Bryan, and took him gently by the arm.

"I'm so sorry, Mr. Scott, but we must hurry on. I do apologize, but we still have an upper story to inspect, and some events have occurred that will demand my presence shortly."

Several of the patients watched them listlessly as they left the room. Only one had failed to react at all. He'd been sitting immobile in a high-backed armchair that many years of seniority had given him the right to have for himself. Only his eyes moved slightly.

Whatever was taking place on the screen had riveted his attention.

CHAPTER 39

The moment they left the room, the man in the armchair continued where he'd left off. He began, as usual, by moving his feet up and down at the ankle. Then he spread out his toes until they hurt, took a deep breath, and relaxed. Next he flexed his calves until they also began to hurt, followed by his shin and thigh muscles. Having flexed and relaxed each set of muscles in his body in turn, he started from the beginning again.

The grainy television screen kept changing color. It seemed the bodies on the screen had been sweating and displaying their exasperation for an eternity. Now it was the third time the same sprinters had lined up for the same race. They slapped their arms and flung their legs about. Some of the track shoes had three stripes and others just one. At the sound of the shot they all took off, pumping their arms forward and back, then upward as they passed the finish line. They were all muscular, especially the colored men. Muscular all over, from top to toe.

Then the man rose carefully from his chair and stretched his hands toward the ceiling. None of the other patients took their eyes off the screen. They ignored him. Then he began flexing his muscles again, group by group. His body was in harmony, top to toe, like the colored men.

Some runners collapsed on the green turf. None of these were colored and they were all wearing light-colored shorts. The light-colored shorts were in the majority. As he stretched his hand toward the ceiling for the tenth time he counted the officials who were lined up at the barrier facing the spectators. For every shift of the camera he counted them again. There were twenty-two.

Then he sat down and began his series of exercises once more.

The runners moved around, arms to their sides, as they loosened up. He had seen this race before as well. None of the athletes looked at one another. Most of them had shoes with three stripes. Only one had settled for a single horizontal stripe. Then he counted the number of officials at the barrier. There were only a few this time. Eight. He recounted them.

In the middle of a break between events he got up again. Bending forward, he took hold of his ankles and pulled his body in toward his thighs. He closed his eyes and listened to the sounds in the room. The buzzing of the spectators was replaced by the silence that boded the appearance of new runners. It was still the same as what he had seen the day before.

He tugged hard at his legs so his forehead struck his knees, and began counting backward. One hundred, ninety-nine, ninety-eight, ninety-seven . . . Once again a shot rang out. He looked to one side and let the picture of the room whirl past him upside down, still counting backward. The features of a face in the chair next to him dissolved as a result of his intense movements. Colors ran together on the screen and again he heard the crowd shouting in broad, deep, inarticulate harmony. He straightened up, fixing in his mind a glimpse of the massive array of arms and colors on the screen. Then he closed his eyes again and began counting the heads from memory. Sounds in the background were fading. He always began to get dizzy at this point in his routine. The last thirty toe touches were performed reflexively. He took a couple of quick, deep breaths and straightened up. After a few spasms in his neck subsided, he again stretched toward the ceiling and didn't sit down until the dots on the screen had again assembled themselves into one picture.

Then he took several deep breaths, holding the last one. This was the reward that followed every round. Total concentration and serenity. All his pores open. At moments like this he became aware of his surroundings.

Afterward he closed his eyes and went through the whole routine backward, movement by movement. When he got back to the start he heard clearly how the steps of the visitors behind him had sounded. He recalled all the movements in the room.

The stranger's shoes had had hard soles. The taps on the floor had been short, the steps many and light. The person had stood still while the director was on the intercom. And then they had exchanged words again.

The man in the big armchair quickly struck his knees together and let his eyes glide out of focus. He exhaled slowly between his teeth, then suddenly took another deep breath. They'd been talking together. Both of them had uttered sounds that felt obtrusive and jarring, now that he recalled them. He focused his eyes again and saw a new set of runners psyching themselves up for the next race. Five of them had shoes with three stripes, two with only one stripe. Next he counted the officials at the barrier. This time there were only four. After the third recount he began breathing more rapidly and looked upward.

Some of the words refused to let go of him.

He looked at the screen again and began from the beginning by wriggling his feet. This time he left out half his routine, got off the chair, and took hold of his ankles. When he heard the steps in the corridor he let go again and straightened up with a jerk. No one had ever caught him carrying out these rituals.

Not until the pock-faced man sat down beside him did he move his head. He allowed his visitor to stroke the back of his hand and counted how many times he did so, as he'd done so often before. This time his visitor was more subdued than usual. "Come, my friend" was all he said. "We're going to see Hermann Müller." Then he gave the hand a squeeze. "Come along, Gerhart, we're going to have our Saturday coffee."

It was the first time in many years that the name seemed wrong to James.

CHAPTER 40

Not until he set foot on the path in Stadtgarten did it dawn on Bryan that the flowers he'd intended for James's grave were now standing in Frau Rehmann's office. After her conversation on the intercom she'd become remarkably more reserved as she showed Bryan around.

A few minutes afterward they'd bidden each other farewell.

The entire venture had been in vain. His wish to learn more about Kröner, or Hans Schmidt, as he now called himself, had not been fulfilled. There had been no opportunity to ask the right questions. Any attempt to couple EEC subsidies with questions of a semiprivate nature would have been running a risk. Frau Rehmann would instantly have been puzzled and known something was wrong. Soon it would reach Kröner's ears. Bryan had no need of such a confrontation.

He would seek out Pock Face when the time was ripe.

All in all, the visit had been a shot in the dark. A waste of time.

As soon as he entered the park Bryan bent down and picked his flower—a crummy, half-withered, nettle-like purple object he'd been able to pull up by its roots without incurring the park attendant's disapproval. He straightened the petals a little. This insignificant growth symbolized his feelings and loneliness better than any store-bought bouquet.

The trip up in the aerial tram seemed endless. The swaying of the gondola made him feel nauseous. A queasiness that still hadn't passed when, according to Petra's instructions, he began following the moss-covered, cobbled path leading up to the colonnade. The artificial Greek columns hugged the slope like some kind of anachronism. They were ringed by low walls topped by iron railings.

Despite its good intentions the construction was indescribably ugly and poorly maintained, with a wistful mustiness that placed the mood and purpose of the site in a state of exalted unanimity.

War memorials in Germany are not normally distinguishable by their anonymity. The gigantic angular column at the bottom of Schlossberg was excellent proof of this. Since the First World War it had honored the fallen, but practical foresight had allowed part of the surface of the column to remain free of engravings. Only two decades were to elapse before World War II took up the prophetically unused remainder of its surface. One counted on not needing more room in the future.

Memorials like this were to be found all over the country, and common to them all was a clear indication as to why they had been erected. Therefore, after having examined every surface of the edifice several times, Bryan wondered why he hadn't found so much as a small brass plate or the tiniest other sign to indicate the purpose for which the structure had been built, or indeed that it was even a burial ground.

He squatted down, resting his arms on his thighs. Then he tipped over onto his knees and scooped up a handful of earth.

It was damp and dark.

CHAPTER 41

Precisely forty-five minutes previously a broad and heavy figure had trod the same path up the slope.

The last steps through the thicket had made him breathe more heavily. It was at least five years since Horst Lankau had been there, and before that, much longer. These columns had witnessed many stolen moments of love. Had Lankau grown up in the town he would doubtlessly have had a different attitude toward the place.

At the moment he hated it.

Throughout three summers his eldest daughter, Patricia, had been crazy about a kid whose family unfortunately had the habit of spending a couple of weeks of their impoverished vacation at a campground south of Schlossberg. From these fluttering tents it was all too easy for the infatuated couple to run up the steps at Schwabentor and along the path to the Grecian-like monument where Lankau now found himself.

The youngster's third summer with his daughter was to be his last summer in Freiburg, and Patricia had never mentioned him since.

Lankau had caught the lovers in the act—with their pants down, as it were—and ever since then the boy hadn't been capable of similar activities. Lankau had been forced to pay dearly, but the kid's parents had been satisfied with the compensation.

Then the fool could at least get himself an education.

Now Patricia was well married and the other two daughters were too smart to try the same stunt.

His son could do what he liked.

Climbing to the platform that constituted the roof of the colonnade, Lankau could clearly see that others still sought out their little adventures here, judging by all the limp, elongated condoms lying vulgarly up against the walls.

A strong contrast to their orgiastic purpose.

It would soon be half past three. Horst Lankau didn't mind waiting. He'd been thirsting for revenge for years.

Arno von der Leyen had suddenly been swallowed up by nothingness that fateful night on the Rhine. Despite Lankau's persistent attempts and excellent connections, his efforts to find the merest trace of the man's subsequent fate had proven futile.

Day in and day out he'd had to live with the physical scars he'd acquired in that crucial clash. He was no longer a handsome man. His closed-up eye made his face look crooked. Women didn't care for him and looked away when he tried to allure them. He felt inferior. The blindness in his right eye prevented him from improving his golf handicap. Every single month his compressed neck vertebrae gave him headaches that made life miserable for both him and his family. The shot in his chest had ripped away muscles, making it difficult for him to raise his left arm higher than his waist and upsetting his stroke up the fairway.

Finally, and worst of all, he was plagued by the wound in his soul known as hatred. It was a source of eternal demoralization and torment.

For the sake of finally avenging all these atrocities, he could easily wait a bit longer.

Lankau had already spotted his victim as he'd bent down to pick the flower at the foot of the pedestrian bridge. He sat down heavily on the roof of the colonnade and laid his binoculars beside his pistol.

The weapon before him was one of the worst ever put into mass production. It was said to have the lives of more friends than foes on its conscience. The Type 94, or the 94 Shiki Kenju, as it correctly was called, was a rare example of how even the Japanese could err when it came to precision mechanics.

The pistol was unreliable. When fully loaded, the weapon was liable to go off with a slight nudge to the safety catch, which was placed in a handy but extremely exposed position, just above the stock.

On the other hand, this was the only pistol in Lankau's collection that was equipped with a silencer.

The first time he had seen it was at the home of one of his oldest business connections, a Japanese man for whom time stood still in order to perpetually honor traditional rituals. One summer day in Toyohashi, Lankau's host had proudly unwrapped it from an old rag and told him how well it had protected him throughout his life, despite its bad reputation.

As the result of Lankau's obvious envy, he had received it as a gift only a month later in a shipment of mixed cargo.

Japanese hospitality had dictated that his host make this gesture to maintain his honor.

But afterward they never did business together again.

Perhaps the Japanese businessman had expected Lankau to return it with a polite protest.

But he hadn't done so.

The weapon had been oiled and tested regularly. The sound of the silenced shots bore no resemblance to the plops usually heard in movies. They simply sounded like shots, short and very quiet, but shots nevertheless. Lankau looked around. There was nothing to be seen within fifty meters' earshot. The activity over at Dattler's—the town's proud landmark and one of the best restaurants in the region—was quite normal. It was seldom anyone felt the urge to wander around the rough outskirts of Schlossberg at this time of year.

Lankau had to grant Peter Stich that.

The broad-faced man looked down the incline and adjusted his defective eye socket. The aerial cableway seemed incredibly slow that day.

Once the gondola finally moved out of view behind the trees, he seized the pistol and lay down flat on the roof. In his experience, the target had to be very close in order to ensure that the Shiki Kenju fired both accurately and lethally. He had tried it out on animals. Since he'd grown overweight through the years, he could no longer run after his prey.

The prey had to come to him, and now it was getting close.

The man was visible for a second before disappearing beneath the treetops. Arno von der Leyen still had the suppleness of youth about him. Naturally he was different from how Lankau remembered, but it was him. Lankau sensed the sweetness on his breath, as though his bloodlust had already found its release. He'd long wanted to meet this man again under circumstances like these.

Unsuspecting, and within firing range.

The footsteps in the building beneath Lankau were slow and hesitant. Apparently Arno von der Leyen was looking for Gerhart Peuckert's grave. Lankau breathed quietly. You could never tell with a man like Leyen. This would be their final confrontation, one way or another, and Lankau was taking no chances. If he could simply get this demon into close range, the matter would be settled. He would shoot without hesitation.

The shouts from the paths above him came from different directions. The voices were young, but not those of children. Lankau cursed inwardly. Young people were good at creating sudden disturbances. They had no respect for natural obstacles and could come crashing out of the underbrush before you knew it.

The crunching steps below him came to a halt.

CHAPTER 42

The damp patches on his knees had been spreading gradually. Sighing plaintively, Bryan leaned back into a squatting position as he tried to take in the landscape below him. The rooftops and green oases in the flat, low-lying countryside merged into one. He hadn't wept like this for years. In the end he had fallen to his knees.

The carefree laughter of the youths farther up the slope, the pungent smell of resin, and the neat landscape before him provoked the most intense loneliness he'd ever felt, for there was no trace of the grave inscription that was supposed to memorialize his best friend.

Bryan bit his upper lip and raised his eyes, cursing himself for not having gotten Petra's address. Maybe he had misunderstood her instructions. Maybe she had expressed herself imprecisely or misled him on purpose.

He stood up, letting his shoulders fall. In this lucid landscape with the town's hectic activity below, he lost his desire to make sense of it all.

This was James's resting place. He was sure of it.

He bowed his head silently in memory of his friend. Then he carefully smoothed out the petals of the wilting flower and looked around for a suitable spot to place it. He would have laid it on top of a gravestone, had there been one.

He stood for a moment at the end of the colonnade and looked beyond the small closed building in the center of the memorial area. A small path disappeared into the foliage a little way up the slope before him as it wound its way upward and around the back of the memorial. The brown soil and the naked, worn roots indicated it was still in use.

Here was an area where he had yet to look.

A few steps up the path he heard the unexpected sound. An insignificant click, almost inaudible. It was a sound that had no business being there.

Suspicion seldom meets resistance. Unlike positive feelings, a suspicion can easily present itself unconditionally and without warning, and even without basis. But in this case there was basis enough.

Petra Wagner, Mariann Devers, and Frau Rehmann: At one time or another they'd all had contact with Kröner—a man who had once sought to take his life and certainly had no wish to be jerked back into the past.

And then there was this sound. This tiny click. Everything could be made to fit with the encouragement of tangible, conclusive suspicion.

So Bryan stopped, squatted down cautiously in the vegetation bordering the path, and waited.

Like a devil that will not be confined to hell, the shape appeared in Bryan's field of vision, less than five meters away. The figure stood for a moment on the narrow platform leading from the roof of the building and scrutinized the path beside which Bryan was crouching. And then Bryan recognized the man.

He had never imagined he would see this repulsive broad face again. Nothing on this Earth could have surprised him more. The cold current of the Rhine should have been his grave for nearly thirty years. Bryan recalled the sight of him disappearing into the waves, wounded and drained of stamina.

His presence was the materialization of a nightmare that had never been dreamt.

Even though the man was more corpulent than ever, the years had treated him kindly. People with weathered skin and color in their cheeks can look youthful even in old age. This would have also applied to the broad-faced man, if it hadn't been for his almost empty eye socket and the white knuckles tightening their grip on a lethal weapon.

The likelihood of this colossus walking past Bryan without noticing him was negligible. He carefully withdrew his foot into the shelter of the underbrush and put his face to the ground, at the same time placing his hands under his chest, ready to spring up like a jack-in-the-box.

He didn't see Lankau's shoe until it was in reach of his arm. Despite Bryan's precisely aimed blow, he didn't succeed in knocking the heavy man's leg out from under him. Almost instantaneously Lankau whirled around violently to confront him, but the impulsive movement made him step back off the flat bit of path and slide awkwardly downward, still standing upright.

But he fired nevertheless.

The impact of the projectile took Bryan by surprise, as did the noise of the shot. He felt no pain at all, nor could he tell where he'd been hit. The echo of the muffled shot had scarcely subsided before Bryan hurled himself at the tottering figure, now almost doing a split with one leg up on the path and the other hugging the side of the slope. Then came the second shot. The tree behind Bryan received it hollowly, its bark opening in a yellowish gape. Bryan grabbed instantly for Lankau's face, kicking him savagely in the chest at the same time.

The cumbersome figure stared at him in openmouthed astonishment. Not a sound escaped him, in spite of the pain the kick must have caused. Then he collapsed and fell backward down the slope, clinging to Bryan. Only the soft undergrowth prevented Bryan from losing consciousness. After the heavy man had tumbled over him several times, the entangled bodies finally came to a halt in the vegetation bordering on the path at the end of the colonnade. Unable to move, they lay side by side in the middle of the thicket, gasping and staring each other in the face. Thin streams of blood trickled down from the scratches in Lankau's head and flowed into the eyelashes of his sound eye. In falling, he had clutched the pistol so frantically to his face that the notch of the sight on the barrel had ripped his flesh. He kept on blinking, but no matter how much he jerked his head he was almost blinded by his own blood. Now the weapon lay less than twenty centimeters away in the churned-up earth.

Bryan reared back his head and began butting the broad-faced man until his own brain exploded in a series of electric flashes.

Then his pursuer uttered a sound for the first time. Bryan tumbled over the huge body and grabbed for the gun, but his head was suddenly and unexpectedly wrenched backward by a firm grip on the hair at the back of his neck.

Lankau's rescue had come from behind. Several youths were standing around, screaming unintelligible abuse, the girls looking on in rapture behind the boys. They'd come in search of excitement and, as usual, the hiding places in the colonnade hadn't disappointed them.

Two of the young men took hold of Lankau, hauled him to his feet and started brushing him down. With blood trickling down his face he put his hand to his bruised head and began looking around distractedly for his weapon, talking nonstop to the youngsters. They let go of Bryan's hair. Without a word, Bryan edged clumsily backward up the slope in a cross-legged position. No one saw the weapon slide under him.

Bryan had no idea what Lankau said to the young people, but he disappeared in a matter of seconds.

The semicircle around Bryan didn't seem in any hurry to disperse.

Cautiously Bryan stretched his arm backward and made contact with the pistol. It was heavier than he'd expected. Just above the grip he found the safety catch. No one heard him push it into place. Then he carefully pushed the barrel down between his waistband and his back and slipped on his jacket. The pain didn't come until he pulled his hand out of his trousers again. An irrepressible moan made everyone stare at him. One of the girls put her hand to her mouth and gasped as Bryan raised his bloody hand and looked at them.

"He shot me," he said simply, not expecting any of them to understand him.

One of the girls began yelling. An almost white-haired young man appeared from behind the others and carefully pulled Bryan to his feet. The red patch on his back pocket was still growing, but to a lesser extent than he had feared. The shot had gone clean through his gluteus maximus, the most fleshy part of the buttock. The wounds where the bullet had entered and left the body had almost closed. The loss of blood was relatively slight. Bryan's left leg felt shaky under him.

Then the semicircle retreated. The fair-haired youth shouted a few words and the rest of the group dispersed almost instantly, running down the path along which Lankau had disappeared. Then he turned toward Bryan. "Can you walk?" he asked, hesitantly. It was a relief to hear him speak English.

"Yes, I can, thanks."

"The others will try and catch him." The young man looked down the path where audible shouts revealed what they were doing. Bryan doubted very much they'd find the man they were looking for. "I'm sorry. We seem to have made a mistake. Did he attack you?"

"Yes."

"Do you know why?"

"Yes."

"Why?"

"Because he wanted to take my money."

"We'll call the police."

"No! Don't do that! I don't think he'll do anything like that again."

"Why don't you think so? Do you know him?"

"In a way, yes."

Although the buttock muscle belongs to a group of muscles large enough to function satisfactorily despite injury, Bryan had to support himself on whatever he could when he took his first steps.

The white-haired youth left him without further comment and rushed off after his companions.

Five minutes later their lively chatter had faded away.

It seemed the path leading to the gondola's end station was longer than before. Bryan stopped after every ten steps and glanced down the back of his legs. The dark patches on his pants were no longer spreading.

By the time the aerial cable appeared behind the treetops he was sure the bleeding had stopped. No need to concern himself with compression bandages or hospital admittance. There were other worries.

The first was keeping alive. There was no way of knowing when, or from where, an attack might come. The only thing he knew was that it couldn't be avoided. It was his life they were after and it was Petra Wagner who had lured him into the trap.

The second worry was: Why?

Why had Petra Wagner lied and why was getting rid of him so imperative that they would risk it in broad daylight?

The third source of worry was some broken branches hanging awkwardly under the bushes. The hollow in the thicket to which they pointed was almost invisible. The bushes above it closed nicely together, but the leaves were quivering in the calm air. Taking careful hold of the grip, Bryan drew out the pistol. He glanced around once more before saying anything. He detected no movement, not even over by the gondola station.

"Come out of there!" he said softly, kicking the toe of his shoe so hard against the graveled path that pebbles flew into the foliage. Lankau got up immediately. The leaves had smeared the blood over his face, which was now almost coated with a brown film.

Then he snarled a few words. Bryan recognized the tone of voice all too well. Despite the many years that had elapsed, his nemesis still possessed the same uninhibited meanness, just below the surface.

"Speak English to me. I presume you can."

"Why?" Aversion burned in Lankau's broad face as he looked at the pistol. Then, as Bryan released the safety catch, the face contorted and the man instantly jumped to one side. Bryan looked at him again and then at the gun. Lankau's reaction puzzled him.

"You can be sure I'll shoot if you do that once more. From now on you'll follow along quietly. One wrong move, deliberate or not, and it'll be your last."

The broad-faced man stared incredulously at Bryan's lips. "Have you forgotten your mother tongue, you swine?" His English was that of the skilled businessman—a torrent of words, yet precise. But his accent was unschooled.

The man heeded Bryan's gesticulation with the pistol. He cut a pathetic figure as he emerged from the bushes, shirt hanging out of trousers with dark stains on the knees and thin, tangled hair pushed to one side. Despite his appearance, Bryan wasn't taking any chances. He struck his enemy twice in the solar plexus with a doctor's authority, so accurately that the giant almost passed out. When Lankau rose to his feet again Bryan shepherded him forward at a meter's distance.

He stuck the pistol in his pocket as they reached the gondola platform and squeezed himself so close to Lankau that the latter could feel the pressure of the barrel despite his well-padded back.

"You keep quiet when we get into the gondola, got it?" Bryan prodded him in the back with the pistol again to emphasize his seriousness. Lankau grumbled something. Then he turned around cautiously and looked Bryan straight in the face. The dead eye was half-open. "Be careful with that Kenju, you dog! It has a habit of going off at the wrong moment."

The man standing beside the gondola booth made no sign to reveal whether he was the ticket taker or not. When he saw Lankau's bloody face he retreated fearfully toward the wall of the building and stood motionless.

"I'm sorry, but I must get this man to the hospital. I'm a doctor." The man shook his head nervously. He didn't understand what Bryan had said. Bryan pushed Lankau into the gondola. "He's had a fall, you see." Not until the swaying gondola had passed the first stage did the man emerge from the shadows to watch their descent.

"Your car!" was Bryan's next order, when they'd finally reached the bottom. Lankau strode across the street and took out his keys. The BMW had been given a parking fine. A bit farther on stood Bryan's Volkswagen. It, too, had acquired a white slip that seemed to fill most of the windshield. That would be the hippie's problem.

Lankau was allowed to drive. As they drove slowly out of town Bryan contemplated his archenemy in this everyday situation, and it seemed to him that man's deeper nature was revealed. Aside from his molested face, Lankau appeared to be the normal family man. Strewn around the car was evidence of an ordinary, unworried life in the form of cigarette packs, toffee wrappings, and empty soft-drink bottles. Here sat an average citizen, a commonplace consumer who enjoyed the good things in life. The golf bag on the backseat spoke for itself. A Wagnerian climax had begun filling the car the moment the ignition was switched on. Here was a murderer, a sadist, a malingerer, and a Wagner fan, as well. How could man be created in God's image, considering how ambiguous, dishonest, and loathsome human beings could be under the surface? And which individual could deny having a Lankau inside him?

"Drive somewhere where we won't be bothered by anyone," Bryan ordered, turning down the volume of the overture's final movement.

"So you can kill me undisturbed, I suppose." The stout man seemed impassive.

"So I can kill you undisturbed, if it suits me, yes," said Bryan, making a mental note of their route.

The sun was still gleaming as Freiburg slid behind them on their way out of town. A tiny child was taking leave of the carefree summer, rolling, dripping wet, in the wide gutters that carried a seemingly unending stream of water alongside the sidewalk. A young woman tried to catch him, practically knocking over a nun in the process.

"Why have you come back? Why are you hunting us? Is it the money?"

The corners of the broad-faced man's mouth turned downward as his cold eyes followed the traffic.

"What money?"

"Petra Wagner says you asked about Gerhart Peuckert. Was he the one who was supposed to show the way to us? Was he supposed to guide you to our goods?"

"Is Gerhart Peuckert still alive, then?" Bryan searched for possible clues in Lankau's face. There were none. Slowly Lankau turned his head toward Bryan.

"No, von der Leyen," he said. He looked at the landscape before him and smiled. "He's not."

When the houses and farms thinned out and the vineyards began to wind through the landscape Bryan had to make a decision. Lankau had said he had more information for him. And he knew somewhere they could talk without being disturbed. There were more than enough signs that Lankau was luring him into yet another trap. Already here, a couple of kilometers from the center of town, it seemed deserted. Despite the numerous side roads and the homeward-bound traffic, each of the houses that lay back from the main road might contain secrets Bryan could well do without.

Every time he glanced at Lankau's impassive face, it struck him that Kröner or Petra might have been initiated into an emergency plan whereby Lankau brought the victim straight into the lion's den.

Lankau was amused when Bryan asked about the farm.

"Goodness no, I don't live there. My family and I live in town. But you won't find them there, if that's what you're after. They're gone." Then he laughed. "This is my little oasis, you understand."

There was a NO TRESPASSING sign at the foot of the road.

Unlike the surrounding farms, the house had only one story, though it was complemented with several wings of small, bungalow-like buildings.

If this was a little oasis, Lankau must be a very wealthy man. It lay well off the road, surrounded by rows of grapevines small enough in number to indicate that wine production was only a hobby.

The courtyard was shaped like a huge ellipse. Bryan ducked down and rammed the pistol into Lankau's side the moment the ignition was switched off. Now his life depended solely on his alertness. If this was a trap, the attack could come from any direction.

"Take it easy, you cowardly cur!" Lankau grumbled, opening the door. "People only come around here to harvest or to hunt."

Already before they reached the living room Bryan struck his hostage so hard on the neck with the pistol butt that he toppled over. The room was incredibly ugly. At least five hundred deer antlers decorated the walls as proof of Lankau's ingrained hunting instinct. There were rows of carved plate racks, thick books, hunting knives and old rifles, heavy oak furniture with striped upholstery, and murky paintings with largely identical and predictable motifs displaying a wealth of nature scenes and dead animals.

The smell was musty. People didn't come here every day.

The limp figure in front of Bryan lay still for only a moment. Bryan struck him again. It was important that he didn't regain consciousness right away.

Then Bryan stood for a long time, listening. Apart from dogs barking in the distance and the whir of tires down on the main road, everything in and around the house was quiet.

They were alone.

An elongated shed stretched the entire length of the yard. Here, too, there were antlers, flayed hides, skulls, daggers, and knives in all shapes and sizes.

The whole back wall was a veritable hardware store, its shelves bulging with paint cans, wallpaper remains, glue pots, and boxes of fittings and nails and screws. There were also bundles of twine of the type once used for binding sheaves of grain at harvesttime.

Bryan tied Lankau firmly to a high-backed chair. He used a whole ball of twine before he felt confident that it would prevent any likely attempt by Lankau to tear himself loose.

Although he was bound uncomfortably and crookedly, Lankau appeared quite unconcerned when he finally woke up. He looked around and merely noted that his arms and legs were tied. Then he turned his head toward Bryan and waited. For that brief moment he seemed old.

For Bryan, the question of survival in any given situation had always been closely connected with the ability to understand and anticipate the reactions of his surroundings as well as possible. Knowing they could expose his and James's deception at the SS hospital, the malingerers were able to go about attempting to kill them. This was merely logical. Like Bryan, they knew what would happen to those found guilty of simulating.

Now all logic had ceased. Sitting in front of him was a man for whom none of this was relevant any longer. So why should he risk his life for ancient history? What could hurt him now? Bryan looked at him. The corners of Lankau's mouth almost reached down to his ample chin. His eyes were ice-cold and expectant. Bryan turned around and stared straight into the glass eyes of a stag. Two of the malingerers had risked their lives trying to catch and kill him on that winter night in 1944. They'd no doubt had their reasons, but Bryan had never been able to understand what made them act the way they did. And it had nearly cost him his life.

That was a mistake he wouldn't make again.

"Tell me everything," he simply said. "If you value your life, tell me everything."

"What is 'everything'?" The big man was breathing with some difficulty. "So that you can get hold of our money?" He grunted with incomprehension. "You won't be able to find it anyway. It's not exactly lying around this house in small chests."

"Money? What money? I don't give a damn about you and your money." Bryan turned around and looked Lankau straight in the face. "You think it's money I'm after? Has it been about money the whole time?" He took a step toward the broad-faced man. "Is there really that much?" Bryan stopped and looked calmly at Lankau, who hadn't batted an eye. He looked like a businessman, negotiating. If so, he'd unwittingly ventured into Bryan's domain. He leaned over the bound man and stared straight at him. "I don't lack money, Lankau. Your piddling amount would probably be just about enough to feed my household pets. If you ever want to see your family again, now's the time to pull yourself together. Tell me what happened that time, and tell me what's happened since." Bryan sat down opposite Lankau and aimed the pistol at his good eye. "I think you should start at the beginning. Start with the hospital."

"The hospital!" There was no mistaking his scorn. "I don't feel like going into it. If it had been up to me, we'd have killed you there. That's all there is to say about that."

"But why? Why didn't you just leave me in peace? How could I have harmed you? I was simulating, just like you."

"You could've done exactly what you did. You could have vanished! And if you'd wanted to, you could also have betrayed the rest of us."

"But I didn't. What would I have gained from that?"

"You could have gone after that railway car, you swine!" Lankau hissed through clenched teeth.

"I didn't hear you; say it again." Bryan took a step back. Then Lankau spat at him, his face radiating contempt. The clumsy attempt left spit running down his chin.

At that moment Bryan aimed the pistol and shot so close to Lankau's face that the barrel flame singed the eyebrow over his good eye. Lankau stared wildly at Bryan, turned his head and tried to comprehend the sight of the almost invisible hole in the back of the chair, a couple of centimeters from his cheekbone.

"If you don't start telling me *now* what's been happening since, I'll kill you." Bryan raised the pistol again and continued: "I know Kröner is here in Freiburg. I know where he lives. I've spoken with his stepdaughter, Mariann. I've seen him together with his new wife and little boy, and I know his comings and goings around town. If you don't tell me what I want to know, I'm pretty sure he will!"

Instead of turning his head to look at his tormentor, Lankau sank down in his chair. The fact that his kidnapper knew Kröner's movements and whereabouts seemed to shake him up more than the shot. Then, apparently having collected himself, he raised his head.

"Where do you want me to begin?" Lankau asked dispassionately. He looked at the man opposite him. The man was a mystery to him. He was resting the Kenju on the back of his other hand, safety catch downward, sitting still. Lankau prayed he would stay like that.

Right now the situation seemed quite hopeless. Lankau winced. His underarms were throbbing.

If the man opposite him was telling the truth, he could know nothing about Peter Stich's role or background. And that was a good thing. If they were to gain the upper hand, perhaps help should come from that quarter.

Despite his frailty, Stich could be a worthy opponent for Arno von der Leyen.

All games set out to win time. It's the first main rule. Arno von der Leyen would get his story.

The second basic rule is to keep your opponent at bay until you've found his weakness. For Lankau, this was yet to come. A person's greatest weakness was often to be found in the motive underlying his actions. The question was, where was Lankau to look? Was Arno von der Leyen avaricious or vindictive? Time would tell.

But the third and most important rule in all games is to keep the size and strength of your own weapons secret as long as possible. Therefore he mustn't mention Peter Stich's true role or identity.

Maybe Arno von der Leyen had heard about the Mailman during the long nights in the hospital. But he couldn't know Peter Stich and the Mailman were one and the same person, for the simple reason that the latter had revealed himself at a time when Arno von der Leyen was in shock treatment.

Bearing these three precautions in mind, Lankau could set about telling his story. He pursed his lips and studied his opponent at length. After a sufficiently long silence his nemesis leaned forward and broke the invisible barrier between them.

"You can start with the Rhine," he said, trying to fix Lankau's gaze as if a kind of intimacy had arisen between them. "I thought you were finished there. Dead and gone and vanished from the face of the Earth. Tell me what happened afterwards," von der Leyen said, nodding encouragement.

Lankau straightened up a bit, scrutinizing his oppressor closely for the first time. The youthful muscularity was gone; his body had deteriorated. Had he not been tied up he could quickly get the better of him. Lankau tested the strength of the twine once more and cautiously pressed his knuckles down into the armrest. "What happened afterwards . . . ? Yeah, what *did* happen?" Von der Leyen moved closer to him and nodded again as Lankau replied. "First and foremost I'd gotten a hole in the side of my chest and lost the one eye." The man opposite him showed no reaction. Lankau pressed his knuckles into the armrest again. "That, quite simply, was the damned situation you left me in, you swine, and yet there was nothing at all simple about it! I couldn't go back to the hospital in that condition, especially not without Dieter Schmidt." Lankau's bad eye narrowed. The skin on his guard's neck was thin and covered with a network of blood vessels, just beneath the surface. "But my hatred of you easily kept me alive, do you realize that, you lout? It was a damned cold winter, wasn't it? I've hardly ever seen so much snow. But the Schwarzwald's embrace is merciful. After two days I knew I would survive. Every farm or laborer's shack has a shed or outdoor pantry in those parts." Lankau smiled. "So I managed—despite the dog patrols they sent after us. But it was a bit harder for those who remained behind, you see. Especially Gerhart Peuckert." Lankau noted with satisfaction how von der Leyen flinched a trifle. An attentiveness he'd been trying to conceal stood out revealingly. The game had begun.

His opponent's weakness was in the process of being exposed.

During the hour that followed, Lankau relived the past. The veil was drawn aside.

Lankau registered Arno von der Leyen's every reaction and movement. He left nothing of importance out of his account apart from the identity of the Mailman, which was never mentioned. He omitted some events and replaced them with others, where necessary.

But the story never lay far from the truth.

When Vonnegut, the orderly, woke up that morning in late November, he discovered to his horror that three men on his floor were missing. He ran from room to room, tearing his hair but touching nothing. The open windows in two of the rooms spoke for themselves. All the remaining patients lay in bed, unconcerned and smiling as always, in anticipation of the washbasins being brought in, followed by breakfast. Calendar Man even stood up and made him a slight bow.

Less than ten minutes later the security guards turned up. They were savage, uncomprehending, and in a rage. Even the doctors had to submit to brutal questioning, as if they were criminals or responsible for what had happened. The four remaining patients in Lankau's room were separated from one another for a couple of days and then brought down one by one to the treatment room below. Here they were interrogated, beaten with a cat-o'-nine-tails, and tortured with whatever instruments were available. The longer it took to make the torturers feel convinced of their innocence, the more severe the torture became. It had taken a particularly long time with Gerhart Peuckert. Although he had a high rank in the security forces— the SD—the chief interrogator showed no signs of collegial understanding. No one escaped—not Peter Stich, Kröner, or Calendar Man. Even the inanimate general on the opposite side of the corridor was brought down. After some hours they let him go. He never uttered a word.

After that Gerhart Peuckert collapsed, and during the days that followed they thought he was going to die.

Then the crisis passed and he showed signs of recovery. Apart from the physical aftereffects of the torture everything returned to normal. Neither Gerhart, the weepy-eyed Calendar Man, nor any of the others could explain to their oppressors what had happened to the three missing patients.

Less than a week later two grave-looking plainclothesmen came for the security officer in charge, who had also held the interrogations. They hauled him off in the middle of a meal and locked themselves in with him for some hours. Then they dragged him out into the courtyard in front of the general hospital wards and hanged him in spite of his high-pitched, blubbering protests. This was an unheard-of dishonor; he wasn't even worth an execution squad. His one, fatal mistake in the course of eight ruthless years had been to allow Arno von der Leyen to disappear in front of their very eyes, and not to have reported the catastrophe to Berlin immediately.

Kröner and Peter Stich began recovering quite quickly and after New Year's they were declared fit for service and discharged with a few hours' warning. For a while now Gerhart Peuckert had not been reacting to anything at all.

Leaving him behind caused them no apprehension.

The fighting at the front was fierce as the Germans steadily retreated. For Kröner it constituted a double risk, because all officers connected with the security service were also potential targets for their own men's bullets, which resulted in many deaths. But despite the fact that Kröner had the authority to do the same dirty work as before, and thereby gain many enemies, he managed to engineer himself into a position where his own men had no chance to stab him in the back. The moment that rumor became reality and the Führer had actually died in his so-called tireless fight against Bolshevism, Kröner disappeared from his camp without warning, without possessions or provisions, and without a scratch.

When he came to relating Peter Stich's subsequent fate, Lankau stared into space for a while. "We never heard anything more from Peter Stich," he said eventually. Arno von der Leyen didn't react. He looked at him with watchful eyes and remained silent. "There were many who were killed in those days."

What Arno von der Leyen didn't have to know was that, after being discharged from the SS reserve hospital in Ortoschwanden, Stich had been sent straight back to Berlin in his original capacity as concentration-camp administrator.

There were two reasons for this.

Firstly, the movement of staff and prisoners between concentration camps had been intensified, while at the same time the need to disband the camps had gradually become more and more obvious. This process required considerable administration, expertise, and a firm hand. And secondly, the panzer divisions in which Stich had most recently been serving were suffering great losses. Many divisions had been pinned down or wiped out. There was no longer any need for him there. However, in the extermination camps his presence was an asset. One could expect his contribution to be one hundred percent.

Thus, right to the end, Stich had played his simulant role better than any of them. He was in safety and had authority.

"Our leader was known as the Mailman, but that hardly surprises you, does it?" said Lankau, noting with mistrust the nod from the man opposite him.

"You needn't worry about what I know or don't know, but what you *don't* want to do is leave anything out. You tell me everything, understand?"

Lankau smiled and licked a corner of his mouth with the tip of his tongue. "His true identity can't mean anything to you because he's no longer alive, but he was useful when it came down to it."

Arno von der Leyen didn't react.

Lankau's audience of one was already in the grip of the story.

. . .

During the last days of the central administration of the Third Reich in Berlin the Mailman had acquired a general knowledge as to which political purges were regularly being carried out in Goebbels's own district. He had the lists of those who had been deported, sentenced to death, executed, or were missing or imprisoned. He knew whose turn was next and for which crime.

In this way he intended to collect four sets of identities whose age and sex would fit himself and his co-conspirators. He had not yet given up the possibility that Lankau and Dieter Schmidt had succeeded in escaping.

He found three of the identities without much effort—opponents of the Third Reich who had recently "disappeared" and had had no relatives. The same people who would be regarded as heroes or freedom fighters when the war finally ended. If they stepped into these men's shoes, they would have nothing to fear in the event of a judicial purge.

It didn't prove difficult for the Mailman to destroy any evidence.

After some fruitless searching the Mailman found a suitable candidate for the fourth identity in a Potsdam jail. It was a coincidence he found both amusing and ironical: a Jew who throughout the entire war had been working under a false name in the middle of town as a top civil servant. A trail of corruption, bribery, and fraud had followed in his wake. Many people had good reason for wishing him dead before the interrogations were over and his transfer to the concentration camps became a reality. A wish the Mailman gladly consented to fulfill.

The Jew disappeared without a trace.

For the Mailman, one person more or less in the greater scheme of things had never made much difference. He had managed to acquire four new identities where age and appearance fit.

During the final collapse of the Third Reich the Mailman disappeared without a trace.

Eight days after the capitulation on May 17, 1945, Kröner and the Mailman met beside a remote and deserted stretch of railway close to a little village in the heart of Germany.

The entire country was in chaos. Shops were being plundered. Wares, livestock, and people were being scattered to the winds in impulsive flight or a last desperate retreat.

A couple of kilometers from the appointed meeting place, where the western Allied troops had by chance come to a halt, Kröner and the Mailman had been separately waiting for the report of surrender. A mere few kilometers farther up the line the railway was under the control of Soviet troops.

After another couple of days in hiding, Lankau turned up as well, emaciated and lice-infested like a tramp. It was a surprise to see him again, yet gratifying. All three had braved Armageddon and the distance involved, exactly according to the plan they'd agreed upon at the hospital. It was here they were to meet when the end of the war became reality. Their future would be determined by a dilapidated railway freight car crammed to the bursting point with the valuables they had bartered their way to at the cost of many a Russian slave laborer's life.

And the freight car was still there. A whole lifetime of events had passed between the day a locomotive had carefully nudged it into place, and now, when all the fighting had ceased.

A trifle overgrown with moss, but untouched, the railway car was tucked away and forgotten on a remote siding close to Hölle, north of Naila in the Frankenwald. It was filled with religious relics, icons, silver altarpieces, and other valuables.

A priceless treasure.

All three were ecstatic. Despite their exhaustion, and in Lankau's case his severe wounds, they were fully capable of putting their plan into practice.

That Dieter Schmidt had been killed was regrettable. But none of them were inconsolable. It meant one less to share with. On the other hand, the Mailman and Kröner were shocked to learn that Arno von der Leyen's attempt to escape had succeeded. The Mailman was furious. The freight car would have to be moved and the remainder of their plan carried out immediately.

The lock on the car's sliding door was rusty but intact. Inside the railcar itself, the remains of a slave laborer who, in the rush of things, had not been heaved out after being liquidated, still lay spread over the first row of cases like an untidy pile of clothing. Behind him, rows of brown cases were stacked from floor to ceiling. Two of the cases in the first row were marked with a faint cross. These the Mailman tore open. After having distributed their content of American dollars, canned food, and civilian clothes, the Mailman opened his briefcase and handed his cohorts their new identities.

The Mailman was well prepared and elucidated his views regarding the coming sequence of events without a single protest. From now on they were other people and could only use their real names when alone with each other. They had to renounce their previous lives and be completely loyal to one another in every way.

Now and always.

On that day Kröner had to swear to his comrades that he would forever keep away from northern Germany, where he was born, had lived all his life, and presumably still had a wife and three children. He had come to the same conclusion himself.

For Lankau there was no decision to make. He had loved his wife before the war. They had been happy, with four children. Now the Russians occupied both his hometown of Demmin on the River Peene and the area where his parents lived in Landryg.

He would never be able to go there again.

In the Mailman's case things were different. Even before the war he was hated in the region he came from. There wasn't much sympathy for the blessings of Nazism and the Third Reich's new order among the simple rural villagers, and the Mailman had informed on those who were anti-Nazi. All too many women had lost their loved ones on account of him.

He would never be able to return home either.

The Mailman was childless but had a woman who followed him in silent admiration, no matter what his life offered her. He impressed on them that she was one they all could trust.

Standing before this freight car and wearing their new clothes, the three swore yet again a sacred oath that from that moment on, they would wipe out the past and regard their families as dead.

Then they divided the tasks among them. The Mailman assumed responsibility for transporting the freight car from the unarticulated zone boundary to Munich. In the meantime Kröner and Lankau were to go to Freiburg and try seeking out Gerhart Peuckert, whom they were certain had knowledge of their undertaking, but whose subsequent fate was unknown.

If they found him alive they were to liquidate him.

For the Mailman, the transport of the freight car went surprisingly smoothly. Several thousand dollars exchanged hands. The American liaison officer who had received the money later disappeared on his way back to base from the town hall in Naila.

Munich itself was seething with signs of dissolution. Black-market dealings and bribes were the order of the day.

Everyone was for sale, as long as the price was right. The unloading of the goods took place with great discretion, and before the month was over most of the valuables had been distributed among five different Swiss bank vaults in Basel.

The task Kröner and Lankau had before them was not as easy.

The landscape was bleak. A country that had been raped, torn to pieces by an idea that now had to be exorcised at all costs. The bicycle trip took them eight days. Four hundred and fifty kilometers in an occupied territory marked by confusion, suspicion, and control after control.

For both Lankau and Kröner, going to Freiburg was like moving from the frying pan into the fire. Even though the town and its surroundings had been barely surviving since the war, it was more than likely that there were still people around who had known of their stay in the hospital.

When they finally reached their goal, their anxiety vanished like dew before the sun. Only twisted steel reinforcements, pulverized rubble, and concrete blocks remained to bear witness to the hospital that had shielded them for a time from the death outside. The town was chaos and confusion. Everyone had their hands full just thinking about themselves and their families. People chose to look forward.

Even in the neighboring villages of Ettenheim and Ortoschwanden, any information as to what had taken place was extremely scanty. The few reports they managed to glean contained the same account of a bomber that had veered off course during the final bombing of Freiburg and dropped its entire load in the hills. Reasonably enough, the general conclusion was that the bombing had been a mistake. A mountain was a mountain, and trees were just trees. A few of the more alert citizens had noticed that from that day on there'd been fewer ambulance transports in the vicinity.

The SS hospital had taken its well-kept secret to the grave, along with those who had perished in the bombardment.

After the reunion in Munich all three lived quite modestly for a while. The city was crowded and the Allies took over its administration with great efficiency. As it became more and more difficult to pass unnoticed, the Mailman came up with the surprising solution of settling in Freiburg, the most beautiful of all Germany's beautiful towns.

Thus they lived a carefree life for some time, until the Mailman learned that just before the eradication of the SS hospital several patients had been transported to the reserve hospital, Ensen bei Porz, in the vicinity of Cologne. Here, during the final phase of the war, doctors had been given the task of investigating the extent to which certain war neuroses and provoked psychoses could have an organic origin. The great majority of patients were found unsuitable as guinea pigs and immediately sent back to active duty after a superficial examination. But the Mailman had been led to understand that a few of the Alphabet House's previous inhabitants were still there.

At Ensen bei Porz they found out that Gerhart Peuckert had not been among the patients transferred from the Alphabet House and that he was already dead.

Lankau leaned back and looked at Arno von der Leyen. His story had ended abruptly. He hadn't revealed the Mailman's true identity with so much as a word. Aside from the fact that he was still bound to the chair, he was pleased with himself.

Arno von der Leyen shook his head. He face had gone pale. "Gerhart Peuckert died, you say?"

"Yes, that's what I said."

"At which hospital?"

"At the reserve hospital at Ortoschwanden, goddammit!"

"Is that what you also call the 'Alphabet House'? Is that the place where we were hospitalized? Was he killed during the bombing raid?"

"Yes, yes, yes!" Lankau sneered. "And so what?"

"I wanted to hear you say it again. I've got to be sure." Von der Leyen's eyes narrowed. It was clear he was trying to catch the slightest revealing twitch in Lankau's face. Lankau regarded him with total impassivity.

Von der Leyen's face went suddenly hard. "An exciting story, Lankau," he said tonelessly. "I'm sure you've had your reasons for being so careful. There must be a lot of money involved."

Lankau looked away. "You bet your life there is! But if you think you can coerce us, you're making a mistake. It'll never work."

"Have you heard me make any demands? The only thing I have to know is what happened to Gerhart Peuckert."

"You've just been told. He died."

"You know what I think, Lankau?"

"Should I care?" Lankau closed his eyes and tried to concentrate on the sound he'd just registered. A slight creak that came if he leaned forward just a bit. Von der Leyen's blow to his chest diverted him instantly from these investigations. The grayness had vanished from Arno von der Leyen's face. He prodded him again with the pistol barrel. Lankau looked at it and held his breath.

"I think I'll shoot you here and now if you don't tell me what's really going on and how Petra Wagner fits into the picture!" Von der Leyen prodded him again. Lankau gasped for air.

"Oh, really? That's a threat I find hard to take seriously." The big man suddenly rocked forward in his chair as if about to butt his interrogator. "But what were you thinking? That you'd force us to hand over what we've scraped together over the years? Shouldn't you have realized it wouldn't be that easy?"

"Until ten minutes ago I hadn't the slightest idea what the whole thing was about. And certainly nothing about any money. I'm here because I want to know what happened to Gerhart Peuckert."

Lankau heard the creaking again. "For God's sake, why don't you shut up, you worm!" he practically screamed as he tried to register the movements of the chair. "You want me to believe that? You seem to forget we lay in the same hospital for months. You think I can't remember how you moved around in bed at night while you were listening to what we talked about? Do you think I've forgotten how you tried to escape the hospital with what you knew?"

"What I knew? I never understood one word of what you were saying to each other! I only understand English. I simply wanted to get away from you and that damned hospital!"

"Oh, shut up!" Lankau didn't believe any of what he was hearing.

The man before him had been playing his game for decades. He was calculating, dangerous, and greedy. Stich's doubts about von der Leyen's identity echoed from a distant past. It was a strong enemy who could sow doubt in his opponent. A superior enemy could make himself invisible. Lankau had never been in doubt. For him, von der Leyen was visible. Now, as then.

He frowned and looked himself over for the first time. His bound legs in their golf socks were completely numb. He tried to flex them without succeeding in restoring the circulation. Nothing hurt anymore. With a jerk that set off the creaking sound again he opened his mouth wide and poured forth a torrent of inarticulate sounds. For a moment the figure opposite looked confused. "And I suppose you didn't understand that, either, Herr von der Leyen." He chuckled over this insult, then was silent for a while. When the color in his face returned to normal he closed his eyes and spoke English again with such deliberate softness, his nemesis could scarcely hear it. "As far as Petra is concerned, I won't tell you a damned thing. Actually, I won't tell you anything more at all. You bore me! Shoot me or leave me alone!"

When their eyes met, Lankau knew that his life would be spared for the time being.

CHAPTER 43

Restaurant Dattler on Schlossberg was not Kröner's favorite eating establishment. Even though the menu was impressive and the food usually what his wife called "choice," the portions were small as a rule and the waiters courteous in a way that could seem condescending. Kröner preferred his meals to be plain, plentiful, and homely. His previous wife, Gisela, hadn't been able to cook. During the almost twenty years they lived together they'd worn out countless cooks with no appreciable results. His present wife, on the other hand, was a dream in the kitchen. This he greatly appreciated and rewarded her for. For that, and much else.

Opposite him, Stich sat glancing at his wristwatch for the fifth time in the course of a few minutes. It had been a hectic day. Kröner could still feel his boy's hug when he'd sent him away with his mother. For this and all future hugs Arno von der Leyen would have to be gotten rid of.

Stich stroked his white beard and again gazed out the panorama windows that laid the whole town at their feet. "I feel the same as you, Wilfried." Turning to look straight at Kröner, he rapped his thin, withered knuckles on the tablecloth beside his coffee cup. "I'd rather it were all over. Now it's up to Lankau. Let's hope things have gone as they should. We've been lucky till now. It was a good thing you fetched Gerhart Peuckert in time. I had a feeling it would prove necessary. But are you sure von der Leyen didn't see you?"

"Absolutely."

"And Frau Rehmann? She couldn't tell you anything more about the purpose of his visit?"

"Nothing more than what I've told you."

"And she believed that story? That he was a psychiatrist? A member of some committee or other?"

"Yes. He gave her no occasion to doubt him."

After a few pensive moments Stich took out his glasses and studied the menu again. It was a quarter past five. Lankau was fifteen minutes late. Then he put down his glasses again. "Lankau's not coming," he ascertained.

Kröner rubbed his forehead, trying to gauge Stich's cold gaze. He felt a sinking feeling in his chest. The boy's hug and his trusting, warm glances were diverting his thoughts again. "You don't think anything's happened to him, do you?" he asked.

"What I think is immaterial. Arno von der Leyen didn't turn up at the sanitarium by chance. And it's not normal for Lankau to be late."

Kröner massaged his forehead once more and looked down toward the aerial cableway. "You think he might be disposing of the body on his own? He can be damned headstrong."

"It's possible. But why doesn't he contact us?"

Even though the years had softened Kröner a bit and he'd come to like his new surroundings, he could scarcely be called naïve. The day's developments, and not least of all Lankau's delay, were extremely worrying. For years the brotherhood of malingerers had been prepared for the possibility of something turning up and threatening their position. With that in mind, there had been times when Horst Lankau had spoken to his family of selling his business and emigrating. Argentina, Paraguay, Brazil, Mozambique, and Indonesia had been named. The descriptions of warmer climates and safe, closed environments were tempting, but his family had been against it.

They didn't know his motives.

For Stich and Kröner, convenience had always come first. Now things were different. Kröner wouldn't take risks merely for the sake of convenience. Recent years, during which he had acquired a new family and learned to give room for feelings, had brought other and more important considerations. He'd grown older, and while the thought of transplanting himself was not appealing, it was nevertheless possible. His wife, on the other hand, was young and could live anywhere. With his consent a new world of mutual agreement and the presence of a small child had pinned him down in his new life.

Now Kröner looked at his watch too. "Petra" was all he said.

"Petra, yes." The old man nodded. "There's no other possibility, is there?" He cleared his throat and wiped the corners of his mouth. "Who knows? Maybe during all these years she's just been waiting for the right opportunity. And now's it's come, apparently."

"She's told him everything."

"Probably, yes."

"Then Lankau's no longer alive."

"Probably not, no." The headwaiter was there instantly when Peter Stich called him. "We're leaving now," he said.

The tracks in the earth beside the colonnade bore clear witness of a fight. As soon as Stich and Kröner were convinced they hadn't overlooked any traces of blood or any other indications of the outcome of the struggle, they drove quickly over to Peter Stich's flat in Luisenstrasse, where earlier in the day they had left Gerhart Peuckert in Andrea's motherly care.

Apart from Petra, Stich's wife was the only one able to get a smile out of Gerhart. It happened only occasionally, and awkwardly, but it happened. And Andrea had to work for the trust he placed in her. Whenever Gerhart Peuckert was installed in Stich's flat Andrea pampered him. Kröner looked up at the building in front of him. He'd never understood why Andrea displayed such magnanimity. It wasn't like her.

Kröner knew she'd regarded Gerhart as dirt during all the years in which her husband and his friends had paid for his stay in the sanitarium. Society should get rid of its scum, she'd always said. She'd seen it put in practice in the concentration camps and it had pleased her. Efficient purging meant fewer costs and less work. It was only her husband's and his friends' curious affection for that madman that made her feign solicitude.

Andrea was good at faking.

All in all, there were many reasons why Kröner was reluctant to let his wife get too close to her.

Andrea noticed their mood as soon as they came through the door. Kröner saw her duck back into the narrow hallway like a shadow. Before she even returned their greeting she had seized Gerhart Peuckert by the arm and led him into the dining room, where he'd often sat in the dark.

This time she switched on a single wall lamp.

"What's happened?" she asked, pointing over at the decanter of port on the sideboard.

Stich shook his head. "Nothing that we can do anything about, I'm afraid."

"Where's Lankau?"

"We don't know. That's the problem."

Andrea Stich dried her hands on a towel and silently fetched her husband's telephone book from the study. He took it without thanks.

He phoned both Lankau's home and his country house without result. Kröner bit the insides of his cheeks. Frowning, he tried to recall his own house and its surroundings when he'd sent his wife and son away. He hadn't noticed anything unusual. A shiver ran through his body that made his shoulders tremble. He'd have to suppress those fears. Lankau was their concern now. It was as if the earth had swallowed him up.

"Let's see, now . . ." said Stich, standing behind Kröner and looking down at the parking spaces in front of the house, and then down along the street that was still bustling with life in the pale afternoon light. "Assuming von der Leyen has gotten rid of Lankau, something will probably happen by itself very soon. Gerhart Peuckert seems to be important to him. But why? Can you tell me, Wilfried? Why will that bastard stop at nothing to find our silent friend here?"

"I think it's the other way around. I'm sure it's us he's after. Peuckert has just been an instrument in his finding us."

"But does that make any sense, Wilfried? Why in the world should he think he could find us through Peuckert? The only thing we can possibly have had in common with Peuckert is a few months in a loony bin. Ages ago, I might add."

"I don't know. But I feel convinced that Leyen is out to blackmail us."

"There I agree with you. At this point I think he's doing it for personal gain. We were hard on him that time, but I don't think he's driven by revenge." Stich turned around and stared out the large window. "I don't think he's the type. Revenge is for irrational people, and whatever else he might be, von der Leyen's not irrational, if you ask me."

All these unanswered questions obviously troubled Stich. The irritation in his face was unmistakable.

"Have you any idea whether Peuckert may be able to help us get on the right track, Peter?" Stich turned to his wife. Kröner knew why she'd been sitting in the far corner of the room. When her husband was in the mood, he could get it into his head to hit her as soon as they were alone. Even though he usually repented afterward and probably didn't deal his blows so authoritatively anymore, Kröner suspected she preferred that others bear the brunt of his displeasure. The idiot sitting in the next room, for example.

In her own way, she, too, had grown softer with age.

After a few more phone calls Stich turned to Kröner and shook his head. They had both accepted the inevitability of the new situation.

The pock-faced man stared at the telephone for some time. By now his wife and child must have reached their destination. Just as he was about to pick up the receiver to call them, Andrea dragged the robotlike figure into the room. Peuckert was still busy chewing some food. Stich took him by the arm and drew him gently down onto the sofa beside him. Then he stroked his hair. It had become a habit over time. This idiot lodger had turned into a kind of pet, their little imprisoned mascot. Their kitten, their little monkey. Lankau was the only one who'd had his suspicions all these years.

"Have you had anything to eat, little Gerhart? Has Andrea seen to you?" Gentleness beamed from the fool's face whenever Andrea's name was mentioned. Peuckert smiled and looked across at Andrea, who had just lit the chandelier. "Do you like sitting here with the rest of us, little Gerhart? Should Kröner come over here and sit with us for a while too?" Stich took his hands and rubbed them as if they were frozen. "There. That's what you like, isn't it, Gerhart?" The old man patted the back of Gerhart's sinewy hand, smiling quietly at him. "Andrea and I would like to know whether Petra still visits you." Kröner noticed the almost imperceptible sign of a smile in the corners of Peuckert's mouth. It spoke for itself. Stich patted his hand again. "And we'd like to know whether she asks you questions, Gerhart. Does she ask you strange questions sometimes? For example, about the old days, or about what we do when we go for an outing in the woods? Does she, little Gerhart?" Gerhart Peuckert pursed his lips and stared at the ceiling, as if in thought. "Well, that may be difficult to remember. But perhaps, my friend, you can tell me if she's ever spoken to you about Arno von der Leyen." The silent figure in the chair looked at him and pursed his lips again.

Stich got up, dropping Gerhart's hands as suddenly as he had taken them. "You understand, this Arno von der Leyen is looking for you, little Gerhart. And we don't understand why. And he calls himself something different. Do you know what Kröner says he calls himself?" Gerhart Peuckert's head rotated slowly toward Kröner in the quiet spell following the question. Kröner couldn't tell whether he recognized him or whether it was a chance look. "He calls himself Bryan Underwood Scott," continued Stich, laughing dryly for a moment before clearing his throat. "Isn't that funny? He's been to St. Ursula's, where he spoke English to dear Frau Rehmann. Surprising, isn't it? Don't you think it's strange?"

Kröner approached Peuckert and bent down in order to take a closer look at his face. As usual it showed no signs of reaction. They would have to take matters into their own hands. "I'll find Petra," he said, standing up.

The old man didn't take his eyes off Peuckert as Kröner straightened his back. Then he opened his eyes wide. "Yes. And when you find her, make sure you squeeze the truth out of her, won't you Wilfried? If you get the feeling she might have let us down, then you'll kill her, right?" he said, jovially clasping Peuckert by the back of the neck with his outstretched hand.

"What about the letter she's always threatened us with?"

"Pick your poison, Wilfried. If we don't do anything, then you're sure to have a problem. And if you pull yourself together and do what you have to, who knows what'll happen afterwards?" The look Stich threw him was mocking. "Almost thirty years have passed, Wilfried! Who would think of taking a piece of paper like that seriously? And who says it really exists? Can we trust the little Wagner girl at all? Go on now and do as I say! Understand?"

"You don't have to order me about, Stich! I can think for myself!" But in fact, this wasn't true. Kröner could no longer think. Regardless of the outcome of his meeting with Petra, they were facing a new situation. One that was new and changeable, and totally unsuitable to his everyday requirements for peace of mind. As he left the room he turned around to face Gerhart Peuckert. The slumped figure's lips trembled as he suffered Stich's comradely grasp. The eyes were devoid of emotion. They looked as if they'd had more than enough for one day.

As he was putting his hat on, Kröner sensed Stich's casual movement in the room behind him. He turned around in the doorway in time to see the blow clobber its helpless victim on the temple. Peuckert fell to the floor, trying desperately to shield his face with both hands.

"What does Arno von der Leyen want with you, you fool? Are you so valuable?" he screamed, kicking him so hard with the toe of his shoe that his frail knee gave a crack. The old man winced and looked coldly down at the figure huddled beneath him.

"What's that swine got to do with you?" Despite his knee, he kicked him again. For a second Kröner caught the expression on Gerhart Peuckert's face. It seemed more astonished than entreating. "What is it about you that could make this son of a bitch spend nearly thirty years abroad without forgetting you? I'd very much like to know! What do you say, little Gerhart? Can you tell me and Andrea?" Then he kicked him once more without expecting an answer. "Can you tell us what the hell this so-called Bryan Underwood Scott wants with you?"

The figure beneath him was beginning to sob. It had happened before. An inarticulate torrent of sound that Kröner knew could incite Stich to hit again, harder than ever. Kröner stepped into the room and took Stich by the shoulder. The gaze that met him told him it had been unnecessary. Stich himself knew it was enough. Time could be short. He would have to calm down.

Andrea Stich walked calmly past Kröner out into the kitchen and poured a colorless, scented shot of schnapps into a grubby glass. Her husband swallowed it in one gulp, whereupon he sat down peacefully in a worn chair in front of his writing desk. After a few moments he rested his chin on his hands and began to think.

As Andrea went to switch off the light in the dining room the battered man got up from the floor and followed her. He sat down at his place in the dim light without a word. In front of him was a small plate with four buttered biscuits they all knew he liked.

He didn't touch them. Instead he began rocking to and fro in his chair, supporting his wrists on the edge of the table. At first almost imperceptibly. Then more and more.

At this point Kröner adjusted his hat and left the room without a word.

CHAPTER 44

It was the pain that made Gerhart rock back and forth, but an agonizing sense of Petra's absence that made him breathe faster and faster.

Strong words had penetrated his armor.

He sat up a bit and began counting the rose ornaments on the stucco ceiling.

After having counted them a couple of times, he stopped rocking.

And then the words came back to him. He tapped his toes under the table and began to count again. This time the words didn't disappear. He touched his earlobe, rocked a bit more, and stopped suddenly.

Glancing around, Gerhart let the room engulf him. He had been in its custody for a long time. The room enveloped him closely and intensely and had a restraining effect. The old man was almost always close by, whether he was counting rosettes, eating cookies, or tapping his toes. Petra never entered that room.

He counted the rosettes again, tapping his toes at the same time. Then he picked up a cookie and broke off a bit into his mouth.

The old man had hurt him.

As the words that had excited the old man grew slowly inside him, Gerhart counted faster. When the room was finally whirling above him at an accelerating tempo, rosette after rosette, he stopped chewing.

Suddenly he surrendered to the thoughts that were overpowering him.

A fragment of an unreal world fluttered past him. Gerhart could understand the name Arno von der Leyen. The name had a length and composition one seldom encountered. And it was a good name. There was a time when he'd repeated it endlessly until it buzzed around in his head and made him dizzy. In the end his brain could no longer deal with it.

And now it was there again, disturbing his peace.

Long chains of thought were not good for him. They were Trojan horses.

Words and feelings could suddenly merge inside him, bringing new thoughts with them. Notions he'd never asked for.

Therefore it was better for these thoughts to live their own lives without outside disturbance.

And now he'd been disturbed.

In this state of mental turmoil a new, disquieting element had appeared.

The name Arno von der Leyen lacked a face. It had been erased years ago. The name bore warmth, but the man behind it radiated coldness. It was a sensation he'd never had about anything else.

While any of the three men who occasionally visited him could shake him up, they didn't make him feel uneasy or confused. The effect of their actions vanished the moment they were gone.

With this name it was different.

He began counting again. The foot tapping under the table accelerated faster than his counting and the name was there again, breaking the eternal silence. Finally he surrendered to the gathering storm within him.

He sat like that for some while.

By the time Andrea came in and gave his plate a contemptuous look, another name had begun swirling around in his head as if it had never been absent. The sound of it had a life of its own. A life that was distant and unattainable. The name Bryan Underwood Scott was the dagger thrust to his consciousness that made all feelings and memories bleed in unison and left him helpless, confused, and apprehensive.

And worst of all: Pock Face had left them to do Petra harm.

Like someone who's lost without his good-luck charm, Gerhart no longer felt invulnerable. His mental armor had been penetrated once and for all. Now that he'd heard all these words, his feelings were shaken free.

He tried to count the rosettes again and felt the hatred forcing its way up from his subconscious. Thoughts were making their chaotic return.

He had been Gerhart Peuckert as long as he could remember. Even though he was also called Erich Blumenfeld, he was still Gerhart Peuckert. The two identities didn't infringe upon each other. But there was also something else in him. He was also someone else. Not just a man with two or three names, but a man who lived a life parallel to the one he was living now. And this man was unhappy. He had always suffered.

Therefore it was good he had been gone so long.

Gerhart took a look at the cookies. He touched one of them absent-mindedly, the butter making his fingertips slippery.

The unhappy man within him was about to take over with all his dormant knowledge and pent-up rage. A young man with hopes that had never been fulfilled. Full of love that had never been nurtured. It was this man who was awakened upon hearing the name Bryan Underwood Scott, but it was still Gerhart Peuckert who sat in the room.

Year after year he had been living with his trivial undertakings and the regular visits. At first he was afraid and regarded his visitors with suspicion. The constant fear of being killed deprived him of his night's sleep, his positive attitude, his vigor. Then, after thousands of days of triviality, he surrendered for several years to the tempting state of relaxed passivity. That was when he began to count and do his physical training, so the days passed in an unbroken rhythm. Finally his routines made him forget where he was, why he was, and why he never said anything. He simply didn't speak. He ate, slept, listened to the radio—children's programs and radio dramas—and watched television when it came into vogue. He smiled now and then or else sat quietly while the others wove wicker baskets or bound the director's books. He could sit for hours on end with his hands folded, cleansed in mind and body. He had become Gerhart Peuckert and occasionally Erich Blumenfeld.

During the first years at the sanitarium in Freiburg it was tiny fragments of a story, a movie, a play, or a book that made life worth living. But every time the stories really got going, they stopped. He lost the thread, could go no further. More and more things confused him and merged in a foggy world. Figures and people became blurred, names disappeared and were replaced by others, actions became meaningless. And then he stopped. Out of all these unfinished and fragmented stories only a single question remained irrationally for some years, tormenting him daily: What was the name of David Copperfield's second wife?

Then one day even that question rolled into the mists of the past, into insignificance and oblivion.

Finally, only a single spark of life remained in his extinguished personality. It was a feeling of security that went hand in hand with happiness. And Petra, who was always nearby—this sweet girl, gradually becoming a woman, who always stroked him tenderly on the cheek—was the only one able to ignite this spark. She was all that remained of his dreams and happiness.

This diminutive woman always spoke about things as if he were a part of her life. She told him about the world outside and about her joys and sorrows. So many things he didn't understand. She spoke about countries he'd never heard of and about people, actors, presidents, and painters whose existence he couldn't imagine.

She left him on rare occasions to travel to other countries. She would come home with impressions strange as fairy tales. Blissful and delicious. But the only thing that mattered was that she came back. Gentle, attentive, and optimistic, with a tender pat on his cheek.

He had grown accustomed to the men who visited him. Their threatening attitude subsided over the years. They no longer clasped his arm and whispered threats into his ear when they were alone. They just became part of everyday life. And each one of them was very different.

The pock-faced one became his friend. Not because the man was always friendly when he visited him or because he always placed some tasty morsel in front of him when they visited his beautiful home. But chiefly because neither the old man nor the man with the broad face ever hit him in Pock Face's presence.

That's how it had been until now.

Lankau was the worst. Even though the old man could plague him for a whole day, he had his redeeming qualities. And he had Andrea.

It was the old man who made the decisions, but Lankau who carried them out. During the first years he looked sinister with his empty eye socket gaping widely during the raging moments he was administering punishment. Whatever the cause or intensity of the beatings, the end result was that Gerhart Peuckert stopped reacting to anything they did to him. And during the course of time they had more or less stopped. The blows had become softer.

Until today.

Gerhart counted the stucco roses again and tried to keep the words at a distance. In the next room the old man was no longer clearing his throat. From time to time his breathing sounded heavy and regular, as if he were sleeping.

By now it was only rarely that all three men gathered around Gerhart.

Occasionally they sang a popular ditty, slapped him on the back, and offered him a small cigar or a schnapps from Lankau's hollowed-out walking stick or from the small hip flask that was always sloshing around inside his alpine jacket. On such occasions they sometimes took him out for a little drive through town or for a short trip home to Kröner, to the old man, or all the way out to Lankau's country house. During these excursions the three men talked business with great enthusiasm. This wrestling with an endless series of unknowns made Gerhart start counting and long to be back in the sanitarium. It usually ended with his making for the car. Then they'd take him gently by the arm and quiet him down with a pill or two.

Gerhart Peuckert, alias Erich Blumenfeld, had always been given pills. In the sanitariums, on trips, and in people's homes. No matter where he found himself, he'd always been given pills. By nurses, orderlies, and by the three men and their families.

Each place had its small cupboard with its pills.

Only once had they taken him somewhere where there were strangers. Petra had come to meet them and had given him a hug. It had been to an air show with thousands of spectators. The shouts and din and the enormous crowd had been terrifying, but the show had fascinated him. For several hours he'd neither pointed nor moved his head, but his eyes shone with wonderment. The spectacle had touched something deep inside him. It was on this occasion, as he followed the fighters that cut across the sky with a tremendous roar, that he'd said something for the first time in nearly fifteen years. All the way until bedtime he repeated his sentence incessantly.

"*So schnell*" were his words.

CHAPTER 45

It had been a strange day for Laureen. The vague feeling that she was about to stir something up that had been lying dormant in her and Bryan's life took greater and greater hold of her. She became convinced that her fate was linked to that small woman Bryan had been talking to in the Stadtpark.

But that wasn't all.

From a distance the encounter with the woman had been reminiscent of a casual reunion that with surprising haste had developed into a confrontation, then an argument. But the outburst of emotion they displayed on parting made Laureen certain they'd soon meet again. She hugged her arms to her body. "It'll be under different circumstances next time," she thought.

Bryan still had his base at Hotel Roseneck on Urachstrasse. This was Laureen's starting point, and this was where she would be able to find him when the time came. The woman was a different matter. Whether Laureen liked it or not, she urgently needed to learn more about this person. Was it her flat Bryan had been watching for such a long time that morning? Who was she? How could it be that a not particularly young woman in a remote German town could interest her husband so much? Where did they know each other from? And how well? Laureen had a mind to find out. Here and now.

Thus it was the woman, not her husband, whom Laureen followed for the next few hours.

There were numerous stops. Twice the woman's black patent-leather coat was swallowed up by a telephone booth. From time to time she disappeared up a flight of stairs, leaving Laureen behind on the busy street, confused and with aching feet. The woman had numerous errands. When she finally entered the wine bar on Münsterplatz and had been staring blankly out the window for some time, Laureen sat down at a table in the corner and removed her new shoes with almost audible relief. Not until now did she have time to study her target closely.

The lady sitting a couple of tables away didn't look particularly desirable.

When Bryan finally came and sat down at her table he seemed very tense. That he appeared didn't surprise Laureen, but their intimacy tormented her. The woman spoke softly, looking down at the table. Then she put her hand on Bryan's arm and stroked it gently. Five minutes after he arrived, he left the wine bar again, looking grimmer than Laureen had ever seen him. Through the blur of the window she watched him disappear, his movements abrupt and uncoordinated, as though he were drunk.

Laureen's dilemma as to whom to follow the rest of the afternoon had thus resolved itself. The woman remained sitting beside the door for a while, staring emptily in front of her. She seemed confused and undecided. Laureen lit a cigarette and turned to face the middle of the room. For the time being, she would remain tucked away in her corner. When the woman finally got up to go, she would too.

CHAPTER 46

Petra was in a quandary. On her rounds in town several of her patients had asked her whether she was ill. "How pale you are, Sister Wagner," they said.

And the truth was that she didn't feel well.

She'd seen the three malingerers from the SS hospital playacting for decades. Even though they were very different individuals, Petra knew for sure that all three would be ruthless if anyone stood in their way.

It had taken Petra a long time to realize this. Without her friend Gisela Devers, whom she still bitterly regretted having introduced to Kröner, she'd probably never have seen things in the proper perspective.

And she was utterly convinced she would never in her life have gotten involved with these three fiends if Gerhart Peuckert hadn't existed.

Because she herself only existed for Gerhart.

She'd been in love with this handsome man since the first day she saw him. An impossible undertaking that had made her a target for derision and gradually isolated her from a normal social life. For years she'd clung to the hope that his traumas would fade and finally disappear. She had lived with the dream of a normal life together with him.

At times she'd felt this possibility breathtakingly close. Brief, happy moments, until the realization came: Gerhart Peuckert's fate was at the mercy of these three men.

This she'd always known. It revolted her.

And it was because of this knowledge and her eternal hopes for Gerhart that she'd betrayed another person today.

It had been a great shock to meet one of the patients from those days. It was the first time this had happened since the three men had reappeared in her life ages ago.

The face was that of Arno von der Leyen, yet he'd seemed a stranger. His language and appearance had scared her. The fear that welled up in her when he questioned her about Gerhart Peuckert was understandable enough, considering her situation.

No one really knew what was going on inside Peuckert. For a long time the doctors had been of the opinion that his mind could best be described as "incubating," that his consciousness lay dormant in the grip of his sub-conscious. Gisela Devers had confided in Petra that Kröner felt convinced that one day Gerhart Peuckert would rise, quite normal, from his sickbed, and he'd also intimated that Peuckert would immediately turn on the three of them. Words like this could provoke a quarrel between husband and wife. Gisela would admonish Kröner, saying, "Leave him in peace." But the brotherhood couldn't afford to lose its grip on Peuckert, because he knew far too much. Things were all right as long as they could control him.

Only because Gerhart was so ill and the condition of his mind so stable did the three men choose to let him exist in peace. This, according to Gisela, was the term they'd used. They let him "exist."

Petra felt uneasy. This was how things were preferably to continue, but now a stranger had arrived. He had connected his past with theirs and asked questions about the one thing on Earth she felt the need to protect with her life. It had been a threat that had caused her to react promptly. Petra sighed and rolled up her blood-pressure kit. She nodded to the patient who lay staring up at her and looked out the window.

Schlossberg had been bathed in sunshine all day. It was as if this insignificant hill wanted to confirm its importance. What would happen to Arno von der Leyen up there, she didn't know. But she could guess. She would hate to be the one to have a score to settle with Hermann Müller when he revealed his true nature as Peter Stich. Anyone who wanted to meet Gerhart Peuckert risked conjuring up Stich's innermost self.

Right now the very thought of it made her sick. The possible consequence of her action had made her not much different from the three men.

It was her friend, little Dot Vanderleen, who'd drawn Petra's attention to the lanky woman across the street. "Look," she'd said, pointing out the window. The woman was standing on one leg, massaging the other foot. "Poor thing," she'd added, empathetically. "She must be wearing new shoes."

Although Petra Wagner was a small woman, the featherweight Frau

Vanderleen reached only to her armpits. Totally fascinated, she'd stood on tiptoe, regarding the woman through the leaves of the potted plants. "New shoes are a curse," she'd said simply, leaving Petra to finish treating her ankle sores. "It's a good thing one doesn't have to put up with new shoes anymore," she'd concluded.

After that, Petra had seen this same woman several more times on her rounds. A quick glance out the window and she'd be standing massaging her feet on the opposite side of the street, regular as clockwork.

Under normal circumstances Petra would have interrupted her Saturday duties for a couple of hours in order to visit Gerhart. It was on these late Saturday afternoons that they seemed closest to each other. For a few seconds every Saturday they loved with their eyes, so to speak. She lived for those few seconds.

At three o'clock Petra visited Herr Franck, an elderly wholesaler with bedsores. According to her schedule he would be the last patient before her break.

But instead of taking the tram down to the sanitarium as usual, she crossed Kartoffelmarkt in the opposite direction, increasing her tempo as she approached a street-theater performance that had attracted a small group of onlookers. As she hurried past the crowd she accidentally bumped into one of the performers, making him stumble.

"Goodness gracious," he exclaimed, adjusting his turquoise leotard. But Petra had given her pursuer the slip.

Petra climbed into an empty taxi opposite the spot where Wasserstrasse and Weberstrasse converge. "He'll only be a jiffy," said the driver in the cab behind. "Fritz is just taking a leak. He'll be right back."

The lanky woman came rushing along Wasserstrasse. She looked harassed. Petra leaned slightly backward to get out of her line of vision. It was clear that the woman didn't know what to do next. She took a few steps, looked down Weberstrasse, and then turned around again. Her untidy hair no longer suited the rest of her elegant appearance. Then she leaned against the wall of a house and bent over, clutching her knees.

Petra recognized that feeling and urge, but knew it wouldn't help tender feet.

The woman was following her all right, but seemed an amateur. She glanced around several times before finally putting her large plastic bag down on the ground beside her, whereupon she sighed so visibly that Petra could almost hear her.

"He's coming now," shouted the other driver, tapping on the taxi's side window. At that moment the woman caught sight of Petra. Her eyes moved from Petra's face to the taxi she was sitting in, then to the taxi behind her and back again. She was clearly aware she'd been discovered.

"Well, missus, you've found a seat, I see. Where shall we go, then?" The chubby man laid his arm on the back of the seat beside him, straining to steal a glance at the woman behind him. Petra had scarcely noticed his arrival. She opened her medical bag and took hold of the scalpel that always lay in the middle pocket of the flap. It had just been furnished with a new blade and could be a deadly weapon. With this in her hand, she was ready to delve further into the day's unfolding mystery.

The woman looked sad as Petra got out of the cab and strode over toward her. "Isn't one allowed to piss?" the driver shouted from the taxi she'd just vacated. "Just two minutes! You could have waited, couldn't you?"

The woman looked completely dumbfounded when Petra let her see the scalpel blade gleam under her arm. She stared at it for a long time, unable to flee.

Then Petra lowered her weapon.

It was the second time that day she had confronted a pursuer, and it was the second time she had been addressed in English. Arno von der Leyen and this woman had something in common besides language, she was sure of it.

"What have I done?" was all the woman said.

"How long have you been following me?"

"Since this morning. Since you met my husband in the park."

"Your husband? What do you mean?"

"You've met him twice today, you can't deny it. First in Stadtgarten and then in Hotel Rappen's wine bar."

"Are you married to Arno von der Leyen?" Petra studied the tall woman. She surprised herself with the question.

The woman seemed to be trying to pull herself together. "Arno von der Leyen? Is that what he calls himself?"

"That's the name I've known him by for nearly thirty years. I've never known him by any other name."

For a second the lanky women seemed completely disoriented. "That's a German name, isn't it?" she said.

"Yes, naturally," said Petra.

"Well, I don't know how natural it is, considering he's my husband, he's English, and his name's got nothing to do with 'Arno.' It's 'Bryan Underwood Scott.' That's the name he's always had. It's written in his birth certificate and it's the name his mother called him until she died. Why do you call him Arno von der Leyen? Are you out to make a fool of me or will you settle for stabbing me with that thing you're waving around?"

The woman's frantic outburst was fascinating. Petra only understood half the torrent of words that had gushed forth. No amount of pricey pancake foundation could hide this woman's red-faced indignation. It seemed more than genuine.

"Try turning around," said Petra. "What do you see?"

"Nothing," said Laureen. "An empty street. Is that what you mean?"

"You can see a big 'C' on the facade over there, can't you? That's Hotel Garni's café. If you promise to accompany me there without making trouble, here and now, I won't need this." Petra swung the scalpel and stuck it under her arm again. "I think we two had better have a talk."

CHAPTER 47

The waiter served the tea in a coffee cup with no apologies. Laureen let it steam for ages before tasting it disapprovingly. Neither of them said anything. The woman across from Laureen seemed about to explode. She glanced at her watch several times, and each time she seemed about to speak, but didn't.

Finally she raised her cup and took a sip. "For me it's a jigsaw puzzle," she said. "Can you understand?"

Laureen nodded.

"And I have a feeling that more than one person may be badly hurt today. Maybe it's already happened and we can't do anything about it. So therefore we must try to fit the pieces together right now. Do you follow me?"

"I think so." Laureen tried to look obliging. "But who's in danger? My husband can't be in any danger, can he?"

"Yes, he can. But you must forgive me if that's of lesser importance to me just now. You see, I trust neither you nor him."

"You don't? Now, listen. I don't know a thing about you! I've never seen you before. You could be anybody. You've known him for thirty years under a different name. And I've got a feeling that you might be in possession of information that may have been affecting our marriage for years. Do you think *I* trust *you*?" Laureen dissolved yet another lump of sugar in the semi-brown liquid the waiter called tea and sent Petra a broad, caustic smile. "But on the other hand, do I have a choice?"

"Nope, I'm afraid not." The woman's burst of laughter hardly corresponded to her diminutive stature. It was deep and resounding and sounded convincing, but it stopped as soon as it began. "My name is Petra. You may call me that. Petra Wagner." She nodded in emphasis. "I met your husband here in Freiburg during the Second World War. He'd been admitted to a big reserve hospital a bit north of town where I was a nurse. I haven't seen him since—not before he turned up today. You witnessed our first meeting in nearly thirty years. Your husband said it was by accident. Was it?"

"I have no idea. I haven't spoken to my husband for days. He doesn't even know I'm here. I know absolutely nothing and I've never heard anything about his being in a German hospital during World War II. On the other hand, I know he was hospitalized for a time when he came home from the war. He'd been missing for nearly a year."

"That must have been the year he was in the hospital here in Freiburg."

The revelation of this part of Bryan's past caught Laureen unawares. It sounded incredible. Still she felt convinced that the woman wasn't lying. "Anxiety and truth go hand in hand, just like lies and arrogance," her father had always used to say. Behind Petra Wagner's calm exterior she seemed fearful.

They would have to win each other's confidence as quickly as possible.

"Good! I believe you, even though it sounds very weird to me." Laureen took another sip of the bitter liquid before continuing. "My name is Laureen Underwood Scott. And you may call me Laureen, if you like," she said. "My husband and I have been married since 1947. We have our silver wedding in less than two months. We live in Canterbury, where my husband was born. He was educated as a doctor and now works in the pharmaceutical industry. We have a daughter and are what one commonly calls unusually privileged. Until two weeks ago my husband hadn't been back to Germany during all the time we've been married. And please forgive me, but until a couple of days ago I'd never even heard of this town." Then, as the two women were looking straight at each other, Laureen pleaded, "Won't you please tell me where my husband is, Petra Wagner?"

———

As far as Petra Wagner was concerned, this Englishwoman could have been speaking Hebrew. She wasn't listening. Instead, she concentrated all her senses on trying to discern weak points in the woman's facade. As a rule, words served as a veil to conceal what was essential. In this case it was a matter of vital importance whether Petra could trust this awkward-looking female or not.

First and foremost she had to think of Gerhart. If she did nothing, she wouldn't be exposing him to any new risk. He would be just as safe as he'd always been.

Naturally she hoped that, when it came down to it, Stich, Kröner, and Lankau would reach an understanding with Arno von der Leyen up there on the mountain. Nevertheless she felt ill at ease, impotent, and far from secure. What if things didn't go as they should, and what if this woman before her had evil intentions no matter what happened on Schlossberg? Then where would she stand? And how would it affect Gerhart?

The woman was no professional, she couldn't possibly be. Presumably she wasn't lying when she said Arno von der Leyen was her husband.

"May I ask you some questions?" she asked, strangely short of breath. Laureen looked surprised, but nodded. "Then answer me quickly. You can regard it as a kind of test. What's the name of your daughter?"

"Ann Lesley Underwood Scott."

"A-n-n-e?" Petra spelled.

"No, without the 'e.'"

"When was she born?"

"On June sixteenth, 1948."

"What day of the week was it?"

"It was a Monday."

"How do you remember that?"

"It just was!"

"What happened on that day?"

"My husband wept."

"And what else?"

"I ate some muffins with jam."

"That's a strange thing to remember, isn't it?"

Laureen shook her head. "Have you any children?"

"No." Apart from the sleazy questions Petra on rare occasion had to put up with when she sat alone in Palmera's Café after having gone shopping, this was the one she hated most.

"If you had, you'd know it wasn't such a strange thing to do. Is that good enough now?"

"No. First tell me what your husband wants with Gerhart Peuckert."

"Quite honestly, I don't know. You must know better than I do." Laureen pressed her lips together, creating lines in the corner of her mouth that caused fissures in her makeup.

"No, I don't."

"Listen here, Petra Wagner . . . !" The waiter passed their table with a tray poised above him. The look he sent Laureen as she took the other woman's hand expressed, if not disapproval, then regret. "Tell me what you know. You can trust me."

Laureen was dazed by astonishment and skepticism. The past she was learning about sank in very slowly. This past her husband had lived was that of a stranger. She had known nothing, absolutely nothing, about it. Petra Wagner was a good guide.

Gradually the hospital, the life there, and the wards in which Bryan lay all became alive and real for Laureen. "How awful," she exclaimed from time to time. "Is that true?" she whispered just as frequently, without expecting an answer.

The account of the months in the reserve hospital in the mountains revealed a yoke of fear. A clinical world of systematic wrong treatment and loneliness, where three men silently terrorized and controlled an entire hospital ward.

And then one day Arno von der Leyen disappeared, and two of the men with him.

"And you're saying my husband and this Gerhart Peuckert had absolutely nothing to do with each other at the hospital?"

"Nothing whatsoever." Petra looked dejected. "On the contrary. Gerhart always used to turn his head away when Arno von der Leyen was in the vicinity."

"And what happened to this Gerhart Peuckert, then?"

The instant the question was put forward, Petra pulled her hand away. She felt unwell. Then she turned around and pulled her scarf from the back of the chair. As she was putting it on, she froze. Almost imperceptibly the color drained from her cheeks.

She took Laureen's handkerchief without hesitation as the tears began to flow.

That afternoon there were minutes that seemed to Petra like hours, and hours that seemed like fractions of a second. These few minutes opened up and screamed of a loneliness and lack of trust that needed to flow unimpeded and be articulated. Finally Petra attempted a smile. Blowing her nose, she laughed in small bursts, shyly and relieved.

"I can trust you, can't I?"

"Yes, you can," said Laureen, taking her hand again. "Apart from the fact that I have no idea whether my daughter was born on a Monday, you can." She laughed apologetically. "Just tell me your story. I think it will be good for both of us."

Petra was in love with Gerhart Peuckert. She had heard terrible things about him, but she loved him just the same. After he and a couple of the other patients had been transferred to Ensen bei Porz near Cologne, Gerhart's health had shown little sign of improvement. It had cost both persuasion and bribery for her to be allowed to accompany him.

When the capitulation was announced, Gerhart was still weak—very weak. He could lie semiconscious for days without knowing where he was. Despite good treatment during the latter days of the war, the shock therapy and hard-handed treatment by the security officers and his fellow patients in Freiburg had nearly done him in. On top of that, he acted as if he were in a kind of chronic anaphylactic shock that no one had time to investigate or enough sense to take seriously. What was worse, after the war ended, Gerhart suddenly was no longer a patient whom the doctors cared about. His status changed from one day to the next. In their eyes he now belonged to a part of the past best left unspoken. There were other patients who didn't have the curse of the swastika hanging over them, and they came first. It was only Petra who worried seriously about Gerhart Peuckert's situation. But she hadn't the insight, training, or intellect to know what should be done in his case. He received the pills he'd always received and was otherwise allowed to sleep all day long.

And so it remained, right until two of the men from the Alphabet House turned up.

At this point in Petra's account Laureen realized why the woman had good reason to be afraid. These two men had come expressly to kill the man she loved. One of them, a big powerfully built man by the name of Lankau, was one of the two who had escaped from the hospital together with Laureen's husband.

The two men walked straight in from the street wearing hospital coats. No one took notice of them, now that so many so-called observers from the occupation forces kept running in and out. They produced no form of identification and yet the hospital staff did exactly as they demanded. It was a strange time, when authorities changed faces quick as a whiplash, in pace with intensified raids and arrests. It was a disorder that preyed on all segments of society.

Everything was teetering and faltering, and no Germans protested.

When Petra went down to the ward to dispense the day's second round of medicine, Gerhart's space was empty. The bed was gone. One of the orderlies pointed toward a linen storeroom, and here she found Kröner and Lankau bent over Gerhart's bed. The instant she saw them she retreated to the doorway so the activity in the corridor behind her could become her defense. She was shocked. Gerhart was trembling and fighting for breath.

A few minutes later she would have been too late.

The two men were forced to leave Gerhart Peuckert in peace because she'd come. She recognized them, and they recognized her with loathing in their eyes. Then they disappeared up the ward's middle gangway. During the following days they turned up one at a time at regular intervals, always smiling and seemingly conciliatory. As long as they came singly Petra couldn't touch them. There would always be the other one to take revenge. And Gerhart was a defenseless target.

Now they were both in the danger zone.

Thus it went for five days, during which Petra kept herself surrounded by colleagues but never left Gerhart Peuckert out of her sight for more than a few minutes at a time. She noted that he grew weaker every day. Since the arrival of the two men he had seemed frightened and numbed and had neither eaten nor drunk to any appreciable extent.

On the sixth day she met the third man from the hospital in Freiburg.

They had waited for her outside. The girlfriend with whom Petra was walking arm in arm began flirting instantly and in an unsolicited way with the pockmarked man named Kröner. This was something she did with all well-dressed men.

It was a grotesque situation.

It was this third patient from Freiburg who spoke to her. A small, friendly man by the name of Peter Stich whom she'd always regarded as incurably ill, right until the doctors discharged him for active service. Meanwhile Lankau stood with arms akimbo, looking around uneasily. It was a dangerous situation, the outcome of which both women risked paying dearly for. Petra listened carefully.

Peter Stich began with a quiet smile: "Gerhart Peuckert should be taken to a safer place, shouldn't he? During times like these, I mean. After all, he's a war criminal, isn't he? And for people like him there's not much sympathy, is there?"

Then he patted her elbow and nodded briefly at Lankau, who promptly disappeared. "Perhaps you'd like to talk to me about it," he continued. "When and where it would suit you."

Petra didn't find it hard to be cooperative. The seriousness of the situation was not foreign to her. Ill or not, Gerhart Peuckert could easily come to pay for his past. Of this there was already daily proof. The search for the most prominent figures of the Nazi regime was in full swing. Several of Cologne's leading citizens had been interned and it was open season for hunting down members of the Gestapo and the special branch of the SS. There was no mercy, let alone help, to be expected from either friends or enemies.

It was a bizarre day at the hospital. A parade of representatives from the Allied forces kept coming and going. In the general confusion several of Petra's colleagues refused to carry out even the most trivial tasks, while uniformed men had hauled yet another of Cologne's finer inhabitants out of his hiding place in the basement. It made Petra sick to her stomach.

They arranged that later in the day she would meet the patients from Freiburg in the railway station's makeshift waiting room. Outside it was almost deserted. Not one of the buses that normally picked up passengers from the station had arrived. Many people were lying asleep or dozing on the waiting-room floor. Strewn around were all sorts of packages, tied-up cardboard boxes, blankets packed with essentials, suitcases, bags, and sacks. The place was well chosen. Petra had insisted that all the malingerers be present, but she would speak only to one of them. And she had insisted that the meeting take place where there were plenty of people around.

She could scarcely have asked for a more crowded spot.

A family was encamped in the middle of the floor. It included at least six small children and a couple of teenagers. The woman's face was lined. She looked worried and weary. The man was asleep. Petra went over and waited in the middle of this group while a couple of the kids tugged at her dress and looked at her teasingly.

Peter Stich saw her immediately. Kröner and Lankau followed a couple of steps behind. Then they came to a halt.

"Where are the other two?" she asked, glancing around quickly. One of the youngsters sat down on the floor between them and looked up, wide-eyed, first under her dress and then at an extremely relaxed Peter Stich.

"Who do you mean?" he asked.

"The two who disappeared the same evening as Lankau. Arno von der Leyen and the other one. I can't remember his name."

"Dieter Schmidt! His name was Dieter Schmidt. They're dead. They died the same night they escaped. Why?"

"Because I don't trust you, so I need to know how many of you there are."

"There are only the three of us, plus you and Gerhart Peuckert. You can count on that."

She glanced around once more. "Here," she said, handing him an open envelope. Stich took out a piece of paper and read it without a word.

"Why have you written this?" he asked, smiling wryly as he handed the paper to Kröner.

"That's a copy. I deposited the original together with my will. It's my guarantee that nothing will happen to me or Gerhart."

"You're wrong there. If we're exposed, we'll expose Gerhart. You realize that, don't you?" She nodded. "So you believe we've got sufficient hold on each other with this note?" She nodded again.

After a moment's discussion with the other two, Stich said, "Unfortunately it would put us in the situation of constantly having to fear something might happen to you. Life insurance between partners ought to be reciprocal. We'll have to ask you to destroy the original. We can't have it deposited with some lawyer."

"What then?"

"We can give you another contract instead, which you can deposit with your lawyer. One that grants you concessions. We can word it in such a way that we would profit greatly from your death. It would throw suspicion on us if you or Gerhart should meet an untimely fate."

"No." Petra could feel Lankau's fury as she shook her head. "I'll deposit the letter somewhere else."

"Where?" Stich cocked his head to the side.

"That's my business."

"We can't possibly agree to that." The words were barely out of his mouth before Petra turned on her heel and made determinedly for the exit. Not until Stich's third shout did she stop.

Then he approached her.

Amid curious glances they talked together the whole evening in the middle of the crowded hall. Peter Stich accepted her conditions and seemed very open, at the same time making no attempt to hide the fact that she and Peuckert would pay dearly if she ever violated their trust.

He managed to reassure her. She knew very well that these men, like Gerhart Peuckert, had all been high-ranking SS officers. People like them risked a life sentence or even execution if they were caught and brought to trial. Their collective source of protection lay in concealing their identities. So if Gerhart were to be allowed to go on living, they all had to stick together—including Petra. She had to guarantee them her and Gerhart's silence.

If she were able to do that, they'd offer her something in return. They would provide Gerhart Peuckert with a new identity, namely the one intended for Dieter Schmidt.

In that event he would come to be called Erich Blumenfeld. With his sharp features he could easily have a little Jewish blood in him, especially if they cut his medium-blond hair short. Nothing would happen to him as long as they stuck to their story. In those days people were beginning to learn why some Jews might need psychiatric help. The malingerers would give him a new life and see that he was taken care of.

There was no reason why Petra shouldn't accompany Gerhart Peuckert and remain close to him.

"And so you wound up in Freiburg?" Laureen shook her head. "Here, of all places, where none of you were safe?"

"That's how it was. The others had already made their decision. And some of my family lives in the area. Anyway, I had no reason to hide." Petra folded her hands and pushed her cup slightly forward with her knuckles. "And it turned out pretty well. Right until you and your husband turned up. For twenty-seven years everything went as it should. Freiburg had many advantages for the malingerers as well. In the first place it's close to Switzerland. Secondly, all the people who could have recognized them were killed when the hospital was bombed—that is, if they hadn't already been transferred. Finally, none of the malingerers had been brought up here or had any other connections with Freiburg. The town was a good choice."

And that's what happened. They all acquired new identities, precisely as Stich had prompted. He, himself, became Hermann Müller. Wilfried Kröner became Hans Schmidt, Horst Lankau became Alex Faber, and Gerhart Peuckert was moved to a private sanitarium as Erich Blumenfeld, the Jew. For the modest sum of two thousand marks the four men's tattoos were removed by an elderly doctor from Stuttgart who had plenty on his conscience, even though he'd been acquitted at Nuremburg. All physical proof of the four men's true identities was gone.

"I think Bryan still has that tattoo," Laureen admitted. It was years since she'd last noticed the blotch that she'd always regarded as being the result of a soldier's foolish whim.

Moving Gerhart Peuckert hadn't caused them any problems. From Cologne he went to Reutlingen, and from there he was transferred to Karlsruhe. By the time they finally brought him to Freiburg, his new identity had long been established.

Petra was glad to have Gerhart back in Freiburg and for a long time she imagined he would get well. Therefore she remained single. Such was the price of love.

But despite Petra's steadfastness and devotion, Gerhart Peuckert's condition remained unchanged. He stayed as he was. Unapproachable, withdrawn. Present and yet distant.

Like a lover in a glass case.

Apart from her, the three men were almost the only contact he had with the outside world. As far as she knew they treated him fairly well. After a few years the men bought the clinic. Then they could come and go as they pleased.

"Are they wealthy?" Laureen had a special way of pronouncing the word. When she was young it was laced with scorn. In Cardiff, wealthy people were those who profited on the backs of the men in the docks and steelworks. By the time she'd risen to a more stable economic stratum, the word had acquired a new dimension that made her hesitate a second before uttering it.

Petra was gazing into space, as if she hadn't heard the question. "At the reserve hospital in Freiburg I had this friend, Gisela, who was a few years older than me. Her husband had been admitted there, a hopeless case. She was relieved to hear he was killed when they bombed the hospital during the final days of the war. We learned to laugh together, that's for sure!" Her smile was faint and sentimental. Laureen imagined Petra had probably not laughed very much since. "As fate would have it, my friend couldn't return to her hometown and then these three men turned up and changed my whole life. One dumb afternoon, years later, I took her with me to an appointment I had with them, just to have some decent company. I should never have done it. It turned out to be her downfall because she wound up marrying one, the pockmarked Kröner. He was certainly the most cultivated of the three, but he tormented her to death. Still, if it hadn't been for her, I would never have understood what it was that drove them to act as they did." Petra took another look at her watch. Then she straightened up and threw off the mood she'd conjured up.

"Yes, they're wealthy," she concluded. "Very wealthy, actually."

Like Stich, Kröner only invested a small part of his fortune. The remainder of the tangible wealth that had given them influence in their new home territory was obtained by hard work. The rest still lay in bank boxes in Basel, untouched. Only Lankau had been eating into his capital regularly, and there was still plenty left, as far as Petra could tell. As his cover, he became owner of a large machine factory that employed many people, even though the factory ran at a loss. It was just his social alibi and a hobby that, like his vineyard, provided him with contacts and hunting companions. He was known as a "character," always good for a joke or an extravagant dinner. Lankau became the quintessential Jekyll and Hyde.

As for Kröner, his business affairs were more widespread and ranged from commerce to real estate. All were types of activity that demanded political influence and many friends. Petra didn't think there was a single baby in Freiburg that Kröner hadn't at some time hugged or patted on the cheek. In this way, he'd spent most of his life building his own ego and neglecting those closest to him.

Stich was another story. Despite his modest lifestyle he was the absolute wealthiest of the three. He had engaged in speculation in the German reconstruction, in the upsurge of trade, and in the paper boom of the sixties. With small risk and great winnings, it was a job that demanded no more than clear-sightedness and determination. As a result he always refrained from mixing with others.

He was an almost unknown entity, even among those closest to him.

During the whole time, relations among the three men were based solely on their common interest in concealing their past. This was why they visited Gerhart Peuckert with precise regularity and made sure they influenced his treatment. It was also why they approved each other's choice of wives and public image.

As far as Gerhart Peuckert was concerned, they all grew accustomed to his condition. Only once did a deeper layer within him make its way to the surface and shock them all. Petra had been present. It had been at an air show. For the first time in many years he had said something. "*So schnell!*" he'd said. That was all. It had been in 1962.

Petra had dreamt about that day many times, hoping it would repeat itself.

"And now's it's 1972. Wilfried Kröner's fifty-eight, Lankau's sixty, Stich is sixty-eight. And Gerhart's fifty, just like me. Nothing has changed. We're just ten years older." Petra sighed. "Time has just rolled along like that—until today."

Laureen sat looking at her for some time. It had been a relief for her to tell that story. Petra's still young-looking eyes were calm now, and sorrowful.

"Petra . . ." she said, and hesitated a moment. "Thank you for telling me your story. I believe every word of it, but I still don't understand what my husband has to do with it all. Would the three men be able to harm him?"

"Yes, they would, and they will, if your husband doesn't accept their conditions."

"What conditions?"

"I don't know. To keep his mouth shut and go home again, I should think. I don't know . . ." She seemed to search for the words. "You say your husband is wealthy?"

"Yes, he is."

"Can he prove it?"

"Naturally. Why do you ask?"

"I think it may be necessary, if he's going to get out of Freiburg alive."

"Get out of Freiburg alive?" Laureen was shocked. "Do you realize what it is you're saying? You have to tell me: What's become of my husband?"

"I can only tell you part of it because I don't know everything. And only on the condition that you swear on your life that neither you nor your husband plan to hurt Gerhart Peuckert."

Within the space of a few hours Laureen was yanked from one reality to the next, at a greater pace than her mind could properly absorb. The extent to which her own role would remain passive was entirely up to this woman who had just spoken so frankly to her. And Bryan was about to present her with yet another reality. Maybe he was in trouble right now. New aspects of her husband were in the process of being revealed. She no longer knew if she could assure Petra that he didn't mean Gerhart Peuckert any harm. Until now she wouldn't have been in doubt.

That was the old days.

"Yes, I'll stake my life on it," she said.

CHAPTER 48

The instant Lankau heard the promising sound of the BMW starting up, his good eye began to smile.

So he'd gotten rid of his tormentor.

Something seemed to indicate they'd overestimated von der Leyen, and that von der Leyen had underestimated him. A suitable combination and an extremely encouraging point of departure.

Horst Lankau was still on home turf. Bound to a good chair with oaken armrests. One that his wife had bought ten years ago from a furniture dealer in Müllheim, a local tradesman and professional charmer who knew how to make an impression on women while he dipped into their husbands' pockets. The chair had looked fantastically solid with its coarse fustian upholstery and massive legs, but the truth turned out to be quite different. The chair was actually a poorly constructed piece of junk and he'd felt like giving the furniture dealer a hiding for having palmed it off on them. In the end, the chair, like so many other items, had been patched up and relegated to service at the vineyard.

In the present situation Lankau wasn't sorry they'd bought the thing. He began jerking the armrests up and down and rocking determinedly backward and forward.

With not so much as a creak both armrests snapped their dowels and flew off backward. With the pieces of wood dangling from his arms he tried in vain to get hold of the knot that kept his torso firmly bound to the back of the chair. The twine and his large stomach prevented him from reaching his feet and untying them. The only alternative was to keep on rocking until the chair disintegrated beneath him into its original components. When the ship's clock above the door struck a quarter past six, the chair collapsed and he was free.

. . .

Peter Stich sounded distant. To judge from his tone of voice when he answered the phone, he'd been sitting and thinking for some time with a schnapps glass in front of him. "Where the hell have you been?" he snapped, the instant he recognized Lankau's voice.

"I've been practicing my English. You should hear how good I am." Lankau held the receiver with his shoulder, rubbing his arms. The scratches were only superficial.

"Just shut up and answer me, dammit! What's going on, Horst?"

"I'm out at the vineyard. That swine Arno von der Leyen overpowered me, but I'm free now. The idiot tied me to Gerda's oak chair!" Lankau allowed himself a laugh.

"Where is he now?"

"That's why I'm calling. He's seen Kröner. He knows where he lives. I've tried to phone Wilfried, but he doesn't answer."

"And what about me? Does he know anything about me?"

"I'm absolutely certain he doesn't."

"Good." He could hear a faint splash at the other end of the line. Presumably Andrea, pouring him another glass. "And you think von der Leyen is on his way to Kröner?" the old man continued after a short burst of coughing.

"That's definitely a possibility, yes."

"Kröner won't be coming home just yet. He's out looking for Petra Wagner."

"Petra? Why Petra?" The day was full of surprises.

"We were afraid she hadn't told us the whole truth. And since we didn't hear anything from you, we had to assume she must have told von der Leyen what awaited him on Schlossberg."

"He didn't know a damn thing! Where's Petra now?"

"I suppose she's out on her rounds. Kröner's busy trying to find out where. When he finds her it's extremely possible he'll liquidate her."

"Too bad for little Petra," grunted Lankau. He couldn't care less. "When Arno von der Leyen has carried out whatever mission he's on, he'll come back here, you can bet on that. And then it'll be my turn to give him some tender, loving care. But right now you've got to see to it that Kröner gets the message. Von der Leyen is driving around in the BMW with my Shiki Kenju in his pocket."

"Good car, rotten pistol; you have a generous nature, Horst. Does he know it can go off if he fiddles with the safety catch?"

Lankau roared with laughter. He could visualize Stich holding the receiver at arm's length from his ear. "God only knows! I don't think so. But at the moment we have to assume that it's loaded with a bullet that Arno von der Leyen wouldn't hesitate sending into Kröner's pockmarked skull. So you'd better get going, Peter."

"You don't have to worry. I've already left," he said quietly before the click.

CHAPTER 49

Since leaving Lankau tied up at his country house Bryan had done some thinking. First of all, he'd have to question Lankau again sooner or later. The circumstances related to James's disappearance were probably correct, but if he were to have any peace of mind he would have to force Lankau to tell him more. Even though the colossus could still fight back, Bryan suspected there were weak points in his defense. If he could find them, he felt sure the various bits of the story would fit together. And then he would let him go.

Before that he would have to go see Kröner and ask him the same questions. Maybe he would be more cooperative, Bryan thought, feeling the pistol that was still lodged in his waistband. And maybe he'd learn more about the mysterious person they called the Mailman. Maybe Kröner would even spit out Petra's whereabouts.

When all that had been accomplished he would phone Canterbury. If Laureen still wasn't home, he'd phone Cardiff in the hope of catching her there. If she was there, he would ask her to pack her suitcase the following morning, take the fast train to London, and continue to Heathrow on the Piccadilly Line. There she would take the first plane to Paris. A couple of nights with him at Hôtel Meurice on the rue de Rivoli, a Sunday stroll in the parks, and evening mass in Saint-Eustache ought to be enough to entice and appease her.

Kröner's house was the only one on the street that lay in total darkness. In all the other houses a light in the hall or over a garden path gave a sign of life. But not here.

And yet, life there was.

Standing just outside the wrought-iron gate in the middle of the drive,

Bryan was totally conspicuous. Twenty meters away an elderly man had just left Kröner's front door and was on his way over to him. Bryan could either walk by or remain where he was and play the game that had already begun. Looking in his direction, the elderly man stopped for a moment as if trying to remember whether he'd locked the door behind him. Then he took another step forward, collected himself, and looked straight at Bryan. He smiled and threw open his arms, almost as if they'd met before. "*Suchen Sie etwas?*" he asked, stopping a couple of paces away to clear his throat.

"Excuse me?" The words popped mechanically out of Bryan's mouth. It was the old man he had seen together with Kröner at the Kuranstalt St. Ursula. The one he subsequently had followed who lived in the house on Luisenstrasse. For a moment the old man seemed puzzled by the foreign language and switched over to English with a smile, as though it were the most natural thing in the world.

"I asked if you were looking for someone."

"Oh! Yes, I am, actually," said Bryan, looking him straight in the face. "I'm looking for Herr Hans Schmidt."

"I see. I wish I could help you, Herr . . . ?"

"Bryan Underwood Scott." Bryan took the old man's outstretched hand, noticing its thin, ice-cold skin.

"I'm sorry, but he and his family have gone away for a couple of days, Herr Scott. I've just been watering their flowers. That has to be done too, hasn't it?" Then he smiled with a twinkle in his eye, friendly and familiarly. "Is there something I can help you with?"

Behind the mask with the white beard was a face that was pricking at Bryan's subconscious. The voice was foreign and unfamiliar, but the features made him feel uneasy without knowing why. "I don't know, really," he said, hesitating. He wasn't going to get another chance like this. "Actually it's not Herr Schmidt I want to talk to, even though it would be interesting, but one of his acquaintances."

"I see. But I may be able to help you nevertheless. I know most of the people in Hans Schmidt's circle as well as he does. Who are you looking for, if I may be so bold?"

"A mutual friend from many years ago. You're hardly likely to know him. His name is Gerhart Peuckert."

The old man scrutinized him for a moment. Then he pursed his lips and his eyes narrowed as he thought. "You know what?" he began finally, raising his eyebrows. "I do believe I remember the man. He was ill, wasn't he?"

This was one development Bryan hadn't expected. He stared at the old man, tongue-tied for a moment. "Yes, I suppose he was," he said at length.

"I think I remember him. Perhaps it's not even so long ago that I heard Hans mention him. Could that be so?"

"I've no idea."

"Well, I can try and find out. My wife's blessed with an excellent memory. I'm sure she can help us. Are you very busy? Do you live here in town?"

"Yes."

"Then perhaps you would do us the pleasure of dining with us. What would you say to half past eight? Would that suit you? In the meantime we'll try and find out where this Gerhart Peuckert can possibly be found. What do you say?"

"It sounds fantastic." The prospects were dizzying. The old man's eyes were kind. "I certainly can't say no to that. It's extremely kind of you."

"Then it's settled. Half past eight. It won't be anything special, you understand. We're not so young, my wife and I, but we'll think of something. We live at 14 Längenhardstrasse. It's not difficult to find. I suggest you cut through Stadtgarten. Do you know Stadtgarten, Herr Scott?"

Bryan swallowed with difficulty. He knew the old man lived on Luisenstrasse. Now he'd just said something different. Avoiding the old man's eyes, Bryan attempted a smile. It was a bad sign to be confronted with a lie just as hope was in sight. Bryan's stomach contracted. An urge to move his bowels took him unawares.

"Yes. Yes, of course I do."

"Then you can't go wrong. From Leopoldring walk straight through the park around the back of the lake and you'll come out at Mozartstrasse. The second turn on the right and you're there. Längenhardstrasse. Number 14, remember that. It says 'Wunderlich' on the door." The old man smiled and they shook hands again. Before he finally disappeared around the corner he'd turned around and waved several times.

CHAPTER 50

One of the more difficult jobs, Kröner was thinking. For years there had been so many opportunities to get rid of Petra Wagner that it was quite painful to think of them now.

All this trouble! At the moment he didn't even know where she was.

The main problem was that it was Saturday, which meant he couldn't get hold of anyone in the staff room or the office. If he called people at home they were always out on some errand or other. He simply couldn't get an answer to his question.

Where was Petra Wagner?

And even if it had been an ordinary weekday, whom could he have asked? Sooner or later someone would be bound to wonder about his curiosity. Especially if she were to disappear immediately afterward.

Kröner felt most of all like turning the car around and driving to Titisee, where his wife and son had probably already been devouring sage cookies at Hotel Schwarzwald all day. He clutched the steering wheel as he approached the traffic light. The road leading to the suburbs on the right looked tempting. But his destination lay straight ahead on the left. When the light changed he slowly put his foot on the gas pedal and drove quickly past the housing blocks toward Petra Wagner's small flat.

Her apartment block was just as deserted as the street. Neither the street door nor the door to her flat was a problem. A quick, firm shove with his body in the right place was enough to sufficiently loosen the doorframe.

Newspapers lay strewn about the entrance. The flat had been deserted some hours ago.

Kröner had never been there before. Both rooms were filled with the pungent scent of a middle-aged woman. The flat was neat, yet depressing.

All but one of the desk drawers was unlocked and strangely empty. A few files stuck out of the bottom shelf of the bookcase and attracted Kröner's attention until several recipes fell out of them. Kröner left the clippings lying on the carpet where they had fallen. In the middle of the bookcase a shelf had been taken out and replaced with an array of framed photographs. They were presumably Petra's family and friends. In the biggest frame in the middle stood a younger version of Petra in uniform—a blue-and-white striped blouse and an old-fashioned white nurse's skirt. Her smile looked more relaxed than Kröner had seen before. In the chair in front of her sat Gerhart Peuckert, staring straight into the camera with a smile so fleeting and feathery that it almost seemed to have been retouched off his face.

In the adjacent room her bed was still unmade. Underwear and what she'd been wearing the day before had been flung at random over the dressing table. Another row of photos was pinned up on the wall over the bed. None of these persons had any connection with the part of her life Kröner knew about.

He looked at the locked drawer again, rummaged around in his pocket, and took out his penknife. A sharp jab straight at the catch followed by a careful twist, and the drawer gave way instantly.

Among a pile of papers lay several more pictures of Gerhart and her. He carefully took everything out of the drawer and placed it on the writing desk. Nothing was more than a few years old. Petra Wagner's souvenirs from the occasional vacation bore witness to her modesty and lack of imagination. Apparently her lifestyle hadn't been enriched much by the money they'd committed themselves to paying her.

Kröner replaced everything, pushed in the drawer, and slowly withdrew the knife until he heard a click. Then he took the wastepaper basket out from under the desk and rummaged through it. As he pushed the basket into place again his eye caught the recipes lying on the floor. Sighing, he knelt down and gathered up the small pile. As he was replacing them in the file on the shelf, a yellowish slip of paper caught his attention.

It was obvious that it didn't belong there.

Even before he had unfolded it, he knew Petra had finally lost her hold on Gerhart's and her own life. He hastily read the short sentences that he remembered word for word, even though it was ages ago since he'd last seen them. He and Stich and Lankau had been worried about that piece of paper for most of their adult lives.

Kröner gave a little smile, then folded the document neatly, stuck it in his inner pocket, and stared for a moment at the telephone dial before lifting the receiver. It took almost a minute before a breathless female voice answered his call.

"Good afternoon, Frau Billinger, this is Hans Schmidt." Folding the penknife with one hand, he replaced it carefully in his pocket. "I don't suppose you could tell me if Petra Wagner has turned up today?" he asked. Frau Billinger was one of the nurses whom they'd had in their employment longest at Kuranstalt St. Ursula. As a rule, when she wasn't sitting in her office she had gone down to the kitchen to make herself a cup of peppermint tea and thereafter padded farther to the dayroom in the A-wing. The television set there was the newest, and the chairs were covered with plastic so the upholstery wouldn't stink of urine. Whenever she sat down and let herself be carried away by a TV series, she often forgot she had a place of her own to go home to.

"Petra Wagner? No, but why should she be here? You drove Erich Blumenfeld home to Hermann Müller, as far as I know. Isn't that correct?"

"Yes, but Petra Wagner doesn't know that."

"I see." Kröner could visualize her thoughtful, shining face. "In that case it's a bit odd, isn't it? It's past six o'clock. She should have been here by now. But why do you ask? Is there something wrong?"

"Not at all, I just had a proposal to make to her."

"A proposal? But what kind of proposal, Herr Schmidt? If you think you can get her to work here for us, you're making a mistake. She's much better paid with the job she has."

"No doubt, Frau Billinger, no doubt. I'd be thankful if you'd just ask her to phone me at home as soon as she comes. Will you do that, Frau Billinger?" The silence at the other end of the line was usually a sign of Frau Billinger's acquiescence.

"And one thing more, Frau Billinger. We'd prefer she didn't leave again when she finds out that Erich Blumenfeld is gone for the weekend. Get one of the orderlies to fetch some pastry. I'll reimburse you. Give her a cup of tea and we'll hurry over in the meantime. Just as long as you remember to phone as soon as she comes."

"Oooh!" Frau Billinger's delight was almost audible on the telephone. "It sounds exciting. I love pastry and I love secrets!"

CHAPTER 51

The conversation, if you could call it that, took place in a hurry. Gerhart raised his head cautiously, stopped counting, and looked into the living room. Andrea was standing there, grimacing. It was a rare sight. Clearly she'd been taken by surprise. In her younger days she probably would have been more on her guard. She swore out loud. Gerhart shrank back in his chair.

There might be hell to pay.

"Goddamn witch!" she hissed. Then it came again. "Goddamn little witch!" she hissed.

Then everything was quiet and Gerhart resumed counting the stucco rosettes. A moment later she came shuffling calmly into the room in her slippers, took Gerhart's arm, and led him into the kitchen.

There he sat, quiet as a mouse, listening to her mumbled complaints until her husband returned. Gerhart's eyes glided out of focus. He tried to let the words pass through him without registering them.

"I've seen him. Arno von der Leyen!" Stich almost shouted. "It was fantastic. He spoke English, just as Lankau said. Fantastic! I nearly fell over when he presented himself as Bryan Underwood Scott, exactly as Kröner said! Not even Lankau knows that. What a name!" Stich tried to laugh but was forced to clear his throat instead. "The fool! Nothing less would do. 'Bryan Underwood Scott'!" Stich stopped abruptly, then continued in a hushed, theatrical voice. "We spoke to each other. 'Excuse me,' he said in English, not realizing who I was." He pinched his wife gently on the cheek. "He didn't know who I was, Andrea! God bless you for getting me to change my appearance. Oh, you just should have heard him!" He sat down heavily and cleared his throat again, snorting from the excitement and the exertion of the quick march back to the flat and up the stairs. "We arranged to meet two hours from now, Andrea." He smiled at her. "He thinks he's coming to dinner. At half past eight at 14 Längenhardstrasse. God knows who lives there." Then he laughed and pulled off one of his boots. "Arno von der Leyen will never get a chance to find that out, either. We two will see to that, won't we, Andrea? I recommended he cut through Stadtgarten."

"She phoned." Andrea spoke the words cautiously, shifting her chair slightly so that Gerhart Peuckert came to be sitting between her and her husband. Peter Stich dropped the other boot and looked straight at her.

"Petra Wagner?"

Gerhart opened his eyes and looked around confusedly until he caught sight of the dots on Andrea's apron. Starting under the front pocket, he began meticulously counting the spots, bottom upward, left to right. Andrea got up quietly. Gerhart's gaze followed her, dot by dot.

"Yes, she phoned ten minutes ago and asked to speak to you."

"And . . . ?"

"She slammed the receiver down when I said you weren't in."

"You idiot!" he yelled, seizing the boot he had just taken off. "You incredible idiot!" The edge of the kitchen table cut into Andrea's thigh as she hastily tried to push herself backward, thereby deforming Gerhart's dotted landscape. Stich's aim could be painfully precise. When his eyes met his wife's, he froze and lowered his arm. "You know Kröner's looking for her, you fool!"

Even if Gerhart had been fully alert, he would never have been able to ward off the blow. The boot was rather old and had been resoled many times. It was heavy and his temple was bare. For a moment he blacked out. When he came to, the figure standing over him was still hitting him.

"It's your fault, all of it!" Stich screamed, striking him again. "You and your bloody English bloodhound. 'Excuse me' here and 'excuse me' there! He's sure as hell not coming here, causing trouble. We've got enough with you, already."

After the final blow he dropped the boot and left the kitchen. Over in her corner Andrea gathered up a couple of cups and went into the living room as if nothing had happened. Gerhart lay motionless with his neck resting against one of the cupboard doors. He didn't touch the numb side of his face. He wriggled first one ankle and then the other. Next he slowly tensed all the muscles in his body, one by one. When Andrea returned to fetch the coffee she mumbled something he couldn't understand and kicked his shin in irritation as she passed by. The moment the pain planted itself in his consciousness, he looked up at her with an expression of surprise.

For some time afterward they left him in peace. He tried to count again in a vain attempt to calm his chaotic thoughts. Sudden whims and strange feelings kept replacing one another, churning him up inside. First, there were the perceptions he'd had. Everyone around him seemed excited and irritable. Kröner had gone off to do away with Petra. Then there were the names: Arno von der Leyen, Bryan Underwood Scott, and again—Petra.

Peter Stich's blows had rained down on him twice that day, but that wasn't what had him aroused. It was the echo of the alien sounds that had come from Stich's mouth.

Then Gerhart Peuckert got up and stood quietly under the humming neon kitchen lights. The words "excuse me" had been like a kiss that awakened him from a magic spell.

Peter Stich continued bawling at his wife, but he stopped pretty quickly, as usual.

There was still some light in the living room, but scarcely enough for what Peter Stich and Andrea were doing. The old man was bent over the desk in concentration. Gerhart glided out of the darkness of the hallway, dimly aware of what was happening. The desk flap was down and half-covered with small pieces of metal. Gerhart had seen it before. Soon the old man would have assembled his pistol, and he would switch on the ceiling light in order to admire his work, well-polished and ready for action. Then Andrea would sigh with pleasure, finally able to see what she was crocheting.

The three men had lived and laughed in these rooms all these years, in spite of the misery they'd inflicted on their surroundings.

"What are you doing here?" Without turning around or looking up, the old man had sensed Gerhart's presence. "Get back to the kitchen, you freak!" he continued when he finally turned around.

"Watch out for the furniture, Peter!" Andrea looked up from her crocheting. Gerhart Peuckert was still standing motionless in the doorway leading to the hallway. He looked disobediently at Stich and made no attempt to obey. Stich got up slowly.

"Did you hear what I said, you idiot?" The old man turned threateningly toward the figure in the doorway, poised and menacing like an old, insolent, snarling dog. Peuckert didn't budge, even when the gun was pointed at him. "Has he had his pills, Andrea?"

"Yes, I put them on the dining-room table when you went out. They're gone now."

Stich approached him with measured steps. Gerhart moved slightly. Neither Stich nor his wife noticed his hand, from which a sudden cascade of pills scattered like stardust. The effect was equally impressive.

Andrea was the first to react. "Goddammit!" was all she said. The old man's jaw dropped. Then, arm raised, he plunged forward and struck Gerhart with the pistol butt even before their bodies collided.

The gash in Gerhart Peuckert's cheek was still dry. It had not yet managed to bleed. Gerhart felt the oncoming confusion and nausea and remained on the floor on all fours like an animal, while the blows from the butt of the pistol rained down on his head and neck. "Now, you eat them, you scum!" Stich shrieked, until he had to sit down, exhausted by his emotional and physical outburst. But Gerhart left the pills lying on the floor as they'd fallen.

"I think I'll fucking kill you," Stich whispered. Andrea shook her head. She took Stich's hand and warned him it would be too messy and noisy.

A quite unnecessary risk.

As she got down on her knees and stopped the bleeding with a bandage she gave Gerhart a cold look. "This is more for the sake of the carpet than for you!" she muttered through clenched teeth. Then she took Gerhart under his arms and heaved him up onto the nearest chair. At a nod from her husband she gathered up the pills.

Peter Stich looked at his watch and put on the safety latch before placing the gun in the pocket of his coat. This time the look he sent Gerhart was gentle. As he drew up a chair beside him, his victim doubled up instinctively. Stich patted him on the shoulder as if he'd been his own son.

"You know you have to do what we tell you, Gerhart. Otherwise we get angry and punish you. That's how it's always been, hasn't it, little Gerhart? Then we beat you or force you in some other way, don't we? Lankau, Kröner, and I are always there, aren't we? But you know that. We can make you do anything at all. Can't you remember how we made you eat your own shit, Gerhart, dear?" Stich put his head close to Gerhart's cheek. "We're not going to have any of that today, are we?"

Andrea almost curtsied as she placed the pills in her husband's out-stretched hand.

"Now, take your pills, Gerhart," said Stich, clearing his throat. "Otherwise I don't know what I'll do with you this time."

Gerhart tried not to resist as Peter Stich forced his dry lips apart. His body was completely passive and drained of energy, burned out by dim thoughts.

"Chew them, Gerhart. Or swallow them whole. I don't care which, so long as they go down!"

When, after the third slap on his neck, Gerhart Peuckert still made no attempt to swallow his pills, the old man got up resolutely and fetched the pistol. As he released the safety his wife took a couple of quick steps toward the sofa as though she'd seen her husband carry out threats like this before. Gerhart was breathing heavily and looking straight at Stich.

"Wait, Peter, take the cushions!" she advised. Sighing, the old man took one that she was holding out to him. He pressed it against Gerhart's temple with the muzzle of the gun. "That'll deaden the noise, all right," he said. The cushion felt cool. Andrea held the other cushion by the corners on the opposite side of Gerhart's head. It felt warmer, as if someone had been leaning against it recently.

"Now, listen, you ape!" Stich said, emphasizing his words by shoving the cushion harder against his cheek with the gun muzzle. "You've played out your role. When we've gotten rid of Petra, what will we need you for? The two of you kept each other under control, which was an excellent arrangement at the time. But what do we need you for without her around?" Despite Stich's firm grip, Gerhart managed to turn his head enough to look the henchman in the face. "It's your last chance," the old man continued. "You can be back in your armchair at St. Ursula's this evening if you swallow those pills now. And if you don't, I don't think we'll have much problem explaining your disappearance. Swallow them! I'm counting to ten!"

By now it was many hours since Gerhart had last had his pills. So much time had never elapsed before. A couple of minutes previously, while he was down on all fours, being pistol-whipped on the kitchen floor and staring at the small white things scattered under the kitchen table, the main sensation he'd felt was one of astonishment.

It was as if the room had grown longer than usual, and he had to keep on swallowing the saliva that had begun flowing unhindered. The sensation of his body growing and shrinking made him giddy. Andrea's steps sounded like the tramping of an ox. All the words came to him as if through a megaphone.

As the old man began to count, Gerhart felt defiance finally taking hold of him. The man's face was in his way. It brought shadow into the room and coaxed disgust up to the surface. He smelled sourish and the stubble around his beard gave him a slovenly appearance.

When he'd counted to five, Stich spat in his face, but there was still no reaction. The old man's face had turned completely colorless with fury and he was frothing at the mouth. Andrea was watching him nervously. "I hate the noise and the mess!" she cried. Then she leaned back precariously as far as she could to make sure the projectile wouldn't hit her when it went through Gerhart's head. The way she was sitting, a gust of wind could have toppled her off her seat.

On the count of seven Gerhart Peuckert raised his arm and dried the spit off his face with the back of his hand. Stich's violent outbursts weren't working as planned. The weaker they were, the greater the effect. Like when the old man had touched him gently on the shoulder. This had inadvertently aroused something in Gerhart that he found impossible to combat.

The desire to feel.

No jigsaw puzzle is complete without the final piece. Without the puzzle, no thoughts. Without thoughts, no feelings. And without feelings, no reactions. This entire sequence was set off by Stich's one tender touch. The soft hands had aroused feelings. Hearing about Petra's intended fate was the final piece. When Peter Stich's tenderness vanished and his threats resumed, they brought Gerhart's reaction with them.

The puzzle was complete.

On the count of nine he spat all the pills into his oppressor's eyes with such force that the old man was temporarily blinded.

A last, fatal mistake.

The old man backed away in surprise. Andrea squealed like a stuck pig, waving the cushion as if it were a deadly weapon.

Gerhart spat again, seized the old man's wrist, and pressed his nails into his leathery skin with all his might.

Gerhart didn't hear the metallic sound of the pistol falling to the floor until it was too late. Within a second everything was quiet. Andrea stood over Gerhart with outstretched arms. She had grabbed the pistol and was intent on using it. Stich's eyes were mad with rage. His entire body shook with indignation. The white, congealing mixture of half-dissolved pills and saliva was still trickling down his cheek, but he didn't notice.

Gerhart turned away from him and looked at Andrea. He stretched out an arm toward her, tilting his head to one side. His eyelashes were glued together and his mouth quivered. "Andrea . . ." he said. It was the first time he'd said her name. Feelings fused and separated again, making him laugh and cry.

"But my dear friend, you seem so upset," came the measured voice from behind. The color returned to Stich's cheeks as he straightened up, and he became his usual controlled self again. "How you can splutter, little Gerhart. In a little while you'll calm down again, I promise. Give me the pistol now, Andrea," he urged, stretching out his hand. "We must put an end to all this!"

In a flash Gerhart reached out and snatched the gun. It happened so fast, one might have thought Andrea had handed it to him of her own free will. Neither Andrea nor her husband had time to react. Then Gerhart took hold of her arm and flung her backward against the wall so hard that she fell to the floor and didn't get up again.

The hatred between the old man and Gerhart Peuckert finally erupted. Without a sound. Stich automatically made for Gerhart's throat with his skeleton-like hands but, despite all his years of passivity, his intended victim danced out of the devilish grip and landed a sledgehammer blow to Stich's jaw.

This pacified the old man.

.   .   .

"What do you want?" Stich asked with difficulty as Peuckert shoved him down into the chair. The belt strapped around his wrists obviously hurt. "What do you want from me?" he repeated.

Peuckert raised a hand to the clear fluid running from one of his nostrils. Calming down, he turned his eyes to the ceiling and let Stich clear his throat. The man studied him a long time, and just as he was about to speak again, Gerhart bent down and picked up the pistol that was lying on the floor between his legs.

Gerhart sighed. Even if he'd tried, not a word could have passed his lips. He would have asked the old man to repeat the name. Not Arno von der Leyen but the other one. The one that had made Stich laugh.

And then it came to him by itself.

Bryan Underwood Scott.

Gerhart got up and without warning struck the old man such a hard blow with the pistol butt that he tumbled out of his chair. Then he sat down and tried counting the rosettes in the ceiling frieze. At every attempt the name came back more and more distinctly. Finally he looked down and thought awhile, whereupon he went into the kitchen and opened several of the drawers. When he found what he was looking for he carefully switched off the light and strode down to the far end of the hallway, where he opened a narrow cupboard and rolled the tinfoil he had just found into a big ball.

Then he screwed one of the fuses out of the electricity meter, switched off the main switch, and switched it on again after quickly replacing the fuse with the tinfoil.

The old man was still lying on the floor when Gerhart heaved the cord of his desk lamp out of its socket. Then he separated the two uninsulated wires and replaced the plug in the socket. The old man groaned a little as he was lifted back into his chair. The two looked into each other's eyes for some time. Stich's were just as red as the time he'd stood wide-eyed under the hospital shower.

But they registered no fear.

Peter Stich looked intently at the pistol and then at the wires Gerhart had stretched toward him. He shook his head and looked away. After a couple more blows to the chest he was too weak to resist. Gerhart pressed the exposed ends of the electric wires into each of his soft palms. Then he stretched the toe of his shoe over toward the switch on the wall. It crackled faintly as Gerhart kicked it on. The old man dropped the wires the instant he received the shock, so Gerhart switched off the current, stuck the wires more firmly into Stich's fists and repeated the procedure. After the fifth jolt the old man's throat began to rattle and he fell to the floor, unconscious, his breath irregular.

The belt had left practically no marks on his wrists. Gerhart Peuckert removed it carefully and replaced it around the old man's waist.

The carpet had been pushed so far up against the wall behind Andrea that it almost covered her. Crumpled curtains and overturned potted plants were strewn on top of the carpet so that only Andrea's ankles and shoes stuck out. She still made no sound when Gerhart dragged her over to her husband. He placed them hand in hand, face-to-face, as though they'd lain down to rest.

The spittle in the corners of Stich's mouth was almost dry when Gerhart opened it and inserted the ends of the wires. Then he stroked Andrea gently on the back of her hand and her cheek. Having looked at her expressionless face one last time, he flipped the switch down. The instant the shock wave reached her, Andrea opened her eyes, horror-struck. The resulting muscle spasms caused her to clutch her husband's hand tighter. He stood for a while, regarding his tormentors' final twitches, until there was a slight smell of burnt flesh. A faint metallic clank from Stich's watchband could be heard as his hand fell to the floor. The hands of the watch continued resolutely on their rounds. It was precisely seven o'clock.

Gerhart went over to the corner and rearranged the curtain and carpet. For a moment he stood looking passively at the plants lying up against the wall, whereupon he brushed the loose earth under the carpet and put the plants back on the windowsill. Finally he went into the hallway, removed the clump of tinfoil, and replaced the fuse. The moment he pressed down the main switch, the fuse leaped with a bang.

Not until he was sitting in the dark living room and everything was quiet did he begin to cry. The combined impression had been too massive, too varied. He had let himself go to such an extent that the immediacy of actions and words was beginning to paralyze him. Then, just as his thoughts were again starting to spin with a centrifugal force, the telephone rang.

Gerhart lifted the receiver. It was Kröner.

"Yes . . . ?" he mouthed hesitantly in German.

"I found your note, Peter. You needn't worry, I'm prepared. On the other hand, I haven't been able to find Petra. I've searched everywhere. She's not at home or at the sanitarium. I've told Frau Billinger to phone me as soon as she turns up there. I'm at home now."

Gerhart breathed deeply. It was far from over. He formed the words slowly before uttering them.

"Stay where you are," he finally said, replacing the receiver.

CHAPTER 52

Even though Petra felt most of all like screaming with frustration, she didn't. For the most part, the tall woman by her side had been quiet and pale, but composed. Their search on Schlossberg had been without result. The sun had slowly set as they searched around the colonnade in hopes of finding some clue that might indicate the outcome of the afternoon's meeting. Petra stood for a while in the reddish glow that accentuated the contrasts and contours of the town beneath her, trying quietly to understand and sum up her impressions of the past couple of hours.

"If your husband's English, then what was he doing in Freiburg during the war?" she asked at length.

"All I know is that he was a pilot and was shot down over Germany together with one of his friends," came Laureen's quiet reply. Suddenly it was so simple and comprehensible. There were so many things that had become easy to explain, it made Petra dizzy. At that moment she could have screamed. In the wake of this revelation new questions were bound to arise.

Questions of such a nature that they had to remain unanswered for the time being.

"And this friend, could he be Gerhart Peuckert?" she asked nonetheless. That was just one of the questions.

Laureen shrugged her shoulders. "Who knows?" she said. Apparently she only had thoughts for her husband.

Petra looked up at Schlossberg and a flock of black, robust birds that were all trying to land in the same treetop. Suddenly she realized how critical the situation really was. The three men who had been playing with her and Gerhart's lives for years stood between the two women and the answers. The first step toward finding the truth inevitably involved a confrontation with them. If there'd ever been any doubt about that in Petra's mind, it was gone now. Laureen's husband must be in grave danger. That is, if he wasn't dead already. Petra had to keep this realization to herself for the time being.

And that, too, made her feel like screaming.

The receptionist at Bryan's hotel was practically friendly. "No, Mr. Scott has not checked out yet. We definitely expect him to stay until tomorrow." The next question made him rack his memory in vain. "As far as I can remember, Mr. Scott has not shown up all day. But I could phone and ask my colleague who was on duty before me," he added without interest, but kindly. "What do you ladies say to that?"

Petra shook her head.

"May I borrow your telephone?" she asked, following the clerk's indifferent wave toward the pay phone behind them.

It was a long time before anyone answered.

"Kuranstalt St. Ursula. Frau Billinger speaking," came the voice.

"Good evening, Frau Billinger. This is Petra Wagner."

"Yes . . . ?"

"I'm a bit late today; perhaps Erich Blumenfeld is worried. Is he all right?"

"Yes, why ever not? Indeed, he is. Oh—apart from the fact that he misses you, of course." Frau Billinger sounded strangely animated. Almost as if she'd just been given another bottle of port by the grateful relative of a patient.

"Hasn't Erich had any visitors today?"

"Not as far as I know."

"Have Hans Schmidt, Hermann Müller, or Alex Faber been there yet?"

"I don't think so. I've not been here the whole day, but I don't think so."

Petra hesitated a moment. "And there hasn't been an English-speaking gentleman to see him either?" she continued.

"An English-speaking gentleman? No, I'm sure there hasn't. But we did have a visitor today who spoke English, now that you mention it. But I believe he was Frau Rehmann's guest, and that was several hours ago."

"You don't remember his name by any chance, Frau Billinger?"

"Goodness, no. I don't even think I heard it mentioned. When are you coming, Fraülein Wagner?"

"I'll be there soon. Just tell Erich that."

Occasionally the three men and Gerhart were together on Saturdays, where they'd go for a drive. Sometimes they even drove as far as Karlsruhe or out to one of the villages near Kaiserstuhl to have a nip at the local inn and sing lieder. In these situations Gerhart would sit in their merry company for hours without moving a muscle.

Petra was relieved to hear that wasn't the case today. As long as Gerhart was at the sanitarium she could concentrate on helping Laureen and thereby possibly herself.

"What did you ask her, Petra?" Laureen spoke even before Petra had replaced the receiver. Petra looked at her. It was the first time she'd called her by her first name.

"I simply asked how Gerhart Peuckert was. He's all right. But I found out something I can't quite understand."

"And that is . . . ?"

"I think your husband was at the sanitarium at some point today."

"I don't understand. If he has already found this Gerhart Peuckert at the sanitarium—this man he's been trying so hard to find—and Peuckert's still there, then where has he been the whole time? Where is my husband now, if not there?"

"I don't know, Laureen." She took the tall woman's hands and squeezed them. They were cold. "Are you sure your husband doesn't want to hurt Gerhart?"

"Mmm . . ." Laureen didn't seem to hear the question. "Tell me, couldn't we go to my hotel now?"

"Do you think he could be there?"

"If only I did. Bryan has no idea I'm in Freiburg, unfortunately. No, there's something I simply can't put off any longer, dammit!"

"What's that?"

"I have to change these shoes. My blisters are killing me!"

It was a rapturous and slightly tipsy Bridget who entertained Petra in Hotel Colombi's lounge while Laureen was up in her room changing into some worn-out shoes. Petra kept glancing at her watch impatiently. She was at her wits' end.

"I really oughtn't be relating such things when my sister-in-law's listening," Bridget said distractedly, noticing Laureen as she strode out of the elevator and headed over to sit down with them again. Laureen pointed at her watch and Petra nodded. "I'm almost ashamed to say so," Bridget continued, unperturbed, "but God, aren't the men in this town gorgeous?"

"You're completely right," said Laureen. "You shouldn't say such things while I'm around. If you're up to something I can't pass on to my brother, I don't want to know about it."

Bridget blushed.

"What do we do now, Petra?" Laureen asked, ignoring her sister-in-law.

"I don't really know. . . ." Petra wasn't looking at her. "I think we'll have to phone one of those three devils." Petra almost bit her lip. "If I'm not mistaken, we'll find Peter Stich at home. He's sure to know what's going on."

"Who're you going to phone?" Bridget looked curious. "Peter Stich? Who is this guy?" Her face lit up for a moment. "What exactly are you up to, Laureen?"

"Oh, keep quiet, Bridget!" She hardly deigned to look at her sister-in-law. "Do you think that's wise, Petra?"

"What else can we do? Your husband's not at his hotel. We have no idea where he is. The only thing we know is that a couple of hours ago he was on his way up to Schlossberg to meet these men. What else can we do?"

"We could phone the police."

"But we've got nothing to report." Petra looked at Laureen. "We can't even report him missing."

"Then phone those men, Petra. Do what you think is best."

As Petra went to find the phone booth in the lounge Bridget took her sister-in-law's hand. Her voice was trembling as she explained. "I must speak to you, Laureen. You've got to help me. I have to get out of this marriage. Sorry, but that's just how it is. Don't you understand?"

"Maybe, maybe not," Laureen replied noncommittally. "It's your life, Bridget. Right now I've got enough with my own life. Sorry, but that's just how it is!"

Bridget's lips quivered a moment.

When Petra returned, she shook her head. Laureen had already guessed, judging by her expression.

"I only managed to get hold of Peter Stich's bitch of a wife. She was alone, so something's got to be wrong."

"What about Kröner and Lankau?"

"I couldn't get hold of them, either."

"What does all this mean?" Laureen could feel the unease growing.

"I don't know."

"It sounds as if you're playing hide-and-seek with someone." Only a little ring of mascara under one eye revealed Bridget's own personal quandary. She smiled her best smile, which she always did when she didn't understand anything.

"Hide-and-seek?" Laureen glanced at Petra. It was nearly a quarter to seven, almost five hours since Petra had spoken to Bryan in the wine bar. The three men apparently had the situation under control. They could be anywhere. "Is hide-and-seek what we're playing now, Petra?"

"Hide-and-seek?" Petra looked at her. Laureen could feel her desperation growing. "Perhaps . . ." Petra said. "Yes, you might as well call it a kind of hide-and-seek."

CHAPTER 53

Had Laureen and Petra bothered to turn their heads a bit as they left Hotel Colombi they would have noticed that the street artists who had been working the shopping streets had moved to the little park across from the hotel. Colombi, as it, too, was called, was the most central green oasis in Freiburg and made an excellent base for visiting artistes. Behind the laughing crowds, the trees and bushes proudly displayed their late-summer green in the fading evening light and formed a garland around yet another hotel.

It was neat and sober-looking, though less exclusive than the Colombi, and bore the pompous name of Hotel Rheingold. Bryan had parked the BMW in front of it five minutes previously. It was here he would take care of the afternoon's most urgent business.

The encounter with the old man in front of Kröner's house had scared him.

Remembering his brazen lie about where he lived made Bryan feel uneasy once again. After the events of the day there could be no doubt about the message that lay behind this lie. Bryan was to be lured into another ambush. He would never have become aware of the deception had he not been driven by intuition—or perhaps more by perplexity—to shadow the old man to his home in Luisenstrasse the previous day.

And by tomorrow morning he would doubtlessly have disappeared from the face of the Earth in the vicinity of a street called Längenhardstrasse.

Apart from the obvious deception, there was something else about the old man that had frightened Bryan. An indefinable feeling where faces, words, impressions, and thoughts struggled to form a synthesis.

But a whole picture refused to materialize, which affected Bryan's concerted effort to get to the bottom of the matter. His eagerness was dissipating imperceptibly but persistently. If he wanted, he could leave Freiburg that same evening and still be able to attend the final ceremony of the

Olympic Games the following day—precisely as originally planned. From there he could drive on to Paris.

One day more or less wouldn't make a difference when the hour of reckoning came.

If, on the other hand, he stayed in Freiburg and were to make the slightest mistake, Kröner, Lankau, and the old man would be ready and waiting. If the risk was that great, then why stay? Now he knew where he had them, so why not come back some other time? The little matter of finding the country house and releasing Lankau could be left to Lankau's confederates. A couple of days' fasting would scarcely harm a man of his constitution and dimensions.

Bryan had thought the whole thing through several times before he happened to stop in front of Hotel Rheingold. The only thing that really mattered now was whether Laureen would agree to meet him in Paris, the romantic capital of the world.

Hotel Rheingold's desk clerk was fat and helpful and overjoyed when he saw the handful of cash. Without hesitation he led Bryan to his cubbyhole behind the desk and left him in peace beside the telephone.

It was Mrs. Armstrong who took the call, which meant Laureen wasn't there. The moment this cleaning lady showed her bony corpus in their home, Laureen usually fetched her bag in the hall and quietly vanished.

"No, the lady of the house is not at home."

"Do you know when she'll be coming back, Mrs. Armstrong?" Bryan was sure she didn't.

"No, unfortunately."

"Do you happen to know where she's gone?" Bryan was sure she wouldn't know that, either.

"No, I haven't looked at the note yet."

"The note . . . which note, Mrs. Armstrong?"

"The one she left before they went to the airport."

"They? Has she gone to the airport with Mrs. Moore?"

"Yes, indeed. They've already flown, both of them."

"I see." Bryan accepted this possibility. "And so they're in Cardiff?"

"No."

"Listen, Mrs. Armstrong, I'd be very grateful if I didn't have to drag everything out of you. Would you kindly tell me where my wife and Bridget Moore are?"

"I don't know. Mrs. Scott said it would be in the note. But I *do* know they're not in Cardiff. They're somewhere or other in Germany."

This bit of information dumbfounded Bryan.

"Would you be so kind as to tell me what is written in the note, Mrs. Armstrong?" asked Bryan, trying to compose himself.

"Just a moment. . . ." One sound after another in the background told him she was working on the matter. He waited impatiently. The telephone was ticking audibly and the desk clerk looked as if he would soon be expecting more cash. He gave a start when Bryan repeated the name of Laureen's lodgings.

"Hotel Colombi? In Freiburg?" he almost shouted.

The clerk followed Bryan to the door, grumbling. He didn't think it proper for a visitor to advertise so loudly for a competitor, especially not after having been entrusted with his private telephone.

Bryan didn't hear him.

It took only a moment before the receptionist at Hotel Colombi knew who Bryan was looking for. "Mrs. Scott is out in town at the moment, but you can find Mrs. Moore right there," she said, pointing with a bright red fingernail toward a corner of the reception lounge.

"But, Bryan!" Bridget exclaimed, obviously astonished. "There, you see? Speak of the devil!"

It wasn't the first time Bryan had seen her a bit tipsy. "Where's Laureen?" he asked.

"She's just gone with that foreign female person. Leaving me to sit here, all alone." She stopped abruptly and began laughing so that the pageboy standing nearest had to make himself look the other way. "Well, maybe not *that* alone. Ebert must be coming down soon."

"I don't know what you're talking about, Bridget! Who's Ebert, and who's Laureen gone out with?" He took hold of her shoulders gently and tried to make her concentrate. "Why are the two of you here? Is it because of me? Who is Laureen together with?"

"Together with? Someone called Petra, as far as I know," she replied, trying to appear normal.

Bryan felt his blood run cold. "Petra?!" He grasped the woman's shoulders tighter and looked her square in the face. "Bridget, pull yourself together. Laureen may be in danger, do you understand?"

"Yes, but aren't you the one who's in danger? I seem to remember that's what they said." She looked at him as if she were just becoming aware of him.

"Do you know where they're going?" She hesitated at his question and stopped concentrating, so he shook her, making the pageboy smile. "Did they say anything about that?"

"They mentioned some people's names. I can't remember them, but I'm quite sure they didn't like them. Petra called them 'the three devils.'"

Not since the birth of their daughter, when Laureen had bled so profusely that one of the nurses began to cry, had Bryan felt the same, stabbing anxiety. He breathed as calmly through his teeth as possible and looked at his sister-in-law, who'd begun blinking more and more slowly as she spoke.

"Did they mention someone called Kröner?"

This woke her up a bit. "How did you know, Bryan?"

"Or Lankau?" Bryan was about to suffocate in his attempt not to hyperventilate.

Her eyes widened slowly. "If you can tell me the third man's name as well, I'll really be impressed."

"No, I can't."

She smiled. "Then it's a good thing it's the only name I can remember. It was such a funny name . . ." Her lips almost formed it. "Like some sound out of a cartoon."

"Come on, Bridget, out with it!"

"His name was Stich! Isn't that a good name? And he was called Peter. That name we know. It was actually him they spoke about most."

Bryan stood still a moment.

Perhaps it was the pageboy behind them who was most surprised when Bryan suddenly went into a fit of coughing so violent that he was frothing at the mouth.

No one attempted to come to his rescue.

Few people have the experience of everything suddenly fitting together to make a whole, where a series of doors are at least momentarily flung open. Yet it was a revelation of this magnitude, brought on by Bridget's mentioning the name, which overpowered Bryan and made him lose his grip.

It was Peter Stich who he'd had a glimpse of in the old man. And it was this subconscious knowledge that had been harassing him for the past few hours. Peter Stich, the old, white-bearded man in Luisenstrasse who owned Hermann Müller Invest. He was the Mailman. The red-eyed man from the Alphabet House.

He was all of them in one.

Bryan felt dizzy. He saw images of a smiling man lying in a bed in a mental hospital, years ago. Glimpses of a man who stood madly with his eyes wide open in a stinging disinfectant shower. Eyes that smiled at him as he hid his pills inside the metal tubing of his bed frame. Recollections of the gentle, cautious man who had twice saved his life. He thought of the first time, where the red-eyed man pointed out the splintered, rough bomb shutters to the security officer, and the second time, when the malingerers wanted to throw him out the window. A series of events that suddenly fit together like a chain reaction, practically causing him to faint.

Each element had played its essential role in one magnificent lie!

Finally Bridget thumped him on the back.

It was several minutes before he came to. After a few vague explanations he realized he couldn't trust anyone anymore, except for Laureen.

And now she must be on her way over to Peter Stich, together with Petra. The same Petra who had sent him straight into the arms of one of the three devils.

CHAPTER 54

Apart from the flat on Luisenstrasse, Kröner's house was the only one Gerhart knew in that part of the town. Outside it was cool, the street lighting massive and strange. Shouts and cries and jeering from a pub drove him over to the opposite sidewalk and slightly off course. He frowned and clutched his flimsy wind jacket close to his body and drew himself up to his full height. Then, instinctively and purposefully like a homing pigeon, he headed directly for Kröner's house, where Kröner would be waiting for Stich.

But it wasn't Stich who'd be coming.

He didn't stop until he got to the palatial entrance. He took stock of the house's entire facade. The only light to be seen was on the second floor. Apart from the window in Kröner's study all the curtains were drawn. A cool breeze was gathering in strength and the entrance afforded only poor shelter. For a long time Gerhart stood looking at his finger, which was pointing undecidedly toward the doorbell.

———

Kröner stood with his back to the window, as was his habit when speaking on the phone. A bad habit, according to his wife. "Why don't you just sit down," she would say. "It's not the Kaiser on the line!" But that was how he felt most comfortable. And today more than ever, with Arno von der Leyen on the loose and liable to turn up at any moment. He was restless. In that position he could at least lean back and look out the window without anyone seeing him from outside.

It was Frau Billinger on the line, speaking more quietly than usual.

"This can't be true! Did Petra Wagner phone you nearly two hours ago? I told you to let me know!"

"No, you merely said I should call and tell you when she turned up."

"You could have assumed I'd be interested in hearing about her phone call, couldn't you?"

"Yes, that's why I'm phoning now."

"Yes, now, and not two hours ago."

"You must forgive me, Herr Schmidt, but I was completely preoccupied by a TV series."

"One episode doesn't last two hours, for heaven's sake!"

"No, but then I became engrossed in the next program, too."

"And now I assume the program's over. Did she say anything else?"

"No, nothing other than that she'd be coming soon. And she inquired about some Englishman."

"What Englishman?"

"I don't know. But I *did* mention that Frau Rehmann had had an English visitor earlier today."

"And . . . ?"

"That's all."

For a moment Kröner was furious. He slammed down the receiver, banged his fist on the table, and swept all the papers onto the floor. Incompetence was unforgivable. In his moment of anger he turned around to open the window and let in some fresh air. Then he stopped and slid behind the curtain, all in one movement. Suddenly Frau Billinger's inefficiency that afternoon no longer mattered. The problem had solved itself, for at that moment Petra Wagner appeared outside the wrought-iron gate. Beside her stood a woman he didn't know.

They were looking up at his house.

He moved away from the window. As he was taking stock of the situation, he heard the doorbell.

One of the *Unterscharführers* in the SS Wehrmacht camps near Kirograd had taught Kröner a special trick that he later made his own. One freezing-cold day this young *Unterscharführer*, along with one of the other junior officers, had stabbed a delinquent to death from sheer boredom just as he was about to be hanged. For that they had received a minor reprimand, but everyone had found it amusing.

It was not so much the deed that Kröner had adopted, but the technique behind the stab itself.

The procedure was simple. All that was required was a little knife and a precise knowledge of how to avoid the ribs and strike the heart. After a little practice he'd become good at it.

The advantage was that it was unnecessary to touch the victim, let alone look the victim in the eye. One did it from behind. First and foremost he'd thought of applying this method to Arno von der Leyen. It was quick and easy and took people by surprise. There was simply no time to react, which was the whole point where Arno von der Leyen was concerned. But this latest surprising turns of events clearly indicated he might have to apply the method to others as well. He would be busy.

But then at least he'd have Petra out of the way.

Kröner stuck his paper knife deep into his side pocket so that only the deer's-foot handle stuck out. It was ready for use. The two women wouldn't cause him any trouble.

Kröner's son had a friend whose father owned a bigger house than theirs. Although the house in itself was impressive enough, it was the glass front door that really made an impact. "You can see who's coming, Daddy! Can't we have one like that?" In Kröner's experience, all such silly demands had their time limit. Others would soon crop up, so he hadn't given the idea any more thought. This was something he might well have regretted now. For glass would have spared him the shock he received when he swung open the massive, carved oaken door.

His smile froze instantly. Instead of the little nurse and her unknown friend, there stood Gerhart Peuckert with drooping shoulders and an apologetic smile on his face.

He was the last person in the world Kröner had expected to see.

"Gerhart!" he exclaimed, pulling him into the hall so quickly that they both nearly fell over the coconut doormat. "Whatever are you doing here?" Without expecting an answer he led the passive and obedient Gerhart upstairs and seated him in front of his desk so that neither of them could be seen from the street.

This extraordinary development made Kröner uneasy. Never before had Gerhart Peuckert been more than a few meters away from his guards. He was most inclined to believe that Petra Wagner had sent him up to the house as some kind of errand boy. But why wasn't he with Peter Stich? Where was Stich?

Apart from his lips, which were dark blue, the creature in front of him was deathly pale. When Kröner took his hands they were cold and trembling.

"What's happened, my friend?" he said gently, putting his face close to Gerhart's. "How did you get here?"

"He registers everything we say and do," Lankau had claimed, time and again. Kröner was still having his doubts. "Have you come here with Petra?" he asked. At the sound of that name Gerhart's mouth tightened and his eyes turned slowly upward and began blinking. A moist film of tears glistened momentarily. Then Gerhart looked straight at him and his mouth relaxed. His dry lips trembled. "Petra!" he said, his jaw hanging for a moment.

"Good Lord!" Kröner shot up from his squatting position and took a step backward. "Petra, yes! You know her name. What does she want with you here? What's happened? Where's Peter Stich?"

Not for a moment did Kröner withdraw his gaze from Gerhart's shaking head, which seemed about to explode. Grabbing the telephone, he noticed Peuckert's knuckles were completely white. His body had started rocking almost imperceptibly.

"Gerhart! You're to sit quietly now until I say otherwise!" Then he dialed Stich's number. When it had rung for a while Kröner cursed quietly. "Come on, Stich, you old asshole, take it!" he whispered. He hung up and tried again. Still no one answered.

"He's not going to answer." The voice was subdued and indistinct.

Kröner whirled around to face Gerhart, managing to see his eyes before the blow hit him.

The eyes were quite calm.

Even before Kröner hit the floor, Gerhart Peuckert struck him again. Kröner was a big man, in comparison with Gerhart, and he fell heavily.

Though he wasn't dazed, he was shaken.

"What the hell . . . !" was the only thing he managed to stammer before instinct took over. As Kröner charged his opponent, Gerhart calmly spread out his arms as if he'd just asked his sweetheart for the next dance. In one mighty embrace Kröner grasped the madman's body and began squeezing with his hands folded around his silent partner's back like he was ready to crush him. Kröner had used the hold before. As a rule it took less than two minutes before his opponent went limp and lifeless.

When Kröner no longer felt Gerhart breathing, he released his grasp and stepped back, expecting the figure would fall over.

But it didn't. Gerhart looked Kröner straight in the face with an empty expression. Then he dropped his arms and quietly drew a deep breath. He didn't show the slightest sign of debilitation.

"A zombie! That's what you remind me of, a zombie!" Kröner exclaimed, taking another step backward as his right hand stole toward the knife in his pocket.

Gerhart uttered a quiet growl. Then, with the mechanical calmness of a zombie he took hold of his belt buckle and drew the belt out of its straps, unaffected as a statue.

"I'm warning you, Gerhart! You know I mean it!" Kröner took another step backward to size him up. He seemed vulnerable. "Let go of that belt!" he commanded, cautiously extracting his knife. If anyone was familiar with the exact moments preceding a personal confrontation, it was Kröner. Calm movements were essential. One quick move and his opponent might react irrationally. So Kröner did nothing sudden or unpremeditated. Gerhart just stood there—still unaffected, almost apathetic—and regarded the knife that was pointed straight at him. He didn't move a muscle and seemed resigned to the inevitability of being stabbed. An assumption that a few seconds later proved to be false.

"Put down that belt!" Kröner managed to say once more. Then Gerhart's face contorted with cramplike spasms that jerked the corners of his mouth downward and wrinkled the bridge of his nose like some animal of prey. The only thing Kröner had time to register was a stinging pain that stretched across his face from ear to ear. The explosion of light when the belt buckle smacked his eyeballs drew his scream of pain into a higher register. He would no longer be able to judge space or substance. So brief a battle, so efficient a blow, so inevitable a defeat.

Next, the figure above him kicked the knife away, dragged him savagely across the floor, and tightened the belt around his wrists. There Kröner lay, stunned most of all by a sudden awareness of the situation.

After a few minutes he drew his legs up under him. Then, with great difficulty he got up into an awkward sideways position. He had let dozens of mishandled victims sit like this on the bare, cold ground, waiting until the merciful shot came.

Now he, too, waited in that position for his redemption.

"Where's Lankau?" said the strange voice above him. Kröner just shrugged his shoulders and squinted his eyes harder to control the pain. The reaction came promptly. This time the backward tug of the belt was so violent that it almost dislocated his shoulders. Despite the pain, he didn't answer.

The experience of being dragged backward down the stairs and through his entire house—blinded and defenseless and crashing into obstacles—was nothing compared to the overwhelming chagrin that engulfed him.

Lankau had warned him and Stich about Gerhart Peuckert for decades. "Why not just kill him? What's there to be afraid of? We can do it easily without being discovered. Crazy people disappear every day in this world. Suddenly their bed is empty. And where are they? You never see them again! And so what? Who's going to miss them? Petra Wagner? We'll get rid of her, too, if there's no alternative. Let's take the chance!" Lankau had been right. Petra Wagner's little note had been unable to do them any harm. They should have gotten rid of both of them long ago.

Kröner felt the doorstep and then the cold and didn't know whether he was being dragged out the kitchen door or into the bathroom. When the bathtub taps began to run he realized that this could be the last room he'd occupy alive.

"Let me go, Gerhart," he said slowly, without begging. "I've always been your friend, you know that. Without me you wouldn't be alive today."

Then everything around Kröner became quiet. The figure directly in front of him was breathing lightly. Kröner's subconscious told him to let Peuckert do what he liked and calmly accept his fate. But both his rage and the will to live were reactivated when Gerhart began screaming his crazy laugh right in his face.

Despite his violent eruptions and wild, groping attempts, his kicks never found their mark.

It wasn't difficult to drag the truth out of Wilfried Kröner. After twenty dunks under the water, the desired information escaped Kröner's gasping, sniveling, blinded and pockmarked face. "Lankau's at his wine farm," he stuttered.

And then Gerhart gave him peace.

As soon as Kröner's feet stopped jerking and floated quietly under the water, Gerhart studied the pockmarked features one last time, turned the drowned man onto his stomach, and removed the belt from his wrists. Then he balanced himself over the enameled bathtub with a foot on each side and bent down toward the flabby form in the water beneath him. He raised the corpse high enough for the water from the soaked clothing to pour out like a small tidal wave, then let the body fall down heavily on the tiled ledge at the head of the tub. The sound was ghastly and the fall so effective that the middle part of the face was partially crushed. Then the dead man slid backward, dragging a plastic animal with him off the edge, and disappeared under the water again. An air bubble lifted his jacket slightly and rose to the surface with a soft plop. A small piece of paper was left spinning around in the center of the ensuing eddy. At every rotation the ink dissolved a bit and spread over the paper like mist. For a moment Gerhart could make out a name. Then it, too, dissolved.

Gerhart stood for a long time, studying Kröner and the little, yellow plastic duck that danced over the dark water beside the neck of the corpse. He wasn't moved by his deed. He'd so often heard the malingerers discuss what they'd do if he, himself, were to be gotten rid of.

Gerhart looked at the subsiding ripples in the tub, closed his eyes and let part of his past disappear. Two virulent thorns in his martyred mind had been extracted. Kröner and Stich. Then he turned around. Before him was the medicine cupboard.

He began to tremble.

The room seemed cold. Everything around him was twisted out of shape. Reality and security were at odds. He studied his face in the cupboard's mirror and saw a stranger.

It took no time to find the big bottle in the cupboard from which the malingerers had fed him so lavishly.

This time he just stuck it in his pocket.

The only visible traces of their encounter were the disarranged carpets throughout the house.

After straightening them, Gerhart returned to Kröner's study. Here he picked up the deer-foot knife from the floor and placed it in the middle of Kröner's desk. In the farthest corner of the room stood a slim basket made of strong plaited bamboo, filled with walking sticks and cardboard tubes. He surveyed the forest of objects for a moment before sticking his hand almost all the way to the bottom. After fumbling for a few seconds he found what he was looking for. A small, slim tube wrapped in heavy brown paper. Kröner had often taken it out playfully to tease him when the malingerers held their drinking parties.

He stuck it inside his wind jacket and hugged it close.

As he was about to leave the house, the doorbell rang. He stood in the middle of the dark hall, devoid of all thought and feeling, until it stopped.

CHAPTER 55

After the women had left Hotel Colombi, Laureen had suddenly begun to cry.

She was quite beside herself.

In an attempt to calm her down Petra had drawn her into a doorway. "Don't worry, we'll find him in time," she said firmly, wondering whether she should slap her.

After ten minutes Laureen was herself again. "Where are you taking us?" she asked, attempting a smile.

"We have to speak to Wilfried Kröner. If we can't get hold of Peter Stich, it's Kröner we have to speak to with."

"You sound worried."

"I've got good reason to be. We both do."

"Then is it wise to go visit him?" The street was brightly lit. The Saturday shoppers had already filled the parking spaces. Laureen looked around. "It's almost like Canterbury," she said distractedly. It was like a melancholy glimpse of a peaceful life several light-years ago.

Laureen leaned up against a flashy, silver-gray car that was parked opposite Kröner's home. Apart from an Audi in the carport and a single illuminated window, the house appeared deserted. "You can see cars like this parked in Tavistock Square," she whispered, mostly to herself. Looking embarrassed, she continued. "It's the street where my husband's accountant has his office." Petra nodded, then looked at the tall woman. She seemed out of balance.

"I don't know whether it's wise to visit him, but we'll soon find out," said Petra after a while. "Did you see anything move by the door just now?" she asked.

"I can't see the door at all from where I'm standing," answered Laureen.

After one of the neighbors nodded to them slightly suspiciously for the second time as he returned from walking his dog, Petra seized Laureen firmly by the arm and pulled her up toward the house. "I don't think there's anyone home, do you?"

"I haven't seen anyone."

"We'll have to ring the bell, I'm afraid."

"And what if there *is* someone home? What could that Kröner take into his head to do to us?"

"I haven't the slightest idea." Petra stopped and looked at Laureen severely. "But remember one thing, Laureen! If anything should happen, you've embarked on this mission of your own free will. Don't tell me later that you didn't know any better."

When Petra rang the doorbell, she noticed the tall woman take a step back.

After having waited for some time, Petra was the first to break the silence. "I'm sure they're all together, all three of them. They're not here. I think Stich and Lankau must have picked Kröner up."

"Why do you think that?"

"Because Kröner's not at home and his car's parked over there," she said, pointing toward the carport.

"Then where can they be?" Laureen shuddered. She usually started freezing after nightfall, no matter the season, and this was an exceptionally mild September evening.

"I don't know, Laureen. Don't you get it? They're usually together with their families on the weekend. And since they're not at home now, one could imagine they were sitting in some restaurant, bawling '*Im grünen Walde*' or something. In fact, they could be doing almost anything, anywhere. Assuming, that is, they really *are* with their families. But they're not, I know it! Not this evening. They're out on their own, God knows where."

"What makes you think that?"

"When I phoned from Hotel Colombi, Andrea Stich was alone at home. Peter Stich doesn't go out in the evening without her. There's a lot you can say about him, but he definitely doesn't leave Andrea at home if those other bastards bring their wives along. On top of which Kröner's wife's car isn't here. She must have been sent on a family visit or something. As for Lankau, I think he's the type who'd send his wife off somewhere." She nodded in agreement with herself. "No, I'm convinced the three of them are together right now."

"And Bryan? Where's he?"

"That's right," she sighed. "And then there's your husband. I'm certain he's one of the reasons why they took off together." Petra fumbled with her purse. She wasn't intending to answer any more questions.

For the first time that day she lit a cigarette. On being offered one, Laureen shook her head.

"Does the house have another exit?" Laureen asked.

"Yes, there's a door to the garden. But the driveway is the only way out of the grounds, if that's what you're thinking."

"It's not."

As Laureen disappeared around the corner of the house, Petra considered what they should do. Living in Freiburg would be difficult for her and Gerhart now. Their entire life together was founded on the relationship built up over the years between them and the three men. If the police were brought in, these fiends would know how to wriggle out of it. The real victim would be Gerhart, and thus her as well. And yet, if they didn't involve the police, the outcome could be violent for all of them. She was convinced that each of the three men could be tackled individually. But if they were together and the situation was getting out of hand, they would be dangerous. Extremely dangerous.

And now that situation was about to arise. The question was, what to do about it and where to begin? When it came down to it, it was Laureen's husband they were trying to find, not hers. In fact, she could just turn around and walk away. She could go visit Gerhart, as she should, then go home to her television, her books, her furniture, and her tedious neighbors.

It was this latter train of thought that frightened Petra the most. She had been stuck in that rut long enough. So, why not? What did she have to lose?

Judging by Laureen's shoes, she'd plowed her way through every centimeter of ground around the house. She had dirt up to her ankles. "We can't get in," she ascertained. "I've tried all the windows and the kitchen door as well," she continued, unaware of the figure that had just pressed itself silently up against the inside of the doorframe only a few centimeters away from her, scarcely breathing.

. . .

Petra called Lankau from a phone booth on the outskirts of the neighbor-hood. There was no answer. For a moment Petra stood stock-still, leaning against the telephone booth. She was puzzled.

"We'll have to wait till tomorrow. They could be anywhere," she said.

"But we can't do that, Petra!"

Petra knew Laureen was right.

"So you have no idea at all where they could have gone?" Laureen con-tinued. "Haven't they some haven where they can go and talk together? An office, a secluded building? Anything at all?"

The smile Petra flashed her was hard to read, but full of sympathy. "Now, listen, Laureen. Between the three of them, Lankau, Kröner, and Stich own a house on pretty much every street in Freiburg. They could be anywhere. They could be back where we've come from, for that matter. At the sanitarium, at Stich's, or at Kröner's place. They could be in Kröner's summer house beside Titisee. They could be out on Lankau's estate, or in Kröner's boat at Sasbach on the Rhine. Or they could be on their way from one place to the other. Let's wait till tomorrow."

"Now, listen to me, Petra!" Laureen took hold of her shoulders and looked at her earnestly. "This concerns my husband! I know there are many things that belong in the past. My husband has never mentioned anything about what you've told me. But do you know what? There's one thing I know for sure when I think about it. Whatever it is Bryan's come here for, he'll see it through to the end. He's like that. And there's one thing more, thank God: Bryan and I have been married for many years, and on many counts we are extremely different. But in one way we're very alike. We're both dedicated pessimists. I always imagine the worst, and Bryan does too, in every situation. So up till now, everything he's done is based on the worst possible scenario." Laureen stopped trembling. "What's the worst imagin-able situation right now?"

Petra was in no doubt. "That Stich, Kröner, and Lankau try to erase all incriminating traces of the past in any way they can. With no scruples!"

"Bryan will have thought of that, Petra. Maybe he never went up on Schlossberg. If he had the chance, maybe he went after them instead.

Where can these malingerers be now? We simply have to find out. Because Bryan's there too."

"That's what I keep saying, Laureen! They could be anywhere and everywhere!" She stared into space. She looked thoughtful and weary, and her voice was toneless as she continued. "But if we use the process of elimination, then Lankau's vineyard could be an obvious possibility. They go there sometimes when they don't want to be disturbed."

"Why there?"

"Why do you think? It's out of the way. There's no one in the vicinity."

"Then phone them."

"I can't, Laureen. Lankau safeguards his privacy. I don't have the number. It's secret."

"How do we get out there? Is it far?"

"It takes twenty minutes on a bicycle."

"Where can I get a bike from?"

"And it takes ten minutes if we take that taxi over there," Petra said, cutting Laureen short and waving her arms.

CHAPTER 56

Despite his age and numerous handicaps, Lankau was still essentially a hardened soldier. He was in charge of the situation. After Arno von der Leyen left, there was little else to do but wait. He had gotten free, warned Stich, and now he waited. The soldier's greatest virtue.

There, under the cover of darkness, sitting beside the window facing the road, he'd often let his imagination take him places. The mountains in Bolivia were teeming with possibilities. A workforce thirsting for orders and impoverished, neglected plains that could be bought for a song. The River Mamoré had been his base of operations the last time he'd been hunting out there, surrounded by mulattos with dark faces and a subservient manner. It was then he had made his decision. The endless variety of vegetation, the promising mineral deposits, the beer joints in San Borja and Exaltación, where the air melted and jukeboxes miraculously poured out scratchy virtuoso interpretations by Elisabeth Schwarzkopf of favorites from the homeland.

All this was to be his future.

Arno von der Leyen's arrival had made this reality more tangible than ever. As soon as this was all over, he would take his final steps.

His last step to safety would be taken by treading softly.

Lankau smiled to himself. The unaccustomed sensation of sitting alone in a completely dark house appealed to him. It strengthened his resolve and his hatred, and the primordial force to be gained from concentration.

Not since he'd taken a nasty spill many years ago on a black piste in St. Ulrich in the Dolomites had his body ached so much. His eye stung, his shoulder hurt, and several of the bloody scrapes were throbbing where the twine had ripped the flesh on his arms and legs. He had also banged the back of his head when the chair collapsed under him.

All in all, he was looking forward to paying Arno von der Leyen back in kind.

He'd return, Lankau was convinced.

So he just waited, alternating between his present hatred and the prospect of future sensations involving young mestiza women and the heavy scent of sugarcane, cocoa, and coffee.

The house was just as Arno von der Leyen had left it. Now it lay in the evening darkness. A single lamp that was never switched off shone faintly in the courtyard. Occasional cones of light from car headlights gleamed suddenly along the road on the other side of the vineyard, illuminating Lankau's hunting trophies and momentarily making them come to life.

As soon as the car slowed down on the main road, Lankau knew he would be receiving a visit. With a deep purr it stopped at the sign in the drive, its lights pointing straight at the house. A moment later it backed away and disappeared toward town.

Lankau took another bite of his apple and put it down on the windowsill, chewing lazily and contentedly. Withdrawing behind the curtain, he looked down toward the main road. The driveway seemed deserted. Perhaps it had merely been someone wanting to turn around, after all. But even though this was a strong possibility, he had to imagine the worst. Maybe the car had let someone off. At best it would be Kröner and Stich.

Endless minutes passed.

Finally hesitant steps crossed the yard, and only then did he catch sight of them. Hesitant, cautious silhouettes. The broad-faced man moved away from the window. He was puzzled. It was Petra Wagner and a strange woman. So Kröner's mission had failed to meet with success.

Lankau groped carefully along the wall from window to window. Everything seemed safe and normal under the shadowy dance of the bushes lit up by passing vehicles.

The women had come alone.

He turned on the table lamp beside the sofa at the same moment as they tried the front door and eased it open.

"Who's there?" he shouted, sticking a short, broad-bladed, double-edged knife inside the elastic of his knee-high socks.

"Petra Wagner! It's me, Petra! I have a friend with me." Lankau blinked when they switched on the strong light in the hall. As Petra stepped into the doorway she seemed to be holding up a finger to shush her companion. Ever since his confrontation with Arno von der Leyen in the Taubergiessen swamp, sudden changes of light had caused his sound eye to play tricks on him.

It made him doubt what he had seen.

"Petra!" He rubbed his eyes. "What an unexpected pleasure!" The voice startled her. As soon as she'd located where it came from, she smiled apologetically.

Lankau's stubby fingers swept through his thin, disheveled hair. "To what do I owe this honor?" he continued, holding out his hand.

It was she who did the talking, even when he bid the stranger welcome. "You must excuse our bursting in like this. This is my friend Laura whom I've told you about. The one who's a deaf-mute." The stranger smiled and kept her eyes trained on her host's mouth. "Did we disturb you?" Petra put her hand to her breast. "Ugh, it was so dark in here when we came. It really gave me a fright just now."

"Now, now, Petra." Lankau stuffed his shirt inside his knee breeches. "I'd just dozed off. Don't think anything of it."

It wasn't difficult to see that Petra and the strange woman were an incongruous pair. And just as undeniable was the fact that Petra had never mentioned she had a friend called Laura, let alone one who was deaf and dumb. On the whole, Petra never mentioned anything about her private life that didn't have to do with Gerhart. If she was in cahoots with Arno von der Leyen, then it was he who had sent her out here. Lankau accepted the possibility.

He could be lurking in the darkness, waiting.

"I don't have your telephone number here," said Petra. Lankau shrugged his shoulders. "And none of you were at home. I just took a chance."

"And here I am. So how can I help you?"

"Are Kröner and Stich here?"

"No, they aren't. Is that all you wanted to know?"

"You have to tell me what happened on Schlossberg."

"Why?"

"Because I have to be sure that Arno von der Leyen is gone for good. Until I know, I can have no peace of mind."

"Really?" Lankau smiled.

"Is he dead?"

"Dead?" Lankau's laughter was boastful and unpleasant. If Petra was trying to set a trap for him, she wasn't going to succeed. "He most certainly isn't."

"Well? Where is he now?"

"I've no idea. Hopefully he's sitting in a plane on his way somewhere far away from here."

"I don't understand. He was so bent on finding Gerhart Peuckert. What *did* happen on Schlossberg?"

"What happened? Why, you know that. He found his Gerhart Peuckert, didn't he?" Lankau smiled at her puzzled expression and spread his hands in the air. "The only thing that happened this afternoon was that my eldest son had a small brass plate engraved with the words, 'In memory of the victims of the bombardment of Freiburg im Breisgau on January 15, 1945.' He fixed it to a small post that he stuck into the ground up in the colonnade." Lankau smiled. "He's clever with his hands, my Rudolph!"

"And what then?"

"And when he removed it a couple of hours later, someone had laid a small bunch of flowers in front of it. Touching, don't you think?" Lankau said, grinning broadly. The women in front of him were looking him straight in the eyes. His experience was that two people are seldom capable of synchronizing a staged deceit, and certainly not two women. If Arno von der Leyen were waiting outside somewhere for the right moment to show up, the expression on the women's faces would have given it away. They would have been more alert, more shifty-eyed. Shifty-eyed and tense. Lankau felt convinced he was alone with them at the vineyard. Which in no way altered the fact that they were not to be trusted. Only the almost imperceptible smile on Petra's face looked genuine.

She appeared relieved.

"When did Rudolph fetch his brass plate again?" she asked with a smile.

"Why do you ask, Petra?"

"Because we were up there around six and we didn't see anything."

"Then Rudolph must have tidied up after himself. He's a good boy. And why were *you* there?"

"For the same reason as we're here now. We had to know what happened. In order to have peace of mind."

"We?"

"I mean 'I,' of course. So that *I* could have peace of mind." Petra's grammatical correction came a bit too promptly for Lankau's liking. "But something like that always has an effect on the people around you, like Laura in my case. That's why I said 'we.' Laura's here on a visit. She's living with me."

"How much does this Laura know, if I may ask?"

"Nothing, Horst, absolutely nothing. You needn't worry. She doesn't understand much of what's going on." Petra smiled just naturally enough to convince Lankau on this count.

"Why didn't you simply phone Stich or Kröner?" Lankau drew closer, noticing how incredibly slender her neck was. Like Arno von der Leyen's, the blood vessels were very close to the surface. "They could have told you what happened up there on Schlossberg."

"I tried. I've already told you. None of you were home. I phoned Stich but could only get hold of Andrea, and she said nothing. You know Andrea." Her gaze wandered over the walls and the trophies. Lankau had made sure there was nothing abnormal to see, apart from the untidy pile of splintered wood beside the fireplace. If Petra had thought about it, she would have noticed Lankau's throne in the middle of the room was missing. In separate bits the chair didn't take up much space. "But where are Stich and Kröner, then?" she asked at length. "Do you know?"

"No."

Petra spread out her arms. She looked at the tall woman and back at Lankau, then gave a faint smile. "That's a relief, at any rate. Thank goodness. Now I won't have to worry about Arno von der Leyen anymore. Could you please phone for a cab for us, Horst? We sent the other one away."

"Of course." The broad-faced man got up, wincing a bit. No matter how things developed now, there was still one unknown factor too many. The deaf woman would undoubtedly be missed if he got rid of them both. Maybe she had relatives. For the time being he would have to restrain himself, even though the opportunity was unique. Gerhart Peuckert and Petra Wagner could always disappear later on, if need be. A tragic little story, a worthy conclusion to a hopeless romance. A Romeo-and-Juliet tale in a callous, present-day setting. There was still time to write that conclusion. But the deaf woman wasn't part of this chapter. He would have to let them go, for now.

"By the way, where's your car, Horst? How'd you come out here?" She was very direct. It was unlike Petra.

The question was so simple. Lankau could have merely smiled and answered, "Just like you, Petra, dear." But in a moment of confusion he felt vulnerable and hesitated. Looking incredulously at the slender woman, he changed the subject.

"You ask a lot of questions, Petra." They stared at each other for a few intense seconds before she smiled shyly and shrugged.

"Perhaps it's your turn to answer *me* now," he continued. On meeting his dark stare the tall woman behind Petra moved back a step. "Why did you say you'd mentioned that woman before? It's not true." As he moved quickly toward Petra, her expression changed. "Is she deaf at all? I'm quite sure I saw you shush her just as you came in." Petra was light as a feather when Lankau took the final step toward her and shoved her aside. The lanky woman behind her put her arms across her face, handbag dangling at her elbow, but it didn't help. A single blow and down she went without saying a word.

She could hardly have said anything, anyway, lying there unconscious with a nearly dislocated jaw.

"Where are you off to?" Even before Petra reached the doorway, his fingers had locked around her wrist like a vise.

"What are you doing, Horst? What's come over you?" she said, tugging at her arm. "Let me go, and for heaven's sake, calm down." He released her and pushed her relatively gently toward the prone woman.

"Who is she?" he asked, pointing.

"It's Laura. We call her Laura, but her name's Laureen."

"Take her handbag and give it to me!"

Petra sighed and slipped the bag off the woman's limp arm. Lankau found it heavier than he'd expected.

Even before the bag was completely emptied, the little sideboard by the door was littered with objects. Lankau promptly thrust his hand into the pile and retrieved a reddish-brown purse whose size promised yet another source of treasure.

The purse contained a multitude of credit cards. Lankau fumbled through them. Sure enough, the woman's name was Laureen. Laureen

Underwood Scott. Lankau studied the name and address for a long time. It didn't ring any bells.

"Your friend is English," said Lankau, waving one of the credit cards.

"No, she's here from Freiburg. Of English extraction and married to an Englishman."

"Strange how many English people are popping up today, don't you think?"

"She's not English, I tell you!"

Lankau turned the purse upside-down. Among the receipts he found a passport-sized photo. Petra held her breath. "She seems to have a daughter" was all he said. "What's her name? You know that, I presume?"

"Her name's Ann."

Lankau looked at the back of the photo, mumbled, and went out into the hall to study it more closely under the ceiling light. "Where do you know this Laureen from? And why have you taken her with you?" The broad-faced man suddenly turned on Petra, seized her arm and squeezed it.

"Who is she, Petra? What's she got to do with Arno von der Leyen?" He squeezed harder, until she began to moan.

Fighting back her tears, she looked him defiantly in the face. "She's got nothing to do with him, you idiot, so let go of me!"

The struggle had been terribly unequal. The heavy man rubbed his neck and stretched it with effort. He knew this pain from the golf course, after an awkward stroke. It always went straight to his neck muscles. But the pain would go away within a few hours. The slender Petra Wagner had not provided enough resistance to his blow.

It had been like hitting air.

He sat the lanky woman precisely where Arno von der Leyen had left him, in a chair not very different from the one Lankau had sat in. Even though he tied her ankles so tightly that the blood began to ooze, she didn't move.

She was still deeply unconscious.

As he passed through his pantry with a dazed Petra slung over his shoulder, he turned off the main switch serving the bungalow. Instantly the light in the yard went out and the starry sky opened above them.

His pride and joy stood in the long middle section of the bungalow. Even though he usually never produced more than a couple hundred bottles of good white wine a year, he'd procured a winepress the previous year that was capable of handling a far greater wine production. In a couple of weeks' time it was to be cleaned and prepared for action again. Until then, it made an excellent place to tie up Petra, who had yet to realize that escaping her bonds would be impossible. Then Lankau tugged slightly at the scarf he'd used to gag her with. It was taut enough.

"You'll be all right as long as you lie very still," said Lankau, patting the gigantic horizontal screw on which she lay. Petra was sure to know its purpose like everyone else in a wine district. As the grapes were drawn toward it, it simply squeezed all the juice out of them. It could easily do that with her as well. "Then you won't hurt yourself on the screw, Petra, dear." Whereupon, to her unmistakable horror, he reached for a relay contact and turned it on. She closed her eyes. "Now, now, little Petra. As long as the main switch is off, you needn't worry. In a few hours it will all be over. In the meantime you're safe and sound here. Then we'll see what happens later."

On his way back across the yard Lankau inhaled the raw coolness of the air. Autumn was hopefully on its way.

A mere two hours ago he might have considered finding space on the wall for another set of antlers or two.

CHAPTER 57

Appalling as it was, it was still a fact.

Laureen was in Freiburg.

Reality in all its horror had returned in an instant. Bryan took a deep breath and drove faster. From now on he would expect the worst. Earlier that evening he'd definitively made up his mind to turn his back on the events in Freiburg, but fate was apparently not going to allow it. The information he'd gotten from Bridget still gave him cold shivers.

It was a disastrously grave situation that no longer involved only him and the men who'd haunted his thoughts for so many years. Now the most awkward and defenseless human being he could possibly imagine had become part of this absurd equation.

Unfortunately it appeared that Laureen in some unfathomable way had got wind of his whereabouts. And now he didn't know where she was, only that she had to be in Freiburg. Bryan shuddered at the thought.

She was incredibly easy prey in the hands of Petra and the malingerers.

Bryan weighed the advantages and disadvantages of the situation. They were extremely unbalanced. As far as he could see, the only advantages were that he was still on the loose, had Lankau under control, was in possession of Stich's correct address, and had a loaded gun.

From Hotel Colombi down to Holzmarkt and Luisenstrasse was only a few minutes' drive. Not the amount of time Bryan usually needed in order to collect his thoughts and be well prepared in a crisis situation.

For a few seconds he considered seeking help. This was precisely the kind of situation for the police. But they'd scarcely believe him. His fragmentary accusations concerning a couple of the town's highly esteemed citizens would astonish them. It would take him a long time to paint a complete and credible picture.

Much too long.

Bryan shook his head. He knew how things worked in real life. No matter where in the world you were, the local police knew its community's rules and played by them. The men who were making his life hell were not exactly nonentities in this town. Besides, neither the pistol with its silencer in his waistband nor the bound-up Lankau would fit too well with the picture of someone who'd been wronged. And by the time help had been mobilized, however reluctantly, the suspects would be long gone after having taken all the necessary precautions.

For the third time within two days he stood viewing the flat on Luisenstrasse from the street. There was no sign of light from within. He found himself overcome by the feeling of having come in vain. He stood for a minute and studied the flat's darkened windows from precisely the spot in which he'd stood that same morning.

Then a detail caught his eye. The overall visual impression had changed. Unlike previously, the total uniformity of the third-floor flat's windows had been disrupted. Bryan's gaze wandered from window to window. The curtains formed a frame around three meticulously arranged potted plants in all the windows except one. The longer he looked, the more chaotic and bare this window seemed, yet there was so little to set it apart from the others. Whereas all the others were adorned with two red geraniums on either side of a white one, this window had two red geraniums leaning toward each other while the white one stood by itself. Bryan shook his head. He simply didn't know what it meant.

Only that something seemed wrong.

Up there lived Peter Stich, the mastermind behind the malingerers' activities and deeds. There was no doubt it was he who had sent Lankau up Schlossberg to kill him. The simulants hadn't forgotten their handicraft or instincts.

His sudden appearance had made Kröner and Stich feel insecure, perhaps even afraid of him. If they found out Laureen was his wife, they would harm her.

Lankau's wings had been clipped, but he could expect the worst from Kröner. However gentle he'd appeared, holding his boy in his arms, he was still a competent killer. There was plenty that could go wrong for Bryan on the malingerers' home turf. They probably knew every street and nook and cranny in Freiburg. It was two against one. They were presumably well prepared and armed. Stich and Kröner must have realized Lankau's attempted assassination had misfired since Stich had seen Bryan outside Kröner's house.

The old man had doubtlessly already planned the next move. In a short while Bryan was expected to pass through Stadtgarten on his way to a street called Längenhardstrasse. Stich had made a point of telling him which route to take.

If Bryan were to do what they expected, he'd have to be very, very alert.

But did he have any choice? If he wasn't mistaken, Stich would be able to lead him to Laureen.

Bryan looked up at the apartment again. A thought struck him. It was the malingerers' turn to make a move now, but maybe the flat contained something that would give him a much-needed head start.

He strode across the street, rang the bell, then quickly strode back to his hiding place under the trees. The flat remained dark. He waited.

Apparently there was no one home. Perhaps they were already preparing their next move.

Stich lived almost too centrally. Holzmarkt and the adjacent streets were still lively on this early Saturday, where the shops had closed and folks were on their way out of town.

Bryan looked around. There were people everywhere, cheerful and busy. But after twenty minutes he was alone on the street.

As far as he could tell.

For even though it wasn't immediately apparent, he had to assume someone was keeping an eye on him. Perhaps even from several positions. Right now the trees prevented him from being discovered from above, but not from street level. So he crossed the street and went around the corner of the building into the backyard.

The entire area behind the building lay in total darkness. The silhouettes from the cypresslike trees and yew bushes ensured that he wouldn't be discovered. Bryan retreated backward toward a small building in the garden and flattened himself against the wall. Here he waited until he'd grown accustomed to the darkness and noises in the vicinity. He looked up at the darkened rear of the building. It was an ideal way in.

There was just one catch.

If anyone was waiting for him up there, this was the way they'd be expecting him to come.

The backstairs door was locked. Bryan shook it and looked up again. There was no movement in the house. The bottom half of the windows to the right of the stairs were furnished with white curtains. Bryan stood on tiptoe and tried to peep over the curtain into the ground floor. Although it was too dark to make out anything inside, he assumed it was a kitchen.

He looked up once more. The drainpipe seemed quite firm as it rose between the stairway and the kitchen windows. He took hold of it. It wasn't the first time he'd had to resort to using this kind of route. He saw the hospital's roof before him. It had been a hundred years ago.

Getting a grip was easy. The drainpipe was dry and solid. Standing flat against the wall, he pushed off with his feet.

He'd gotten heavier than he thought and could scarcely muster enough strength.

He was already losing courage by the time he reached the cornice of the ground floor. His heart was beating menacingly hard and the tips of his toes ached terribly. Each of the stories was at least three meters high. There was still a long way to go.

When he reached the third floor his fingers were numb. Just as he leaned down toward the kitchen window, the fittings that fastened the drainpipe to the wall began to creak. He pressed against the bottom pane of the kitchen window. The pipe's joints and fittings protested at each nudge. At the sixth try the pipe shifted, sending a cascade of fine plaster down into his face. After this he decided to change hands so that his left hand, closest to the backstairs windows, was left free. The frame was rotten and pliable. With the flat of his hand he pressed cautiously but firmly against the pane until it finally gave way.

There was no mistaking the noise.

Then he unlatched the window and crawled in.

The back stairs were damp and the plaster fell off the wall in large flakes as he fumbled his way up the few steps to the landing. He paused for a moment before gingerly trying the kitchen door. It was locked. He thrust his foot carefully against the bottom corner of the door farthest from the hinges. It gave way a trifle. Then he pressed the middle of the door beside the lock, where there was the most resistance. Luckily the door had only one lock. Bryan assessed the narrow door's strength as he'd so often seen in the movies. It was just a matter of a hard kick to the bottom of the door while pressing the door handle down and inward as much as possible. At the same time he'd have to fall forward into a room he knew nothing about.

That's all there was to it. He shuddered at the thought.

If anyone was waiting for him inside, the only way he'd be able to defend himself was to kick out in all directions as he fell.

It seemed extremely risky. Bryan began sweating and drew out his pistol. First the door. Then, once into the room, he would stand still and wait.

A second later he lay writhing on the wooden floor, still out on the stairs. His toe hurt like hell. He must have broken something. There hadn't been much noise. Or much headway made. The door was still standing.

Bryan pricked up his ears. The only thing he could hear was his own stifled groans. No one came out on the landing, attempting to kill him. No one on the floor below yelled, "Burglar!" Nothing happened.

He got up again with difficulty and began shoving the bottom of the door repeatedly with his sound foot. That was a better idea. To and fro, like a child fingering a loose tooth.

The door burst quietly open, allowing him to look into a dark room. He waited out on the stairs for a couple of minutes.

Still nothing happened.

The smell in the kitchen was indefinable, moldy and acrid. He switched on the neon light and was almost blinded by its cold glare. The room was a relic from the past. Plate racks, pale-green colors, enameled saucepans and a thick, scratched kitchen counter. A jar of butter and a package of cookies still lay on the table. Bryan took the few steps into the dark hallway and groped his way to the light switch.

Nothing happened when he turned it on. This unpleasant discovery made him hug the wall and extend his gun in front of him. The kitchen light reached only a little way into the adjoining room, where there was a round table with a plastic tablecloth. Four cookies on a plate were sitting on a table in front of a shabby dining-room chair.

A bite had been taken out of one of the cookies.

Bryan swallowed a couple of times. His mouth was completely dry. It seemed like all activity in the room had suddenly ceased. The deserted seat and the light that didn't work were both ominous signs. Bryan wiped the sweat off his brow with his free hand and sank cautiously to his knees. From this position he could just barely stick his hand through the crack in the door to the adjacent room. After a few tries along the doorframe his fingers touched the light switch. Its mechanical click was distinct, but no light came on.

Without hesitating to think he pushed the door wide open, then immediately lunged after it as though he'd regretted the move and wanted to pull the door shut again. The glow from the streetlights struck him as he tumbled forward.

The double doors to the next room were opened wide, making space for his headlong entrance. Once inside the large room, he tripped over something soft.

He turned his head wildly in all directions to see if his opponent was above him or behind him. Having made sure that neither was the case, he turned and looked straight into the wide-eyed stare of a dead woman.

It took at least five minutes for Bryan to collect himself. The bodies beside him were lifeless. He didn't recognize the woman, but the man she was clinging to with her contorted hand was the red-eyed Stich. He, too, was dead. Still warm, but dead.

Despite the darkness, there was no mistaking the sight. The convulsions of the two dead people were still painted on their faces and the sallow eyes were as dull as the skin of musty egg yolk.

The red-eyed man was still clutching the implement that had killed them. That was why the lights hadn't worked. Bryan looked at the two wires and nearly threw up. A white stripe of burnt flesh ran across Stich's lips. The bodies had a sour, characteristic stench, as if someone had been frying food and hadn't cleaned the stove. Stich's death had been just as appalling as he himself had been in life.

And he'd taken the poor woman with him.

CHAPTER 58

When I get to the vineyard I'll park the BMW down by the main road," thought Bryan as he assessed the situation. It was best to be cautious. He had been through much too much during the past few hours.

And had gotten no further.

Laureen and Petra had been swallowed up by the unknown.

He'd made many ghastly finds during his careful inspection of Stich's flat. Despite the scant illumination from his lighter, there was no mistaking the evidence of Peter Stich's true self. Drawer after drawer, shelf after shelf and room after room revealed that the old man had still been living in his grim past. Pictures of dead people, weapons, medals, flags, banners, figurines, periodicals, books, and still more photographs of more dead people.

Bryan had left Stich's flat unobserved. From Luisenstrasse he'd resolutely set off for Kröner's little mansion, which he'd already had under surveillance twice before. He was sure this time would be the last.

Kröner's big garden had been pitch-dark when Bryan reached his house, almost making him lose his nerve. The only sign of life came from a small light on the second floor.

Otherwise the place would've looked dead and deserted.

After ringing the doorbell a couple of times he'd stepped back into the front garden, where he picked up a pebble from the garden path and took aim. The windowpane on the second floor only rattled for a fraction of a second. Then he'd thrown several more. Eventually he had bombarded all the windows, the pebbles ricocheting back onto the lawn.

Then he realized how stupid he'd been.

Bryan looked out of the car's side window. The moon had not yet risen. The house and vineyard lay under cover of darkness.

Even before he reached the drive leading to Lankau's country home, Bryan noticed the light in the yard was no longer burning. When he switched off the car lights, everything was dark. Bent almost double, he groped his way a couple hundred meters over the ditch and alongside the grapevines. Under the cover of the foremost row of vines he made it halfway around the back of the house, so close to it that he could catch a glimpse into the room where he'd left Lankau tied to his chair.

It was dark and quiet inside.

He'd have to begin his pursuit of the truth yet again. While he was lurking around Kröner's house twenty minutes previously, he'd realized Lankau was probably the only one who could help him in his quest. The big house in town had been empty. Kröner had left his nest and had presumably already made sure Petra and Laureen were under his control.

Bryan sat listening for a long time. There was nothing to indicate Kröner's having gotten there first. The only sound that reached his ears was the hoarse screech of birds he'd so often heard on his nightly walks in Dover. The vineyard was their domain.

He looked at the dark sky and sneaked the last twenty meters to the corner wall facing the courtyard.

CHAPTER 59

This time Lankau was determined not to be caught off guard. After leaving Petra he'd spent most of the time peering into the darkness from his hunting-room window. At one point the lanky woman in the chair had been a bit hysterical. She'd awoken with a start and looked around in the dark, bewildered. When she realized she was tied up, she tugged at her bonds and made some guttural sounds behind her gag, but she stopped as if by magic the instant Lankau emerged from his corner. Her eyes expressed astonishment rather than horror or surprise. Lankau smiled. "Unable to speak, she is not," he whispered to himself. She drew back her head in disgust as he loosened the tight scarf that cut into the corners of her mouth. "So you're not completely dumb," he tried again, this time in English.

"Yes, you're quite alone," he continued, alternating between German and English. "Little Petra's not here. Do you miss her?" Lankau laughed, but the woman in the chair didn't react.

"May I hear you say something again, my dear Laura, or whatever your name is?" He squatted down in front of her. "What about a little scream, for example?" He raised his fist and spread out his fingers right in front of her face. Then he took hold of it as if it were a big stone he was about to throw. A scream came when he began squeezing, but no words.

"I think I can make you say something when I want to," he said, getting up and looking down at her. He knew he could. The main switch to the bungalow and the winepress was out in the pantry. If he made it clear to her what would happen to Petra if he turned it on, she was bound to talk. If she could.

Then he tightened the gag again and took up his position by the window.

The first glimpse he got of Arno von der Leyen was when he got out of the BMW down on the main road. The sight of the bent-over figure set him off. Lankau slid his hand slowly along the windowsill without taking his eyes off his victim. Then, seizing the knife that had lain ready beside his half-eaten apple, he turned resolutely toward the bound woman. After speculating briefly about how drastic were the measures he should take, he decided to let her live for the time being.

A single blow to her neck just over the collarbone, and she sank into the chair, unconscious.

For a while the figure was hidden from view behind the vines. Failing to detect any movement in the vegetation, Lankau stepped back from the window.

Although it was dry enough outside, the cobblestones in the courtyard felt slippery. Bryan made his way carefully, though he nearly slipped a few times on their mossy covering. The thought of entering the house without knowing why the light in the yard had been switched off worried him. In spite of the Shiki Kenju that lay in his hand with the safety catch off, he couldn't help feeling uneasy. Darkness had been his constant companion ever since he'd crept into Stich's flat.

But now it didn't suit him anymore.

He registered something familiar the moment he stepped into the hall. But before he managed to make out what it was, he felt a deep stab in his side. As he was tumbling into the room, he sensed the same familiar thing again. It was intense now.

Suddenly the pistol was kicked out of his hand and the light switched on.

The only thing Bryan could see above him was Lankau's silhouette. The ceiling light surrounded him like an aura. Bryan was blinded and rolled instinctively to one side, into something hard and irregular. In one movement he snatched and flung the object up at the silhouette's head with all the strength he could muster.

The result was enormous. The figure toppled over with a roar.

Bryan sat up with difficulty and tried to pull himself over against the wall as fast as he could. The contours and arrangement of the room came to him in a flash. Lankau lay on the floor in front of him, staring at him maliciously. He was still holding the knife, but wasn't ready to jump at him yet. It was easy to see why. A short, deep gash over the bridge of his nose had exposed bluish-white cartilage.

Bryan felt a jab of pain in his side and looked down. He'd been stabbed underneath the third rib. If he had made it three centimeters farther into the room, the thrust would have perforated his lung. Five centimeters, and he would have been dead. Then and there.

The blood was only trickling out of him slowly, but his left arm was locked in position.

Just as he discovered this, Lankau started crawling toward him. Bryan groped around and found another piece of wood similar to the one he'd just hurled at him. As Lankau leaned forward, slashing at him, Bryan whacked his arm and both the wood and the knife flew out of sight.

"You swine!" Lankau roared, forcing his heavy body up on one knee. Both of them were breathing heavily as they glowered at each other. There were only a couple of meters between them.

"You won't find it!" Lankau snarled as Bryan started scanning the floor. Bryan's eyes moved fast. Neither the knife nor the Kenju could have landed very far off. Then he stiffened when his eyes spotted the lighter he'd given his wife only two months previously. A variety of Laureen's small possessions littered the floor. Turning his head, he caught sight of the feet of a bound figure and got the shock of his life. At that moment he knew what he had sensed upon entering the room, something pervasive and insistent that should have warned him. The enticing whiff of the perfume Laureen had used every day for nearly ten years.

Perfume he had bought for her himself.

The gasp he was about to utter upon seeing his wife bound and gagged, her face white and eyes blank, never got a chance to pass his lips.

In that unguarded moment Lankau threw himself forward with such colossal force that the wound in Bryan's side started bleeding more profusely.

With his nose damaged, Lankau's mouth was open all the time, spewing nauseating breath and sticky saliva. He was concentrating solely on his attack, his entire physiognomy inflamed with the lust to inflict pain. Bryan's hands sought feverishly for a way of warding him off and mounting a counterattack. He had to duck punches, intercept slashes, and parry kicks from Lankau's feet and jolts from his knees.

Centrifugal force flung the interlocked bodies across the contents of Laureen's bag—packs of cigarettes and tampons, eyeliner, makeup compacts, notebooks, and other indeterminate bits and pieces. The men banged into furniture, tore the curtains down over them and overturned black wooden carvings from Kenya. A quiver of Zulu arrows broke like matchsticks.

Just as Bryan managed to wriggle one arm free so he could grab outward toward Lankau's crotch, the big man rolled onto his side and pushed Bryan away.

They sat a couple of meters apart, each weighing his options as they recovered their breath. An old man who knew what there was to know about killing and a middle-aged doctor who knew luck was not eternal. Lankau was looking for anything that might serve as a weapon. Bryan was looking solely for the Kenju.

Lankau was the first to succeed. Bryan never saw it coming. The hallway sideboard hit him hard on the collarbone, knocking the wind out of him. Instantly the big man flew at him as if he'd grown wings.

Punching him in the stomach with one arm, Lankau slid the other around Bryan's neck and seized the neck hairs that Laureen had so often tried to make him trim. The grip of the arm, huge as a pillar, nearly broke his neck. Then Lankau got up and flung Bryan with inhuman force against the wall with all the antlers. One of the trophies was at chest height. The small, sharp points shredded Bryan's jacket as if it had been moldering for centuries.

Laureen's scream made Bryan turn his head for a second. The next thing he felt was the collision with Lankau's total weight. One of the antler's points broke off on Bryan's backbone with a snap, making Lankau roar with delight and intensify his attack.

It may have been pain that made Bryan stretch both arms into the air, or intuition. In any case his hands brushed against the bony armor of another of Lankau's trophies.

Warm blood was already streaming down his back. With all the weight and strength he could muster, he wrenched the antler off the wall and swept it downward in a single movement, with such force that its points bore deep into Lankau's thick, muscular neck. The broad-faced man instantly jumped backward in astonishment, the deer's skull sticking up above his head like some kind of deformity.

The effect was clear. The man tottered another couple of steps with a swaying movement characteristic of someone about to lose consciousness. But as he teetered backward toward Laureen, Bryan realized Lankau had yet another ace up his sleeve.

Before he could react, the heavy man had moved behind Laureen and was standing semi-upright, leaning against the back of her chair. His right arm already lay poised across her neck, his hand gripping her chin. It wasn't hard to figure out what could happen next. A single jerk of that arm and it would be the end of her.

Lankau said nothing. Breathing heavily and staring Bryan straight in the face, his left hand groped for the antler that dangled from his fleshy neck. Bryan detached himself from the wall at the same moment as Lankau yanked his left hand upward. Their roars of pain were indistinguishable.

"Stay where you are!" Lankau screamed, as Bryan took a step forward. "One wrong move and I'll break her neck!"

"I don't doubt it!" Bryan knew it was no empty threat.

"Bring the twine from over there. You know where it is!"

"I'll bleed to death if I don't bandage my back first!"

Lankau's bad eye opened a trifle as he raised his eyebrows. There was no mercy to be had from that quarter. Both of them stood still, sizing each other up.

The expression in Laureen's eyes was heartrending. The grip on her neck made the tendons stand out in taut lines. Breaking her neck would not mean the end of the fight. They both realized this, so Bryan could afford to defy him and slowly remove his pullover. The knife stab in his side was pumping blood slowly and steadily over his thigh. He felt carefully across his back. The wounds caused by the antler tips were jagged, the gouges deep. He stripped all the clothes off his upper body.

The bandaging job was extremely provisional. Lankau smiled as Bryan tore his shirt into strips and attempted to patch himself up with almost acrobatic dexterity. Finally Bryan slipped the pullover back over his head and fetched the twine.

"I'm afraid all that bandaging won't do you much good." Lankau laughed, putting his hand to his neck.

Bryan ignored him. "And now I'll bet you want me to tie myself up."

"Start with your feet, you bastard!"

Bryan bent down with difficulty. "You realize you won't get away with this, don't you?"

"Who's to prevent me?"

"People know I'm out here!"

Lankau looked at him indulgently. "Oh, do they, really? And I suppose there's a whole cavalry regiment stationed out there on the edge of Münstertal?" He laughed again loudly. "Maybe there's already someone behind me, ready to shoot. Is that going to be your next practical joke?"

"I told the clerk at the hotel where I'd be this evening."

"Oh, yeah?" Lankau sneered. "Then thanks for the information, Herr von der Leyen. We'll have to find a reasonable explanation for your disappearance, won't we? That shouldn't be too hard, should it?"

"My name's not von der Leyen. Can't you get that through your thick skull?"

"Tie up your feet and quit talking!"

"You know she's my wife, don't you?"

"I know many things! Oh, yes. That she's deaf, for example. Also that she can't say anything unless she's gagged. Then she manages to talk quite well. And I know her name's Laura, but in reality it's Laureen, and that she comes from Freiburg, yet prefers living in Canterbury. You happen to live in Canterbury too, I would imagine."

"I've lived there all my life except for the few months during the war when you know very well where I was!"

"And so you two turtledoves thought you should come over here on a little tourist jaunt? How cozy!" His sarcastic smile vanished and he drew a deep breath. "Have you finished yet? Have you tied it tightly?"

"Yeah!"

"Then get up, take the rest of the twine, and hop over here to the table. Let me see if it's tight enough. Put your hands behind your back while you hop!"

Lankau's tug at the rope confirmed that part of the job was accomplished.

His rapid breathing betrayed his excitement. "Lean over the table, you got that?" Bryan laid his chin on the tabletop. The quick jerk to his right arm almost broke it.

"Stay like that," Lankau warned. "If you make the slightest move, I'll break your arm!"

Whereupon he wound the twine around Bryan's right wrist and continued around his thumb, then through Bryan's belt. Bryan howled as his hand was fastened to his back.

"You're quite a couple, you two," Lankau continued, turning Bryan over so the edge of the table stuck into the punctures in his back. Bryan bore the pain without flinching. "Why, you're almost like Peter and Andrea. There's a pair of charmers for you! Friendly and kind and ever so sweet!" He laughed. "You know them, I suppose?"

"Stich is dead," Bryan said tonelessly as his left arm was tied to his belt in the same manner, only this time in front of his stomach.

Lankau froze. He looked as if he were contemplating hitting him. "So, here we go again, you swine. Always full of surprises!"

"He's dead. I found him and a woman in a flat on Luisenstrasse about an hour ago. They were still warm." Bryan shut his eyes tight as Lankau raised his fist. The blow was calculated and brutal. Then the broad-faced man lugged him over in front of the woman and let him fall at her feet.

"Let me see the two of you." He clutched his neck, rubbed it a bit, and then removed the gag from Laureen's mouth. The woman began sobbing before he managed to apply the scarf to the wound in his neck.

"Bryan, forgive me!" she said, with great difficulty. She had tears in her eyes. "I'm so sorry, I'm so sorry!"

"Isn't that what I said?" Lankau's burst of laughter made him cough. "For a deaf and dumb German woman she speaks pretty good English." He sat down at the back of the room, breathing heavily as he listened to Laureen's loving, despairing voice.

Bryan tilted his head and tried to caress her knee with his cheek. Attempting to control herself, she whispered pleas for forgiveness without listening to his reassurances. By now Lankau was breathing almost soundlessly in the corner. The calm before the storm, thought Bryan, and nodded up at Laureen. He had no illusions. This was the act where the culprits bid each other farewell. Judging from Laureen's mildness and sudden irrational quietness, he was sure she knew it too. Now they were going to die. The past twenty-four hours hadn't been kind to their executioner, either.

It had to end soon.

"Time's up, friends!" he finally said, clapping his hands as he got up.

Bryan turned toward him. His eyes were as moist as his wife's, who hardly dared look up. "You can still manage to avoid making a bad mistake," he said. "My wife and I don't wish you any harm. I just want to find Gerhart Peuckert. He was my friend. He was an Englishman, just as we are. My wife followed after me to Freiburg. I knew nothing about it, I assure you. She hasn't done anyone any harm. If you let us go we'll help you."

"You can't quit, huh?" Lankau shook his head and bared his nicotine-stained teeth. "You? Help me? With what, may I ask? You know what you are now? You're pathetic!"

"When they find Stich, they'll find a number of things that link him to you. You'll be interrogated. They'll go through all Stich's belongings. Who knows what they may find? Maybe you and your family need to move somewhere else. Somewhere far away from here. Very far away. And perhaps we can help you with that." Bryan saw a momentary element of doubt creep into Lankau's nasty smile. "Can you be sure Stich hasn't left anything that could incriminate you?" he added.

"Shut up!" Lankau roared, jumping out of his chair. His kick made Bryan's body turn a half somersault.

Laureen's gaze was rigid as Bryan rolled toward her. She gasped for breath, wide-eyed but hardly looking at him, trying to control her breathing. Bryan knew immediately that this wasn't caused solely by fear. Had that been the case, she wouldn't be restraining herself.

She'd be screaming and crying.

Bryan tried to read her lips. Barely moving, they were whispering inaudible words. He couldn't make out what they were. Then she bit her lip, a sign of despair. She rolled her eyes upward as if in resignation, then let them drop a couple of times in quick succession.

Bryan sensed her desperation as Lankau made a move to approach them. "I'm sorry, Laureen," he burst out, noticing Lankau had stopped. "I should have been more open with you. I should have told you everything. About the hospital in Freiburg and about James . . ." The shake of her head made him stop short. She didn't want to hear it. She knocked her knees together and Bryan followed the movement. Then it stopped and Bryan's eyes reached the floor.

Behind her bound feet lay the Kenju. Just a meter away.

She must have just noticed it.

Lankau was standing behind him. Bryan turned around and looked up at him with haughty defiance. "You'll come to the same end as Stich, you fat pig. And a good thing, too, when you won't listen to reason!" The gob of spit he aimed at Lankau never made it past his chin, but there was no mistaking the intent. Lankau returned the greeting with still another kick, so that Bryan rolled against Laureen's legs.

Just as he'd expected.

As he lay gasping for breath, he drew the gun imperceptibly forward with the right arm that was tied behind his back. He could use only his index and middle finger. Then Bryan heaved himself a bit upright, and with the help of Laureen's nudging toes managed to edge the weapon behind him and over toward his left side, where his arm was tied in front. A moist, sweaty feeling was spreading down his arms. Lankau had begun breathing heavily again.

"Do you think I'm a fool, von der Leyen?" he said, touching the root of his nose where the wound had already stopped bleeding. "I don't believe a damn bit of the nonsense you're trying to make me swallow. Of course, it's possible that this stick of English bamboo is your wife, and it's possible that you call yourself Underwood Scott these days. After all, there are plenty of us who changed identities after the war. But von der Leyen you were, and von der Leyen you remain. The question is what I'm going to do with you. I can't just let you disappear. Or can I? I'm no spring chicken anymore. I don't take the kind of chances I used to. We must do the right thing."

"We? Don't expect any help from us!" Bryan leaned farther to the side, gasping once more as his face contorted with pain. Finally, drained of strength and submissive, he lay down on the floor on his left side. Precisely so the gun was just under his elbow.

The expression on Lankau's face was inscrutable, dark and calculating. "What if there really *is* someone who knows you're here tonight? You're probably just lying again, as usual. But what if there isn't? What then? Am

I going to break your neck or drown you in the pool? And what about that skinny specter there? Shall I take her out to the winepress to join little Petra? Does your hotel porter know she's here, too? I doubt it!"

Bryan tried to get some life back into his numb left hand. Once he got hold of the pistol he'd only get one chance. And he mustn't let it pass.

"Where is Petra?" came Laureen's surprising question. She seemed composed now and was looking straight at Lankau for the first time.

"How about that, little lady! I thought you'd never ask. Kind of strange, considering the two of you were such good friends. Ever since childhood, right?"

"I've never set eyes on her before today. Where is she?"

"Do you know what? I think all that concern should be rewarded. You shall be reunited, so to speak. In a kind of unique and figurative sense to be sure, but better than nothing."

"What the hell are you talking about?" Bryan coughed so hard, his whole body shook. As he worked his fingers for all he was worth.

"There's a main electricity switch right out there in the pantry. I've turned it off. Perhaps you noticed the light in the yard wasn't on when you returned?"

Bryan looked at him. "And . . . ?"

"And that switch is the main switch for the bungalow, the garage, and the winepress that's standing in the middle of that wing."

"The winepress? What do you mean?"

"Come on, you know. Those things you drop bunches of grapes into. The grapes circle around and around so nicely until they're mashed. Quite a practical appliance, I must say."

"You bastard!" Laureen blurted out. She lunged forward in the chair as though trying to attack Lankau. Her eyes were glowing with fury. "You don't mean to say that Petra . . . ?" Then her body went totally limp and she began to sob.

"No, I don't. However, if I flip the switch out there it'll be a different matter." His face grew darker. "But that's going to have to wait a bit. I haven't quite finished with her, not that it's going to matter in the end."

"Laureen, take it easy!" Bryan leaned his head against her legs and tried to caress her by moving it from side to side. "Things won't get that far. Did the two of you come here together?"

"Yes."

"And she's not in collusion with them?"

"No!"

Bryan looked up at Lankau. A bit of feeling was starting to return to the index finger of his left hand. It wouldn't be long before he'd make his attempt. The timing had to be perfect.

"What has Sister Petra done to any of you?" he asked.

"That's something I can only answer after you're gone from here, Herr von der Leyen. I'm afraid you'll never know." Lankau laughed. "Bad timing!" he said in English. "Isn't that what you call it where you come from? But whatever she's done, the outcome will be the same." He turned around. "You see, one of my friends has a nice kennel near Schwarzach. I've got three choice Dobermans there. Bad hunting dogs to be sure, but very good watchdogs when necessary. What a pity I don't have them here this weekend. Then we could get everything over all at once."

Laureen looked down. Bryan was lying quite still at her feet. She worked to control her breathing. This was no time to scream.

"Three dogs like that, they've got good appetites," Lankau continued, baring his discolored set of teeth again. "They'd certainly be able to eat someone little Petra's size within a couple of days, not to mention you, you skinny ghost. And if they don't manage it all in one go, there's certainly no lack of freezers here."

CHAPTER 60

The doorbell rang just as Gerhart was about to leave Kröner's house. Its sound reached his ears with diabolical force and the urge to cringe was hard to suppress. On the other side of the door everything was quiet. Someone was waiting for it to be opened.

And then a miracle happened.

Suddenly, for the few seconds he basked in the comforting sound of Petra's voice outside the door, he existed. The corpse in the bathtub a few steps away was revived in life and soul. The nightmare was exorcised. At the sound of that voice the gruesome resolve he'd been nurturing in every fiber of his body, the vengeance, and the struggle against the years of mistrust and systematic maltreatment, vanished altogether.

The moment of bliss was brief. Reality returned as he realized treachery could still be lurking nearby. Her next words felt like being stuck with an awl. The language she spoke provoked pain and fear in him. Each word and every syllable made him more hypersensitive and vulnerable. It was the spirit of evil, come to life. Gerhart bowed his head and covered his ears. The other woman's voice was sharper, enhancing his anxiety. It was bold and direct. Gerhart stood still, with his hands clasped to his ears, counting the seconds until their voices died away.

The image of the small, fair-haired woman who meant so much to him began to flicker and become distorted. The eternal smile was suddenly difficult to recall. Increasing giddiness made him back up along the wall. Finally he squatted down in a corner of the hallway, leaning his head against the oaken door.

Gerhart felt most of all like going home. There he could find food. There he could sleep. His home was the sanitarium.

There he was safe.

He shook his head and began to whimper. What he had just heard wouldn't go away. Could he trust anyone ever again? Who wanted to hurt him?

There was still the broad-faced monster who had abused him for so long. Kröner was no longer there to parry the hefty man's blows. This would please Lankau. Gerhart had seen it so often. The man was forever lying in wait, his eyes radiating evil. A devil who tyrannized everyone around him, except Kröner and Stich. And now they were gone.

They'd got what they deserved.

Gerhart was about to count the row of boards in the wall panel, then stopped. He regretted nothing.

He stood up and began flexing all his muscle groups by turn. He had to be prepared. For Lankau and the other one. He wouldn't think about Petra and her companion just now. That would have to come later.

First Lankau and then Arno von der Leyen. The one would lead to the other. It was so simple. As long as the two of them existed he'd never be sure of finding peace of mind. And that was the only thing he wanted. But how? At the sanitarium they would be able to fetch him and do things to him. They'd do him harm and force him to return to the past. And they would succeed.

This was something he couldn't allow.

In the past lay only evil.

Gerhart stopped exercising and let his shoulders drop. The ship's clock chimed in Kröner's living room. It was time to go.

Lankau was at his country house. Those had been Kröner's last words. The little farmstead just outside of town. Surrounded by vineyards.

Gerhart couldn't remember having walked so far before. Although he wasn't tired, the feeling of emptiness was burdensome company. For countless years, as long as he could remember, he'd always had an assisting hand by his side.

The stars above him had carpeted the sky hours ago. The mist and darkness didn't scare him. The moon lay snugly over the landscape. The scent of the earth was strong. It would soon be harvesttime.

An event Stich and Kröner would have celebrated.

Gerhart listened to his footsteps. He was out in the open. There was no way back. At every step his hatred of the two men increased. He pulled the wind jacket up around his ears.

At the time, Arno von der Leyen's disappearance had been a source of great misery. But the years had worn the feeling down. And now, somehow, the man was back and had stirred up that misery again. Which was why he had to hate him.

Without him, everything would have been as before.

Petra would still stand out clearly in his visions.

There was light on in the house. Gerhart looked toward it. Lights in all the windows as if there were a party going on.

At the first gentle curve in the drive he threw himself down into the roadside ditch and crawled forward on his stomach. It wouldn't be the first time Lankau had amused himself by letting his dogs loose outside when he had guests. Then he could stand out in the courtyard with his hands on his hips, making the curs grovel before him while his guests tried not break stride as they made for their cars.

His amusement had been hard to conceal.

It was completely quiet. Even the sounds of traffic on the main road had ceased. He gave a brief, high whistle. Sudden noises could make the largest and meanest of the dogs go berserk and bark hysterically. At the second whistle he felt sure the dogs were not outdoors that evening.

The ditch led directly around behind the outer buildings. Gerhart moved along the last damp stretch and saw the courtyard open before him. It was not lit up as usual. Gerhart knew this was wrong. The light was always burning when there was someone in the house. A new feeling of nervousness spread over him.

One mustn't ever overlook Lankau's signals.

The pantry light shone dull and faintly over the cobblestones. There were no parked vehicles. Not even Lankau's.

He got up carefully and took a good look around. There could easily be someone observing him behind one of the small rectangular windows in the various sections of the wooden bungalow. In one quick sideways movement he reached the door to the toolshed.

Gerhart had been there many times before. Compared with the clinical and orderly occupational therapy he was subjected to at the sanitarium, this room was an El Dorado of untidiness, flickering visual impressions, garden tools and other work implements, plus odds and ends of used materials. A short-handled knife whose blade had been honed down to practically nothing usually hung in the corner.

It was still razor-sharp. Gerhart leaned against one of the supporting beams as he felt along its edge. He breathed calmly. The contours around him were emerging in three dimensions.

The knife was not his only weapon. When he confronted Lankau he would act submissive and calm, as always. He would make the mountain of flesh feel safe and superior. He would get him to tell about Arno von der Leyen. Quietly and calmly.

Not until then would he start speaking normally. Gerhart was sure he could. The words were coming to him now almost without hesitation. He felt his mind's presence. The pills were no longer separating him from his ability to think.

Finally he would work Lankau up into his true odious self, where he was easiest to hate. And then he would strike. The moment and means would come. The dagger was there only if needed. Gerhart flexed his muscles again one by one and drew a deep breath, so the almost-extinguished scent of last season's grape harvest permeated his senses.

The sound penetrated the darkness like a rat scurrying across gravel, but the accompanying groan was human. Gerhart clutched the knife. Was there something he had overlooked? Was Lankau lurking in the darkness? He pressed himself against the beam and examined all the murky corners, one by one.

The next time he heard the sound he knew where it came from. The door was open to the room with the winepress. Had it been harvesttime, this would have been unthinkable.

Gerhart stepped into the room and immediately saw the white figure lying on the screw of the winepress with pleading, terrified eyes. When they met his gaze, the fear in them softened for a moment.

It was Petra.

Gerhart stood stock-still.

CHAPTER 61

Lankau stepped over Bryan, who lay doubled up on the floor. Behind him Laureen sat still, shaking. She was paralyzed by the prospect of ending up as dog food.

Suddenly Lankau kicked aside the remains of his chair, which had been used as weapons in the heat of battle. Bryan leaned his head back and caught a glimpse of a couple of taut animal hides stretched out on the wall behind him. In between the hides was an almost invisible handle, painted the same color as the wall. As Lankau took hold of it, a rush of fresh air entered the room that made Bryan feel dizzy. Double doors opened onto a terrace, revealing the moon rising in half darkness. Lankau flipped a switch on the outer wall of the house, at which point a flood of light revealed the outdoor facilities in sharp detail. He took a step onto the terrace.

At last Bryan felt the Kenju lying snugly in his left hand. He would have to turn around and pull himself up to precisely the right angle if he were to have a hope of hitting his target. It was almost impossible to fire upward at a sharp angle with his hand tied at waist-level. Bryan turned cautiously toward the double doors, waiting for Lankau to step backward into the room. Laureen had almost stopped breathing.

The distance was less than four meters when Lankau backed in. The shot was fired just as he was about to turn around.

The dull thud of the bullet hitting the beam just beside his head made him look back in astonishment.

At the next shot he had vanished back onto the terrace.

"Did you hit him?" Laureen asked, getting hysterical. She'd been hyperventilating for a couple of seconds before daring to speak. "He's gonna kill us, Bryan!" She was sobbing now.

Bryan wasn't sure. Maybe the second shot had hit. He turned toward the window facing the road, but saw only the faint outlines of some tall trees.

For a long time he was certain Lankau was just waiting. In fact, that was all he needed to do. Although Bryan had a wild card in his hand, his situation was not good. Laureen constituted a weapon to be used against him. Lankau would attack her instantly if he left her side. That would be the wrong way to play the wild card. And it was just as well. His mobility was greatly restricted by his bound feet. His arms weren't too useful either.

After Laureen's final sniffle everything was quiet. Night birds were on the move in the distance. A faint hum from the swimming pool's filtering system was practically all that could be heard. There was no sound of breathing, no movement, no trace of life beyond the double doors.

"He's gonna kill us, Bryan," Laureen repeated, this time much fainter. Bryan shushed her sharply. There was no doubt the front door had been opened. Silently. But there was no mistaking the draft that suddenly swept the floor.

Bryan turned onto his back and tried to take aim at the door to the entrance hall. The thought that Lankau might have a gun hidden somewhere made him turn ice-cold. He fired the moment the figure stepped into the room. The dry wood of the doorframe splintered, leaving a hole bigger than a teacup.

Bryan's heart stopped beating the instant the figure acquired form. His finger froze on the trigger, drained of will and intent.

He could have fainted.

Fully illuminated by the light from outside stood the person over whom he'd been brooding, for whom he'd been mourning and sacrificing himself for a lifetime in a bottomless feeling of loss. The brother he'd lost so long ago. The friend he had failed, deserted and betrayed.

The torn earlobe was the first thing Bryan registered.

It was James.

He stood there like a ghost, looking him straight in the eyes. He hardly looked older, merely different. The shot hadn't made him flinch in the slightest. He simply stood completely still, trying to comprehend what he saw.

As the figure stepped forward, Bryan stammered his name repeatedly.

Laureen was holding her breath again, looking alternately at the stranger and at the door to the terrace.

Bryan didn't notice her. The hand holding the Kenju had quit obeying him. His eyes were blinded by tears.

"James . . . !" he whispered.

As the figure in front of him knelt down, Bryan tried to absorb every single one of his features, as though James might vanish just as quickly as he'd appeared. "You're alive," his eyes said, laughing.

The figure in front of him expressed nothing.

James glanced at Laureen and over toward the open door. Then he turned and looked Bryan straight in the eyes, but his gaze was dead. "Watch out for Lankau," Bryan pleaded, feeling his friend's breath on his face. "He's here!"

At these words James gently took the gun out of his hand. Bryan sighed deeply. It was incredibly wonderful and incomprehensible. He looked up at his friend again and wriggled his left arm. "Untie me, James. Quickly!"

The spit hit Bryan in the face like a whiplash. In a second James's face contorted and became completely unrecognizable. The Kenju quivered as it pointed straight at Bryan's temple. The turnaround came so quickly that Bryan was still wearing a frozen smile.

The next moment Lankau stepped back inside, obscuring the light from the terrace.

James looked at him without changing expression.

CHAPTER 62

Gerhart! What the hell are you doing here?" Despite his coarse manner, Lankau addressed him in a friendly fashion. "Not that you've chosen the wrong moment. Not at all!" He came closer, at the same time guarding himself against any new, unpleasant moves from the recumbent von der Leyen. "It's good you've come, my friend!" He raised his hand slowly in a cordial, accommodating fashion, his face ever watchful. "You've done the right thing. You've helped me. Well done!"

Von der Leyen appeared unable to stop trembling. He seemed paralyzed, a pleading expression on his face. "Please . . . !" was all that passed his lips.

The word hit Gerhart Peuckert like a smack in the face. He backed his way toward the entrance hall in the midst of snarled exchanges between Lankau and the figure lying prone on the floor. There was no sign of agitation. His face was blank.

"Come now, Gerhart," Lankau said, smiling broadly to disguise his excitement and anger, "give me that gun. It's not such a good thing to be walking around with."

Lankau looked at him imploringly, stretching out his hand tentatively. Gerhart shook his head. "Just calm down, Gerhart. Let me put the safety on for you. You mustn't do that on your own. Come. Everything's good now."

Lankau looked him in the eyes. The defiance he saw was something new. "Come on now, Gerhart. Give it to me or else I'll get angry!" Lankau went right up to him. "Give it to me!" he demanded, with outstretched hand. The defiance in Gerhart Peuckert's eyes intensified. He put on the Kenju's safety latch but didn't hand it over.

Lankau retreated to the middle of the room and looked at Peuckert as if he were a naughty schoolboy. "Gerhart," he tried again, "what do you think Stich and Kröner would say if they saw you like this? You give me that pistol now, okay?"

The words that came left him completely dumbfounded. "They wouldn't say anything. They're dead."

Lankau's jaw dropped. It was the first time he'd heard Gerhart Peuckert speak coherently.

This was a hellish situation. Could what the idiot said really be true? Lankau went over to the telephone and dialed Stich's number. After several fruitless attempts he phoned Kröner. No one answered there, either. Lankau replaced the receiver and nodded quietly without looking directly at Gerhart. "No, there's nobody home." He frowned. "Maybe you're right." Gerhart looked at him as if his chain of thought had been interrupted. The multitude of impressions had apparently begun to confuse him. "I don't know what to believe," Lankau continued, tilting his head. "How did you get out here, Gerhart?"

"I walked," Gerhart answered promptly, pursing his lips.

Lankau looked at him guardedly. "You did the right thing, Gerhart," he finally said, his face lighting up in a big, ugly grin. "Absolutely! But why aren't you with Peter and Andrea? What's happened?" Lankau studied him. The idiot's atypical shrug and upturned gaze would get on anyone's nerves. "Did you see anything?" Lankau persisted. He shook his head as he saw Peuckert's expression. "What about Petra? Why didn't you go to her? She lives much closer to Stich's flat."

"Petra was together with that one over there," Gerhart said, pointing accusingly at Laureen, who sat with closed eyes.

"Do you think Petra's in league with these two?" Lankau left the question hanging for a moment and glanced once more at the weapon lying loosely in Gerhart's hand.

The gun barrel pointed more and more upward with each step Lankau took forward. "We can trust each other, can't we, little Gerhart? No, you needn't be afraid that I'll take the pistol from you. Why should you harm me? I'm the only one you can trust."

Gerhart's eyebrows rose slowly. "It's okay to put the gun down, Gerhart. Put it on the table and come help me with von der Leyen." Lankau watched with satisfaction as Gerhart complied. "We're going to write his last chapter."

· · ·

Despite the woman's despairing look, Arno von der Leyen made no attempt to resist. He fell limply into Peuckert's and Lankau's grasp.

The terrace was grayish white. The swimming pool fit naturally into the architectonic layout. Leaves were already floating on its surface. Lankau, who was carrying Bryan's foot end, snorted as he made straight for the edge. The water level was high. The pool had not yet been drained after the long summer.

Von der Leyen struck his head as they dropped him on the tiled edge of the pool. Peuckert stood over him, looking him straight in the eyes. Von der Leyen returned his look with one of distress until his eyes rolled up and he mercifully lost consciousness.

"It serves him right!" Lankau said, straightening up. "Now we've just got to make it look more or less natural, don't we?" he added to himself. "Someone might come looking for him and they'd be bound to find something they shouldn't. Like fingerprints and such," he muttered merrily. "So it's better that he's all they find." Lankau nudged the unconscious body disdainfully with the toe of his broad shoe.

"And what, in fact, will they find?" he muttered again. "A drowned foreigner with a belly full of alcohol, that's what." He bared his crooked teeth.

Her eyes were so swollen that Laureen could scarcely see Lankau when he reentered the room. "Hey," he said, glancing at her mischievously, "this ought to do it!" He held up the magnum bottle for her to see and went out into the night air again.

"What do you say, Gerhart?" he asked the motionless man, who stood studying the unconscious figure. "Isn't this just the answer? Come to think of it, that's how the bastard had planned to get rid of me!" He knelt down beside the swimming pool and scooped up a handful of chlorinated water. "If it'd been up to this swine, I'd have drowned in the Rhine, hadn't I?" He nodded to himself in answer.

CHAPTER 63

Bryan jerked to the side when the cold water struck him in the face. For a moment he was confused. He wasn't afraid until he saw James's blue eyes riveted on him.

Then reality returned.

The years had robbed him of his childhood friend and given him a monster instead. And it was his own fault. It was an insight that destroyed his peace of mind, a realization that would prevent him from returning to his old life, even if he managed to survive his present nightmare. Bryan shook his head at the thought. He tugged at his bound arms.

"That's right, Herr von der Leyen!" came from above him. "Time to wake up, because now you're going to drown like a rat. You're going to get a taste of your own medicine!"

Bryan tried in vain to defend himself. A quick jerk backward loosened his neck vertebrae with a faint crunching sound, like at a chiropractor's. The bottle had no trouble finding his lips. Every time he pulled his head away, Lankau squeezed his neck tighter with his free hand. His fingers closed off the carotid arteries with deadly precision until Bryan began to black out and his lower jaw drooped.

Finally he stopped resisting.

After a long gulp his throat began to burn and the vodka almost choked him. Lankau loosened his hold and let him cough. "We can't have you suffocate, can we? That's not the plan."

"There'll be an inquest," Bryan sputtered. "They'll find marks on my body. I have deep wounds. They'll be hard to explain, you pig!"

"Maybe, and maybe not. Who knows whether they'll find anything? Perhaps the pathologist will have a bad day. He sometimes does. I happen to know all about that!" Lankau took a single swig from the enormous bottle. "Perhaps I even know him. Yes, come to think of it, I know him pretty well." He took another swig. "Aaah!" he said, exhaling deeply. "We'd better say that you and I were drinking together, but you were a bit less seaworthy!" He laughed so hard, his whole stomach shook.

Bryan felt his surroundings losing their meaning.

Still laughing, Lankau pushed Bryan forward until he hung halfway over the edge of the pool. Again he wrenched Bryan's head back and forced a big gulp into him. "You might as well drink, my friend. It'll be easier for you that way."

The vodka warmed his lips. The bottle had done its job and would soon be empty. The water below him was almost beautiful with its delicate, green reflections. He scarcely felt Lankau push his head underwater. It swaddled him, cool and soft, like the feeling of a fresh pillow in a feverish sleep. The second before he'd have to give up and breathe the water into his lungs, Lankau heaved him up again.

After another two plunges he succumbed to a feeling of indifference. The alcohol had had its redeeming effect.

"I don't hear you complaining!" Lankau's acrid breath was close to him as the water streamed off Bryan. "Are you still there, you swine, or have you had too much to drink? Are you going to deny me the pleasure?" He shook Bryan's head back and forth. Bryan saw only flickering images.

More determined than irritated, Lankau flung him down again. "Then we must have another go, I'm afraid. I want you screaming for mercy!" His eyes bored through Bryan's foggy gaze. "You're going to get to see that female of yours crushed to death in the winepress over there. And Petra, too. We'll take her first, since she's already been prepared. In the meantime you can come to yourself a bit so you'll be fresher when it's Wifey's turn. A little flip of the switch out in the pantry, and hey, presto! All over! That's what can happen when someone rubs me the wrong way. Maybe it'll affect your tenacity." He thrust out his jaw, clutching the magnum bottle. "It's a pity for Stich and Kröner that I didn't get to you a little earlier, but never mind. He who laughs last, laughs best."

Lankau snorted and took another swig. His hair was tangled, his whole upper body wet with chlorinated water. With extreme difficulty he got up and leaned over Bryan. "You take hold of him there, Gerhart. We've got to get him over to the shed!"

CHAPTER 64

Lankau saw the shadow move across the terrace as he was lifting up one end of his semiconscious victim. The next thing he felt was a violent blow that made his legs give way under him and sent him hurtling sideways over the edge of the pool.

"Goddamn you, Gerhart, you imbecile! You're gonna pay for that!" he gasped as he grabbed hold of the ladder and let the water stream off him.

Not until he'd brushed water off his body with unconcealed irritation did he realize what had happened. It had been a simple, ridiculous mistake. He'd let Gerhart overhear what he intended to do with Petra. He suddenly remembered that the gun had been left lying on the table inside, but by then it was too late. Behind his kneeling, near-senseless prey, Gerhart was standing like a pillar of salt, pointing the pistol straight at him.

"What is it, Gerhart?" he asked, stretching out his hands in a gesture of reconciliation. "Are we no longer friends?" He rose slowly to his wet feet and approached the tall man. "Was it what I said about Petra, Gerhart? Then I apologize." Peuckert's eyes were burning with hatred. Lankau assessed his possibilities. "I was only joking. What did you think? It was merely a matter of getting that swine von der Leyen to squeal, you know that!" He had a single step left, then he would strike. "Petra's a good girl. . . ."

That was the last thing he said before Gerhart began screaming.

The anguished, hateful cry was so bloodcurdling that the birds flew into the air, chattering, and Lankau stiffened. Even as it still echoed across the landscape he saw that Gerhart Peuckert had no intention of letting him get any closer. Peuckert's face was bluish red, his lips pulled back with teeth completely bared. Lankau retreated a couple of steps and nearly slipped in one of his own puddles. He stretched out his arms and continued backing away in a big curve toward the double doors to the living room. The figure in front of him did nothing but stand there, breathing deeply, watching his clumsy attempt to make his way backward.

When he reached the room he turned and ran to the pantry.

His pursuer caught up with him just as his hand reached the main switch to the bungalow. Precisely as Lankau had hoped.

"Give me that gun, Gerhart! Otherwise I'll turn it on," he said, crooking his finger. "And then you'll never see Petra again. Is it worth it?"

"I heard what you said before!" Gerhart's face was still twitching. "You'll do it anyway!" He pressed the pistol hard against Lankau's temple.

"Nonsense, Gerhart! You're not well enough to tell the difference between reality and fantasy!" The tiny beads of sweat on Lankau's face stood in sharp contrast to his calm voice. It was a wonder he could speak at all.

Gerhart Peuckert stretched his hand slowly up toward Lankau's, which was still resting on the switch. "If you touch me, I'll press it!" Lankau said, sweating as he watched the hand stretch past him.

When at last the sinewy, almost spidery hand lay on top of his, Lankau gave up all resistance. Gerhart Peuckert's eyes were calm, attentive, and cold.

Lankau jerked involuntarily as Gerhart threw the switch. The sharp bang from the shred of gears set into motion was accompanied by the gleam of the light in the yard. Lankau wasn't sure if he'd heard a scream. The characteristic rumble of the winepress meant that its methodical, deadly rotation had begun.

During the next few minutes Lankau obeyed Gerhart Peuckert's orders without hesitation. He prayed that the madman wouldn't start fiddling with the safety catch while he was aiming the weapon at him. Every breath was transformed into thoughts of how he could escape his precarious predicament.

On Peuckert's command, he dragged von der Leyen into the house and over to the blubbering woman. Meanwhile he tried to remember where his wife's toylike hunting rifle could be hidden. As he passed the exotic weapons hanging on the wall behind the bound woman, he considered staking his life on a desperate grab for one of them.

Gerhart Peuckert never gave him the chance.

"Sit down at the table," Peuckert said. It had become silent in the room.

Arno von der Leyen was slumped on the floor, his eyes trying to smile up at Laureen.

However irritating, Lankau felt an increasing admiration for Peuckert's cold nonchalance, coupled with imperceptible bursts of burning hatred that, for the time being, had to be suppressed.

"Put your legs all the way under the table," Gerhart ordered without looking at him, "and pull your chair in with you." Lankau grimaced and squeezed his bulging belly against the rough edge of the oaken table. The idiot was rummaging in his wife's bureau.

"Write on this!" Peuckert threw a sheet of lined paper on the table in front of him.

"You don't know what you're doing, Gerhart! Wouldn't it be nice if I drove you back to the sanitarium? Remember, if it hadn't been for these two, nothing would have happened. It's not my fault!" He swore as he looked up at Gerhart. "If it hadn't been for them, you and Petra would still be having a good time together, wouldn't you? And whatever happened to Kröner and Stich wouldn't have happened. Isn't that so?"

The ballpoint pen Gerhart threw onto the table in front of him belonged to the Englishwoman. It had been lying on the floor at Gerhart's feet.

"Shoot those two instead." Lankau jerked his head in the direction of the tied-up man and woman. "Just shoot them, man! They haven't brought us anything but misery. What could possibly be the harm in that? I know you can do it, Herr Standartenführer Peuckert. No one could hold you responsible, anyhow. How could they? You'll get back to the sanitarium, I promise. It'll be just the same as before. You'll be Erich Blumenfeld again. Reconsider, Gerhart. Don't you remember? We were the ones who looked after you all these years."

Peuckert calmly tightened his grip on the pistol. Bending his head slightly, he looked at Lankau, frowning. "I remember," he replied, pushing the paper toward Lankau's belly. "Write what I dictate!"

"Maybe," answered the broad-faced man, trying to figure out how many bullets were left in the Shiki Kenju.

"We, citizens of Freiburg im Breisgau," Peuckert drawled slowly, "Horst Lankau, *Standartenführer* in the Mountain Commando Corps, alias Alex Faber; Obersturmbannführer Peter Stich of the SS Wehrmacht and

Sonderdienst, alias Hermann Müller; and Wilfried Kröner, *Obersturmbann-führer* in the SS Wehrmacht, alias Hans Schmidt . . ."

"I'll write nothing!" Lankau said, and threw down the pen.

"I'll kill your wife if you don't!"

"So what? What do I care?" Lankau shifted slightly in his chair. The massive table was heavier than he had reckoned with. To throw it at Peuckert would require superhuman strength. He took a deep breath.

"And your son, too!"

"Oh, really?" Lankau flipped the pen farther away in defiance.

Gerhart stood staring at him for some time until, with a grimace, he added, "It was I who killed Kröner and Stich." Peuckert didn't take his eyes off Lankau, who was now breathing calmly, his face no longer so defiant. "I electrocuted Stich. And Andrea, too. And you know what? They were pitiful from start to finish. In the end they didn't even smell good." He paused for a moment. Spittle had formed a crust in the corners of his mouth. He delved deep into his pocket and shook it. There was the familiar rattling of a bottle of pills. For a moment his eyes clouded over. Lankau watched. He seemed to be having withdrawal symptoms, as if the urge to take a pill or two was becoming increasingly strong.

"Don't you feel well, Gerhart? Tell me. Shouldn't I help you?" Lankau heard his words die away.

"And I drowned Kröner," Gerhart finally added softly, straightening his back. "In the same way as you intended to drown that swine over there. Very slowly."

"I think you're lying!" Lankau was not unaffected, but still he leaned nonchalantly back in his chair as far as his uncomfortable position allowed. If he could combine the movement with a strong heave of the table, he was sure he'd break free.

"I've had excellent teachers."

The smile that spread across Lankau's lips was almost one of pride. But Gerhart's statement was a dangerous truth. "What do you mean?" he asked.

"You know very well." Gerhart wiped the corners of his mouth and spat on the floor.

"Are you thirsty, Gerhart? I have some good Rhine wine in the bungalow. Do you feel like having some?" Lankau moistened his lips and winked.

"Shut up!" came the prompt reply.

The wet figure on the floor made sounds of pathetic vomiting attempts. Neither Lankau nor Gerhart turned their heads. "Don't you remember how you used to entertain each other with stories about how to kill people?" Peuckert continued. "I think you do. I do, at any rate. You threatened to kill me as well!"

"Nonsense! We've never threatened you. Well, perhaps years and years ago." Lankau looked apologetic. "That was before we knew we could trust you."

"You're full of shit!" Peuckert hissed at the broad face, which was watching him vigilantly. Lankau was making ready to push off.

The stink of vomit was becoming noticeable. Bryan groaned, regurgitated an extra time, and tried to sit up. "Kill him, James," he coaxed quietly.

But he couldn't get through to him.

"You were the worst one, Lankau." The madman radiated contempt. "Can't you remember you made me drink the blood of the animals you'd just been out hunting?" Peuckert took a step to one side. He was furious. Lankau remembered, but did his utmost not to react. Now Peuckert was standing behind him. "And the dog piss? And my own shit?" he yelled.

Telltale beads of sweat formed on Lankau's forehead. He was still convinced he could reason with the fool. But in a game like this, sweat was an irrational factor. Impossible to control and all-revealing. Lankau raised his arm cautiously and wiped his brow. "I can't remember any of what you're talking about. It must have been Stich. He could be an evil devil when the urge came over him."

The man standing behind him was silent for a moment. Then he struck him hard on the neck with the Kenju. The shot went off instantly. Lankau threw his head back, wondering how he could still be alive. His ears were howling. He looked to the side. The projectile had struck above Arno von der Leyen's head. The woman was silent but still crying.

Gerhart Peuckert looked at the pistol in astonishment. He hadn't pulled the trigger.

"Be careful with that thing, I told you! It can go off for no reason." The sweat on Lankau's forehead was turning cold. He shook his head.

"Are you afraid of it, Lankau? You shouldn't be." Gerhart Peuckert's agitation made Lankau's ears buzz even more. "You'll be begging me to use it! I'm not forgetting what you said out on the terrace."

"It was you who killed Petra, remember that. It was you who started up the winepress!"

"And I've thought of an even worse fate for you if you don't write what I dictate. Can you remember how you threatened me with caustic soda? Teasing me by threatening to make me drink it?"

Lankau twisted his body around as much as he could. The sweat had broken out again. Gerhart turned and strode up to Arno von der Leyen. "Get up!" he ordered, addressing the drunken man who was lying in his own vomit.

"I don't understand what you're saying," came the quiet response from the floor. "Speak English, James. Talk to me."

Gerhart stood for a while, regarding the figure beneath him.

"Get up!" he then said slowly, in English. Lankau was overcome with horror. At once it dawned on him how fatally he'd misjudged the situation and how wrong his decisions had been.

Arno von der Leyen looked up immediately. Lankau noted that Peuckert's eyes were still evil-looking and cold as he watched the bound man. If there were any ties between them, it was a mystery to him.

"James!" was all that came from the man on the floor.

"Get up!" The Kenju lay firmly in Peuckert's hand. He took a deep breath. Lankau noted his excitement with unease. "You're going to get something for me from the kitchen. I'll untie one of your hands." He stepped to the side and slugged Lankau on the back. "Don't get any bright ideas, you hear?"

Even though Lankau didn't doubt Peuckert would carry out his threat, he chose to ignore the warning. He'd gotten a good grip on the table in front of him. All his strength was mobilized.

Arno von der Leyen scrambled to his knees. He didn't seem to understand what Gerhart wanted him to do. The wounds in his side and back seemed to be plaguing him intensely. Peuckert made no move to help him.

The clamminess on Lankau's back began to cool.

"You're to fetch the caustic soda from the kitchen cupboard. It's labeled ÄTZMITTEL. Bring it along with a glass of water, you understand? And don't try anything smart. You won't get away with it." Arno von der Leyen got to his feet and tried to straighten himself up. Leaning painfully to one side, he again glanced at Peuckert's impassive face. "Perhaps I'll give you a more merciful death if you do as I say. The woman, too."

"Death?" Arno von der Leyen looked as if he were trying to shake off the alcoholic fog. "What are you talking about, James?"

"Save yourself the trouble, you drunken swine!" Lankau heard himself say. "He's raving mad!"

Von der Leyen leaned his face against Peuckert's chest. "James, it's me, Bryan! I came to find you. Listen to me." His confused eyes were begging. Peuckert didn't react. Suddenly von der Leyen drew himself up, making his wounds burst open again and trace dark shadows on the side of his pullover. "We're friends, James!" he pleaded. "You're coming home now. To Canterbury. Petra can come too, if you like." He shook his head in bewilderment. He couldn't understand what was happening.

Peuckert turned to face Lankau. "He refuses to prepare the caustic soda that you're to drink."

"That, I understand." The mockery in Lankau's voice suppressed his desperation. His grip on the table was now perfect.

"And you don't think I can make him do it?"

"Who knows?"

"Are you going to write?"

"No, I'll be damned if I am!"

Gerhart pushed von der Leyen over as he went over to the woman. She trembled as he looked at her, trying awkwardly to back away. The dark smudges of makeup around her eyes ran slowly down her face. "So I'll have to find another method! I'll hit her if you don't help me," he said slowly.

"Caustic soda?" Arno von der Leyen said tonelessly. "Why that?" He flinched when Peuckert struck her. The woman began to sob.

"You still won't?"

Von der Leyen shook his head and flinched again at the next blow.

"Do what he tells you, Bryan!" the woman suddenly spat out. Her outburst made Lankau's blood run cold. "Do it!" Von der Leyen looked down at her. She was leaning on her side, gasping for breath. Peuckert had hit her in the chest.

Arno von der Leyen straightened up slowly.

Lankau tried to stay composed. A steadily increasing pain in his midriff pulsated with every breath. He already had the table resting its full weight on his palms and hairy lower arms. He looked up when the two men stood before him. "Aren't you going to untie your friend?" he said, addressing Gerhart with a quiet smile. "Then we'll see if he's capable of holding a glass."

Peuckert's alert blue eyes scrutinized Lankau for a moment. It took some time for him to loosen the knot in the belt with the gun in one hand. Leaning back, Lankau took up a position whereby he could concentrate every muscle fiber on sending the table precisely in von der Leyen and Peuckert's direction.

The shock effect when he sprang up with the table resting on his lower arms was amazing. Reflexively Peuckert released the safety catch and fired the gun twice, but it was already too late. The table absorbed the shots as it flew forward. Its massive weight flung the two men backward and they landed beneath it on the floor. The Shiki Kenju flipped out of Gerhart's hand and ended in the doorway to the entrance hall. Lankau was already on his feet before the men could begin struggling free of their heavy burden.

He roared triumphantly and jumped around the table to take possession of the pistol. There were still three bullets left. He wouldn't hesitate in using every last one. One for each of them. The dogs would get more to eat than they could manage.

And then his world collapsed. Once and for all.

"Stop" was all she needed to say.

Facing him stood Petra.

There was no mistaking the expression in her eyes. The weapon already lay snugly in her hand.

"Let me do it, Gerhart! I know where the bottle is." She looked authoritatively at the tall man and gave him back the pistol.

Lankau felt the pain intensify in his stomach and breathed more and more heavily. This time they placed him at the end of the table, right up against the wall.

The bound woman sitting in the chair was still trembling with shock. Petra looked neither at her nor at Arno von der Leyen, who was again crouched at the woman's feet.

"You leave the woman alone, Gerhart! I'll do what needs to be done."

"I told you to stay away until the whole thing was over." Gerhart Peuckert was white in the face.

"I know you did. But we're going to do it my way, Gerhart."

A little plop could be heard a moment or two after Petra had gone out to the kitchen, like the discharge of a vacuum. Lankau looked at the poster on the wall. Cordillera de la Paz. A world of adventure that was fast receding from him. The distance was becoming insurmountable.

He grabbed the pen and began to write.". . . *Obersturmbannführer* in the SS Wehrmacht, alias Hans Schmidt . . ." When he'd completed the sentence he looked at them. "Is that all?" he asked defiantly.

Gerhart Peuckert looked at him calmly and dictated the conclusion. "I beg my family's forgiveness. The pressure from the others was too great. I had no choice."

Lankau looked back at him. He raised his eyebrows and put down the pen. These words were to be his last to the outside world. They were going to take his life no matter what he did.

He closed his eyes and let himself be carried away by the smell of coffee beans, dry earth, and the breeze from the primeval forest's valleys. The cacao tree provided him with shade. The sounds from the Indians' huts reached him like an incarnation of reality. Then he felt the pressure in his chest again, this time higher up. His skin grew cold. They dared not use the caustic soda, he knew that. "Write it yourself, you louse!" he screamed, opening his eyes as he tried in vain to push back his chair. The shot came instantly and bored deep into the beam above him. Gerhart Peuckert hadn't hesitated a second.

Horst Lankau looked toward the door, where Petra stood with the glass in her hand. "No one's going to believe someone would commit suicide with caustic soda!"

"We'll see." Gerhart turned toward the woman in the doorway. "Come here, Petra," he said.

Lankau sat still for a while, pulling at the corners of his mouth. The glass was now resting heavily in Gerhart's hand. Lankau breathed deeply between his teeth.

Then he seized the pen again and wrote. When Lankau put it down his expression was vacant.

Gerhart Peuckert looked over his shoulder. It took him some time to read the few sentences. Then Lankau noticed his nod.

"Get it over with!" Lankau hissed, the words' intended vehemence hampered by the pains in his stomach and heart. He shifted to one side as Gerhart pressed the muzzle of the Kenju into his ear. "Now I've kept my end of the bargain!"

"So you thought you could escape, you dog," Gerhart Peuckert said, controlling himself. "Can you remember what you always used to say? 'It only starts to get interesting when the victim is softened up by fear.' That's what you said." He pressed the weapon harder. Lankau constricted his nostrils so he didn't have to inhale the smell from the glass.

"Why should I drink this?" Lankau felt the sweat trickling again. "Shoot me. You won't get me to drink!"

"Then I'll pour it over you!"

Lankau looked up at him with a hateful expression and took a deep breath. The nauseating, pungent odor failed to materialize. Lankau sniffed the glass again. Petra stood beside him, looking away. Then Lankau threw back his head and began to laugh. No longer noticing the cold steel in his ear, the roars grew louder. Behind him, the woman in the chair began whimpering again.

"That's a good one! There's no damned caustic soda in that glass! You couldn't do it, could you, Petra?" He stared triumphantly at his assailant. "Did the two of you plan that one, too, little Gerhart? I wonder what you poured in the glass? Bath salts?" As he laughed he glanced at Petra, who was biting her lip.

"Ha!" Lankau stuck out his tongue and thrust it teasingly down toward the glass. "She couldn't do it, Gerhart, dear! The little chick would never be able to do something like that." At that moment the pistol muzzle was removed from his ear. Gerhart Peuckert's eyes were feverish and wavering, aimlessly inspecting everything in the room. Finally they met Petra's gaze.

She looked at him pleadingly. "Don't do it, Gerhart! For my sake!"

For a moment Gerhart Peuckert stood perfectly still, staring at the glass in perplexity. Then he calmed down. "In that case, do it," he commanded. "Stick your tongue right in!"

Lankau smiled up at him and confidently put his mouth to the glass. Teasingly and extremely slowly, he pointed his tongue at the surface of the liquid. When it finally reached the surface it gave a violent jerk by reflex. Lankau's face changed immediately. "What the hell?" he yelped. His face went bloodred as he waved his tongue, pulled it back in his mouth and began spitting and swallowing. The pain bored into his flesh and made his mouth burn. He began salivating uncontrollably. A moment later he started to groan, gasping ever more quickly for breath.

Gerhart's laughter reached the surface slowly, as though he'd forgotten how. It was hollow and deep and accompanied Lankau's increasingly labored breathing. "So she wouldn't dare, would she? I was almost beginning to wonder. Are you thirsty, Lankau?" he howled. "I think we have a nice Rhine wine out in the shed. Wasn't that what you were going to offer me? Or perhaps you'd prefer to drink the contents of this glass? Maybe you don't think it smells as it usually does, but never mind. As long as it works, as they say!"

CHAPTER 65

Petra looked at Gerhart in horror and shrank away from him. He stopped the instant he noticed her expression. His jaw muscles pulsated visibly until he got hold of himself. Then he handed her the glass with the deadly liquid.

Lankau followed Gerhart's movements from his seat. He was still short of breath. Gerhart fixed his eyes on the windowsill as he paced around Petra. "Enough of that!" he said, picking up the remains of Lankau's apple as carefully as if it were a tiny living creature. "You're right," he continued. "No one would believe anybody could consider committing suicide with caustic soda. Not even someone like you!" He looked straight at Lankau. "Shall we try and think back, Lankau? Can you remember the nights in the hospital when you talked about how to kill people with ordinary, everyday objects? Knitting needles, hammers, and wet clothes among other things, as I recall. Do you remember how you and Kröner laughed? How you tried to outdo each other with your repulsive methods? Your imagination knew no bounds." He clutched the apple and stared into space. Petra stood stock-still, listening. She'd never imagined hearing so many words pass his lips. His voice was beautiful, but the moment was ugly.

And she could have done without the coldness in his eyes.

"When I think back, it was the simplest methods that made the greatest impression on me." He tossed the apple in the air and caught it a couple of times in front of his victim's eyes. "I'll bet you know what I'm thinking of now." He smiled. Lankau's face darkened. Even though his breathing came in labored wheezes, his eyes were alert. "Wasn't it actually Kröner who thought the method up? I'm sure you know better than I. All I can remember is that vivid description of the victim who got a piece of apple forced down his throat. It takes a while, but it sure is simple. And no one suspects anything. It can happen to anyone. Not murder, not suicide. Just so long as it looks natural, right?"

The simplicity of the question was frightening. Gerhart was obviously capable of carrying out his threat. Petra felt paralyzed. When Gerhart had released her from the winepress, he assured her she needn't fear Stich or Kröner any longer. Her feeling of relief had been so restorative.

Now that feeling was gone.

Lankau's eyes slowly clouded over. It was the first time Petra noticed how aged they were. The cornea was matte, the whites yellowed. Gerhart took a bite of the apple. The broad-faced man flopped backward and stared in disbelief at the piece of apple Gerhart had spat into his hand. Then Lankau's neck muscles twitched and his arms struck out wildly. He took a deep, wheezing breath and threw his head to the side as Gerhart determinedly guided the piece of apple toward his mouth. He tried to say something and raised his arm. His eyes were feverish.

Before Gerhart could try forcing his lips apart, Lankau jerked one last time. Then, with a look of astonishment on his face, his head dropped slowly forward until his chin lolled on his chest.

For a moment Gerhart was at a loss. He pushed at the drooping cheek and saw how passively the head followed the movement.

Lankau was already dead before Gerhart had carried out his revenge.

Petra refused to believe what she'd just seen. She was overwhelmed by a mixture of doubt, helplessness, relief, and sorrow.

When Gerhart realized what had happened he turned toward the other man, who was also trying to fathom what he'd just seen. He leapt at him without warning, hitting him repeatedly and roaring in frustration like a wounded animal.

Thanks to the vodka, von der Leyen had no idea where the blows were coming from. He was too weak to defend himself and fell against Laureen, who was shaking her head hysterically from side to side.

"Stop it, Gerhart!" Petra screamed, but it wasn't until she grabbed his arm that he seemed to understand what she meant. He stepped back, crouching, his knuckles white and his agitation fed by deep breathing. The gun was still in his hand. He was unable to compose himself.

Despite her continued pleas, he took a firm hold on von der Leyen's neck and dragged him out onto the garden terrace.

Petra turned immediately to Laureen, who was about to lose consciousness. Then she made for the kitchen. The knife she found was intended for skinning rabbits. The bonds around Laureen's ankles and wrists fell away like sewing thread.

"I think he's gone mad," she whispered to Laureen, trying not to cry. "You've got to help me!"

Laureen tried to get up. All her limbs were numb. Petra knelt in front of her and rubbed her legs. "Come on, Laureen!"

———

The blow that sent Bryan facedown on the terrace at the edge of the pool was swallowed up in the vodka haze. James's yanks on his neck forced him up to his knees. Bryan smiled and shook his head. The effect of the alcohol swept over him in waves. He didn't even notice the pistol pointed at him. He still had a nasty taste in his mouth. He coughed and leaned back. The dampness of the night and the breeze were doing wonders to clear his brain. Bryan turned his head to face his assailant. He understood nothing. His friend's profile was blurred.

"Is it you, James?" he said. "Help me get out of this," he said, wriggling his left arm. He smiled.

"Yes, it's me," said the voice above him, muffled and subdued. And in English.

"James . . ." Bryan whispered, trying to focus. Never before had his voice been so gentle. Then he leaned on his side and rested his chin against his friend's leg. "Thank God," he whispered.

"You two stay over there!" came James's sharp retort. From far away Bryan could hear Laureen shout his name. He tried to turn toward the sound and took a deep breath. The two indistinct figures over by the house stood still. "If you come any closer I'll push him into the water. Don't move, understand?"

James stepped aside and Bryan nearly fell. The outline of the object James was holding slowly came into focus. It was a gun. Bryan tried to grasp the situation. He couldn't. "Why don't you untie me, James?" he asked again.

James knelt in front of him. "Arno von der Leyen? Bryan?" he barked. "Who is this person who's asking me this?" His eyes looked cursed. "Did you help me? Did *you* free *me*, by any chance?"

Bryan raised his eyebrows, preparing to answer.

"Don't you dare open your mouth!" James got up, the gun still trained on his prisoner. "You deserted me, sick and tormented! I could have lain there forever, couldn't I? Like a discarded relic!" The movement came suddenly and violently. James ripped Bryan's sleeve off with a single jerk, making him feel sick all over again. "You've still got it!" he said, looking at the faint remains of the tattoo in Bryan's armpit. "That surprises me." Bryan vomited a couple of times, letting the slime hang in the corners of his mouth. "You've been going around with that for a long time, Bryan. Wouldn't it have been better to remove it entirely? Like the memories?" James let Bryan's arm fall.

"Can't you remember at all what it was like at the hospital, Bryan? Weren't you there for six months, maybe a bit longer? And so what?" James glanced at the women. Petra gave him a pleading look and let go of the other woman, who was still leaning against her. "Can you imagine nearly thirty years of that?" he continued. "Do you have children now, Bryan?" He sneered, looking at the muck dripping off Bryan's nodding chin. "All that time! While you were having children, while you were making love, while you were experiencing the world, while you were enjoying life, while you slept, while you took walks in your parents' garden, while you became one with your dreams and fulfilled them—here I was sitting. For thirty years!" He screamed out the last sentence, tearing Bryan out of his dull indifference with a start. He looked up at his friend, who stuck his hand in his pocket.

A big bottle of pills appeared. "Would you like to relive that time? Would you like to know what it was like for me while you were living your life? Would you like to know where I disappeared to?"

Bryan opened his mouth without resistance. With the very first pill he recalled the chlorine-based medicine's characteristic dryness.

After thirty years, his salivation reflex was aroused instantly.

"Take one!" James shouted and stuffed another pill in him. "Take one for every year you let me down!" James thrust the pills firmly into the back of Bryan's mouth until he nearly vomited. In his still drunken state he was unable to resist. "And take these for good measure!" James pushed still more down his throat. Bryan swallowed them all. When the bottle was empty he could tell it wouldn't be long before he began slipping into unconsciousness.

The next few minutes were an inferno of noises. Women's cries, and James's ceaseless insults, curses, and impossible questions. Bryan didn't answer them, nor could he understand them. He turned to look up at his friend. There was no mercy in his eyes.

And Bryan couldn't care less.

CHAPTER 66

Laureen was beginning to get some color in her cheeks. The scene beside the swimming pool had her clinging to Petra as she kept repeating her prayers, again and again. Petra shook her head, grasping the rabbit knife firmly. She intended to use it if there was no alternative.

Petra squeezed Laureen's hand so hard, it hurt. None of Gerhart's words made it easier to understand why her life had turned out as it had. But the sentences clarified the years that had passed. Explained the self-deception. Put the events of recent hours into perspective. And made her want fervently to understand more.

Even though it might be too late.

Laureen stamped the terrace tiles in impotence as Gerhart forced the pills into her semiconscious husband. When he stopped, his victim began swaying gently from side to side.

Petra was clearly horrified. If they didn't do something, the dose James had given Bryan would be lethal. She begged Gerhart to listen, pleaded with her beloved to stop. Tried to make him understand it still wasn't too late. That they would be able to get away and bury the past. That they had a life in front of them to be lived. That this was something he owed her.

And still he waited passively as he watched Bryan slowly doze off. Madness and revenge had become one.

Laureen's hold on Petra's hand was convulsive, tightening and relaxing, tightening and relaxing. Finally she let go. She took a quick, impulsive step to the side, then stopped abruptly. Just as she was about to make a last, hopeless attempt to rescue her husband, Petra lunged forward with her knife raised. If she stabbed Gerhart, she would have no reason to go on living. Gerhart aimed the gun at her face as he followed her gaze. He looked from Petra to Laureen and back again. Petra didn't hear his warning. Not until the knife was heading for his throat did she become lost in the bottomless depths of his eyes. By the time her hand reached his face she'd dropped the knife.

The blow on his cheek fell as gently as a mother's slap. Gerhart seized Petra's hand and clutched it hard until she relaxed completely. Then he dropped her hand, gave her a soul-penetrating look, let the pistol fall, and stumbled onto the lawn. He stood there, stock-still, hyperventilating.

Laureen was already holding Bryan's head in her lap as Petra came to herself.

"Lift him up!" Petra ordered, sticking most of her hand roughly down Bryan's throat. She made Laureen take a firm grip around her husband's waist, and press. The third attempt worked. A fit of coughing was accompanied by acid, slime and half-dissolved white clumps. He was blue in the face. "Help him," she ordered again, demonstrating how to force his face backward and try to make him breathe normally by means of artificial respiration.

Behind them, Gerhart had become very quiet. Then he groaned and sank to his knees.

Petra was at his side immediately. "Gerhart, it's over," she sobbed, as she put her arms around his head, stroked his cheek and kissed him.

She smiled at him and stroked his cheek again. She called him Gerhart, James, Erich. He was pale. His eyes were vacant. She took hold of him, hugged him, and looked at him again. He didn't react.

"Gerhart!" she shouted, shaking him. She begged him, admonished him, alternated between his names, caressed him, and addressed him in German, English, and then German again.

He was kneeling very quietly, his pants soaking up moisture from the ground. He was in another world again. Withdrawn into himself. Swallowed up by nothingness. He stared emptily into space.

Over by the edge of the pool Laureen's husband's speedy return to consciousness took her unawares. He awoke with a start, almost as drunk as before. He smiled when he saw her and drew her instantly to him, unaware of his state and unappetizing appearance. She let him kiss her greedily, laughing and crying at the same time. Then they sat, hugging each other without a word.

Petra's face lay buried in James's shoulder. They hadn't moved for some time. She looked up and saw Laureen reaching cautiously to one side in search of the gun.

Finding it, she got up carefully, pulling her tipsy husband after her. It was only after Petra mouthed a silent prayer that Laureen let the weapon fall again.

———

Bryan stared around as if realizing where he was for the first time, and tottered over to the couple on the lawn. He sank to his knees so close to them that he almost pushed them over. Inserting his arm between Petra's face and James's neck, he turned his friend's face toward him. James made no attempt to resist.

Then he bent forward and babbled drunken nonsense in his ear. Petra loosened her hold and buried her face in her hands.

"Well, James, this time I'm not leaving you behind, am I?" Bryan bumped his nose against his friend's cheek. James had an alien smell. "Can't you say something, James? Come on, don't be such a wet blanket." He took hold of his face with both hands and shook it, then patted him on the cheek. "C'mon, say something!" Bryan didn't protest when Petra pushed him away. His present state made him oblivious to her scorn and despair.

She took hold of her loved one again. He didn't react. Neither Gerhart, Erich, nor James had been liberated in this kneeling man.

Laureen noticed Petra's dismay and wept freely as Bryan flopped down on his back in the dew-soaked grass and began to laugh. Then he whistled a couple of snuffled bars and laughed some more.

His state of intoxication was a blissful one.

Bit by bit it came back. The song they had made their own when they were boys. The irrational, crazy and trivial words came back to him. "'I don't know what they have to say, it makes no difference anyway!'" Bryan howled with laughter at its meaninglessness.

The starry sky was infinitely deep and magnificent in spite of the moonlight. The darkness drew the meaning of all that had happened out into the universe and swallowed it up. Bryan turned onto his side, looked at his childhood friend and sang as if the past had returned. Fragments of memories came to him from when they were young and used to climb the cliffs of Dover. The roar of the sea below them, the warmth and smell of the urine spreading embarrassingly in the crotch of his short pants.

"Can you remember, James?" He laughed and continued: "'I'm against it!'"

Laureen squatted down beside him and pulled him up a bit more vertically as he bawled out his song so loudly that it re-echoed from the fringe of the Schwarzwald. "'Your proposition may be good, but let's have one thing understood. Whatever it is, I'm against it!'"

When he finished, he sang it all over again. At the last beat he laughed with relief.

The figure a few meters away lay immobile in Petra's embrace. She raised her head and looked at Bryan as though he'd desecrated a sacred moment. Her tear-swollen face had aged. James's body twitched violently as she laid her head back on his shoulder, making her jerk as if she'd received an electric shock. She clutched him tightly before he fell over. Something rattled deep inside James's chest. He shook as if he were in the midst of a malaria attack. Again and again he let out a sobbing roar.

Petra held him to her and stroked his neck, trying to catch his glance. She wiped away his tears as his body trembled like a leaf and his eyes sought the ground, manifesting all the pain that had been inside him. It was impossible to express in any other way.

Bryan stared at him in confusion and crawled toward him on his knees. Petra and James couldn't stop crying. They sat together like that for some time. Laureen began to freeze and hugged her arms to her body.

Then James raised his head so slowly that even Bryan could follow its movement. Laureen pulled Bryan gently away from the two. James was looking straight into Petra's eyes. He stroked the skin on her cheek and kissed her gently on the mouth. She closed her eyes and hugged herself to him. There they sat, letting the moment pass in silence.

A fit of shivering made Bryan tremble repeatedly. A few snowy white clouds were floating above the dark foothills of the Schwarzwald's magnificent panorama. The September night became increasingly clear.

Then James sighed, staring out into space. He tried to clear his throat and raised his head hesitantly toward Bryan. He looked at him for some time. The muddled expression that met Bryan's gaze made him smile. James couldn't quite get hold of the words. He stammered a couple of times and paused. After a couple of minutes it came out quietly. "Bryan," he said, with a voice that sounded as familiar as his own father's. "Tell me: What was the name of David Copperfield's second wife?"

Petra and Bryan looked at him, moved and bewildered. Bryan closed his eyes and tried to grasp what was going on. The question seemed infinitely trivial to him. Looking at his friend, he tried to find an expression that would reflect his assortment of mixed-up feelings. His smile turned out apologetic.

Laureen pulled her husband's confused head toward her and ran her fingers through his hair. "Her name was Agnes, James," she said. "Her name was Agnes."

CHAPTER 67

The events of the previous day were still vivid for them both. The nausea was wearing off but the physical pains were much in evidence. The shot, the stabs, blows, and kicks would take months to heal. Bryan had had to change his bandages three times during the night. He gave Laureen an anxious look. She hadn't slept a wink either, and had a headache that was killing her. Repeated attempts to put on makeup hadn't been able to hide the beating she'd taken.

Bryan fumbled with his cigarettes. He was white as chalk as he grabbed the receiver again.

"Couldn't we just fly home?" she'd suggested.

Ever since Bryan had checked out of his hotel that morning, he'd sat glued to the telephone in Laureen's hotel room.

Laureen finished packing, though she was forced to sit down several times during the process. It had been a hectic morning. Having Bridget around had been a colossal irritation. She was ready to attack Bryan physically when she saw the bruises on Laureen's face, but settled for giving him a tongue-lashing. They let her believe what she liked. She'd understood nothing of the previous day's events, thank God.

Finally Laureen sent Bridget into town with five hundred marks in her pocket, declaring that she and Bryan had a lot to discuss.

Bridget was dumbfounded. Though it was Sunday, she'd have no problem using up the money.

Just as Bryan replaced the receiver, the phone rang again. After a few seconds he began to chuckle. Laureen was startled and looked at him aghast as he clutched his sides with laughter.

"It was Welles," he said, when he hung up. Laureen nodded, partly relieved, partly uninterested. "He wanted to tell me he'd found a psychiatric patient in Erfurt named Gerhart Peuckert." He attempted another smile, but gave his shirt a worried glance instead. It had stopped turning red. "What do you think of that? In Erfurt!"

Laureen shrugged. "Did you get the passport?"

"I found one that should work," he said, dialing the next number. "We'll take the train to Stuttgart and fly from there. I don't think we should fly from Basel-Mulhouse." He stopped and held up his hand, requesting silence. He'd finally gotten through.

"Petra Wagner," came the voice. She sounded worn-out.

"How far have you gotten?" Bryan took a last puff and stubbed out the cigarette.

"It'll be expensive, that's all I can tell you," came the cool response.

"That doesn't matter. Can we trust her?"

"I'm quite convinced you can."

"Then do what you have to do. And James? Or perhaps I should say 'Gerhart'?"

"You can say 'James,'" she said tonelessly. "Yes, I think it'll work out."

Bryan looked at Laureen several times during the remainder of the conversation. She was sitting on the edge of the bed, hands resting limply in her lap.

"How's it going, Laureen?" he said, finally. He lit another cigarette and felt his side.

She shrugged and didn't answer.

"Frau Rehmann, the director of St. Ursula's, demands half a million pounds to discharge him and remove the case records."

"That's quite an amount," Laureen answered apathetically. "I assume you're going to pay."

Bryan knew her. She didn't expect an answer. Of course he was going to.

"As far as I can tell from Petra, there hasn't been anything on the radio yet about the dead bodies. She doesn't think they've found them."

"They will, sooner or later," she said.

"By then we'll be far away. They won't connect us with what happened. They probably won't be able to figure out what happened at all."

"Are you sure?" She stared into space. "The taxi driver who drove Petra and me out there thought we had some business on the farm opposite Lankau's. I don't think he'll be a problem. But there's so much else." She looked worried.

"The letter James forced Lankau to write will be very important evidence. They're bound to connect the other two deaths with his. You needn't worry about that."

"You told Lankau you'd left a message at your hotel saying you were out at his country house."

"You were the only one who believed that, Laureen."

She frowned and stared up at the ceiling.

"The fingerprints, Bryan! What about them?"

"In the car? There aren't any. I took precautions."

"And around the house and the bungalow and on the terrace? There must be thousands of traces!"

"I don't think they'll find anything. We were very thorough. You know that."

She sighed, then tried to think the whole thing through once again. "Are you sure, Bryan? It was dark when we cleaned up. You were drunk. Petra was beside herself. I can't spend the rest of our life worrying that they might find out what happened."

"Lankau killed the other two! That's what they'll believe. They'll find his letter and they'll establish that he's the one who wrote it."

"They'll presume he intended to shoot himself with the small hunting rifle Petra found out there. Is that the idea?"

"That was our intention, yes. And that he didn't manage to carry it out before he collapsed. The postmortem will reveal a perfectly natural heart attack."

"And the wounds on his body?"

"You saw all the scars! Lankau was hard on himself. They'll wonder, but they won't find any answer."

"And the hunting rifle and bullets?"

"There'll be only his own fingerprints on them."

"What about the other places? At Kröner's and Stich's? What'll they find there? Are you sure they're not brimming with evidence? James's fingerprints must be everywhere."

"I'm sure they are! But they won't find him anywhere. They won't know where to look or who they're looking for. It's not even certain they'll try. They'll be busy enough trying to grasp the extent of the scandal these men's double lives are bound to create. You shouldn't worry about that at all!" He sat thinking for a moment. Then the words came quietly: "In any case, should the unthinkable occur where the investigation puts them on the track of what's happened, only James would be held responsible. Not you or me. But that won't happen, Laureen, be sure of it."

"When that Frau Rehmann realizes how many skeletons are in the closet of this whole affair, she's bound to confess." Laureen dabbed the tip of her nose carefully with her handkerchief.

"No, she won't. Bribery and abuse of authority wouldn't make good advertising in terms of her career. She'll keep her mouth shut." Bryan patted his suitcase. Now all he had to do was phone the Olympic delegation and then they could be off. "Laureen," he said. "Frau Rehmann knows what she's doing. She knows she'll be able to live comfortably and securely for the rest of her life, provided she doesn't react. She knew precisely how she wanted the half million pounds to be paid. It was as if she'd been planning for this to happen all along. She doesn't want a check, does she? No, the money is to be transferred in her name directly to an account in Zürich. After that, it'll be too late. She'll have to keep quiet, even if she gets qualms of conscience."

It wasn't the first time Laureen had gone over to the window that morning. Bryan got up, walked over, and took hold of her shoulders. The sigh that escaped her was one of exasperation. The green lawn in front of Hotel Colombi was completely deserted. On the other side of the park, in the distance, came the faint sound of a train toiling its way over the railway's many track crossings.

"And Bridget?" she asked quietly. "Doesn't she know a bit too much? She was there yesterday, you know. She heard the malingerers mentioned by name."

"Bridget won't be able to remember a thing, even if she'd had it chiseled into her brain. She was drunk yesterday and got even drunker during the evening, judging by her appearance this morning. Besides, it's quite unlikely that the English newspapers would go into detail about the death of three ex-Nazis. She'll never get to know."

She dropped her arms to her side and tried to breathe deeply. The bruised rib was hurting more and more. "And he's really supposed to come back with us?" She locked her eyes on his.

The question had been a long time coming.

"Yes, Laureen, he is. That's why I came here."

"And Petra, what does she say to that?"

"She knows it's best for James."

Laureen bit her lip and looked straight through Bryan. Her mind was reeling with a multitude of doubts and notions. "Do you think Petra can handle him, Bryan?"

"She thinks so herself. We'll have to see. He's coming home with us."

"We can't have him being near us, Bryan, do you hear?" Again she fixed his gaze.

"We'll see, Laureen. I'll work something out."

Petra and James were already standing on the platform when Laureen and Bryan arrived at the station. James was freshly bathed. He stood like a rock, casting sidelong glances down the endless row of railway ties. He didn't return their greeting and didn't let go of Petra's hand for a second.

"Is everything taken care of?" Bryan asked.

Petra shrugged.

James avoided looking at them. Laureen watched him from behind her sunglasses, making sure Bryan stood between her and the others.

"He's a bit sad just now," Petra explained.

"Anything in particular?" Bryan tried to catch James's eye in the bright sun. His face was wreathed in light. Rows of baggage trolleys and mail trucks were lined up on the adjacent platform, ready for the next working day. Their train had to be arriving soon.

"He keeps talking about a scarf that's disappeared. It's the only thing he's spoken about all morning. He'd expected to find it at Kröner's place. Gerhart thought . . ." Petra paused. "*James* thought Kröner had hidden it in a little cardboard tube that he found in Kröner's home. He carried that tube around under his wind jacket the whole time until we came home to my place. I think he got up twenty times last night to look in it."

"Was it Jill's scarf, James?" Bryan went up close to him. James nodded and was silent. Bryan held his side and turned to Petra again. "It was a scarf he got when he was a boy. The malingerers stole it from him while we were in the hospital."

"He was sure Kröner had put it inside the cardboard roll, but there were only drawings inside. That knocked him out completely."

Bryan shook his head sadly. "Jill was his sister. She died during the war."

Bridget arrived pretty late, strutting along the platform with such uncertain steps that under different circumstances Laureen would have hidden in one of the mail trucks. Instead she greeted her as if they hadn't seen each other for years. "Bridget, you silly girl. At last!" she said, hugging her and her baggage. Bridget nodded feebly to Petra and the man standing beside her, and completed her greetings by sending Bryan a look that would turn glowing coals to ice.

When they got on the train it was as if their seating had been prearranged. James sat down at one end of the compartment while Laureen sat down at the other.

Bridget stood at an open window to get some fresh air while Petra tried to peep out the window under Bridget's arm.

"Are you expecting someone?" Bryan asked. Petra stared sadly ahead of her.

"We're sure now, aren't we?" Laureen said, almost inaudibly.

"Sure about what, dear?" asked Bridget, looking curiously over her shoulder.

"Sure that it's the right train, Bridget!" said Bryan curtly, cutting short Laureen's half protest with a determined look. Sitting diagonally across from him, James hadn't reacted at all to any of the sounds or movements in the train car. He seemed uncomfortable in the clothes Petra had found for him, and inspected all the passersby on the platform for slightly less than a second each, as if he were counting them.

Petra leaned her face against the window, trying discreetly to stave off the beginnings of a tear. Then she sighed and leaned back into her seat.

"Good Lord!" exclaimed Bridget. "Have you ever seen such a hippie? You'd think she was some kind of African with that bundle she's got on her head." She drew away from the window a bit so the others could see what had caught her attention. Petra sprang to her feet when she caught sight of the woman and broke into a broad smile. "I'll be back in a moment," she said, addressing James. "You stay here!"

The reunion on the platform set off a lively commentary by Bridget, who didn't budge from her seat, thereby filling the entire window.

James's face lit up momentarily when the two women entered the car. Laureen immediately noticed Bryan's astonishment. "Who is it?" she whispered in Bryan's ear.

"Hello, again," said the woman, giving Bryan her hand.

"Mariann Devers!" Bryan was flabbergasted.

"We obviously have more in common than just my mother." She smiled and embraced James. She adjusted her layers of clothing and looked into James's eyes as she spoke tender words to him. Then she gave him another hug and studied Petra for a while until she was composed enough to bid them farewell.

Just as she was about to leave the compartment, she turned to Bryan. "It's rather a pity that you and my mother didn't become a couple that time. What a family we would have been! Instead, now you're taking my very best friend and my dear Erich from me. What do you think you're doing?" Her eyes were friendly, but she was obviously moved by this reunion. After hugging Petra again she disappeared off the train.

"What happened?" said Laureen, finally removing her sunglasses. "Who was that woman? What was all that about her mother, Bryan?"

Bryan didn't answer right away. He was looking at Petra. "That was Gisela Devers's daughter" was all he said. Petra nodded.

"Do you know her?" he asked.

Petra nodded again. "I knew her mother, yes. She was my best friend. When she died I took care of Mariann. She's like a daughter to me."

Bryan took a deep breath. "And she knew James?"

"Erich, she called him. Yes, ever since she was a little girl. She used to visit him often, didn't she . . . James?"

The figure beside her gave a curt nod.

"So she could have already led me to James the first day." Bryan took a deep breath and immediately clasped his side. It was a difficult fact to accept.

"Yes, that's right, if you'd shown her a photo of him." Petra thrust out her bottom lip. "She probably has several pictures of him tucked away somewhere. It wasn't unusual for Gisela to take him along to family gatherings." She smiled quietly, stroking the back of James's hand tenderly. He hadn't taken his eyes off the window since Mariann Devers's exit. "Sometimes he was even allowed to take the picture."

Bryan closed his eyes and could see Gisela's blurred face before him in the first photo he'd studied at Mariann Devers's place. The photographer hadn't been very experienced. He fell back in his seat and knocked his head several times against the headrest, mumbling to himself.

Bridget looked from him to Laureen and back again. Just as she was about to say something, she was interrupted by a knock on the window.

"Erich!" Mariann Devers called out from the platform. James looked at her apathetically and tried to return her smile. "I nearly forgot. I think this belongs to you." She unraveled her multitude of scarves. "I've been wearing it for years. I stole it from Kröner. He bragged about having stolen it from you. It amused me to wear it when I was with him. He never discovered it!" She hurled the piece of cloth in through the window, smiled at Petra again, and turned away without a word.

"Strange woman," said Bridget, just managing to duck in time. She had no desire to touch the object that had just flown onto the floor. James looked at it. The scarf was worn thin. It was blue with a decorative border and had a little heart embroidered in one corner. He picked it up gingerly and held it before him, as though it were something fragile and alive.

CHAPTER 68

Winter was not yet over. Laureen had been staring worriedly at the road as they drove the last few kilometers up to the house. Until now the trip had been no pleasure.

"Must we, Bryan?" she asked for the fourth time.

"*I* must, yes. But *you* can still change your mind." Bryan splayed his fingers on the steering wheel, then gripped it firmly again.

"How can we know he won't turn nasty again?"

"We've already discussed that, Laureen. It's all over."

"Discussed, yes. But do we *know*?"

"Petra says so, and so does his doctor."

Laureen sighed. Bryan knew quite well that she'd been dreading meeting James again for over four months now.

Ever since they'd come home.

"I'm glad he settled in Dover and not Canterbury," she added.

"I know you are, Laureen." Bryan checked the intersecting side roads. The traffic was thinning out, so their destination couldn't be far. It wasn't the first time he'd been in that part of the country, but it wasn't the part of Dover he knew best. He shook his head. "And why would he have wanted to live there?" he continued, without looking at her. "He has neither a childhood home nor any family left in Canterbury, and his sister Elizabeth lives in London."

"Why?" The windshield was fogging up inside and she wiped it clear.

"I'll tell you why." Bryan felt her looking at him. "Because *you* live in Canterbury!"

Bryan smiled quietly. "That's probably not much of a reason, Laureen." Heavy clouds behind the mist heralded the cliffs and the Channel behind them. "Petra says he never mentions me."

Laureen looked down at her hands. Their restlessness clearly revealed her state of mind. "Bryan, how's it going with him, actually?" she asked.

Bryan shrugged. "The doctors think the scars they discovered when they scanned his brain were caused by a number of tiny blood clots. That wouldn't surprise me."

"What are you thinking?"

Bryan saw the image of a motionless figure before him, lying in bed with blank eyes, suffering the effects of electroshock and pills, the harassment by his fellow patients, plus isolation and constant fear. "I'm thinking about a lot of things, but primarily the blood transfusions they gave him. It's a miracle he survived them."

"And how's it going for him now?"

"As well as possible, I suppose. Petra says he's making progress."

Laureen took a deep breath. "That's comforting to know. Also when you think of how much you're spending on his treatment." She frowned and shook her head.

Bryan knew she had noticed his uneasiness.

"I'm sure it's going to go all right today, darling," she finally said, as the landscape swept past. "Just wait!"

The house was not big. Several of the properties Bryan had contemplated buying were considerably larger. Young evergreens stood along the stone wall, stiff and tinged with white by the frost of the previous day.

When Petra came out to meet them, it was clear she had grown older. She gave a faint smile as she shook Bryan's hand.

"We've been looking so forward to this," said Laureen, returning her hug.

"Thank you for the invitation, Petra." Bryan looked at her rather self-consciously. "I'm glad you're ready to see us now." She nodded. "How's it going?" he asked, looking toward the house.

"Okay, I suppose." Petra half closed her eyes. "He won't speak German anymore."

"That was to be expected, wasn't it?" Bryan looked straight at her.

"Yes, I guess so. But it's difficult for me."

"I'm very grateful to you, Petra."

"I know," she said, smiling faintly again. "I know that, Bryan."

"Are things more peaceful now?"

"Yes, but it was bad in the beginning. Everybody had to come here and see him." She pointed toward the land stretching toward the cliff. "They parked their cars right up to the rear garden."

"Bryan has told me that, in a way, the Second World War lasted longer for James than for the Japanese they found on an island in the Pacific a few years ago." Laureen tried to seem impressed.

"That's what they said, yes. Which is why all the curious people had to come!" Petra gestured toward the front door in invitation. It was biting cold. She had no coat on.

"We could have kept it secret if it hadn't been for the authorities," said Bryan. "If only they could have found out which account to draw his pension from." James had yet to show himself. "Oh, well, he got it in the end, paid retroactively. A kind of consolation, one might say."

"Yes," said Petra, opening the door.

James sat in the living room, gazing out the window. Light didn't penetrate, even though the window faced directly toward the cliffs. Bryan sensed Laureen's uneasiness as soon as she saw him, and she quickly retreated to the kitchen, which was Petra's domain.

Bryan tried to relax. James was looking better. He had put on weight and his eyes were kinder. Petra had been taking good care of him.

He gave a start when Bryan spoke. "Hello, James" was all he managed to say.

James turned his head. He eyes dwelled on Bryan for a long time, as if trying to arrange the separate elements of Bryan's face into a coherent whole. He nodded briefly in return, then continued staring out the window.

Bryan sat at his side for half an hour, watching his chest heave up and down.

The women were enjoying themselves in the kitchen. It was clear that their informal chat was doing Petra good, and Laureen had no intention of stopping. They looked at Bryan with curiosity when he came out to them.

"He didn't say so much as a word to me." Bryan made his way to the little dining table and sat down heavily.

"He doesn't say much, Bryan."

"Is he never happy?"

"Sometimes, yes. But rarely. He hasn't felt much like laughing recently." Petra took another cup from the cupboard. "I'm sure it'll come back again. Others would say James is already much better. But I think it's going slowly."

Bryan looked at his cup as it was filled up. "If there's anything I can do, please tell me."

"You needn't do anything."

"What about money?"

"You give us plenty. And we have the pension, too."

"Just let me know."

"I will. And besides that, there are the drawings." Bryan noticed an undertone of skepticism in this last comment.

"The drawings?"

"Yes, the drawings that were inside the cardboard roll James took from Kröner." His face took on a puzzled look. Holding up her hand as a sign for him to wait, she disappeared upstairs.

"Is he strange, Bryan?" Laureen gave him an anxious look that didn't appear to want an answer.

"A bit, yes."

"Perhaps we should have waited before coming here."

"Perhaps. I think I'll try and get him to go for a walk after lunch. Maybe we'll be able to talk a little then."

Laureen put down her cup. "Are you mad?"

"What do you mean?"

"I simply won't allow it! You're not going out to the cliffs with James!"

"Why ever not, Laureen?"

"It just won't do. He'll do you harm, I know he will!" She spoke the words emphatically. Petra came down the stairs and noticed Laureen's flushed cheeks.

"I'm sorry . . ." Petra said, preparing to go again.

"There's nothing to be sorry about," said Bryan. "I was just suggesting I'd go for a walk with James after lunch."

Petra caught Laureen's eye briefly, then looked out into the yard.

"Does he still hate me?" Bryan almost dared not hear the reply.

"I don't know, Bryan." She frowned. "He never speaks about you."

"But it's a possibility?"

"With James everything is possible." She turned and handed Bryan the parcel she'd fetched. "Here, look at this."

The paper was yellowed and crumpled, the string thin and presumably just as ancient. An old newspaper came to view. *Unterhaltungs-Beilage* it said in Gothic letters. Bryan turned the first page. The drawings lay there in a small bundle. He looked at them, then placed them carefully side by side on the kitchen table. He examined the paper and the signatures, looking several times at Petra. Then he sat down.

"I can see why Kröner kept them for himself," he said. "Have you had them appraised?"

"James says they can't be appraised, not just like that." Petra laid her hand on the drawings.

Laureen stared at the smallest of them. She shook her head. "Doesn't it say 'Leonardo da Vinci' there?"

Petra nodded quietly.

"Yes, and there, and there. And this one's signed by Bernardino Luini." Laureen stopped and looked determinedly at Petra. "You can't have them lying around here, Petra!" she exclaimed.

"It wasn't my decision" was all Petra said.

James still didn't utter a word during the entire lunch. Laureen gave up trying to talk to him after a single attempt but followed every one of his movements attentively and with disapproval. James ate lustily. When he wasn't staring at his plate, he was looking at the serving dish, and took a second helping without asking.

"Bryan suggests you should take a walk together, James," said Petra when they were eating their dessert. Laureen glanced at her in dismay. Bryan put down his spoon and looked across at James, who was now sitting quite still, staring at his plate.

"What do you say, James? Shall we?" Bryan tried to sound enthusiastic. The face that turned toward him looked indifferent, almost apathetic.

Laureen drew him to one side while Petra was fetching James's overcoat. "I don't like it, Bryan," she whispered. "I don't think you ought to."

"Stop it, now, Laureen!"

"You know how I feel about him. Do you have to? Shouldn't the rest of us come with you, at least? He hasn't said a word all day. He's weird!" she said, emphasizing every word.

"He hasn't been outdoors since last week when they went to London for his treatment, Petra says."

"I still don't think you should, Bryan. Don't do it—for my sake!" She was pleading with him. "Didn't you see the look he gave you?"

The wind had died out. An easterly breeze filled their lungs with sea air. The earth was still so frozen that it was difficult to find footing on the cliffs where there was so little vegetation.

They walked a pace apart, silent and reserved. Bryan looked at James several times and tried to reach him with a smile.

"Petra showed me the drawings, James," he said quietly.

The scream of gulls suddenly rose up above them, drawing their gaze out to sea. Bryan went over what he wanted to say several times before he finally said it. "They're not authentic, did you know that?" James didn't answer. He nodded briefly, without interest.

The waves were breaking cold and violently beneath them when they reached the edge of the cliff. Bryan turned up his collar and glanced at his friend.

"I don't think it was far from here that we put the balloon up, James. Do you remember?" As Bryan expected, there was no reply. "We were happy then. Even though it nearly ended in disaster." Bryan lit his first cigarette of the day. The mild tobacco was refreshing. There was no one to be seen all the way back to town. The sea was an orgy of cool colors.

Several times James emitted a small grunt. He clutched his coat tightly.

"Shall we go home, James? You're not enjoying this, are you?"

Bryan was answered by yet another grunt. Then James picked up the pace.

He stopped at a spot where they'd obviously been before, many years ago. James stood looking straight down into the depths. Then he turned around.

"No," he said suddenly, inspecting the ground beneath him. "I don't remember all of it. Only parts."

Bryan inhaled deeply, the smoke blending with his words. "Of what, James? Our balloon trip?"

"I can only remember that you let me hang on the cliff." A brief look of clarity vanished immediately from James's face.

"But I got you up, James! Don't you remember that? It was simply an accident. We were just two foolish boys."

James started to clear his throat. One moment he was standing quite relaxed, the next moment he was flexing all his muscles methodically, one by one. His behavior and facial expressions changed constantly. It couldn't be easy on Petra.

"I remember things, and I don't remember them," said James, coming to a halt. "You don't know the story of the malingerers yet, do you?" he said suddenly, cutting short his own chain of thought.

"Probably not all of it. I only know what I've heard from Laureen. What Petra told her."

James took a couple of steps onto the plateau as Bryan followed him with his eyes. "That story is the most important element of my life." He stared in front of him, shaking his head, letting sorrow take over again. "And it's not even my own story. That's not so good to think about, is it?" The edge of the cliff was less than a meter away. James came and stood in front of him and looked him straight in the eyes for the first time. "Petra tells me you became a doctor, Bryan," he said suddenly.

"Yes, I did."

"And that you made a lot of money."

"Yes, that's also true, James. I own a pharmaceutical firm."

"And that your brothers and sisters are well."

"Yes, they're well."

"There's a great difference between us, isn't there, Bryan?"

As Bryan looked into his eyes, their color changed with the reflections of the sea. "I don't know, James. I suppose there is." Bryan regretted his dishonesty the moment James looked at him.

"You don't think I know that?" James said very quietly, taking a step closer. Their faces were almost touching. James's breath was sweetish. "I think I can live with my wasted life," he said, pursing his lips. "But there are many things I find difficult."

"What, for example."

"What?" He wasn't smiling. "You, for example. And withdrawal symptoms from the pills, needless to say. That people speak to me. And that they expect me to answer. That I'm Gerhart and Erich and James, all at the same time!"

"Yes."

The sinews in James's neck stood out. He raised his hands slowly toward Bryan's torso. "But that's not the worst thing." Bryan took a step backward and planted his feet. Then he took a deep breath.

"The worst thing . . ." James continued, carefully taking hold of Bryan's upper arms, "The worst thing is that you didn't come and get me!"

"I didn't know where to look, James! And that's a fact! I tried, but you'd completely vanished." The grip on Bryan's arms tightened.

For a moment James's eyes took on a vacant look. Then he pulled himself together and whispered so quietly that the screaming of the gulls almost swallowed up the words. "But the absolute worst thing of all is knowing that I did nothing myself."

A twitching in James's face that lived and died in a split second drew Bryan down into the depths of the past, where a hollow-cheeked boy with lively eyes and freckled, golden skin tried desperately to taunt him into helping him as the balloon's canvas was being torn to shreds above him. "Trust me," James had said, wincing just before it happened. "It'll turn out all right." It was this wince Bryan saw again in James's face now. Imploring and full of self-contempt.

"But you couldn't, James," he whispered, almost to himself. "You were ill."

"Like hell I was!" His exclamation was unexpectedly explosive, affecting his whole face. Now his eyes were desperate. "Maybe in the beginning, yes! And maybe also at the end! But it took years. Some bloody long years. The only peace I got during those years was from the pills. It was a terrible kind of peace. I was James, I was Gerhart, I was Erich. But ill, I was not." His grip tightened, stopping Bryan from interrupting. "Not most of the time, anyway," he concluded.

They stood looking at each other. There was anger, uncertainty, and sorrow in James's eyes. Bryan felt him shifting his weight to his clenching hands. James tried twice to formulate the next sentence with a half-open mouth before it finally came.

"And now you ask me whether I can remember the balloon! And you'll keep asking me one thing after another! Things you and others know about, that only a ridiculously little part of me faintly remembers. It's as if people are trying to force me to turn my back on all those years when I was sitting and waiting!"

"Why do you think such things? Why should we want that?" Bryan looked intensely at the trembling man. He raised his hands slowly and gripped James's lower arms.

James shut his eyes tight. After a while they flew open, eyebrows raised. They still reflected agitation, even though his face had calmed down. He gave a short laugh. "In the end, things come back in bits and pieces anyway." James pressed his upper arms in toward Bryan's body. Bryan had to concentrate on maintaining his balance. "I've been seeing the dog patrols again lately, which I haven't done for years. I see them trying to catch us, Bryan. They get closer and closer. And then I see the two trains passing each other down in the valley. One heading west, the other heading east. Our salvation, we thought at the time." Bryan nodded, trying as hard as he could to shift his fixated body.

"And then I think maybe we shouldn't have jumped on it."

"You shouldn't think that, James. It makes no sense."

James leaned toward Bryan so his chin almost rested on his shoulder. Behind them the cliff was now almost enveloped in mist. Beneath them the waves were shoveling in from the east. Bryan felt them beckon.

A seabird flapped up from the foot of the cliffs, protesting audibly. At that moment James's firm grip wavered. His body trembled like the calm before the storm.

He suddenly burst into laughter and Bryan forced his left leg behind him in a feverish reflex movement, sliding on the frozen earth. James appeared to be lost in thought. His eyes grew distant and his laughter ceased as suddenly as it had begun. The abrupt change of mood seemed both crazy and logical.

As the waves' crashing subsided, their enticement died out as well. Gingerly, as in a waltz step, Bryan shifted his weight to his right foot and moved behind James, who scarcely noticed. It was as if a mist of lethargy had drawn the tension out of him.

James's shoulders fell. He released his grasp.

The face Bryan saw looked calm. "It's good we jumped on that train, James," he finally said. "You mustn't think otherwise." Bryan tilted his head and tried to catch James's eye. "And it's good we jumped on the train we did, rather than the other one," he added gently. James gazed up at the sky, the breeze ruffling his hair. He breathed deeply, nostrils dilating. His closed eyes reflected harmony.

"And do you know why, James . . . ?" He looked at his friend for some time. The wind dropped momentarily. James's eyes opened and caught Bryan's. He was waiting, not the least bit curious.

"Because if we had taken the eastbound train, I'd bloody well have had to fetch you from Siberia!"

James looked at Bryan for a while, then turned his head away. From the way his eyes danced across the sky it almost looked as if he were counting the clouds, one by one, in their wild, disorderly flight.

Then he smiled quietly and turned away from the wind, bending his head back so the late rays of the sun covered his face.

After James had left him alone, Bryan stood motionless and watched him walk down to the house, step by step, in the pale refractive light of the setting sun. The figure didn't turn around a single time.

The definitive slam of the door didn't reach him until ages afterward, muffled and infernal at the same time. Bryan closed his eyes and took a deep breath. He lacked oxygen.

The trembling in his body came in waves.

When he finally let his shoulders fall, Laureen was standing before him.

She looked deep into his eyes as never before. It felt as if she were seeing all the way into him. Clutching her coat collar to her neck, she tried to smile. "I think the drawings are fakes, Bryan," she said after a brief silence, trying to keep the hair out of her face. "I advised Petra to have them examined."

"I was afraid of that." Bryan was listening to the screams of the gulls. They were getting hungry now.

"I don't know if she will. James told her he'd get them sold, that she should just trust him and he would take care of it."

The words came to Bryan in fragments. They merged to give another, yet significant, meaning.

"Take care of it?" Bryan breathed quietly. "That sounds familiar, somehow."

Laureen took his arm. She squeezed it repeatedly as she tried to control her windswept hair with her other hand.

"You don't feel so good, do you Bryan?" she asked cautiously.

He shrugged. Isolated splashes of froth swept up the surface of the cliff in gusts. All in all, Laureen was mistaken. But it was strange, the mood that was taking hold of him.

"Do you feel let down, Bryan?" she asked quietly.

Bryan delved deep into his pocket. The packet of cigarettes emerged from under his bunch of keys. For a while he stood with the unlit cigarette in his mouth. It quivered in the wind and flew away. He pondered the curious inversion of her question. Although he hadn't formulated it so simply himself, a similar question had been ready and waiting since James turned his back on him and left.

"Do I feel let down?" He bit the inside of his cheek as it began to tremble. "What's that feel like? I don't know. But I've felt a breach of faith. The whole time! That feeling I *do* know."

Echoes of broken promises filed through his brain and wrestled with his good upbringing, phony boarding-school manners, and adult codes of honor—all of them comforting memories of solidarity. And now the latest memory of James's back, retreating toward the house.

Bryan stood in the throes of this struggle for some time. And conquered it in the end.

"I'm wondering why it should take thirty years for that question to be posed correctly . . ." he mused.

Laureen stood motionless for a long time.

The sun was positioned like an aura around his head as the sea darkened. "But if you'd asked it before, I wouldn't have known the answer."

"And now?"

"Now?" He shielded himself against the wind. "Now I'm free!" He stood for a moment, then put his arm around Laureen's shoulders. He drew her carefully to him and held her tenderly until he felt her relax.

Then he pulled out his bunch of keys with a metallic rustling. "Would you do me the favor of fetching the car, Laureen? You can pick me up down the road," he said, pointing at a cluster of trees. He handed her the keys. "I just want to stand here a moment."

Bryan had already let go of her as she was about to protest, and he turned to face the increasingly cold wind. He barely noticed when she took his hand and put it up to her cheek. A short way down the path she paused. She turned toward him and called his name. When he turned around, she was gazing back tenderly. "You're not planning to see him again, are you?" she asked.

The cliff beneath him would probably last forever. His epoch was just an intermezzo in its eternal, proud swagger.

That's how fast things could be relegated to the past. From one minute to the next.

He leaned back, listening to the fading echo of happy cries from a far-distant past as the car started up behind the ridge.

The realization—that it takes two to make a friendship, but only one to break it—grew and spread, becoming one with the surroundings, and then lingered on the edge of the precipice for a single, ethereal moment until only the present remained.

Two small boys smiled at him in farewell and he smiled in return. Alive, naked, whole, and ready to face the future in the fading glow of the setting sun.

The rays danced the final steps of a languid tango for the Alphabet House's very last simulant.

APPENDIX I

The Background for the Title, *The Alphabet House:*

With typical German thoroughness, everyone inducted into military service in the Third Reich was classified according to an ingenious alphabet system by the medical examiners, and also later, if they were wounded in relation to the war. This precise and cryptic system determined the degree to which the examinee was fit for duty.

In the course of the war it turned out that some of these "labels" could have fatal consequences for the bearer, including liquidation. This was particularly true for the insane and mentally retarded.

According to *Die Krankenbataillone* by Rolf Valentin (Düsseldorf: Droste Verlag 1981), the following designations were used, among others:

Designations for Fitness for Service:

1. k.v. = *kriegsverwendungsfähig* = fit for active duty. In some cases the "k.v." classification resulted in peculiarities, like L40: Great speech impediment, or B54,1: Bed wetter (L54,1: Incurable bed wetter).
2. g.v.F. = *garnisonverwendungsfähig* = fit for garrison duty. In other words, office or kitchen duty, or suitable for flak duty, supply duty, construction work, etc.
3. g.v.H. = *garnisonverwendungsfähig heimat* = fit for homeland garrison duty. For example, hospital orderlies at the Alphabet House who took care of the SS officers. This was also the designation for dispatch carriers, workshop workers, overseers, etc.
4. a.v. = *arbeitsverwendungsfähig* = fit for work duty. Usually skilled laborers, often slightly disabled.

Designations for Rejection from Service:

Z.U. = *zeitlich untauglich* = temporarily unfit for duty. Designation for someone with one or more temporary ailments at the time of examination who will soon be fit for active duty.

Subclassification:

z.b. = Currently unfit for duty. To be examined again after two months. If they were still deemed unfit after two months, they were given the designation "*zeitlich g.v.*" or "*zeitlich a.v.*" (reexamined after two months and found permanently unfit for military duty), or w.u. = *wehruntauglich* (unfit for military duty).

Those found unfit for military duty were further classified according to the reason for rejection under the designations "vU-*fehlern* (ailment)" and "L-" and "U-*fehlern.*" vU ailments, plus U15,2 and U16, meant unconditional rejection from military service. After treatment the rest could often be designated fit for "g.v.H." or "a.v." duty. A large number of these designations dealt only with physical ailments. The designations for psychogenic ailments, such as those suffered by the patients of the Alphabet House, were basically classified as follows:

w.u.:   Unfit for duty (although suited to join the reserves as of the fall of 1944).

A15,1:   Inherent elated nervous agitation.

A15,2:   Low intelligence.

A15,3:   Psychologically deviant (usually considered fit for active duty).

Z15,1:   Temporary nervous exhaustion caused by external circumstances.

Z15,2:   Alcoholism or other ailments caused by habit-forming drugs.

L15,1:   Neuropathy (nervous condition), psychasthenia (phobia or anxiety symptomized in particular by tiredness, which in turn could be symptomized by loss of sleep, concentration, and memory, and the increased feeling of pain). A condition where normal bodily functions that are usually automatic and unconscious become consciously irritating, symptomized by pounding heartbeat or shortness of breath, for example. The patient is often also anxious, unsure of himself, and likely to evade difficult or demanding situations.

L15,2:   Mental retardation to a lesser degree, debility (often considered fit for duty).

U15,2:   More advanced mental retardation, imbecility.

U16:   Mental retardation and epilepsy.

vU15,1:   Designation for both past and current mental disease.

vU15,2:   Severe mental retardation, idiocy.

vU15,3:   Morbid, extreme mental deviation, like compulsion neurosis, extreme congenital depressions, or phobias.

L,U/vU17:   Suffering from chronic brain and spinal-cord conditions, with effects such as continued paralysis following infantile paralysis.

A18:   Minor chronic paralysis in the peripheral nervous system.

k.v.U/vU18: Serious chronic paralysis in the peripheral nervous system.

A19:   Healed cranial fracture, or concussion without aftereffects.

Z19:   Same as A19, before possible aftereffects have been established.

L19:   Abnormal cranial shape, including bumps and indentations, tissue damage, and past concussions that make the use of a helmet or other headgear difficult, whose effect is otherwise limited to stupor or dizziness.

U/vU19:   The same kind of case as L19, but with occasional effects of dizziness and approaching unconsciousness.

These are some of the letter/number combinations that gave the nickname "Alphabet House" to the ward in which this novel's two main characters were hospitalized.

APPENDIX II

Designations of Rank in the SS during the Second World War:

SS-Schütze: Private
SS-Sturmmann: Lance Corporal
SS-Rottenführer: Corporal
SS-Unterscharführer: Sergeant
SS-Scharführer: Platoon Sergeant Major
SS-Oberscharführer: Company Sergeant Major
SS-Hauptscharführer: Battalion Sergeant Major
SS-Sturmscharführer: Regimental Sergeant Major
SS-Untersturmführer: Second Lieutenant
SS-Obersturmführer: Lieutenant
SS-Hauptsturmführer: Captain
SS-Sturmbannführer: Major
SS-Obersturmbannführer: Lieutenant Colonel
SS-Standartenführer: Colonel
SS-Oberführer: No equivalent U.S. military rank
SS-Brigadenführer: Brigadier
SS-Gruppenführer: Major General
SS-Obergruppenführer: General
SS-Oberstgruppenführer: Lieutenant General
SS-Reichsführer: Special title and SS rank; no equivalent
    U.S. military rank

When Bruce Jansen ascends to the White House after the assassination of his wife on election night, he is a changed man, determined to end gun violence by any means necessary. Rights are taken away as quickly as weapons. International travel becomes impossible. Checkpoints and roadblocks destroy infrastructure. The media is censored. Militias declare civil war on the government. The country is in chaos, and Jansen's former friends each find themselves fighting a very different battle, for themselves, their rights, and their country. . . .

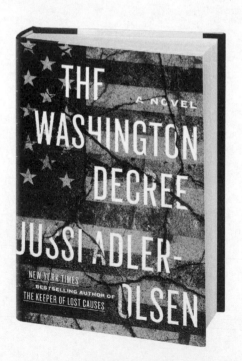

Penguin
Random
House

CHAPTER 1

Even though she was still only fourteen years old, Doggie knew: Just as every adventure has a beginning, it also has an ending. In Doggie's case the ending couldn't have been worse.

It all began with Governor Jansen's office sending Virginia's biggest local television station a suggestion for a new quiz show, plus the capital to get it off the ground.

It was to be a geographical quiz where everyone who could correctly name China's most populous city was invited to participate. The TV station went for the idea.

After the initial elimination round, only forty-eight participants were left, and among them—quite sensationally—was a fourteen-year-old girl. The excitement rose for four weeks: Both the sponsor, Leatherman Auto Tires, and Governor Jansen's campaign office wanted to get their money's worth.

The first programs were broadcast in the afternoon, but the show quickly found its way into prime time. A good three-quarters of Virginians followed the event on their TV screens. This was a new viewer record.

Throughout the Commonwealth of Virginia, people bet on the outcome. Each had his or her favorite. But most, by far, backed the girl with the dimples, who was also the youngest contestant: Dorothy Curtis, also known as Doggie.

Three weeks and three episodes later, Virginia's TV audience finally got their three winners—and what winners they were! Governor Jansen beamed like a Hollywood star, the host had his wages doubled, and the newspapers went crazy. With the exception of a blonde with silicone breasts and full hips who lost out in the last round (but instead got her own talk show on which to display her attributes), the winners couldn't have been more popular.

First prize went to Rosalie Lee, a big African American woman from New York who happened to be in Virginia for the first time, visiting her sister Josefine. Rosalie was a showpiece of a woman, with pearly teeth, roaring laughter, and winks to the audience, and few could match her talent of using so much time to answer a question that the audience was about to go crazy.

Only one point behind her came T. Perkins, a pale-faced, practically albino sheriff who came from one of the smallest counties in the northwestern part of the state. A man who, in his youth, had been one of the nation's best dart players. And finally, in an impressive third place came Doggie Curtis, the girl with the dimples. What a triumph! The winners couldn't have been more different, and everyone involved with the show was pleased. How could any part of the population feel overlooked with those three? It simply wasn't possible.

The lucky winners couldn't believe it when they heard their prize being announced live on the show. Along with the graduated cash jackpots came nothing less than a trip to the other side of the world for the three of them.

For Doggie especially, it was all unreal and incredible. They were to travel to China with Governor Bruce Jansen, his staff, and an official Chinese delegation. They'd be entering a closed world, and everything would be paid for.

It sounded like a fairy tale.

Doggie's father was proud about his daughter being so bright, but not about her prize. He was a right-wing Republican and hated Bruce Jansen, who was "old money" and a Democrat besides.

"Jansen? That swine?" he yelled at her. "You don't plan to participate in a PR stunt like that, advancing the ambitions of that fucking untrustworthy

Democrat, do you?!" He forbid her going, and Doggie's mother was forced to use all her powers of persuasion to make him change his mind.

As fate would have it, this was the last time Doggie heard them quarrel. Her parents were divorced just five months later, a divorce that descended into a fight over money and custody of their child. Doggie ended up being installed in her mother's house with her mother's maiden name.

In a way her father was right. It *was* all a PR stunt, but so what? Governor Jansen was a clever man. He'd taken three ordinary people and made them everybody's darlings, and via them, invited Virginia's entire population of seven million souls along to a far-off, enigmatic land. It was practically the only thing folks talked and read about. School newspapers, ladies' magazines, and even Doggie's father's boring hotel business newsletter wrote about it. And everyone wanted to talk with Doggie. She'd been approached by twenty-one of Virginia's thirty-four newspapers, either for interviews or to publish the last month's entries in her diary.

It was quite an achievement: Bruce Jansen had embraced the entire population all at once, and vice versa. He may have been calculating, but a swine he was not. He was quite fantastic, actually.

Doggie's heart was pounding as she bid her mother farewell and ascended the portable stairway to the huge airplane, glittering in the sunshine. She'd flown at least twenty times within the States, plus to Mexico and Puerto Rico, but never in a plane that size. It was a little frightening.

When she reached her seat, Sheriff T. Perkins was already in the next seat by the window, looking sleepy and absentmindedly cleaning his fingernails with the point of a gilded dart. Governor Jansen's wife, Caroll Jansen, came over and patted her on the cheek. "You're a clever girl, Doggie," she said. "It was wonderful, you winning third place. Just magnificent. I think we're going to have a fine time together, we two." She nodded graciously to a few of the passengers and sat down a couple of rows forward, between her husband and his indispensable right hand, Thomas Sunderland.

Then Rosalie Lee came blustering down the aisle. She gave everyone a hearty greeting and planted herself next to Doggie, her bulk flowing over onto Doggie's seat. She immediately emptied a giant paper bag of Coca-Cola cans, crackers, chips, and a great variety of candy bars and began offering goodies to all her neighbors. It had been like that in the TV studio, too. No one in Rosalie Lee's company was going to go hungry if she had anything to say about it.

Chewing away on her portable feast, she entertained Doggie with talk of New York, her little apartment in the Bronx, and her three wonderful sons, finishing with peals of laughter as she described how she'd kicked her loser of a husband out of her home, ass first.

Rosalie's unrestrained laughter woke Sheriff T. Perkins up a bit, and he looked around in bewilderment. He was pretty easygoing—slept now and then and didn't say much. He'd clearly been the most knowledgeable of the three quiz winners, but even though Rosalie Lee had sometimes seemed slow-witted, appearances were deceptive. Her brain was capable of changing gears suddenly and leaving everyone in the dust, and that was how she wound up winning the contest.

A couple of hours later, a young man who'd been sleeping since takeoff leaned his head towards the row of prizewinners in front of him. "Wesley Barefoot." He presented himself with luminous teeth. "Well, looks like we're going to be together the next couple of weeks. Maybe you know my mother—she's Governor Jansen's secretary." The three shook their heads politely.

"Congratulations, by the way," he continued. "I watched all the episodes, just like everybody else. You were all brilliant!"

They smiled obligingly—just the cue the man needed to launch into his life story. He was studying law and loved politics and British rock bands. Et cetera, et cetera, et cetera.

Doggie thought he was nice and smelled good.

Bruce Jansen took one female prizewinner under each arm as they walked towards the welcoming deputation of photographers, cameramen, and journalists in Beijing's airport. The weather was cold and gray, and everyone was talking at once. After the obligatory questions from the Chinese press, the governor turned to face the international press that was standing behind a row of blue-clad Chinese soldiers.

Doggie quickly noticed one of the journalists, a very little man with intense, dark eyes and a receding hairline. A man who was obviously receiving more attention than the others and got all his questions answered, one after the other. When the interview was over, the governor and his wife disappeared in a black limousine, along with two Chinese officials. The rest of his staff followed in another official car, and the crowd of journalists began breaking up. Apparently, the diminutive, dark-eyed journalist was the only one who seemed interested in the rest of Jansen's party. He waved to his photographer and made straight for the little group.

"Hey, my name's John Bugatti," he said with a hoarse voice, and cleared his throat. "I work for NBC. I'm supposed to follow along with you and Jansen on the whole tour, so I thought I'd say hello." Close up, Doggie could see he had more freckles than she'd ever seen. An irresistible little guy. She was really enjoying this trip—her father's objections had been completely unfounded.

Doggie Curtis's last day in Beijing began like a fairy tale, just like all the others. As usual, the little group of Americans had begun by eating breakfast in the hotel's dining room, surrounded by smiling waiters. Aside from Rosalie Lee and Caroll Jansen, whose finer motor functions seemed to be on the level of a stranded jellyfish, everyone was eating with chopsticks.

Doggie gazed through the large windows at the city's skyline, with its scalelike tiled roofs on clusters of hutongs. They had wandered through the Summer Palace's enchanting, long corridors, breathed the air at Beihai Lake, and silently contemplated the calm that enveloped the Hall of Prayer for Good Harvests. The days had flown by, and now they were going to take a bus ride to the silk market, followed by a walk along the market's narrow streets to the nearby American consulate. That evening they were going to the circus, and the next day they would begin a trip around the Chinese countryside—Xi'an, the Yellow River, Hangzhou, Shanghai, and back again. It was a question of getting as much out of these remaining days as possible.

The market seemed remarkably quiet. Even the few curious people who were following along after the group were silent. None called out to them; no one was pushy.

"They sure do business in an orderly fashion here," whispered John Bugatti at Doggie's side. "You should see how they assault you in Hong Kong or Taipei. It'll probably be like that here in a couple of years, just wait and see."

She nodded and let her eyes wander over counters overflowing with bolts of material and multicolored silk dresses and scarves. One she saw would look perfect on her mother.

"What do you think that one costs? What's that say?" she asked Bugatti, pointing at a sign written in Chinese.

Suddenly, Caroll Jansen came out of nowhere and put her arm around Doggie's shoulder. "That one would look perfect on you!" She smiled, took out her wallet, gave the seller some money, and chose to ignore the fact that he didn't smile back as he folded up the scarf and handed it over the counter's rough planks.

"Come over here, Doggie!" called out Governor Jansen, who was standing before a large population of small Chinese figurines of an indeterminable material. "Look! This one brings good luck. May I have permission to give you one?"

The shopping took only a few more minutes and they were on their way towards the consulate, Doggie with a new scarf over her shoulder and a little, hollow Buddha figurine under her arm. She was proud and happy. Governor Jansen had looked her deep in the eyes and assured her that the little icon symbolized an eternal bond of friendship between them. "You just come to me if you ever need help," he said. It was amazing.

She hunched her shoulders and took a deep breath of the sharp morning air. Everything was perfect: her traveling companions, the exotic trees, and all the people going about their business. She smiled at the workers sitting on the edge of the sidewalk with chopsticks and small bowls, eating warm food from the stalls lined up behind them.

Wesley Barefoot was walking in front of her with a smile so broad, she could see it from behind.

He was pointing in all directions with one eye glued to a cheap, newly acquired camera. T. Perkins was walking along beside him, eyes alert, a plastic bag in each hand filled with all kinds of toys for nieces and nephews. At the head of the procession strode Governor Bruce Jansen in the best of moods with his wife under his arm. As they approached the consulate, he waved to one of the officials who was on his way across the street to greet them. Doggie looked up at the building. As she expected, it was smaller than the embassy on Xiushui Bei'jie where they'd eaten a delicious welcoming dinner two days before, but it still made a vivid, pompous impression in the sunshine, with the Stars and Stripes flapping in the breeze and an erect Chinese sentry standing on a low platform before the entry gate.

Doggie glanced over her shoulder, back down the crowded, narrow street of tradesmen and their stalls. There was a world of difference between the Western-style, official opulence of the consulate and the flimsy, thrown-together stalls of the silk market. It revealed a huge gulf in wealth and customs.

A little street seller was casting one of his many colorful dragon kites up into the breeze, and the group paused to watch it wriggle towards the sky.

Then it happened.

Caroll Jansen suddenly screamed and struck out with both arms, her purse clutched in one hand. Doggie whirled around as her cry ended abruptly and she sank to the ground, blood squirting from her neck, while Governor Jansen's advisor, Thomas Sunderland, lunged after the young Chinese attacker. Sheriff T. Perkins flung away his plastic bags, so the sidewalk in front of the consulate came to life with bouncing rubber balls and small, plastic animals of every description, and in one leap he succeeded in cutting off the man's escape route back into the teaming silk market. Doggie would always remember the assailant's bloody knife, still gleaming as he tried to ward off the charging sheriff.

Next she saw Governor Jansen falling to his knees, the figure in his arms already lifeless. Her lips moved silently as people rushed from all directions to help. She saw everything: Rosalie Lee shredding her best blouse into strips to try and stem Caroll Jansen's bleeding, the soldiers racing over to T. Perkins, who, with blood running down his arm, had pinned the kicking, howling killer to the ground. And she saw Wesley Barefoot, standing still as a statue in the middle of everything, his face white as a corpse.

She was also witnessing the moment when Wesley Barefoot became a man. The toothpaste smile would never be the same.

There was a crowd growing and a tumult of cries and confusion as John Bugatti and the governor's advisor, Thomas Sunderland, struggled to carry Caroll Jansen into the consulate building. People were left standing in shock with their heads in their hands, in stark contrast to the quiet whimpering of the captured assassin.

Doggie sank down on the sentries' platform, her back against a pillar bearing a gigantic brass plate identifying the US consulate. And there she remained.

"Come here, my girl!" T. Perkins was calling to Doggie. By now it was ten minutes since the fatal attack. He kneeled down, put his arm around her, and held her close. "Did you see it happen?" he asked.

She nodded.

"I'm afraid she died, Doggie." He kept still a moment as though to see her reaction, but Doggie said nothing. She already knew.

He got her into a large, white room in the consulate where a couple of employees had been assigned to try and help them. The atmosphere was hectic and crackling with tension. Most of the officials were wearing grim expressions as they pecked at their computers or talked on the phone. This was clearly a serious crisis. A great number of authorities in China and the United States had to be contacted and consulted. Secretary of State James Baker's name was mentioned several times.

Outside, one could hear the hurried steps of people running back and forth on the street. The young Chinese attacker was now standing under guard, pressed up against a wall, shaking. His wild eyes suggested he had no idea what was happening.

"I don't think he's normal, Doggie," said Rosalie Lee, who then squeezed her arm.

They watched as men in uniform screamed their rage and contempt in his face. Then a flatbed truck came with more men in uniform, and they tossed him in the back. The young man's eyes were terrified.

"A shot in the back of his head within two days, wanna bet?" grunted one of the consulate employees.

Doggie stood up, trying not to lose sight of the doomed assailant. Nothing was making sense; all she knew was that she wanted to go home. Then she sat down quietly again and stared into space until John Bugatti stuck a cup of steaming tea in her hand.

"It's a terrible thing that's happened, Doggie," he said, attempting a smile. "We're all so sorry you had to witness this, but you mustn't let it shatter your soul, do you hear me?"

She nodded. It was a strange way of putting it, but she understood him.

"It's just by chance you were here, that's all. I can understand if right now you're feeling small and afraid and very, very sad, but it's over now. In a couple of days we'll be home again."

Doggie took a deep breath. "Yes, but we were supposed to go see all kinds of things. . . ." She was just beginning to realize that the great adventure was over. "The mountains and the Ming graves and the terra-cotta soldiers . . . We were supposed to see all that, weren't we?" Now she could feel that pain in her soul.

Bugatti laid his arm on her shoulder. "Listen, Doggie, what happened will bind us all closer together," he said, as Rosalie Lee nodded her agreement. "Because of what we've experienced today, we belong together from now on. All of us: you and me and T. Perkins and Rosalie Lee and Wesley. Do you understand?"

Doggie looked at them. Each was sitting there with his or her own version of confirmation of Bugatti's statement painted on their face. Wesley tried to nod his agreement, but he couldn't. It was like his body was paralyzed.

Bugatti cleared his throat. "I think from now on we'll belong together in a special way, and we'll always be able to seek each other out if we need comforting. Remember that, Doggie. From now on you'll always be able to call me if you need my help. I'm sure the others feel the same way."

Rosalie and T. Perkins both nodded.

Doggie gave them a dejected look. That was just something people said. "How would I ever be able to get hold of you?" she asked. "You're probably always in China or New York or Camp David or somewhere." She shook her head. "You're a famous journalist, and I'm only me! Don't you think I know that?"

Bugatti nodded. Then, with permission, he took the Buddha figurine that Bruce Jansen had given her only a half hour ago and put it in his lap. Again asking permission, he borrowed T's gilded dart and scratched a little paint off the Buddha's parted lips, thus making a small opening into its hollow insides. Then he pulled a notebook out of his breast pocket. "Look, Doggie," he said. "I'm going to give you the phone number of my dear uncle

Danny. You can always call Danny, because if there's one person who knows where I am, he's the man." He rolled the slip of paper tightly together and forced it into the figurine's mouth. "There! Now you can always get hold of me if you need me."

At that moment Governor Jansen stepped into the room, closely followed by Thomas Sunderland. Neither of them looked well.

Jansen stood still for a moment, shoulders sagging, with sad, empty eyes staring straight ahead. Next he straightened up in a way that made everyone avert his gaze, and then came the part Doggie would never forget:

"My dear friends," he said. "You did what you could. May God bless you for . . . for . . ." Then no more words would come.

JUSSI
ADLER-OLSEN

"Adler-Olsen merges story lines . . . with ingenious aplomb, effortlessly mixing hilarities with horrors."
—*Publishers Weekly* (starred review)

For a complete list of titles,
please visit prh.com/JussiAdlerOlsen